FALL INTO DARKNESS

Nermesa chopped apart his inhuman adversaries without pause. Much to his distress, though, his arm grew heavy, his legs weary. Yet there was still no end in sight to the demon's woodland horde.

He struggled up a ridge, the upward path slowing his pace, enabling the monstrous imps to gain on him. Several grabbed hold of his legs, his torso, and wrapped around his helmet, obscuring his vision. Unable to see exactly where he was going, Nermesa waved his weapon about wildly.

Then his left foot touched not earth but air. He toppled forward, still in the clutches of his inhuman adversaries. Nermesa frantically swung the sword, determined to fight until the end.

His helmet slipped from his head. A moment later, Nermesa's skull impacted against something harder than it . . .

Millions of readers have enjoyed Robert E. Howard's stories about Conan. Twelve thousand years ago, after the sinking of Atlantis, there was an age undreamed of when shining kingdoms lay spread across the world. This was an age of magic, wars, and adventure, but above all this was an age of heroes! The Age of Conan series features the tales of other legendary heroes in Hyboria.

*Don't miss these thrilling adventures
set in the world of Conan!*

The Marauders Saga

GHOST OF THE WALL

WINDS OF THE WILD SEA

DAWN OF THE ICE BEAR

*The Adventures of Anok,
Heretic of Stygia*

SCION OF THE SERPENT

HERETIC OF SET

VENOM OF LUXUR

The Legends of Kern

BLOOD OF WOLVES

CIMMERIAN RAGE

SONGS OF VICTORY

A Soldier's Quest

THE GOD IN THE MOON

THE EYE OF CHARON

AGE OF
CONAN™
HYBORIAN ADVENTURES

A SOLDIER'S QUEST
Volume II

THE EYE
OF CHARON

Richard A. Knaak

ACE BOOKS, NEW YORK

THE BERKLEY PUBLISHING GROUP
Published by the Penguin Group
Penguin Group (USA) Inc.
375 Hudson Street, New York, New York 10014, USA

Penguin Group (Canada), 90 Eglinton Avenue East, Suite 700, Toronto, Ontario M4P 2Y3, Canada
(a division of Pearson Penguin Canada Inc.)
Penguin Books Ltd., 80 Strand, London WC2R 0RL, England
Penguin Group Ireland, 25 St. Stephen's Green, Dublin 2, Ireland
(a division of Penguin Books Ltd.)
Penguin Group (Australia), 250 Camberwell Road, Camberwell, Victoria 3124, Australia
(a division of Pearson Australia Group Pty. Ltd.)
Penguin Books India Pvt. Ltd., 11 Community Centre, Panchsheel Park, New Delhi—110 017, India
Penguin Group (NZ), Cnr. Airborne and Rosedale Roads, Albany, Auckland 1310, New Zealand
(a division of Pearson New Zealand Ltd.)
Penguin Books (South Africa) (Pty.) Ltd., 24 Sturdee Avenue, Rosebank, Johannesburg 2196, South
Africa

Penguin Books Ltd., Registered Offices: 80 Strand, London WC2R 0RL, England

This is a work of fiction. Names, characters, places, and incidents either are the product of the author's imagination or are used fictitiously, and any resemblance to actual persons, living or dead, business establishments, events, or locales is entirely coincidental. The publisher does not have any control over and does not assume any responsibility for author or third-party websites or their content.

THE EYE OF CHARON

An Ace Book / published by arrangement with Conan Properties International, LLC.

PRINTING HISTORY
Ace mass-market edition / October 2006

ISBN: 0-441-01445-3

ACE
Ace Books are published by The Berkley Publishing Group,
a division of Penguin Group (USA) Inc.,
375 Hudson Street, New York, New York 10014.
ACE and the "A" design are trademarks belonging to Penguin Group (USA) Inc.

PRINTED IN THE UNITED STATES OF AMERICA

10 9 8 7 6 5 4 3 2 1

1

ONCE, WHEN HE had been just past his tenth year, one of Nermesa's instructors, a philosopher, had told the young heir to House Klandes, "Eternity is forever, but it is the minutes that change lives."

Standing in the court of Conan, King of Aquilonia, the captain finally thought that he understood just what the man had meant. While the great expanse of time itself might fill the discourses of the learned, for the common man—such as himself—a single moment's decision could mean an entirely different future, for good or ill. More to the point, there was never just *one* such decision. There was a series, each forever altering what might have been and ultimately complicating life to the point of utter frustration.

Or at least that seemed to be the case with Nermesa's life.

One such decision, nearly two years ago, had been to leave one of the oldest families in all Tarantia— Aquilonia's capital—to seek to join the military and serve the Cimmerian-born ruler of his beloved homeland. That had led to a number of drastic choices out in the western frontier, where more than once the tall, brown-haired son of Bolontes had nearly lost his head to brigands and Picts. Another choice during that time had had to do with breaking his arranged betrothal to the Lady Orena Lenaro, the beautiful but cold woman to whom he had been engaged since childhood. From that had come her sudden decision to accept the proposal of the ambitious Baron Antonus Sibelio, a prominent trading rival of House Klandes.

And finally, there had been his acceptance a year prior of the offer by King Conan and General Pallantides not only to serve as a Black Dragon—one of the king's elite— but to be one of the very select to stay constantly on hand near Conan himself. The consequences of that were still being played out.

Of course, as Nermesa's blue eyes studied the throng of courtiers and diplomats, he wondered why the king even needed anyone nearby. Of those here to see the ruler of Aquilonia, there were only three of interest to Nermesa. One was the Nemedian ambassador, the snobbish, gray-haired Zoran. While with his garish, billowing robes and perfumed body, the man had an effete look to him, Nermesa had seen him handle a sword once during a duel with an Ophirian count with a reputation for a swift, able blade.

It had taken Zoran all of five seconds to break the man's guard and not only cut him through the heart but also across the throat for good measure.

At present, Zoran drank wine from a golden goblet while talking down his long nose at a squat local merchant who likely was trying to do his best to profit from the relaxed trade restrictions King Conan had just this evening announced. Nemedia had still not recovered from its failed invasion of Aquilonia some years past and in order to keep its eastern neighbor from collapsing—despite no love for King Tarascus by Conan *or* Queen Zenobia—the latter had finally negotiated a treaty opening up Aquilonia to Nemedian goods. Of course, in turn, the Nemedians needed to buy materials and foodstuffs that only Aquilonia could best supply, so matters still worked out to Tarantia's advantage.

Not far from the Nemedian ambassador was a bearded,

broad-shouldered man wearing a blue cloak over his leather-armored torso and clad in matching kilt with blue metal tips. Thomal Dekalatos was the ambassador from the city-state of Sarta, part of the land of Corinthia, just south of Nemedia. Although his basic style of dress was akin to several other figures there—all also ambassadors from one Corinthian city-state or another—not once through the evening had he mingled with his fellow countrymen. In a bold move, Sarta, located near one of the mountain passes leading to both Nemedia and Aquilonia, had finally taken advantage of their location to seize by arms the most valuable trade route. Once relatively obscure and of little military might, Sarta now threatened to become the dominant force in its native land and much of the credit or blame for that fell upon Lord Dekalatos' shoulders. It was said that he had been the one to engineer the plan, although some thought that he had had assistance. Now the other Corinthian states debated whether to join Sarta in a new league or rise up against it.

The third figure whom Nermesa eyed spoke with King Conan himself and was none other than Baron Antonus Sibelio. Although only a dozen or so years younger than Nermesa's father, the baron looked nearly the same age as the Black Dragon officer. Pale brown of hair and clean-shaven, he presented a regal figure in his rich, blue-and-black-colored silks. On one hand he wore his favored ring with the glistening emerald, surely worth a fortune in itself. As ever, clasping his wide cloak at the neck was a golden disk upon which had been embossed a heron with one leg raised. In the bird's talons, it held a sword which it looked prepared to expertly use. The crest of House Sibelio, a House once almost as obscure in Aquilonia as Corinthian Sarta, but now among the most influential.

As tall and as fit as the lupine Antonus was—Nermesa could not deny that Orena had chosen well after he had broken their betrothal—the baron was dwarfed by the Cimmerian. With his square-cut black mane and sun-browned countenance, Conan was clearly an outlander, something that still rankled some of the older families of Aquilonia. He had been born up in the harsh, cold climes beyond Gunderland and the Border Kingdoms, a place of barbarians and mythic tales. His blue, smoldering eyes not only focused on the man to whom he spoke, but also surreptitiously studied every aspect of the chamber. The rich-yet-simple blue garments failed to mask his muscular build, the results of years as a mercenary, officer, and, as some whispered, a *thief*. Like all save the Black Dragons, Conan was unarmed, a fact made more noticeable by his hand, which kept slipping down to seek the hilt of the sword that usually hung there. Since the ambassadors could not come armed, the king had declared—much to the dismay of Queen Zenobia, General Pallantides, and Nermesa—that he would not wear a weapon, either.

"Crom!" the Cimmerian had declared when those protests had come from those most loyal to him. "Am I a cowardly knave among men that I'd carry a sword when they can't?"

"But you are *ruler* of Aquilonia," Pallantides, a dark-complexioned man of possible Ophirian origins had insisted. The vulpine-featured commander shook his head vehemently, his long, flowing black hair accenting his distress. "Whereas this lot *is* just a bunch of jackals seeking some meaty bone to gnaw upon . . ."

"We have much more to lose than they do," had added the queen, a swarthy, dark-haired beauty from, of all places, Nemedia. As part of a harem, she had rescued Conan from his enemies. Seeing a spirit matching his own and certainly noticing her physical attributes, the Cimmerian had quickly announced her as his queen. They were an able pair, well matched in all ways. "*I* have much to lose," she had concluded more pointedly.

But even her words fell on deaf ears. Conan resisted all arguments and so Pallantides countered his decision by adding half again as many men to watch over the occasion. An even bigger surprise to Nermesa than the king's refusal to wear a weapon had been when his general had chosen the heir to Klandes—one of the newest members of the Dragons—to command the contingent.

"After Khatak and the Picts, how could I trust anyone else more?" Pallantides had declared.

Of course, the general was there, too, standing with her majesty. One could have almost mistaken *them* for the royal couple. Pallantides was clad in his laced silver armor, the black, hissing wyrm on the breastplate marking him as leader of the elite knights. A rich purple cloak with silver lining draped over his shoulders nearly to the marble floor. Like the king's, his narrow, brown eyes surveyed everything even as he attended to Queen Zenobia.

She was, in Nermesa's estimation, one of the most arresting women that he had ever met. It was not simply her beauty or the curves that the green, silken gown accented to perfection. She also had a keen mind, one as quick as any man's, including her beloved husband. Zenobia could match wits with any courtier or ambassador and come out the clear victor.

However, somewhere in the crowd was a woman of whom late Nermesa had found himself more intrigued than his queen. Once she had been to him only the mousy young sibling of Orena, yet now she was a woman herself and one who, in his opinion, far outshone her glamorous but arrogant sister.

Unfortunately, of Telaria Lenaro, he saw no sign. With her lush auburn hair and soft green eyes, she should have stood out, but the young lady-in-waiting was absent from Zenobia's side.

But he *did* suddenly spy Orena. The features so similar to Telaria's yet more defined had the opposite effect than the younger sister's did on the captain. Even the eyes, the same in shape and color, held such a severity that he immediately turned from the statuesque blond woman rather than have their gazes accidentally meet.

In doing so, Nermesa suddenly found himself facing someone much associated with the Lady Lenaro but much more welcome.

The gray-eyed figure with the square jaw and very patient look was a Gunderman. Gundermen came from the northernmost part of the kingdom and were known for their trustworthy service to their employers, be that employer a noble such as Orena or the king of all Aquilonia. Everyone hired Gundermen. They were practical-minded and, as a people, had never risen up against the conquering Aquilonians. In fact, they even made up a good part of its army.

As was often the custom among his kind, this Gunderman had his long, fair hair bound behind him. He wore the blue-and-black uniform of a servant of House Sibelio even though when last the pair had met it had been the Lenaro family for whom he had worked as bodyguard. Of course, his true loyalty had not changed, for he had been—and still was—Orena's man.

"Good evening, my lord," the Gunderman murmured politely.

"It's good to see you, Morannus. How do you fare in your new dwelling and capacity?" Although Orena still held control of House Lenaro's holdings, she was very much now the Baroness Sibelio. Her personal belongings had been transferred to Antonus' outlying estate and her family home sealed up for the time being.

"I survive," Morannus said, with a hint of a smile. "The home of the baron *is* a bit more comfortable."

"And his own servants? There is no rancor?" Nermesa recalled one time when he had almost run afoul of the baron's own chief Gunderman, Betavio. The muscular bodyguard had the foul temper of a pit dog.

"My duty is to see to my mistress's needs," Morannus replied with a guarded expression. "Nothing else matters."

That, to the captain, meant that the two Gundermen did not get along. Not a surprise, when both were used to being in command of the rest of the household.

"May I extend my congratulations to you, my lord, for your posting. Well deserved. I always believed that you were destined for great things."

The admission from Morannus startled Nermesa, who

considered the man something of a friend despite the differences in their stations. "Thank you."

"A pity you and my mistress had a parting of the ways. I had high hopes for that union." The ponytailed Gunderman cocked his head. "But Klandes and Lenaro might yet be bound together, if what I hear has truth."

"I don't know what you mean," muttered the officer, certain that his face was reddening.

Morannus bowed his head. "I've overstepped my bounds! Forgive me—"

At that moment, there came raised voices from the direction where the knight had last seen Lord Dekalatos. Morannus stepped back as Nermesa, hand already on the hilt of his sword, turned to deal with the matter.

A balding Corinthian in green cloak and brown garments confronted Dekalatos. He had clearly had one cup of wine too many and was on the verge of striking the ambassador from Sarta. Nermesa made a quick study of the shouting man and recognized him as the representative from Tebes, the city-state most affected by Sarta's seizing of the pass.

"Your cutthroats are charging a monstrous toll now! This is the final straw! Remove them from the pass immediately, or Tebes will have to declare—"

"Be cautious, be wise," Dekalatos suggested. "Your words will be noted with the first hint of hostility clearly made by Tebes."

The second ambassador faltered, and his expression grew more adamant in its fury. "Spare me your 'kind' warning! I know what happened to Koron! He—"

As Nermesa rushed forward, he quickly glanced at the king and queen. Two Black Dragons stood with Conan and the baron, while Pallantides had pulled Zenobia from the crowd. Satisfied that the royal pair were safe, Nermesa interceded.

"My lords," he said confidentially to the two. "This is not an occasion for such disagreements. You are guests of his majesty!"

"Quite right, quite right," replied Thomal Dekalatos. His hand strayed to a silver pin on the shoulder of his cloak. "As I was just telling the Count Stafano—"

"You were doing no such thing! I came here to talk reason, in a calm voice, and you told me to go prostate myself to your horse if I hoped to appease Sarta! You insult me so to my face at a royal affair!"

The Sartan piously looked around. "Did anyone hear me say such a base thing to this man? Anyone?"

No one, especially the other Corinthians, gave any indication of having heard the foul words. Most of them likely had not, but Nermesa suspected that Stafano's countrymen would have denied hearing anything no matter the truth. Sarta now held that much of an upper hand over the rest of Corinthia.

"Come, my lord," Nermesa quietly said to the enraged count, "There is some fine food over on the table yonder! Please partake of some of Aquilonia's finest dishes . . ."

"Yes, do that," the bearded Dekalatos urged politely.

Count Stafano's eyes all but bulged. His face went red with renewed fury. "You—you *hear* him? By Mitra! I'll have your throat for this!"

He ripped free from Nermesa, thick hands seeking his counterpart's neck. Thomal Dekalatos started to back away, but not quickly enough. His one hand remained by his shoulder.

With trained reflexes, Nermesa not only regained his hold, but increased it. He pulled the count from his intended victim.

But at the same time, the Sartan's hand pulled away from his shoulder . . . taking with it the pin. Like a viper, the hand darted forward and back in an instant.

Count Stafano let out a gasp of pain. Glancing at the man's hand, Nermesa saw a tiny dot of blood form near the base of the thumb.

With his gauntleted hand, he grabbed the pin from Lord Dekalatos, but it was already too late. The count fell back into Nermesa's arm. Another of the Black Dragons helped the captain set the stricken Corinthian to a chair. Stafano's face was completely ashen.

"I—I—" he stammered.

The count fell back, and he let out a terrible groan. His tongue, now an ominous shade of purple, thrust out.

Count Stafano let out one last, feeble gasp, and stilled.

"You saw," Thomal Dekalatos calmly declared. "He was coming at me with murder in mind! The man was clearly in a deranged rage! I had no choice!"

Pallantides strode toward him. "But it is forbidden to bring a weapon of any kind in the presence of the king and queen at such an event! That pin is clearly poisoned."

"Merely a personal protection. And well needed, I might point out!" He thrust a finger toward Nermesa. "If that man had done his task as he should have, I wouldn't have been forced to such a drastic measure to save myself!"

More than one eye turned to Nermesa, who had already been berating himself for having missed the pin. True, no one could have guessed that the decorative piece could be so lethal, but as the officer in charge, any lapse was *surely* his responsibility.

"Nevertheless," continued Nermesa's commander, "I must ask that you come with me, my lord. Now." Pallantides reached out to take the Sartan's arm. "This matter must be dealt with."

Keeping out of reach of the general, the ambassador vehemently shook his head. "I am a citizen of Sarta and protected by my rank. Do not presume to treat me like a suspected brigand."

"No one is doing that, but you must—"

"Now, Thomal," came another voice from behind the Sartan. "Keep your head, man. The general's only doing his duty."

Keeping one hand on Lord Dekalatos' shoulder, Baron Sibelio came around in front of the man. Pallantides started to say something, but the baron turned to him first. "There's no need to make more of a scene out of this, is there, General?" He pulled his hand from the ambassador's shoulder.

"Thomal will cooperate as long as you respect his station, won't you, Thomal?"

Lord Dekalatos stirred himself. "Yes. We of Sarta are not barbarians and butchers, as some would think us. This was unintentional, and I will personally compensate Stafano's family if need be."

He could hardly buy them a new Stafano, thought Nermesa, but from what he had seen of Corinthians' greed, perhaps money *would* prove a more-than-adequate substitute for the late ambassador's "loved ones."

"Good man," remarked Antonus. "General?"

"Thank you, Baron." The commander of the Black Dragons waved back the two subordinates who had stepped up to assist him with the Sartan. "If you'll come with me, my lord?"

"Of course." Lord Dekalatos walked alongside Nermesa's superior as if the two were about to embark on a companionable conversation.

Nermesa had other men quickly but respectfully remove the body of the late Teban representative. As Lord Stafano was brought away, Baron Sibelio quietly commented, "Not what you were hoping for tonight, was it? I'm sorry, Captain Nermesa."

"I should've paid more attention. This is my fault." He glanced in the direction of the king . . . only to find Conan eyeing him in turn.

The Cimmerian had his goblet to his mouth, but was not drinking. His eyes bored into Nermesa's own and, in the Aquilonian's mind, condemned the younger man's ineptitude.

"You shouldn't be so hard on yourself," responded Antonus. "I'm sure no one else would."

No one but my liege, the heir to Klandes thought, eyes still caught by those of King Conan.

The rest of the guests all stood silent, expectant. Conan abruptly tore his gaze from Nermesa and glanced around at the gathered guests. Without warning, he smiled broadly to them and at last drank.

The crowd suddenly became animated again. It was as if the fight between the Corinthians and the subsequent death of one had never occurred.

But as he excused himself from Baron Sibelio and once more took up his position, Nermesa knew that the repercussions of the terrible incident would play out for some time to come.

And he would certainly be at their center.

2

NERMESA WAS NOT summoned to answer for his failure the next day nor the day after that. In fact, General Pallantides acted as if all were well between them and that he was not deeply disappointed in the young officer's abilities and conduct.

Somehow, that only made Nermesa feel more concerned. When his punishment did come, he expected it to be more severe, even possibly dismissal from the Black Dragons. The heir to Klandes was not certain he could live with such shame. More important, he was not certain that his parents, especially his father—who had served in the military with distinction and honor—could either.

That made it all the more difficult to meet with them this day.

The banner of his House hung high above as Nermesa reached the walled gates. Upon the banner's golden field reared a red lion with twin swords—also red—crossed over the beast. When Conan had seized the crown from the despot Namedides and placed his own lion on its black field on the flags over the palace, Bolontes had actually considered changing the generations-old emblem of his clan simply so no one would think it linked at all to this upstart usurper. Fortunately, he had never followed through, and in the time since his son had willingly gone to serve the Cimmerian, the elder Klandes had mellowed to the point of respecting his king.

Nermesa prayed for some of that calm as he handed a servant the reins of his horse. He trotted up the marble steps and past the fluted columns, where a House guard saluted him and opened the doors for him.

In the wide, marbled corridor within, his mother, Callista, met him. A tall, handsome woman with a slight hint of gray in her bound, brown hair and clad in a favored alabaster gown, she hugged her son tightly.

"How are you, Nermesa? Have they rectified that frightful problem with the Corinthians? Has Pallantides said anything about it to you?"

"Nothing yet, Mother." He peered past her at a doorway farther down. "Is Father in the great room?"

"Yes, he had much work to do. Things are not all well with our holdings."

It was what Nermesa feared. "I can't stay long. I'd better go talk with him immediately, then."

"Try to keep him calm," his mother pleaded, kissing him on the cheek. "It's always wonderful to see you."

Nermesa marched up to the doors to his father's study, where a servant stood at attention. "Don't bother to announce me. I'm sure he knows that I'm here."

"Yes, Master Nermesa . . ." The balding man opened the way.

The great room was not only where Bolontes, head of House Klandes, did his work, but also something of a shrine to the clan's lengthy history. Each wall paid tribute to its past patriarchs and members of note. Lifelike, painted busts of Nermesa's grandfather, great-grandfather, and many others sat proudly atop marble stands. To the right, the captain noticed the bust of his father's eldest brother, whose death had forced Bolontes to take on the reins of the House. The family resemblance was there in both brothers, as it was in Nermesa. The eyes, the well-angled nose, the proud patrician features, almost unchanged despite the centuries. Both men were over six feet, tall even for many of their race; but Bolontes was yet another two inches more than his son, ever making Nermesa feel like a child.

The elder Klandes had risen at the entrance of his only child. He gave Nermesa a nod and a quick survey. "The armor of the Black Dragons suits you well." He eyed the plumed, visored helm in his son's arm, the sleek, black breastplate with the small but savage dragon embossed on the center. Nermesa was armored from head to toe as if ready to do battle—which, as one of the king's elite, he had to be. At the slightest call of the horns from the towers of the palace, the younger Klandes had to race back to defend his lord. "As I thought it would."

"Thank you, Father."

Bolontes had never much been one for physical greetings, but since his son's near death fighting the witch Khati's Picts and bandits, that had changed. Clad in his white tunic and red, gold-lined cloak, he came around and strongly hugged his son. "Good to see you."

"I told Mother that I can't stay long. I'm certain that the general will be asking for me. There was some hint earlier."

"And you think it has to do with what happened at the gathering." The gray-haired Bolontes frowned. "A grim business, that, and naturally convoluted, dealing with ambassadors, of course."

"Yes. But no one will speak against the Sartan, especially the other Corinthians," Nermesa explained. "I suspect that Lord Dekalatos will be sent home, reprimanded, then returned here as if nothing happened."

His father snorted. "And some wonder why I never sought to enter the political arena. Running Klandes is battle enough."

Nermesa eyed the documents on the huge oak table that served as the elder Klandes' desk. More than one quill lay discarded on the side and a second bottle of ink sat unstoppered, clear evidence of the long day's work. "You asked me here to discuss our business and to sign some agreements?"

"Yes, as my heir, you already have a say in several of our ventures, and to have both our marks on the documents will guarantee our word even more."

The son's brow arched. "*Your* mark isn't enough for some?"

"Of late, no." Bolontes guided Nermesa around the desk, then reached for one of the parchments. Nermesa immediately saw that it was a new agreement between his House and their partners in the granaries. He read it over quickly, his eyes narrowing at the changes. "Concessions? We've less control over the granaries than in all previous agreements."

"It's a unified demand . . . or they make a new agreement with House Sibelio."

"Sibelio . . ."

"The good baron's everywhere we are, Nermesa, undercutting our prices, offering incentives . . . it's a wonder the man is making any profit at all, but, by Mitra, he seems to be."

"He has contacts in Ophir, Nemedia, Brythunia, and as far away as Kush, as I understand it, Father." Nermesa rubbed his chin. "He was very helpful and considerate during the chaos at the gathering. He's always so." The captain gritted his teeth. "No, not always. Not when Orena's with him . . ."

Bolontes made a face. "A woman scorned, my son. I won't ask you again why you broke off with her, but I do admit I wish it had been otherwise."

Trying to stifle his growing anger, Nermesa pretended to reread the agreement. Orena had planned this well, as she always had everything. His leaving her had been the first time she had been caught off guard, and she was determined to make him pay. He had originally assumed that she had married the ambitious baron both to spite him and gain more prestige, but Nermesa had realized too late that Orena had intended to use her husband's influence and wealth to seek revenge. Face-to-face, Antonus had never treated his rival with anything other than respect and friendliness, but to placate his bride he intended to ruin the entire Klandes family.

"It has to stop," muttered Nermesa.

"What's that?"

The son steeled himself. "I'll talk to Orena. I'll settle this with her."

"Maybe you can use Telaria as a mediator," suggested Bolontes, studying Nermesa. "Unlike her sister, she still seems to have quite a fondness for you."

"I'd rather not include her in this. This is between Orena and me."

His father said no more about it, but Nermesa could not help suspect that Bolontes knew the truth. The breaking point between him and his betrothed had been when he had discovered her beating her younger sibling. That was also the reason that Nermesa had pushed for the queen to take Telaria Lenaro on as a lady-in-waiting.

The situation with Orena could wait for the moment, though. Despite his determination to end their feud, the officer knew that he had to sign the papers his father presented him. Any delay to do so would further endanger the dealings of House Klandes.

Dipping one of the unbroken quills in ink, Nermesa signed under the seal of the House as his father had done. Like the senior Klandes, he was left-handed, unusual in Aquilonia.

"These also," Bolontes said, handing him two other parchments. They were of a similar nature to the first.

Nermesa set down the quill. "I'll speak with Orena as soon as possible."

"I doubt that she will even see you, my son."

Nermesa considered. "If I talk to the baron separately first, he might arrange a meeting with her." He cursed himself for not having known of these most recent matters before having run into the baron at the gathering. Antonus had given no sign of his latest dealings, and even Morannus had hinted nothing. But then, Orena had a way of readily controlling *most* men. "I think he'll do it."

Not looking quite convinced, Bolontes nonetheless remarked, "Perhaps undercutting us so much is hurting him more than I imagine. See what you can do." He stacked the documents. "How fares the trading agreement the Cimmerians negotiated? Will it stand after the Corinthian trouble?"

"It should. Ophir, Nemedia, and Brythunia have expressed no reservations, and the last I heard from General Pallantides, Lord Dekalatos insisted that what happened would not change the decision he made in the name of his king. No matter their hatred for Sarta, I believe most of the other city-states will fall into line. To do otherwise would be to provoke war between them."

"Let us pray to Mitra that they keep sensible. That agreement opens many new vistas for us, Nermesa. Klandes would profit well by its adoption."

Nermesa patted his father on the shoulder. "All will go well. You'll see! All will go well . . ."

IT PROVED TO be the worst prediction Nermesa had ever made.

The trading agreement began to unravel but two days later. It came not, as the captain would have supposed, from the incident between Sarta and Tebes, but rather from the southeast, between Ophir and Koth. Accusations flowed from the latter that their caravans, which had to depart from the city of Khorshemish, were being waylaid south of the Karpash Mountains before being able to enter Aquilonia. Blood between the two realms had long been bad. Koth's previous king, Strabonus, had perished after he and Ophir's ruler, Almarus, had both attacked Conan's realm. Koth's current lord, Strabonus' nephew, Gorald, believed that his uncle had been betrayed by the Ophirians despite the fact that Almarus had also been slain. The missing caravans had merely brought the matter to a head.

And as the ambassadors of both kingdoms flung accusations at one another, Brythunia declared that it, too, had lost caravans, these traveling through Nemedia and Corinthia. With a barely concealed sneer, Zoran suggested that it was odd that nearly everyone else had lost good numbers of men and merchandise and that Aquilonia should consider itself very fortunate not to have had much in the way of such troubles. The fact that he had said so in the presence of King Conan made it all the more remarkable that he still lived, for the Cimmerian was known to be very proud of his reputation for honor.

Over the following month, the king and his trusted advisors sought any way they could to keep the trade agreement alive. In the end, though, it was Baron Sibelio of all people who managed to at least keep the parties from withdrawing, even if actually accepting the proposal now appeared questionable.

Nermesa had no chance to speak with the baron, for the very day after the captain visited his father, Pallantides assigned him to oversee the patrols. This meant that Nermesa spent much of his time beyond the gates of the palace making certain that order was kept in the near vicinity. It was not enough for the Black Dragons to defend their monarch should someone breach the palace; the general preferred that any assassins not even make it over the outer walls.

It did not take long for Nermesa to ascertain that all was in order, but his duties insisted that he constantly recheck each post. On the trek from one to the next, he himself studied every person and building around him as if all might be of a suspicious nature. Having failed King Conan and Pallantides once, Nermesa would not do so again. He saw this task as a chance to redeem himself in their eyes.

It was no simple task, either. Around him swarmed people from a dozen lands and more. Tarantia was the pinnacle of civilization. Here pilgrims came to learn and to marvel, scholars came to debate, and merchants came to buy and sell. The capital of Aquilonia was surrounded by a great stone wall with battlements and four gateways allowing entrance from the vast, surrounding plains. Originally known as Tamar—and still called so by some of the most elderly—it was a place dominated by tall marble towers, many of them painted in the traditional blue and gold. The majority of buildings, whether towers or not, had entrances flanked by high, fluted columns and great bronze doors. Over those entrances hung brilliant carved reliefs of heroes and mythic beasts.

Tarantia was also filled with statues, so many that a young Nermesa had once wondered if they outnumbered the living. They were most often found standing before the steps of public structures and were generally of past important citizens involved with that particular place. Others raised in more open venues consisted of famous generals, past kings still admired, and the like. All were painted to appear very lifelike, even to the strands in their garments and the color of their eyes. Often, people would glance in the direction of one, feeling as if that figure stared down at them. Even Nermesa, born and raised in Tarantia, more than once found himself meeting the gaze of this statue or that.

The palace itself, situated behind him on somewhat of a hill, was a towering, walled edifice with battlements. The banner of King Conan fluttered atop many points, including the palace's own high towers, the tallest in all Aquilonia. Guards walked the outer walls of the king's residence, most of them Black Dragons like him.

Not all that far away from the palace stood another tower, an ominous dank leviathan whose lit upper windows at night gave it the semblance of some terrible demon's visage. The Iron Tower was where the worst criminals were imprisoned. Originally built as a keep, it had, under the tyrant Namedides, been a feared place into which many enemies of the king had vanished. Under Conan, it now served a more noble purpose, but still the captain was never very comfortable around it.

Nermesa paused at the vast stone bridge over the Khorotas River, watching briefly as boats laden with Aquilonia's best goods headed south toward Argos. It did not surprise him at all that the three largest bore the armed heron of Sibelio.

Beyond the post where five Black Dragons stood watch, Nermesa spotted a contingent of breastplated Gundermen, a part of the normal City Guard. One of the men reminded him of Morannus, which gave Nermesa an idea. Perhaps he could speak to Morannus alone and convince him to whisper in the ear of Orena. The Gunderman was one of the few who might have influence over her. Of course, it likely went against the bodyguard's loyalty even where Nermesa was concerned, but at present it was the only notion the captain had.

As usual, the crowd was a mix of many types, from short, broadly built Argossean traders to swarthy Bossonian archers in their traditional brown-and-green forest garb. Like the Gundermen, the Bossonians made up a large and valuable part of the kingdom's military. Nermesa had met several of their kinsmen in the Marches, located just east of the Pictish wilderness and a natural buffer against incursions by the tattooed barbarians of the west. They were trustworthy fighters and good men. Many of them had sacrificed themselves against the Picts, Nemedians, and other foes in the name of King Conan.

Nermesa had just begun to leave the area of the bridge when he saw another Black Dragon approaching on horseback. The long blond hair and jutting chin told him that it could only be Paulo, a member of the fabled unit for even less time than Nermesa. Their relative newness in the ranks had brought them together as friends. In some ways, Paulo reminded Nermesa of a more noble-born Quentus, his servant and good companion who had joined the military with the young Klandes, only to be gruesomely killed in the west.

"There you be!" called the other knight, eyes brooding. "Been looking all over for you, I have!" Paulo hailed from a northern part of Aquilonia near the Border Kingdoms, but his accent and manner of speech were due to his mother's being from some still more northerly land.

Paulo's grim manner immediately put Nermesa on highest alert. Gripping the hilt of his sword—a sword given to him as a gift for meritorious duty by Conan himself—the captain asked, "What is it? Has something happened to his majesty?"

This momentarily brought a grin to the blond knight's ugly face. "Always worried about him, aren't you? No, nothing like that! Himself wants to see you!"

"Himself" was how some of the other Black Dragons referred to Pallantides . . . at least when the general was not within earshot.

Nermesa grimaced. It was too soon to hope that he had made amends for the earlier debacle. Surely, Pallantides had decided on some even lower post for him as further punishment.

The pair returned to the palace, where the general actually stood waiting for Nermesa. The young Klandes prepared for the worst.

"There you are! About time, Captain Nermesa! Don't go far away, Sir Paulo. This concerns you as well."

"Me?" The blond knight gave Nermesa a quick glance that seemed to condemn his friend for somehow drawing him into his troubles.

"Give your horses over to someone else and come with me."

Doing as commanded, the pair followed Pallantides deep into the palace. Even with his limp—the result of a much harsher injury at the Battle of Valkia—the tall commander nearly outpaced the two younger men. As they walked the long, marble halls, Nermesa sought to keep his mind off his imminent fate by eyeing the various reliefs lining the walls. Some were of past kings and their accomplishments, but many were new and dealt with the colored-yet-admirable past of Aquilonia's Cimmerian-born monarch. There was Conan against Xaltotun, the undead wizard. Conan leading his army against the Nemedians. Conan and the Black Dragons fighting off King Strabonus. The king by himself, slaying some monstrous serpentlike creature. And on and on.

They were the pet project of Queen Zenobia, a woman very intent on reminding all of the exploits of her husband. More than once in the past, many Aquilonians had seemed to forget what the former mercenary had done for them, thus allowing pretenders and outsiders to wreak havoc on the kingdom. Zenobia sought to have this never happen again, and she was aided in her efforts by Pallantides, Count Trocero, and Sir Prospero of the southwestern province of Poitain—an area ardently supporting Conan—and even Publius, the heavyset high councilor and chancellor.

But while the reliefs reinforced Nermesa's admiration for his lord, they also served to remind him of his failure. That failure further magnified when he realized just where they were heading.

King Conan had been born in a vast, untamed land, and so, even after many years among the "civilized" peoples, sometimes he acted as if the walls closed in on him. The Black Dragons understood and respected this, for they saw their liege as the great cat he utilized as his symbol. The palace was a beautiful cage, a necessary evil, and, like a caged lion, Conan *had* to pace it or find a place where he could at least pretend he was out in the open. Thus it was that he spent much time alone or with Zenobia on the wide, banistered balcony that gave him the best view of the rolling plains and woods north of Tarantia. It was always the balcony facing north, even if in the opinions of some the views in other directions were more breathtaking.

There was no need for Pallantides or the guards on duty at the entrance to announce them. Conan had apparently known of their presence long before they reached the entrance, for he had already turned to face them.

"About time, Pallantides," he remarked gruffly. Under a stern brow, he eyed the other two. "Captain Nermesa. Sir Paulo."

Next to Nermesa, the other knight swallowed in surprise.

The king seemed to know the name of every man serving him, even if that man had not been with him long. In Nermesa's mind, it was yet another reason why Conan commanded such loyalty. Those willing to die for him were not simply nameless drones; they were brothers in arms.

"The delay was unavoidable, your majesty," returned the general. Neither he nor the men with him knelt before Conan. Public affairs demanded such protocol lest outsiders think the king's followers respected him little, but, in private, the former soldier felt it demeaning to his men.

Conan grunted. "Get on with it, then."

"As you command." When it came to the Black Dragons, the king often let Pallantides relate his wishes. The king would interject when he thought necessary. "What I say is for your ears alone. Even those you travel with must not know the full extent. Understood?" When both men nodded, Pallantides continued, "Captain Nermesa. Sir Paulo. The trade agreement teeters on the brink of failure. With it, the king hoped to build a common need among the lands, one that might stave off future bloodshed. Without it, we are certain to face new conflicts with many of our neighbors, something which *cannot*, even if victory is ours in each case, be good for Aquilonia in the long run."

The two knights quickly glanced at one another. They knew what stock Conan put in the agreement and its passing. How, though, did that affect them?

"Captain Nermesa. You know the reports of missing or slaughtered caravans coming from nearly every realm. Even Nemedia has evidence that their people were slain . . . and after they had brought their goods to Tarantia and headed back laden with valuables purchased here. Those cases mirror most of the others dealing with Aquilonia itself."

The suggestion was clear. If most of the lost wagons had only recently left inner Aquilonia, then it gave the appearance that their country was at least in part responsible for the crimes.

"If I may," remarked Nermesa, recalling something. When General Pallantides indicated he should go on, the captain said, "My own House—and I believe that of the Baron Sibelio—have both reported lost men and goods, too. Aquilonia is not untouched, as some might claim." He did not mention any name, but knew that all would think of the Nemedian ambassador, Zoran, and his foul words.

"All lost within the borders of Aquilonia and far less in total value than what many of our neighbors reported." The general looked to the king. "Though not unconsidered, yes, your majesty?"

"We've lost few, but even one is too much." Conan turned to face the north again. "Too much when you're a king."

Nermesa knew that he was speaking more about the lives than the valuables. "How may we serve, your majesty?"

The muscular king looked back, but it was Pallantides who answered. "There is a caravan leaving for southern Nemedia. Zoran plans to go with it, bearing with him missives for King Tarascus. Zoran's personal guard is good, but too small under the circumstances. There are also men accompanying the caravans, but they are mostly hirelings of the House owning the wagons. King Conan has offered a contingent of the Black Dragons to ride with the caravan—using the ambassador as part of the reason—and the owner has agreed."

So Nermesa was to be a guard for an arrogant foreigner, little better than the man's own help. It pained him that Paulo and other comrades had to share his misfortune.

But then, Pallantides added, "That is your *official* capacity. What the king truly desires—and what his majesty is placing you, Captain Nermesa, in charge of—is finding out the truth about these charges."

The captain straightened. "Sir?"

"We need a trusted man who's experienced commanding in the field, someone who's adaptable. His majesty decided on you."

Nermesa looked to the king, who nodded grimly. "I will not let you down this time!" Bolontes' son blurted. "I swear!"

"No one here thinks that you did that evening, Nermesa." The corner of Pallantides's mouth curled up. "But I'm certain that Zoran and many others do. They will misjudge you. The king is interested to find out what their error in judgment might cause to happen. What it might reveal about these attacks."

He had not disappointed his lord after all! Nermesa tried to stay focused, but *hearing* that with King Conan standing before him and thus giving it validity almost overwhelmed the young Klandes.

But it would not do to create another disaster by not paying attention. He listened carefully to the general's final words.

"Captain Nermesa, you will treat Zoran very respectfully and not take anger at any words he or anyone else in the caravan may say about the Teban ambassador's death. You must pretend to know your place. Sir Paulo, I've seen you fight alongside the captain and have recommended to his majesty that you would be a good second." It was a promotion for the newest member of the elite unit, and Paulo thrust out his already-prominent jaw in a smile. Returning his attention to Nermesa, the veteran officer added, "Watch and listen. Should you make it to Nemedia without incident, you will travel back with the next caravan. We have the word of the owner that it will take a trail leading it along where the last caravan was likely ambushed. Investigate all you can, but at the same time, I expect you to do your part to keep the wagons and their drivers safe. Is everything clear?"

"Aye, General."

"You may decline this mission if you like. This is beyond the dictates of the Black Dragons—" He nodded proudly when Nermesa immediately shook his head. "As I thought. You have a good head on your shoulders, young Klandes. You proved that not only in the Westermarck, but here at home. That's why the king trusts you with this task." General Pallantides looked to King Conan. "I believe that covers the essentials, your majesty. The lesser details I can give them as they prepare."

The Cimmerian, arms behind him and legs spread in a military stance, again studied the duo. To Paulo, he gave another nod, but to Nermesa, he said, "May your sword be strong, Captain, and your wit stronger."

Nermesa bowed his head. "Your majesty."

Conan once more turned to the rail. Pallantides indicated that the audience was over, but as the trio stepped into the palace and beyond the guards, he said, "Paulo, you go ahead. I've a last detail I forgot to discuss with the captain."

"Yes, sir."

When the northern knight had departed, the general leaned close to Nermesa. "One thing I didn't bother to mention, because it is of a personal nature to you. The wagons of both the caravan you leave with and the one with which you return are the property of House Sibelio. Baron Antonus Sibelio, married little more than a year to a certain Lady Orena Lenaro, whom I recall you know." The veteran knight's expression revealed nothing. "This will not be a problem, will it?"

At first, the revelation made Nermesa wonder the same thing, but immediately after it occurred to him that perhaps this was a blessing in disguise. If he kept Antonus' caravans safe, it would give him a decided advantage when he sought reconciliation with Orena through her husband. "No, General. Definitely not."

"Good man."

They were suddenly interrupted by one of the sentries near the balcony entrance. "General Pallantides, his majesty just commanded me to find you! He requests your presence back on the balcony. Said it concerns the trial of Baron Brocas of Torh."

Pallantides' dark face grew darker yet at mention of the man. He looked Nermesa's way. "Another fool caught up in an ill-advised plot against the king. In the end, his greed was greater than his cleverness. I'm suggesting that if he's found guilty—which he will be, with the evidence I have—that he be executed and his body left at Traitor's Common." Traitor's Common was an area outside the city where, traditionally, the corpses of men such as Brocas were thrown there as a warning to others. However, Conan was not as eager to use the Common as his predecessors. With a sigh, Pallantides added, "But his majesty will likely decide on Os Harku, since the island prison is near the Bossonian Marches and the people hurt most by the plot were all innocent Bossonians."

Captain Nermesa knew little of the events, but nodded understanding. "I'll begin gathering my things, General."

"Good man. I'll meet with you later." The commander of the Black Dragons started to limp off, then suddenly called back, "Oh, Nermesa?"

"Yes, my lord?" He waited for Pallantides to give him some last-minute change in orders, but the elder knight had something else in mind.

"I said you have a good head on your shoulders, young Klandes. Be exceptionally wary. For the sake of many, I'd like you to keep it there."

And with that, he walked off.

3

THERE WAS ENOUGH time to bid farewell to his parents, but the one other person with whom Nermesa would have liked to have spoken he was unable to meet with owing to his duties and his imminent departure. Nermesa had much he desired to say to Telaria, but the opportunity never arose. Even when he had a free moment, her duties to the queen kept the young lady-in-waiting from him.

He was in the midst of saddling his horse for the journey when the note came through one of the palace servants. The young servingwoman scurried off immediately after giving it to him, allowing no chance for her to explain the contents.

Telaria's handwriting was familiar to him. The note was short and clearly written in haste, but it still said much.

My heart goes on this journey with you. Please be careful, Nermesa.

Underneath, she left only the first letter of her name. The missive lightened his heart, even if he had no time in which to compose a response. Stuffing the note in his saddlebag, Bolontes' son quickly mounted, then joined his men.

Nermesa rode to the eastern gate of the city, where the caravan awaited. He was followed by a contingent of twenty other Black Dragons. Nermesa arrived at his destination to find Ambassador Zoran already quite impatient even though the Black Dragons were more than an hour ahead of schedule.

"I trust this is not a precursor of what to expect from you, Captain," he said, gazing down his nose at the Aquilonian from atop his elegant chestnut mare. Zoran wore robes of red and gold, and the chains dangling from around his neck incorporated rubies and sapphires. His long, thick mane of gray hair had been freshly brushed by one of two servants who rode a few paces behind. He wore a scarf to shield his face from the sun. Only the sword in the gleaming sheath at his side gave any indication that he might be other than a helpless, jaded aristocrat. It was Nermesa's suspicion that much of Zoran's appearance and manner were an act for others, but he could prove nothing.

"I will not fail in my duty," the captain answered, acting as if still frustrated by his failure to save the Teban representative.

Zoran gave him a bland smile. "Let us hope not, for all our sakes."

Nermesa met with the caravan master, a gruff, eye-patched former soldier named Darius, hired on a year before by House Sibelio. Lighting a long, clay pipe, he welcomed Nermesa, then pointed the pipe toward the Nemedian, who was engrossed in giving some last instructions to the assistant he was leaving in his place. "I seen you two talkin' before you came to me. Friend of yours?"

"I only know the ambassador through official channels," Nermesa responded carefully.

"Which means you find him as much a dolt as I do, eh, lad? If we're lucky, maybe a rabbit will cause his dandy horse to shy and we'll be rid of 'im."

The captain made a noncommittal sound, then bid the

caravan master good-bye. Returning to Paulo and the other Dragons, he set out getting everyone into their proper positions. Nermesa sent four men to the front of the column, then spread all but himself, Paulo, and the third officer—a Pellian named Augustus—along the two flanks of the caravan. Nermesa had Paulo take command of those on the right, leaving the left to the stern-faced Augustus.

As for Nermesa, he took up a position on the left where he could keep an eye not only on both the front and rear, but the good ambassador. The caravan's own guards, mostly hired mercenaries, kept closest to the wagons, although a pair each did ride up front and at the rear.

The column got under way by midmorning. Some onlookers eyed the party with minor interest, Black Dragons were not the usual escort for anything but a royal excursion. Of course, the presence of the Nemedian ambassador gave some excuse.

With over a dozen wagons laden with trading goods, the pace was slow but at least steady. The wagon master proved a diligent man whose military training soon showed. Under his control, the hired guards kept alert and ready. Baron Sibelio had hired well, and Nermesa began to wonder if he would accomplish anything at all on this journey.

If the first three days were any indication, his concerns had merit. The weather was pleasant, and the trek toward the mountains between Nemedia and Corinthia went without incident. The only thieves that the wooded areas through which they passed offered were squirrels who sought to investigate the wagons for nuts.

There were three main routes by which to reach Belverus, Nemedia's capital. One was to ride north near the Border Kingdoms and circle around the mountains there, passing the city of Hanumar before reaching Belverus. Had the baron sought business in Hanumar, they would have taken that route. However, much to Paulo's disappointment—he still having family along that path—that was not to be.

The second route would have taken them directly through the mountains; but while in Aquilonia it was spring, in the high passes winter still clung to its reign. Another month, and the snow would melt, but at this point it was still far too treacherous for heavy wagons.

And so, it was to the southeast they traveled. The chain ended just shy of the borders of not only the two kingdoms, but Ophir as well. Nermesa hoped that, so near to the three other borders, he might pick up some word pertaining to his investigations. He also saw the area as an ideal place where cutthroats might finally attempt to take the caravan. He alerted Paulo and Augustus of this notion, and both agreed with the soundness of his reasoning. The wagon master, too, believed that they would be at their greatest danger there and had already prepared his own men with that in mind.

But the area was some days away, and so the guardians of the caravan could only watch and wait as they journeyed. Nermesa almost welcomed the first hints of the mountain range, his tension having grown with each quiet day.

Every night that the caravan made camp, the Black Dragons set up a perimeter watch of their own beyond that of the wagon's contingent. The elite fighters kept in contact by a series of whistled signals known only to their own, each with subtle intonations that would make it all but impossible for anyone to imitate them properly without extensive practice. As commander, Nermesa also checked in with each man through a set of his own personal signals, further complicating any hope that listening brigands might have of tricking the knights.

Confident in their safety, Nermesa met with Darius to discuss what, if anything, he knew about wagons lost near their present vicinity.

"Aye, there was one small caravan taken about an hour's ride from here," answered the grizzled veteran. "Leastwise, that was its last known location."

"Will we pass the site in the morning?"

"Should come close enough so that you can take a look at the area—if 'n there's anything to look at, that is."

Nermesa was determined to do just that. It would be his

first chance to actually try to do something to accomplish his mission.

Making the rounds one last time, Nermesa left Paulo and Augustus in charge of the perimeter. Each evening, the three commanding knights used staggered shifts to ensure that there were always two of them on duty. Certain that any attempt to raid the caravan would come much later in the night, Nermesa always wanted to get his first rest period over so that he would be awake and on hand later.

But before he could reach his bedroll, he crossed paths with the ambassador. Zoran gave him an indifferent nod.

"All well, Captain?"

"The camp is well guarded, Ambassador."

"I should hope so." The Nemedian sniffed the air. "The stench of Ophir already reaches us, and if the wind changes, so will that of Corinthia."

Nermesa was careful only to nod for fear that any remark would draw Aquilonia into Zoran's observations. Fortunately, the ambassador seemed to lose interest in him after that, striding off to his wide sumptuous tent without the least farewell.

Finally reaching his more modest arrangements, Nermesa bedded down. He had quickly grown accustomed to sleeping on a thin blanket in full armor, something that would have made his mother aghast. It had been a necessary learning experience; those fighters who could not quickly learn to get rest wherever they could soon made fatal mistakes as a result of exhaustion.

Nermesa at first lay there—helmet at his side—calculating his next possible move now that they were near the shared border. However, as he had already done so more than once during the day, his thoughts soon drifted to images of home—including his parents, his favored haunts . . . and Telaria Lenaro. With the words of her brief missive playing through his mind, Nermesa gradually fell off into slumber—

And snapped up into a sitting position after what seemed to him only a moment as shouts and cries filled the night.

In the light of the nearest fire, hooded men *swarmed* into the campsite.

He flung aside his blanket and drew the gleaming sword given to him for slaying the bandit, Khatak. The three emeralds in the silver hilt glittered even in the dim light of the campfire, and the rearing lion etched farther in seemed to strengthen Nermesa's hand as he grabbed his helmet and raced to meet the first attacker.

The knight confronted a figure whose hood was pulled tight over his head, with only eyeholes giving evidence of any humanity underneath. Leather armor covered the torso and legs. The bandit came roaring at Nermesa, three wicked slashes of his curved sword momentarily forcing the Black Dragon back.

But Nermesa quickly recovered, parrying the last strike, then counterattacking. He forced his adversary to the defensive, finally running him through when the latter's booted foot stumbled over a rock.

No sooner did Nermesa slay that one than another leapt at him out of the dark. More alert now, the captain made short work of this new threat, thrusting the keen blade through the shadowed figure's throat.

Taking a moment to collect his thoughts, Nermesa listened. From all around him came the sounds of battle. In the light of the fires, he made out murky forms struggling with one another. More than one body lay sprawled on the ground, and several of those appeared to be the hired guards.

But what had happened with the other Black Dragons? How could the situation have grown so dire so swiftly?

He let out a shrill whistle and was greeted a moment later by Paulo's own signal. However, there was no similar response from Augustus. Cursing, Nermesa turned to where the Pellian should have been posted.

On his way, he passed the Nemedian's tent. Duty forced him to detour to the entrance in order to see if Zoran was in danger. "Ambassador! Ambassador! Are you—"

But there was no sign of Zoran or his servants in the tent. The Nemedian's belongings were strewn about as if by a whirlwind, and several pouches lay slashed open. Nermesa belatedly noticed that two of the walls within had been severely cut, the gaps large enough for men to slip through. Whether that meant Zoran had fled or others had entered and kidnapped him, Bolontes' son could not say.

He could no longer concern himself about the ambassador. The fate of the entire caravan was at stake. Tearing away from the tent, Nermesa continued on to Augustus' location.

As he neared, the captain came across two men struggling. One was Darius, the other a hooded brigand. Darius was an able man, but his attacker loomed over him. The two were locked close, with the wagon master's adversary clearly gaining the advantage.

Wasting not the slightest thought, Nermesa fell upon Darius' foe. Caught now from two directions, the bandit sought to flee. The wagon master quickly ran him through from the side.

As the man fell, Darius grinned at the Black Dragon. "Thanks for the assist, lad!"

"Have you seen Sir Augustus? He was supposed to be in charge of this area!"

"That's not the ugly soul with the pale hair is it? If you mean the other one, the last I saw 'im, 'e was heading out to speak with one of your sentries there." Darius pointed with his weapon.

Nermesa started off in the direction. "My thanks! Tighten your forces! Keep them from the wagons!"

Darius shouted something, but it was lost in the sounds of struggle. Ahead, Nermesa heard swordplay. In the wooded area before him, he made out a dim form doing battle against not one, but three villains. His hopes rose.

But while it was a Black Dragon, it turned out not to be Sir Augustus. In the dark, Nermesa did not recognize the man's face, but one Black Dragon always came to the aid of another, and so he leapt next to his comrade. Two of the hooded attackers took him on, enabling the other man to concentrate better on the remaining one.

Gritting his teeth, Nermesa met one blade after another. He quickly judged the man on the left as the better sword and focused his attention accordingly.

To his side, the other Black Dragon darted in, wounding his own foe in the arm. As the attacker pulled away, the other Aquilonian finished him off with a deep stripe across the stomach.

But, in doing so, he left himself open to the better of Nermesa's own adversaries. The villain pulled back from Nermesa, lunging for the distracted soldier.

"No!" the captain shouted, but there was nothing he could do. The other Black Dragon twisted in an attempt to avoid the strike, but too late. The bandit's blade cut a red river across his throat.

Snarling, Nermesa instinctively thrust, putting a sudden end to his lesser opponent. He turned on the final fighter, beating him back relentlessly. The bandit tried twice to slow the captain, but Nermesa's attack was fueled by anger and determination to such a degree that each attempt by his foe now seemed laughingly slow and inept. He cut one bloody arc over the man's chest, then another, the leather armor doing little to stop the Aquilonian's keenly honed blade.

His adversary turned to flee. Not caring at his unchivalrous behavior, Nermesa caught the man in the back.

Only when he was the last left standing did Nermesa pause to catch his breath. Behind him, the battle still raged, but, at the moment, all he could do was stand.

As the pounding in his chest eased some, the Aquilonian suddenly became aware that he was not alone anymore. Tightening his grip on the sword, he spun to face his new enemy—

And beheld what he could not imagine as anything human.

It was clad in black robes that flowed with and against the wind as if they themselves had life. Although the shadowed, hooded figure had arms and the general shape of a man, those arms ended in twisted limbs with taloned fingers . . . fingers pointed at Nermesa.

But worst was what lurked within that hood. A deep blackness, as if nothing existed.

Nothing, that is, save one gleaming, monstrous crimson orb situated just above where the nose would have been.

The captain froze, so stunned was he by the unearthly sight. Only when he heard the low, unintelligible whispering and noticed that the fingers gestured, did Nermesa of Klandes register the imminent danger.

With a cry, he threw himself toward the specter, demon—whatever it might be. Unfortunately, his momentum was short-lived, for his foot caught some large, heavy object on the ground. Nermesa toppled, falling flat on his face. His sword slid from his hand.

He immediately rolled over . . . and at last discovered the reason why Sir Augustus had not given any warning. The Pellian lay flat on the ground, eyes staring up into the night heavens. Nermesa could see no immediate mark on him, but one touch was enough to assure him that Augustus was very, very dead.

A fate surely awaiting Nermesa if he did not act quickly.

Flinging himself to where he had last seen his sword, Nermesa tried to decide what to do against the one-eyed fiend. If it could slay a steady fighter such as the Pellian with but a glance, then Nermesa would be hard-pressed to defeat it. Still, he could not just stand there and die.

He rose to discover the ghostly form gone. Nermesa spun in a circle, certain that in some direction he would find it waiting.

But although it was nowhere to be found, the Aquilonian quickly realized that not all was well. The area had grown deathly quiet. There was no sound of battle. Nothing. Not even the creatures of the night.

Until there came whispering.

It was identical to the voice of the fiery-eyed demon. It came low, and from all sides of him. Again, Nermesa turned fruitlessly in a circle.

Then, a rustling noise arose from the ground to his right. Yet, as the captain turned to face it, it arose from behind, too. No sooner did he look there, then Nermesa heard it from another direction.

It was everywhere. A sound like a parchment unfolding or leaves scraping against one another. The whispering continued unabated, never changing tone or intensity.

Something stirred in the woods. Unwilling to wait for more of a threat, Nermesa charged at it, swinging the blade in two savage strokes.

For his quick action, he was rewarded with several severed grass stalks.

The same sound continued to come from everywhere and, worse, the Aquilonian again detected movement. A figure darted behind a tree, a figure far too short for a man. Not in the least, though, did Nermesa believe it to be a child.

"Come and fight me, then!" he growled, threatening with the blade. "Quit skulking in the shadows!"

And to his sudden horror, they *did* come.

In the dimness of night, it was impossible to make them out clearly, but they were nothing human. At first, Nermesa simply believed he saw only bushes and grass shaking, as if some animal moved among them. Yet not only was he aware that these plants had not been there a moment before, but they *themselves* moved as if with intent.

A glance over his shoulder verified that the view was the same no matter where he looked.

The whispering finally grew stronger. With a sense of foreboding, the Black Dragon turned his gaze to his right and saw the fiendish shade atop a nearby ridge. The eye glittered evilly.

Ra shana du karos, ashtur Charon . . . came the whisper. *Zeta catar Charon . . .*

Nermesa tried to head toward the demon, only to have something seize his leg. He slashed down blindly at it and heard the cracking of branches, the ripping of leaves.

From all over, the small figures converged. In Nermesa's mind, it was as if the woods themselves attacked him. He did not know whether what he saw was real or the product of some foul mesmerism, but his soldier's instinct made him fight as if every grasping limb was as solid as a bandit's blade.

He chopped again and again, momentarily breaking their monstrous hold. They scampered about like devilish imps, ever seeking a blind spot or unwary moment.

Although Nermesa desired to reach that which had summoned them, he was forced to run in the opposite direction. This also took him away from the caravan, but to stand his ground was to be overwhelmed. Leafy limbs wrapped over his mouth. Strong, vinelike ropes sought to tangle his feet. He chopped through shadowy form after shadowy form. All the while, the Aquilonian heard the whisper in his ears, the same dread voice urging on the horde.

"Away from me, damn you!" Nermesa snapped, shoving off a sudden growth swarming over his breastplate. His sword hand became entangled despite his efforts, and he nearly lost the weapon again. Such a loss would be fatal, he knew, for nothing had an effect save the blade's sharp edge.

He hacked and slashed and cut at all within range, more than once slicing into a tree trunk by accident. The smith who had forged the sword at King Conan's command had surely been exceptional for his trade, for despite all the mishaps, the weapon remained as sharp as the first day Nermesa had received it.

But however excellent the sword was, it was only one weapon against an ever-growing torrent of greenery in the guise of men. They rose ahead of Nermesa, seeking to block his way. By sheer determination, the Black Dragon kept some path open, but often just barely.

Ra shana du karos, ashtur Charon . . . zeta catar Charon . . . The words continued to mock Nermesa from both within and without his head. He chopped apart his inhuman adversaries without pause. Much to his distress, though, his arm began to grow heavy, his legs weary. Yet there was still no end in sight to the demon's woodland horde.

Nermesa struggled up a ridge, leaving in his wake a thick trail of ruined foliage. The upward path slowed his pace, enabling more of the monstrous imps to gain on him. Several grabbed hold of his legs, his torso. Another fell upon his head, wrapping around his helmet and obscuring his vision.

Unable to see exactly where he was going, the Aquilonian waved his weapon about wildly. With his other, he ripped at the leaves and branches, snapping those he could.

Then his left foot touched not earth but empty air. He toppled forward, still in the clutches of his inhuman adversaries. Nermesa frantically swung the sword, determined to fight until the end.

His helmet slipped from his head. A moment later, Nermesa's skull impacted against something harder than it . . .

SILENCE REIGNED IN the darkened woods. Along the path carved out by the Aquilonian lay a half-visible scene of devastation. From trees hung ruined, nearly severed branches. Smaller shrubs had been hacked into pieces. Leaves lay scattered everywhere.

But through the ruined greenery came another form, the shadowy form witnessed by Nermesa. It moved as if gliding along, its long robes trailing well behind it. Yet, despite its voluminous garb, the figure was not hindered by branches snagging the material. It was almost as if what passed through was not mortal.

The specter followed the route taken by the battling soldier, following it all the way to the top of the high ridge. There, it paused to peer down into the black depths. The ridge off which a blinded Nermesa had stepped ended over a precipice many times the height of a tall Aquilonian. So great was it that, in the night, it was impossible to see the bottom.

Impossible to see, even with one blazing, sinister red orb.

The cloaked figure muttered something in a tongue the

likes of which Nermesa had never heard. However, there was a foul, triumphant tone to those words that no one could have mistaken . . . if they could still hear them.

And with that, the specter vanished into the forest.

4

NERMESA WAS NOT dead, but in some sense he differed little from a corpse. Through a painful haze, a part of him struggled to rise, to continue to do his duty. It was not merely for him, but for his king, his family, and everyone important to the knight.

And so, mind still mostly lost, the Black Dragon slowly rose. How much time had passed, Nermesa did not know or care. He knew nothing, save that he had to move on.

Covered with leaves and other forest refuse, the knight staggered forward. A large welt thrust from the right side of his head, but he was beyond noticing.

His foot shoved against something that rattled of metal. Nermesa unconsciously reached down for it, grasping his sword like a sleepy child would a favored toy. Then he stumbled on, only knowing that a good soldier did not retreat. Therefore, he went forward, even if forward was *not* the direction back to the caravan.

How long his trek lasted was impossible to say. He walked for as long as his battered body and addled mind would allow him, then simply stopped, dropped to his knees . . . and then onto his face again.

WATER TRICKLED. IT was the first true sound to penetrate the darkness enveloping the Aquilonian. The trickling made Nermesa lick his lips. He felt thirst, overwhelming thirst.

With the incessant desire for water came the first hints of waking. Other noises slowly registered. The call of a bird. The wind. The distant howl of a wolf or dog. Small animals moving in the background, unconcerned over the armored body lying in their midst. A low, pained moan . . .

A moan that was his.

Something crawled over the right side of Nermesa's face. He shook his head, dislodging it. With bones and muscles that screamed, Bolontes' son used his hands to push himself up slightly.

When he found this feat possible, Nermesa attempted a more intricate one . . . that of trying to open his eyes. This required effort a hundredfold to raising himself up, but at last the beaten soldier succeeded.

He saw immediately that he was still in a wooded area. It was also daytime, although slightly overcast. There appeared no sign of the imps or their demonic summoner. Nermesa felt some vague wonder that he lived, but that wonder was outweighed by the need for water.

Straining, Nermesa managed a kneeling position. He could not see the water, but he could tell that the source lay somewhere just ahead of him. Nermesa started crawling, then paused when he realized that he did not have his sword.

At first he saw no sign of it, but then a glitter of green caught his eye. Stretching, he seized the weapon by the pommel and dragged it back.

A part of him noted that there was no hint of blood or anything akin to it on the blade. A little bit of sap, but nothing else. Yet Nermesa felt certain that he had fought solid enemies, even if they were not human. It had not been his imagination . . . had it?

Then he thought of Augustus and the one-eyed fiend. Certainly that dread scene had not been any figment of his imagination.

The memory stirred him on. Clutching the sword in his left hand, he crawled on his knees toward the trickling. A few low shrubs blocked his path, but Nermesa found the strength with which to hack them apart.

Ahead, a stream beckoned him. Its clear waters bounded over smoothed rocks. The knight pushed himself forward, eager to kiss its pure surface.

The water was almost as cold as ice. It served not only to satiate Nermesa but to clear much of the haze away.

Unfortunately, it also brought to light the pain in his head.

The sudden surge of agony nearly made him sink his face into the stream. Coughing, Nermesa rolled onto his back. Shaking off his right gauntlet, he gingerly touched the wound.

The lump was nearly the size of an egg and tender to the touch. Cupping some water, Nermesa brought it to his wound. Memories stirred. The sudden lack of footing. His helmet slipping free. His body half-enveloped by the forest creatures raised up by the demon.

His head striking the ground.

Nermesa could only imagine that the fall had not been as great as he had thought or that some of the foliage clinging to him had in part protected his body from injury. Those were the only explanations he could think of to explain the miracle of his being alive.

But they did not explain his present whereabouts. Looking behind him, the Aquilonian saw no sign of any ridge. In fact, instead of a ridge, he saw something *far* taller jutting out above the tree line.

A mountain range.

Its perspective did not match what he recalled from the day before. There were some details that looked vaguely familiar, but they were at the wrong angles and much too close.

The throbbing grew incessant again. Nermesa located a deeper part of the stream and gingerly dipped his head into it. The cool water soothed him. When he was finished, the Aquilonian found a secure spot nearby and laid back to rest for a moment.

His supposedly brief respite turned into sleep. It was the sound of an animal in the distance that finally stirred the battered officer again. Ignoring his injuries, Nermesa jolted to a sitting position as he listened.

The sound repeated. It was not the call of a wolf or some bird, but that of a creature of far more importance to him.

It was the whinny of a horse.

Nermesa knew not whether the horse was wild or tame, only that it might be his key to survival. Taking his sword in hand, he forced himself to his feet, then started off in the direction of the call.

The way proved difficult going, but, driven by his concern for the rest of the caravan and the mission itself, Nermesa pushed on. Several times he had to halt and take a breath, but always he kept his ear open for any further cry.

And, at last, the weary Aquilonian heard one.

It was close. So very close that Nermesa nearly called out in response, so relieved was he. The Aquilonian trudged forward, praying that the animal would not run off.

But as Nermesa wended his way past several trees, he heard other sounds . . . the lowered voices of men.

His grip on the sword instinctively tightened.

There were at least three voices, and one of them he found vaguely familiar. Moving cautiously, Nermesa closed on the others' location.

His heart nearly stopped when he saw the contingent of riders. At least a dozen and, from their look, hardened fighters. Despite their cloaks, they were surely soldiers, possibly cavalry.

Their leader was a grim-faced man with a scar across

his chin. He kept his helm clutched tight in his cloaked arm, which prevented Nermesa from identifying him.

There were two other riders across from him. Judging by their positions, they had arrived separately. The conversation was actually a three-sided one, Nermesa realized, but what any of them were saying, he could not make out.

As the Black Dragon edged nearer, the military officer muttered something to the nearer of the two. Whatever he said provoked an annoyed reaction from that figure, for the latter suddenly gestured ferociously at the soldier. As he did, his face became partially clear.

Ambassador Zoran . . .

Sight of the Nemedian filled Nermesa with fury. If Zoran was here, that surely spelled disaster for the rest of the caravan, including those under Nermesa's command. For all he knew, they were even *dead*.

A couple of the horses suddenly snorted. The officer and Zoran both looked in Nermesa's direction. In turning, the officer revealed part of the armor underneath his travel cloak. Not at all to Nermesa's surprise, it was Nemedian.

The other rider also turned in the saddle, and although his face remained obscured by his hood, enough of his garments showed to give the Aquilonian something of a start. The third man wore *Corinthian* garb.

The Nemedian officer barked a command, then pointed toward where Nermesa hid. Backing up, the captain turned and ran. Behind him, he heard shouts and the clatter of hooves.

Although his body protested, Nermesa ran. To stay would be to invite certain death or, worse, torture. The Nemedians would love nothing better than to take an officer of the Black Dragons and try to peel from him his secrets.

Crashing sounds arose from the position he had abandoned. Glancing over his shoulder, he spotted at least four men on horseback giving chase. Nermesa had the momentary advantage of the thick woods, but ahead lay areas where the riders would surely catch up.

One man did not even need that long. The Aquilonian suddenly felt hot breath on his neck and heard the thick snort of a horse in his ear. Nermesa threw himself aside just in time to avoid being scalped by a sword.

The Nemedian fought to turn his steed around, the woods giving the mounted soldier much interference. Leaping to his feet, Nermesa charged into his opponent. The rider tried to parry his attack, but Nermesa cut low. His blade severed the saddle strap.

As the saddle slid, the soldier tumbled off. Nermesa slapped the animal on the flank and as it rushed past, he lunged at the fallen Nemedian. His blade caught the soldier through the throat.

Too late, Nermesa realized that he had lost a chance to have a horse of his own. He turned and ran even as two of the other riders neared. More soldiers could be heard farther back.

Nermesa leapt down a small ravine, his feet landing in water that he had to assume was from the same stream he had earlier used. The splash echoed in the woods.

Above him, one rider reined his horse to a halt. He could not see Nermesa—who was planted below him against the side of the ravine—but clearly suspected that his quarry had not moved on. The Aquilonian caught glimpses of the hunter above through outstretched roots from trees atop the ravine. The Nemedian's animal paced back and forth as his master peered down, seeking some sign of Nermesa.

A second rider suddenly arrived. He muttered something to the first, and the pair started off to the west.

Momentarily safe, Nermesa quickly crossed the stream and headed farther away from where he had seen Zoran and the others. Piecing together his view of the mountains with the uniforms of the soldiers, he believed that he was in Nemedia—but how, then, did the Corinthian fit in? Was he a spy in the service of Nemedia? That seemed the most obvious choice, but for some reason the captain was not satisfied.

Keeping an eye out for soldiers, Nermesa climbed up a

ridge. Somehow, he had to find a way out of this place and return to Tarantia. Whatever his original mission, the king and General Pallantides would be very much interested in the Nemedians' activities, especially where Ambassador Zoran and the mysterious Corinthian were concerned. After what had likely happened to the caravan, Nemedia's link to the other lost wagons appeared very strong.

Hoofbeats warned him of imminent danger. Nermesa threw himself to the ground, flattening out as best he could so as not to be seen.

However, the lone rider who raced past was not one of the soldiers, but rather the faceless Corinthian. He sped along a woodland trail as if pursued by a thousand Pict warriors.

Barely had the Corinthian vanished from sight when another horse appeared. This one ran at a much less brisk pace and as Nermesa dared look up, he saw that it was the animal whose saddle he had cut.

Risking discovery, the Aquilonian leapt up in front of the riderless horse. The animal shied, kicking at him. The hooves came within inches of his chest, and Nermesa had no illusions as to the breastplate's ability to protect its wearer from damage should those hooves have hit.

Using his long experience with horses, Nermesa managed to calm the beast down. The saddle still hung precariously from the animal, but was clearly of no use. Nermesa quickly removed it. He disliked riding any horse bareback, especially in armor. It served neither him nor the poor creature well, but he had no choice.

The horse protested as he climbed up, but quieted once Nermesa was completely mounted. Prodding the animal in the sides, the Aquilonian quickly departed the area. He was still too near the meeting place for his tastes.

One part of him desired to turn west and head back to Tarantia, but another was curious about the sinister Corinthian. Following his instincts—and the fact that if he headed in the other direction he would likely run into the Nemedians—Nermesa headed along the other rider's trail as fast as he dared let the horse run.

There was a possibility that the Corinthian had turned off elsewhere, but Nermesa saw no sign and so kept to the beaten path. By the location of the sun, he estimated the route to be winding southeast, which made sense. How far he was from the border, though, Nermesa had no way of knowing.

A freshly tossed pile of earth was the first hint that his quarry was indeed ahead. Encouraged, Nermesa urged the horse faster.

Then, something made him suddenly glance back . . . just in time to see the other two soldiers catching up. The Nemedians grinned, like wolves certain of their kill. They beat the flanks of their horses with the flats of their blades in order to force the animals to run faster. The gap between the Aquilonian and the pair rapidly shrank.

As they neared, the soldiers split up, coming at Nermesa from two sides. Rather than be caught between them, the captain pulled the reins hard. With his free arm, Nermesa clung on for dear life as the animal came to a sudden stop.

Startled by his audacity, one of the riders kept going for several paces. The other managed to slow, but not as quickly as the Black Dragon had. It put him a few feet ahead of Nermesa and gave the Aquilonian the opening for which he had hoped.

He lashed the soldier in the arm, then, as the latter sought to turn, cut into his sword hand. With a yelp, the Nemedian dropped his weapon.

Nermesa had hoped that the man would retreat, but instead, the soldier reached for a dagger. The captain had no choice but to gut his foe before the second soldier returned. As it was, Nermesa barely succeeded in pulling his blade free before he had to defend himself from a furious assault by the surviving Nemedian. The clang of their blades resounded in the woods, worrying Nermesa that other soldiers would come in response to the racket. Yet, try as he might, he could not break the soldier's defense.

"Aquilonian spy!" snapped the bearded Nemedian. "Surrender and my commander may still grant you some mercy!"

"I am no spy!" retorted the Black Dragon, although his mission did bring him close to being one. "Nor am I a brigand like you, plundering innocent caravans and slaying all in them!"

"Dog! We do no such thing!"

Perhaps this soldier believed that, but that did not change matters. Nermesa had to finish the fight and finish it fast.

Without warning, he slid off the opposite side of his horse. Lacking a saddle, the action proved a swift one that took his adversary off guard. Cursing, the Nemedian tried to kick the riderless mount away.

As he did, Nermesa came around and seized his outstretched leg. He threw the soldier off the back of the horse.

The Nemedian struck the ground headfirst. Nermesa stood over him, expecting to do battle, but his foe simply lay where he had fallen. After carefully prodding the body with the tip of his sword and finding no trickery, the Black Dragon knelt closer. Turning the head to the side, Nermesa surmised that the soldier had broken his neck in the fall. The death was a reminder to Nermesa how fortunate he had been to survive his own, much greater fall with so little injury.

Rising, the Aquilonian seized the dead man's horse by the reins and leapt up. He peered around, but saw no further signs of pursuit. Nermesa again contemplated riding toward his homeland but felt certain that the truth about what was happening could best be unveiled by following the Corinthian.

The general trail was not hard to pick up again. Although he had ridden hard, the Corinthian clearly did not travel like a man fearful of being followed. That gave Nermesa hope; the other's ignorance would surely work to his advantage.

But although Bolontes' son urged his new mount on to great speed, after more than an hour, he saw no sign that he was gaining on the Corinthian. Worse, his head had started to ache, and the rumble in his stomach warned him that he had to find sustenance soon. Slowing his steed, Nermesa checked the saddlebags, but was rewarded with only a small handful of dried fruit. This he devoured with no sense of alleviating his hunger.

Nermesa had a choice of seeking food or continuing the chase. Choosing the former would mean rummaging around in the woods with the possibility of not even finding anything immediately edible. Still, how long could he continue before weakness made him careless?

Aware that he was likely making a potentially fatal mistake, Nermesa took up the chase. He assuaged himself by swearing that if he saw anything worth eating, then he would immediately halt his pursuit.

As if to mock his decision, a fog began to rise. Despite there being still two or three hours of daylight, over the next few miles, visibility faded to just a few yards. Forced to slow his pace, Nermesa eyed the mist like an enemy. It made any possible change in the Corinthian's route more difficult to sense.

Another precious hour passed without any noticeable change to the fog or any sign of the other rider. Nermesa began to think more about food. At this point, even hunting for berries in the mist was likely to be more rewarding.

With an exasperated sigh, the Aquilonian turned off the trail. Dismounting, he led the horse toward an area that looked promising. Sure enough, a few minutes later, a bush with black berries materialized out of the fog as if by magic. Nermesa immediately went about the task of plucking a few to taste. They were sweet and reminded him of some similar berries he had eaten back home.

It was not the most elegant meal, but Nermesa devoured as many as he felt safe doing. His head gradually throbbed less, and he felt some of his hunger subside.

While he had eaten the fruit, the horse had munched on some grass nearby. Now, though, the animal sniffed the air as if smelling something better. On a hunch, the weary officer let his mount lead.

For his patience, Nermesa was rewarded by another

stream. Letting the horse drink, the Aquilonian took up a position just a little upstream and, setting down his sword, splashed his face. Only then did he also drink.

As he wiped his mouth off, he heard the horse suddenly snort. Every muscle immediately taut, Nermesa seized his weapon and the horse's reins. He quickly shushed the horse, then paused to listen.

The clink of metal made his eyes narrow. When he heard it again, Nermesa focused on the direction from which it had come. Quietly tying the horse's reins to an oak, he slowly moved on.

The fog thickened, and in it Nermesa now and then *saw* shapes that seemed not of the mortal world. One he dared touch with the tip of his sword, only to find it a twisted tree. Cursing himself for his overwrought imagination, the Aquilonian moved on toward where he thought the sound had originated.

Again, came the clinking of metal. Nermesa kept his sword hand steady. The ground became treacherous, and he struggled not to slip as he suddenly descended a hillside.

Near the bottom, his foot caught on something. Despite Nermesa's best efforts, he tumbled to his knees. His hands pressed against metal as the Aquilonian fought to keep from falling forward. Nermesa smelled a foul odor.

A slack-mouthed, nearly fleshless face stared up at him.

With a startled gasp, Nermesa pulled back. He looked down and discovered that his knees pressed against the armor of the corpse. The knight leapt up, gaze still held by the horrific sight at his feet.

Only the armor truly kept any shape resembling what had once been a man. The legs and hands had been torn away, apparently by large, scavenging animals. The helmet hung lopsided on the skull, which still seemed to be caught in its death scream. Dried stains indicated where a sword had burrowed through a joint in the armor, slaying the man.

By the armor and insignia, Nermesa immediately recognized him as a Nemedian soldier.

How long the man had been dead, Nermesa could not say. Weeks, even months. Long enough for nature to feed on the bounty caused by his slaying.

But just as Nermesa began to wonder what the corpse was doing out in so empty a place, he heard again the clink. This time it came from much closer and to his right. Stepping over the skeleton, Nermesa peered into the fog—

And suddenly realized that he stood in the midst of a horrific scene of carnage.

There were hints of bodies wherever the mist gave glimpses of his surroundings. They lay sprawled in all manner of poses, as if indifferently tossed by some specter of death.

Nermesa's brow furrowed deeply. Some specter of death . . . or perhaps the brigands who had captured their caravans.

Covering his mouth and nose, he walked among the dead, seeing ghoulish bodies in both armor and civilian garb. Some of the latter were certainly merchants, their torn, bloodstained robes still revealing marks of wealth. Others wore more common clothes and had, no doubt, been drivers or servants.

All had been brutally slain.

At last, Nermesa located the source of the clinking. A guard's remains had become entangled in a small bush—likely when he had been tossed down—and part of one ruined gauntlet hung so that when the wind blew, the bony fingers could no longer prevent some parts of the glove from swinging into one another.

Nermesa gently moved the skeleton's hand so that the clinking stopped. Only then did he notice that the armor was not Nemedian but rather from Corinthia. Turning to survey those twisted forms nearest, the captain saw that not only were there more Corinthians, but also some armor that could have originated in Ophir or maybe Koth.

He shuddered. Small wonder little trace had been found of the caravans taken in the south. The villains had carried off the bodies, then brought them to this place for disposal like so much garbage. Nermesa could imagine only one reason for the effort, and that was to keep the various kingdoms involved wary and nervous. Mystery always increased tensions.

Somehow, there was more to the attacks than mere profit.

With a sense of foreboding, he continued his search. Sure enough, there were some Aquilonian bodies, but, they, too, were older, nearly stripped of flesh. Had they been from his own caravan, they would have been nearly whole. It gave Nermesa some hope that Paulo and the rest had survived their struggle.

He knelt by one of the Aquilonian bodies, trying to find anything to help him in his mission. However, as he touched the body, his gaze fell upon several long, savage scratches across not only the armor but the bones as well. In fact, something had taken special interest in gnawing on the body, which explained why one arm and one leg were missing.

Nermesa suddenly recalled the clinking to which he had put an end.

The Black Dragon straightened, peering into the fog around him. He had earlier registered the notion of scavengers only peripherally, his greatest concerns that of discovering the truth about the monstrous scene before him. However, such a grisly larder as this would surely catch the attention of a more huge creature. Certainly the scratches and bites gave indication of a beast at least as large as a hound . . .

Nermesa started back. Best he return to the horse and leave this foul place only a memory. It was not that he feared an animal, but only a fool stayed to fight a predator in its own lair, especially a lair so shrouded.

As he stepped quickly over the bodies, he prayed to Mitra to watch over the dead men's souls. Such barbaric treatment he had not seen even out west among the Picts. At least they had some respect for the enemy dead, even if they showed it by hanging the heads of their foes atop stakes. Of course, the witch, Khati, had been less respectful, but then she had been in league with her half brother, the savage bandit, Khatak, whose evil had known no bounds.

Far ahead, a shriek filled the silent wood, the shriek of a horse.

Nermesa's horse.

He started running toward it, now unmindful of what lay at his feet save to keep from tripping against them. The horse was his life; without it he was alone in the middle of hostile country.

But as he started up the slope, something passed through the fog above, then vanished. Nermesa hesitated. What he had seen looked almost as large as a bear . . . but had not moved like one.

The Aquilonian backed up.

A roar echoed throughout the area, one seeming to come from everywhere. Nermesa retreated back into the makeshift graveyard.

He heard movement to his right. The Black Dragon turned—

And a huge creature with two massive, saberlike teeth and crimson, feline eyes fell upon him.

5

IT WAS THE dead that saved Nermesa at that moment, in particular, a skull against which his hand struck. As the horrific cat lunged for his throat, the desperate Aquilonian seized the object and swung it at his foe. The skull caught the beast hard in the temple. Startled, the cat slipped off Nermesa's armored torso, giving its intended meal the chance to pull free.

Coming up on one knee, Bolontes' son thrust at the fearsome carnivore. A cat it was, but larger than any lion or tiger he had seen in the zoo in Tarantia. Moreover, never had he come across one with such massive incisors. They looked easily capable of puncturing a breastplate, and only luck had kept Nermesa from becoming a fresh addition to the cat's larder.

Savage feline orbs sized up the Aquilonian. The animal stood almost to Nermesa's shoulder and likely weighed four or five times as much as the soldier. That it hesitated at all was probably due to the fact that most of its prey did not fight back; the men left here were already dead. It had no doubt steered clear of the brigands themselves, there being too many for even its tastes. Besides, why fight for food when it was brought to you?

Perhaps it even thought of Nermesa as one of those who had thrown the bodies into the depression. That confusion would not save the captain long, for even had he been one of the killers, he was only a single human. Such odds were greatly in the cat's favor.

The animal tensed. Nermesa immediately understood what that meant. Even as the cat leapt again, he threw himself far to the side. The huge creature slashed at him; fortunately, the long, wicked claws only glanced off the back of Nermesa's breastplate.

The Aquilonian also tried to attack as he jumped, but his blade missed completely. He rolled to a kneeling position even as the cat came around to attack again.

Positioning himself much like a pikeman meeting cavalry, Nermesa held the sword on an upward angle toward the beast.

Unable to stop its momentum, the cat fell on the blade. Nermesa had hoped that he would impale his foe, but while the wound was a deep one, it missed both the heart and lungs.

Nevertheless, it did greatly slow the saber-toothed giant. The cat fell to the side, panting. Pulling his sword free, the Aquilonian jumped atop the injured animal.

Feeling the weight atop him, the cat grew animated again. It twisted, trying to claw off Nermesa's face. Because of its wound, the cat's reach was not as great as it once would have been, but the long claws tore off the armor protecting the human's right leg and left several red but shallow trails in the skin.

Gritting his teeth, Nermesa pointed his sword point down and plunged it into the beast's neck.

The cat hissed in utter anguish. It writhed madly now. In its convulsions, it tossed the Aquilonian off. Nermesa went crashing into several ruined corpses in Corinthian gear.

Spitting and hissing, the savage feline tried to dislodge the sword by rolling over it. When that only succeeded in driving the weapon deeper, it stood awkwardly, then shook as if wet.

The sword at last came free, but the exertions proved too much for the badly wounded animal. Even as it turned to a half-stunned Nermesa, its front leg on the side of the gaping chest wound gave out. The cat tried once more to stand, but to no avail. Its other front leg gave in . . . then, with an almost pitiful sigh, the saber-toothed feline fell on its side and grew still.

Gasping for air, Nermesa kept one eye on the cat as he crawled toward his sword. Each second, he expected the beast suddenly to rear to life and decapitate him with one slash of the claws. Yet the great feline did not move even when the soldier grabbed his blade.

Unfortunately, from somewhere in the distance came *another* roar.

Nermesa's eyes rounded as he contemplated his chances against what was surely the dead cat's mate. Turning in the opposite direction of the new call, he staggered among the dead, seeking a path out. Nermesa had some hope that his own scent would mix enough with that of the corpses to slow the other creature, but knew that the animal would eventually still be able to tell fresh meat from rotting cadavers.

He thanked Mitra when the last of the ruined skeletons gave way to empty woods again. In the fog, each shadowed form Nermesa saw seemed to take on the shape of the beast he was certain was about to pounce on him. That they all proved to be trees, bushes, or rocky growths did nothing to calm the beaten officer.

Where he headed, Nermesa had no idea. He just kept moving, trying to put as much distance as he could between himself and certain, horrific doom.

The second cat howled again, but whether the sound came from nearer or farther away, the Aquilonian could not guess. Rather than give himself any excuse to slow, Nermesa moved as if he were only a step ahead.

Daylight began to recede, plunging him into a world

where he could not even see his own hand. Using the sword as a blind man did his staff, Nermesa wended his way through the awkward terrain. It had been some time now since the last call by the dead beast's mate, but still Nermesa pushed himself on as best as his screaming muscles allowed.

But somewhere along the way, his strength gave out. He paused against a tree, keeping the sword out in front of him. Deciding that perhaps he could spare a few moments more, Nermesa slid down to a sitting position.

He fell asleep almost immediately.

NERMESA WAS BACK among the dead, only this time there were hundreds upon hundreds of corpses strewn about in the most grisly of manners. There were so many dead that in some places they lay piled, one on top of the other, for several layers.

The Aquilonian tried his best to find a way out of the grisly pit, but not only did stacks of bodies block his path, but his boots seemed all but glued to the muddy ground. Each step was a struggle of titanic proportions.

Then howls filled the air from every direction. Burning, feline eyes appeared in the mist above the pit, *hundreds* of pairs of inhuman orbs.

In desperation, Nermesa shoved aside a pile of bodies. He crawled over what remained and finally saw an opening far ahead.

But then something snagged his foot. He tugged at it to no avail, finally looking down to see on what he had caught himself.

The skeletal hand of a rotting Nemedian cavalryman was wrapped tightly around his ankle.

Nermesa sliced at the gruesome limb. Pieces of bone went flying. However, no sooner had he freed himself than another hand seized his leg at the same point.

Horrified, the Aquilonian slashed again and, when the hand shattered, immediately threw himself off the pile. He landed in a small, clear spot, where the Black Dragon quickly went into a fighting stance.

The mounds of dead began to shake. A decaying hand wielding a rusting ax burst from one. A skeletal limb brandishing a sword thrust out from another. In seconds, ghastly figures started tearing themselves free from all around Nermesa.

Without hesitation, he swung at one before it even fully emerged. The ghoul shattered like so much dry kindling, but almost instantly another started to rise from behind its ruined form. Nermesa slashed that one, but the process merely repeated itself.

Again the howling filled the air, this time coming from the knight's back. He whirled. Three more monstrous warriors shambled toward him. Although their faces were as fleshless as those of the ones he had destroyed, they were not the countenances of men but savage cats with saberlike incisors. One after another, the three opened their empty maws and howled at him.

"Keep away!" Nermesa shouted, swinging furiously. The Aquilonian decapitated one, but the headless fiend continued on. He tried to back away, only at the last moment realizing that the undead were converging on him from that direction, too. In fact, he was completely surrounded, with the horrific throngs multiplying tenfold with each breath he took.

With a roar of his own, Nermesa hacked and cut at everything within reach. He battled blade against blade, blade against claw. His foes fell before him as if nothing . . .

Despite that, their numbers continued to swell. They closed the circle tighter. It became harder to swing the sword. The ghoulish cat faces leered hungrily. They filled Nermesa's view—

NERMESA WOKE WITH a cry, leaping to his feet and thrusting wildly at adversaries who were not there. He swung blindly for nearly a minute before finally coming to his senses. Then, using the sword for a crutch, he fought for breath.

It was day again, although how far into it, the bedraggled officer could not yet hazard a guess. Certainly well into the morning, at least. A mist still covered the land, but not quite as thick as that through which he had plunged in the dark. He listened for some sign of the other cat, but heard nothing.

His stomach rumbled, and the pounding in his head reminded him that he again had to search for food and water. The berries and the small bit of rations he had found in the saddlebag of the one horse had been his only food in more than a day. While he could survive on that for at least another day or two, the lack of sustenance would continue to have a debilitating effect on his mind and skills.

On unsteady legs, the Aquilonian began traversing the woods in search of anything edible. Twice he came upon berries, but past knowledge quickly identified them as unfit for human consumption. Despite lingering desires to take a chance with them, both times Nermesa moved on.

A rabbit crossed his path at one point. Nermesa lunged at the small animal, only to have it easily evade his laughable efforts. The Black Dragon cursed the escaping animal as he would have a foe in battle, then realized his foolishness.

He did at last come across a pool of water, and although it looked a little brackish, Nermesa dared drink. Feeling a bit relieved, Bolontes' son studied the vicinity. It appeared that Mitra finally smiled down at him, for near the pool Nermesa spotted a bush with edible berries. Not caring what might happen if he ate too many, the starving knight devoured all he could find, even a few that were not yet quite ripe.

Although not completely satisfying him, the berries served to return to the Aquilonian some of his strength and presence of mind. He studied his surroundings again, seeking a better understanding of his location. He assumed that he was still in Nemedia, but exactly where was an excellent question.

He started up a hill in hopes of getting a more useful

perspective. The woods—and the mist—looked thinner up there, giving Nermesa hope that he might spot a village or at least smoke from one.

But his first glance around once he had reached the top was anything but promising. More tree-lined hills greeted Nermesa, several of them taller than the one upon which he stood. Worse, mountains stretched north of some of those.

To the southeast, though, a faint wisp that might have been smoke or merely an interesting cloud formation enticed him. With no other notion as to where to head, Nermesa started that way. Even if this was Nemedia, where an Aquilonian officer—especially one of the fabled Black Dragons—was likely to be attacked en masse by the locals—Nermesa understood that he had no hope of returning home unless he found proper food and a mount.

Even if he had to steal both.

The path was highly uneven, but Nermesa at first managed a good pace. He kept the sword handy, although not once since starting out had he seen anything remotely resembling a threat. Still, in a strange, likely hostile land, it paid not to become complacent.

Atop the hill, Nermesa had been better able to estimate the time of day. As he had surmised, it was very late morning. He had originally had hopes of reaching the vicinity of the unknown settlement before nightfall, but as the day waned, he saw that his progress would not be sufficient. Even though twice along the way the Aquilonian had fed himself on more berries and some bird eggs from a nest, and had even found water again, the pace with which he had begun slowed as the hours passed. Despite his best efforts, Nermesa finally had to stop to rest for a time.

He was now certain that some settlement lay ahead, possibly even one of impressive size. The one tendril of smoke—it was definitely smoke—had split off into nearly half a dozen, possibly more. Nermesa believed that the nearer he got, the more those tendrils would further divide.

But before that could be verified, the last vestiges of day gave way. Despite that, Nermesa pushed on, determined to cut the distance as much as possible before the last of his energy gave out.

He managed perhaps two, even three hours more, then finally realized he could go no farther. Propping himself against a tree, Nermesa debated continuing after a small respite, but finally decided against it. Seeing no better place to settle down, the exhausted captain again slid down into a sitting position right where he was.

As on the previous night, he had barely done so when slumber claimed him. This time, fortunately, there came no nightmares of monstrous, undead warriors mixed with fiendish beasts. Nermesa's sleep was a vague collection of images from his life, none of which he retained for more than a moment. His taut nerves finally began to relax—

"I commanded you to *stand,* Aquilonian!" bellowed an accented voice in his ear.

Nermesa started, his sword hand instinctively coming up.

With a sharp clatter, another blade expertly forced his down. A large figure silhouetted by the sun stood over him like a fearsome deity. As Nermesa's sleepy eyes focused, he made out armor and the cloak of an officer.

A Corinthian officer.

"Come on, you!" demanded the helmed figure, a bearded veteran twice Nermesa's age and with a face as ugly as the gorilla-god of the Picts, Gullah. "Rise up, spy!"

"I'm no spy!" Nermesa managed to blurt.

"If not one, then what does a Black Dragon, one of the Aquilonian king's most trusted, do so near Tebes, eh?"

"Tebes?" Bolontes' son eyed the man in confusion. He was still adjusting to the notion that he had crossed into Corinthia somehow, much less that he was farther south— near Tebes, not *Sarta*, as would have seemed more likely.

"Still playin' games, eh?" The officer pointed his blade at Nermesa's throat. "Hand over your weapon, and we'll head back to the city! You can prove your innocence there!"

Nermesa loathed giving up King Conan's gift, but the Cimmerian-born ruler would have been the first to point out that life had far more value than refusing to surrender even the finest sword. Nermesa hoped that, assuming he proved he was no spy, somehow he would regain the weapon that had already saved his skin more than once.

He dropped the sword at the feet of the officer. The man snapped his fingers. Glancing past him, Nermesa saw half a dozen soldiers on horseback. One leapt down and retrieved the blade, immediately returning to his mount thereafter.

"Where's your own steed, Aquilonian?"

"Lost." Nermesa chose to say no more. It was possible that the Corinthians would know where the fearsome cats made their home. Should they go there and find the skeletons, they would surely think him partially responsible for the slayings.

The officer took his response at face value. He eyed his captive. "Doubt you'd make it if you walked, and I'd wager the magistrate would want you alive for questioning. Koras! Double up with Athenus! I want this one on a horse next to me . . ." The Teban commander grinned, revealing several gaps in his teeth. ". . . with his hands bound tightly behind him, naturally!"

The expert soldiers quickly took care of the situation. Nermesa offered no resistance and even helped wherever possible. He hoped that his good behavior would work to his advantage. With Sarta advancing its own cause with the takeover of the pass, the leaders of Tebes were actively seeking Aquilonia's favor.

The patrol took a winding path toward home, but it was still a much quicker journey than Nermesa could have hoped for on foot. In fact, he realized that he would have likely taken more than one wrong turn, forcing himself over more inhospitable terrain than needed to be crossed.

A thought occurred to Nermesa.

"I wish to speak with the ambassador from Aquilonia," he said to the patrol leader, whose name was Agamendion. "The moment we arrive."

"You'll need a seer, then," retorted the brutish captain. "Your precious ambassador's been dead a week."

"What?" The blood faded from Nermesa's face.

"Accident, they say. There's a messenger on his way to your capital with the news."

Agamendion shut his mouth and looked ahead again, a clear signal that, for him at least, the conversation was at an end. Nermesa sat in the saddle, staring inward. He had not counted on the ambassador's dying. One look at Nermesa and the uniform he wore, and the man would have vouched for him. Now, it was simply Nermesa's word . . . which, as one who had seen foreigners in trouble in his own country, he knew would not be much help at all.

But all thought of his predicament momentarily faded into the background as the party left the wooded hills and entered a vast, flat agricultural region . . . and Nermesa beheld in the distance the tall walls of Tebes.

Even more so than a place like Tarantia, a self-governing city-state such as Tebes or Sarta made ample use of the fertile soil around it. Thus it was that the region circling the city had little in the way of simple estates, where the wealthy went to enjoy the peace one could not find within Tebes itself. Instead, every estate that Nermesa saw seemed to be in a competition to grow the most of some crop or raise the largest of some animal—or both. Countless workers toiled in the fields, and Nermesa was reminded that the distinction in classes was even more absolute among the Corinthians. The serfs worked like slaves and, in some cases, likely lived little better. The garments of most of those the Aquilonian surveyed were simple cloth tunics with flat, open sandals. Few looked up as the party passed, a sign of just how much work their masters demanded of them.

Another party of riders came up from the direction of the city. Their captain, a man almost as fierce-looking as Agamendion, saluted Nermesa's captor, then led his own troops on. The Aquilonian soon noticed other armed contingents riding here and there. In addition, each estate he passed had its own organized force . . . and Nermesa knew that they were not there to mind the serfs.

The city-states of Corinthia were constantly at odds with one another, various confederations rising up and changing with the wind . . . at least, that was the view in Tarantia. The situation with Sarta was only the latest shift in political control, but its implications reached well beyond Corinthia's borders.

The walls of Tebes had a solid look to them, as if carved from one gargantuan stone. The vision was a false one. The skillful craftsmanship of the builders had covered the true stone with a clay mixture that, when hardened, was almost impossible to crack. Other realms had tried over the years to discover Tebes' secret formula, but to no avail. Nermesa even recalled General Pallantides once speaking of it, the commander of the Black Dragons wishing that the walls surrounding the palace could be likewise reinforced.

The gateway the party approached was sharply arched and with two high, wooden doors that swung open to the sides. As Captain Agamendion led the riders through, Nermesa saw that, when shut, the doors were secured by two huge beams—one at about waist level, the other just above a man's head—sliding across from opposite directions. A platform on each side of the gateway enabled men easily to maneuver the upper bar.

Although Nermesa had never been to Corinthia, he had learned something of its architecture from his tutors. The ancestors of the Tebans and their Corinthian counterparts shared a similar background with Aquilonia's, but there were differences. The Tebans, it seemed, like to build upward in a manner different than Bolontes' son had seen back in Tarantia. They made use of every hill or rise, seeming to accentuate those areas to the extreme. Streets rose and wound around buildings in manners that, to the practical Aquilonian, seemed haphazard and unduly complicated. There were none of the sleek towers such as at home, the taller buildings here seeming a series of boxes stacked one on top of another for anywhere up to a dozen stories. The only towers akin to Tarantian design were the ones near the walls that were used to watch for invaders.

They were gaunt, unprepossessing shadows of the proud giants Nermesa had grown up around.

Most of the basic structures—inns, smithies, and such—were more near what the captive knight was used to, but even with them there were alterations. Roofs were of a green copper and arched almost violently. The columns at the front entrances were slimmer and characterized by a top decorated with a design fashioned after the thorny leaves of the acanthus plant, native to both lands.

Statues dominated various front steps of public buildings much the way they did in Tarantia, although none of the faces were, of course, familiar to Nermesa. Most were clad in the fashion of the Corinthians—dramatic cloaks pinned at one or both shoulders draping over the gownlike tunics still popular among most of the citizens.

Several people paused to eye the captive, no doubt trying to place his own distinctive armor. Some might be able to identify him as Aquilonian, but few would realize that he was a member—however sorry—of the Black Dragons. A ragged figure sweeping refuse into the sewer—Corinthians were famed for the complexity of their water systems, which rivaled even that of Tarantia—gaped at Nermesa as if the knight sported fangs and horns.

As they headed deeper into Tebes, Nermesa dared ask, "When will I be able to see the magistrate?"

Agamendion chuckled. "Sooner than we both thought!" He pointed ahead at a dour marble structure with a foreboding, sooty look to the stone from which it had been built. Men clad in gray armor and visored helms and holding spears at attention stared malevolently at the approaching riders, but they were not at whom the Teban captain now pointed. That honor went to a slim, bald man whom Nermesa might have taken for a clerk in the king's counting-house. Yet, as the watery-eyed figure in the dark blue tunic slowly descended the wide, well-worn steps, each of the grim guards straightened with clear respect and not a little fear.

"Here comes Lord Carolinus now," declared Agamendion. "You may regret your desire to see him, Aquilonian! He looks not to be in a good mood."

Indeed, as Carolinus noticed them, his expression turned sour. He especially seemed to mark Nermesa as the focus of his dislike.

"What is this, man? Who've you brought me? An Aquilonian by his looks . . . and that armor is for no common soldier . . ."

Nermesa decided to take the matter in hand. "My lord Carolinus—"

He got no farther, for at that point Captain Agamendion angrily slapped him across the mouth, drawing blood. "You'll be silent until spoken to directly, understand? And it's 'Magistrate Carolinus' to those in your position!"

Nermesa angrily struggled with his bonds. Two of Agamendion's men drew their weapons, and one of the guards on the steps started down, his intention clearly to run the arrogant prisoner through.

But a single wave of Carolinus' hand made the Teban soldiers freeze. "Away with the weapons. The man is an officer of Aquilonia. Whatever his faults with protocol, I'd like to hear what he intended to say . . . and judge from there."

Something in the magistrate's eyes warned Nermesa that he had better explain well.

But before he could begin, someone else caught Lord Carolinus' attention. "Wait," he ordered the Aquilonian. "I was on my way to meet someone. Here he comes now. I will speak to him, then deal with your situation."

The magistrate walked on past Nermesa. Bolontes' son started to look over his shoulder to where Lord Carolinus headed, but Captain Agamendion gave him a warning glare.

With nothing else to do, Nermesa ran over his story. He had to be cautious about his mission, but certainly could explain that his party had ridden with the caravan as part of a special escort because of the rash of attacks. Whether or not to mention Ambassador Zoran, the Nemedians, and the mysterious Corinthian was still a matter of debate, though. He did not want to be the unintentional instigator of a new series of arguments between the kingdoms, especially since tempers were already near the boiling point.

What *could* he tell the magistrate, then? Nermesa would have to pick each word and thought carefully. Carolinus did not strike him as a man who missed much.

From behind him, the magistrate called, "Captain Agamendion! Come here!"

Turning control of Nermesa over to another soldier, the officer dismounted and hurried over to his superior. Nermesa leaned back, trying to hear what they discussed. Unfortunately, he could understand nothing, not even what the tone of their voices meant.

Without warning, the Corinthian captain returned to him. To the Black Dragon's surprise, Agamendion began cutting his bonds.

"You're free," grumbled the patrol leader. "And I'm to apologize for any trouble you've had." The bearded officer spat on the street. "Consider yourself apologized to."

Nermesa was just pleased to be free. Rubbing his wrists, he nodded to the captain. "My sword?"

With a scowl, Agamendion sent a man to retrieve the elegant blade. Clearly, the Corinthian had intended to claim it for his own.

As Nermesa sheathed his weapon, Lord Carolinus returned. The senior magistrate's attitude, while still officious, was more respectful than previously. He indicated Captain Agamendion and the other soldiers who had captured the Aquilonian.

"The state of Tebes extends its apologies for any undue stress placed upon an emissary of his majesty, King Conan. While the guards can be forgiven for not expecting to find a member of the august Black Dragons wandering our realm on foot, they should have escorted you with dignity to us as they would any visitor of significance."

While not exactly certain that he had as grand a status

as the balding magistrate indicated, Nermesa thanked Lord Carolinus.

"New matters have been brought to my attention; otherwise, I would speak more with you, Captain Nermesa"—Carolinus ignored the Aquilonian's startled expression upon hearing his name—"thus, I will leave you in the company of a fellow countryman, whom both you and I have the pleasure of knowing well. He'll treat you accordingly, I'm certain."

And with that, he stretched his hand out to the side and brought into Nermesa's view a fellow countryman that the Black Dragon did indeed know well . . . and hardly would have expected to come across now.

"Quite a journey you've had, Nermesa Klandes," remarked the Baron Antonus Sibelio with a smile. "You really must tell me about it over some wine . . ."

6

"AN INTERESTING TALE," the baron said, after hearing Nermesa's somewhat-abbreviated story. He poured some more of the sweet red wine he favored into the captain's silver chalice. "One for the bards, if I do say so myself."

Nermesa left the new wine untouched, his thoughts deeply involved in the events he had just related. "Nothing epic about it, my lord. Mostly a story of failure and ineptitude."

"Hardly that . . . unless you've left out something significant?"

The pair of them sat in a city villa owned by the other noble. Antonus had offhandedly mentioned to Nermesa that, in addition to Tebes, he had villas in Sarta and two other major cities of Corinthia.

"A stupid necessity," Antonus had told him. "But when dealing with Corinthians, it's not good to put all your eggs in the proverbial basket. I generally make certain to have a presence in whichever state suddenly finds a way to claw to the top of this land, such as Sarta is doing now."

"How do the Tebans feel about that?"

"They need my goods and influence." The baron had grinned, then. "How do you think they feel?"

Nermesa still did not know how the Tebans felt, but at the moment he certainly envied Antonus' life . . . save where the man's marriage was concerned. As he sat there, purposely ignoring Baron Sibelio's suggestion that there was more to the story than Bolontes' son had indicated—and which was so very true—Nermesa wondered how he could bring up mention of Orena's obsessive vengeance to his savior.

His eyes darted around the sitting room favored by Antonus for personal chats. While the outside was pure Corinthian, the interior was very much that of Aquilonia, especially the capital. Antonus had installed all the latest fashions that Nermesa recalled from home, including wide silken curtains colored royal blue, something just becoming popular in Tarantia.

"You live well here, my lord baron," he finally commented.

Antonus smiled, the only indication that he noted how Nermesa had sidestepped his question. "I refuse to live like a man on the run when I come to do business, even if my trip was a last-minute decision."

"Trouble?"

"Precautions," returned the baron. "With matters heating up not only in Corinthia, but Nemedia and elsewhere, I felt it important to come here. As a matter of fact, the request to send your Black Dragons along to escort the caravan heading to Nemedia came just as I was myself mounting up."

Nermesa had not known that. "I apologize for failing in my duty to protect your property, my lord baron."

"We are both nobles, Klandes. I will call you Nermesa and you will call me Antonus. There is no enmity between us . . . not even with the history you have with my bride."

It was the opening for which the captain had hoped. "I wish that I could mend ways with the Lady Orena, Antonus."

"And thereby keep me from constantly attacking House Klandes?" The lupine mouth curled into a wider grin as

Nermesa opened his mouth to protest. "Merely my jest! It would be my pleasure to put an end to our competition. Trying to counter House Klandes at every turn is putting more of a strain on me than you might think. I do cover my troubles well, Nermesa—"

At that moment, there was a knock on the door. At Baron Sibelio's call, his man Betavio entered. The muscular Gunderman's presence had come as no surprise to Nermesa. Betavio's first and foremost duty was protecting his baron.

"What is it, Betavio?"

"You asked me to see about the return caravan to Tarantia. It will be fully laden in three days and can leave the fourth."

Antonus nodded approval. "Splendid. You may go."

Betavio bowed his head to his master, then, almost as an afterthought, Nermesa. After the Gunderman had departed, the baron turned back to his guest. "I didn't wish to say anything until I could be certain matters could be arranged. I arrived here just to find out that our ambassador had passed away unexpectedly. My good friend, the Magistrate Carolinus, contacted me about sending his remains back to Tarantia, which I came this evening to tell him I would do." Antonus shook his head. "The dear ambassador's death seems to have been serendipity for you! I can now tell you that I've had Betavio fixing it so that you will be able to return to Tarantia with us at the same time."

"I—I'm grateful, Antonus, but my mission—"

Baron Sibelio waved off his protest. "While I'm certainly not privy to everything involved in your mission, I think that it would be best if you returned home and conferred with General Pallantides. I've already sent a messenger bird to Nemedia, to see about the caravan. It may be that it yet made it to its destination. Whatever the case, the news will then be dispatched to Tarantia in time for me to obtain it and turn it over to you and the general."

"I don't know what to say. I don't even know if I can accept your offer. I should continue on. This may be the only chance I have of still discovering *something*."

"You've three more days to think it over, Nermesa. In the meantime, as you haven't been in Tebes before—or even Corinthia as a whole, if I recall—I insist you be my guest and charge any expenses you have to my account. You'll find House Sibelio's name opens many doors here. The baron hesitated, then added, "And when we return home, I'll also see to it that peace can come between our families. If Aquilonians cannot live together, what does that say about the chances for the king's trade agreement and the Corinthians' squabbling?" He leaned forward. "Well? Will you at least take my hospitality? You can consider it a partial apology for what I've done to your family business."

The captain realized that his host would not accept any other answer and, in truth, Nermesa was not certain where to continue. He should have perhaps ridden for Nemedia, but if Zoran was involved in the caravan attacks, then the ambassador likely had men watching for a lone Black Dragon. Besides, if Paulo and the others were dead, as Nermesa feared, then there would be no one to back up his story once he did arrive. Again, if Zoran was indeed a villain, then he might use the Aquilonian as a scapegoat, claiming that somehow Nermesa was a traitor and one of the murderous brigands.

His head felt as if it were spinning. He tried to straighten, but could not.

Antonus saw his predicament. "I've been remiss! You've been through too much these past few days!" The noble leapt to his feet. "Betavio! Betavio!"

The Gunderman burst into the chamber. He stared at Nermesa. The knight also tried to rise, but his legs proved unsteady.

"I'm . . . I'm all right," he nonetheless insisted.

Coming around to the front of Nermesa, the Baron Sibelio took hold of his guest's shoulder with one hand. With the other, he rubbed his own chin in thought. The glitter of his emerald ring caught a dazed Nermesa's eyes.

"You've not eaten right," began Antonus quietly. "and you certainly haven't slept properly. The best thing for you would be a good night's rest! I think that you're likely to fall asleep even before you hit the pillow . . ."

Nermesa nodded, seeing his point. He *had* been through a lot. Would it shame him before his king if he finally allowed himself to recuperate a little?

He never had the opportunity to answer his own question, for, a moment later, Nermesa collapsed into the baron's arms.

WHEN THE CAPTAIN woke again, it was to find himself in a plush feather bed in a room Antonus had set aside for guests. He also soon discovered that he had slept through an entire day.

The baron was away from the villa on business, but the gruff Betavio had remained behind. Nermesa thought this odd since the man was a bodyguard.

"My lord baron's confident of his safety in Tebes," the Gunderman responded much too sharply to the captain's question. "He ordered me to stay with you, though . . ." His expression indicated he would have preferred *any* other duty.

If the Gunderman was supposed to act as his nursemaid, then both he and the Baron Sibelio had matters all wrong. Against the bodyguard's strong objections, Nermesa dressed in his full uniform. "It would be better if you wore some garb borrowed from my lord baron," insisted Betavio, what little politeness he attempted quickly dwindling away. "A Black Dragon in the streets of Tebes makes a good target, my lord . . ."

"I will not shame my comrades and my king by hiding what I am. Besides, the Magistrate Carolinus did welcome me to the city." In the end, though, Nermesa did agree to wear a travel cloak. However, the knight did not bind it closed, as the Gunderman suggested.

It was well past midday when Nermesa at last stepped out into the street. A slim woman in a long, flowing tunic and accompanied by two stern guards eyed him as he stood at the gates of the villa trying to decide which direction to go. The woman's expression did not show the distrust that Betavio had suggested. Rather, it held an invitation Nermesa could not miss. He smiled politely and immediately chose the opposite direction she was going in order not to give any mistaken impression as to his interest.

He had left Betavio with the notion that he planned to see the sights of Tebes. Antonus had given him the idea. However, Nermesa's true intentions were to seek out any clue—no matter how minute—that might lead to finding out about the hooded bandits and their intentions.

Already, he had a few notions. The Corinthians were all but up in arms against one another, mostly because of Sarta's taking of the pass. Perhaps Tebes or one of the other city-states—Athun was a likely candidate, its rivalry with Sarta going far back—had arranged the attacks to make Sarta regret its actions. Maintaining the pass militarily had to be straining Sarta; if enough caravans did not come through it, then the profit the city-state sought would never materialize. That might send Sarta into ruin, making it easy pickings for its enemies.

It was also possible that Nemedia had plotted all this. Certainly, Zoran's actions hinted so, but right now the king of Nemedia actually needed trade between his realm and those of his neighbors—even Aquilonia—to flow well. Tarascus sat precariously on his throne, his treachery against King Conan years before having lost him much support among his most influential followers. If Tarascus could not keep Nemedia stable, he risked a coup.

The Tebans actually seemed quite willing to converse with the officer from Aquilonia, and it soon became clear that they saw King Conan as someone who would side with them against Sarta. Nermesa doubted that the veteran warrior-turned-monarch would risk his nation so unless there was absolute proof that Sarta was responsible for the deaths of Conan's subjects. Then, the miscreants involved would pay with much blood. Conan was caring toward his people, relentless against his enemies.

Unfortunately, although he soon enough ascertained that the inhabitants believed a war between city-states was brewing and that it was all Sarta's fault, about matters concerning his own mission the Black Dragon learned nothing. If he mentioned the caravans, they were the work of the Sartans or, from a few merchants who had just come from the southwestern areas of Corinthia, the foul deeds of envious Ophirians. Nermesa marked Ophir as a point to further investigate, but otherwise felt that he had more or less wasted his day.

There *was* one other clue, but he was not certain what to make of it or even if it would lead anywhere. Two of the last people with whom he had spoken had mentioned something called *the Waste*. Nermesa believed it to be a location in the city, but neither had been willing to talk more about it, as if doing so brought bad luck.

He came back to the villa to find the Baron Sibelio already dining. Antonus gestured with a knife for Nermesa to join him, then insisted on hearing about the officer's day.

"You can spare me wide-eyed details of how interesting the city is. You went in search of information, didn't you?"

"Yes."

"You found none, did you? Dressed like that, I'm not surprised. You should have borrowed some of my clothes, as Betavio tells me he tried to insist."

"I did not want to appear a spy," Nermesa returned rather defiantly. "The Teban soldiers seem quite eager in their duties. I didn't wish to make their acquaintance again dressed as something I'm not."

Antonus took a sip of wine. "Noble. Well, did you discover anything of value?"

Taking a bit of his own food, the knight hesitated, then asked, "Have you ever heard of a place in Tebes called *the Waste*? I believe it to be an inn or—"

The baron cut him off. "It's not an inn. It's an area. I'm surprised that you heard about it. The Tebans like to pretend that it doesn't exist.

"Why is that? And why call any place by such a name?"

"Because if there's someone somebody else no longer wants, if there's something that needs to be hidden from the eyes of others, it's done so there. Just as there are places where the refuse of the wealthy is taken so as to no longer abuse their sensibilities, so, too, is this area used to dispose of the dirt and secrets that could ruin the greatest reputations. Not to mention unwanted relatives, spouses, rivals, and such . . ."

Nermesa shook his head in disbelief. "Disgusting!"

"You think Tarantia has no such place now that Conan is ruler? Trust me, it merely moved to a less noticeable location. No matter who rules, there will always be a need of some for a place like the Waste."

If such a dire place did exist in Tebes, it certainly was the kind of area where, for a price, someone might be able to tell Nermesa what he needed to know. At the very least, it gave him some hope.

"I need to go there, then. Is it far?"

The other Aquilonian's eyes widened momentarily. "Not far enough, unfortunately. You can reach it in reasonable time, not that reason has anything to do with the Waste." He put down his knife and looked serious. "I'd advise against it, but I doubt you'd listen. If you must go, then I ask you to take someone with you for added protection. Betavio, if you like. He knows the city well."

Aware that, unlike with Morannus, he and Betavio were not on the best of terms, Nermesa politely refused the offer. He did not, of course, tell his host why.

Antonus frowned, but returned to his meal. Shaking his head, he remarked, "Be careful, then. I know you mean much to one member of my family, if not another."

Nermesa did not pursue his host's last statement, unwilling to focus on anything but his quest. Only if he succeeded—and survived—could he even think about an auburn-haired lady-in-waiting to the queen.

First, Nermesa had to concern himself with the Waste.

• • •

THE AQUILONIAN'S DESTINATION lived up to its name in its appearance, too. Nermesa quickly recognized the moment that he crossed from the more safe areas to the Waste. A grayness suddenly covered the buildings which he passed, a grayness that might have been soot, but that seemed something almost *alive*. The buildings that followed also needed more and more repairs. Cracks ran like veins across walls and roofs of some buildings that looked near to caving in. The change was so dramatic that Nermesa even halted the horse Baron Sibelio had lent him in order to peer back. Sure enough, only a block past, things appeared *cleaner*, more wholesome even.

But despite the unsettling shift in his surroundings, Nermesa pushed on. He soon saw that the Waste did have a life of its own, one with a veneer of cheerfulness that he quickly noticed seemed to have a harsh edge to it. There were taverns and inns, something that the Aquilonian had not initially expected, and from them emanated music and raucous laughter.

But there were signs that this merriment came with a heavy price. No establishment had less than two burly guards at the doorways. As Nermesa watched, from one tavern came the hurtling body of a patron. His airborne exit was followed by the emergence of two more giant guards, men with faces so disturbing that they made Captain Agamendion seem more like the dashing hero in one of the plays shown in the amphitheaters of Tarantia.

There were bodies, too, although whether alive or not was not always clear. Most were propped up in sitting positions against walls or curbs, but a few lay sprawled among the heaps of rotting refuse in the corners and alley entrances. They might have merely been sleeping off a drunk, but the Black Dragon nonetheless kept one hand close to the hilt of his weapon.

He chose two taverns to start his hunt, but quickly abandoned both as useless. In a third, Nermesa nearly got into a fight with a mountain of a man who thought that the officer was trying to steal away with his woman, a prostitute whom the Aquilonian judged to be twice his own age and looking far older. Fortunately, the offer to buy an ale for *both* quickly ended the matter, but left Nermesa wondering whether or not he had just been played for a fool by the pair.

At the next tavern, a servingwoman with a passable face—but yellowed teeth—finally gave him his first hope.

"Ye'll want to talk to Arno over there," she said with a shake of her hips in the direction in question. "He hears everything."

Nermesa gave her an extra coin for her information but declined the woman's offer of a room for a reasonable price after his business with Arno was through. Carrying an extra ale with him—a suggestion by the server as a way to gain the informant's goodwill—the cloaked Aquilonian walked over to the potbellied, beady-eyed figure nursing a nearly empty mug in a corner table.

"You be the sword of the Cimmerian who rules the north realm," Arno said in way of grumbled greeting. "A little lost, you be, to come here."

The squat figure's recognition of him did not impress Nermesa. The Black Dragon's armor was evident underneath the cloak.

"I am Captain Nermesa of Aquilonia, yes."

Arno's eyes looked not at him, but at the mugs in his hand. "A thirsty, thirsty man, or is one of those for this honest soul?"

Nermesa set the extra mug in front of the informant. Arno immediately swallowed the rest of his own drink, then cast aside the empty cup for the fresh one. He took a careful sip, smiled slightly, then gestured for the Aquilonian to sit with him.

"Smart lad. You bring the good stuff . . . as goes in this swamp of a place, anyway."

As the knight studied the man across from him, he noted a few telltale things. Although now soiled and discolored, Arno's garments had once been of the finest quality . . . and looked as if they were not hand-me-downs, but made for him in particular. He also saw that, behind the ragged beard lurked a face more like his own than that of a Corinthian.

"You're Aquilonian . . ." the officer muttered.

"As much as its king is," growled Arno. "I belong nowhere and everywhere! You want idle talk or you want word of those who plunder their own?"

For the first time, Nermesa had some hope that he might at last be on the right trail. He leaned forward, whispering, "What will it cost me?"

Arno took a deep swallow. "Another ale's good for a start. More of this stuff, in fact." He signaled the serving-woman over. "Marya, my generous friend's inclined to purchase me a brother to this one. Bring it will you?" As she started to turn, he took hold of her wrist. "And he's also offered to pay for time in the back, so don't go making plans with another, eh?"

Marya gave the fat man what Nermesa supposed was for her a winning smile and went off to get the new drink. Arno watched her vanish into the crowd, then gave his client a penetrating stare.

"Much better than her I used to have, boy," he snarled. "But for my state here, she's gold compared to the rest."

Unwilling to argue, Nermesa pulled out a coin for the ale, then what Marya had earlier told him the room with her would cost.

Arno tapped the last amount three times. "I like to take my time with my pleasures."

"The rest when you tell me something worthwhile."

"Done." The expatriate Aquilonian leaned close. "There's been things I heard, from different ends. Many a caravan taken and coming from many lands. Corinthian, Ophirian, Nemedian, Aquilonian—"

Nermesa frowned. "Tell me something I *don't* know."

"You're looking for a Corinthian," Arno said with a malicious grin, "who be not a Corinthian."

The Black Dragon was suddenly alert. "What do you mean?"

The man across him tapped the coins again. With frustration, Nermesa added one of those Arno had demanded. "No more until I hear more."

"A Corinthian who is not a Corinthian. Nor is he Aquilonian, Nemedian—"

"Spare me the list!" the knight hissed. "If not those, then what is he?"

But Arno leaned back and took a drink from his ale. "I can tell you something worth all the money still owed and more, but only if it's all on the table."

"Very well, but it stays in the center until I believe your information worth this game!"

The bearded informer licked his lips as he watched Nermesa count out the rest. His eyes pored over the coins as if they were Marya's hips.

"Well?" demanded Nermesa.

One fat hand started to reach for the coins, but the officer planted his own gauntleted one over the payment.

Shrugging, Arno drank some more. At that point, the servingwoman returned. She not only brought Arno his new ale, but, with a giggle, whispered something in his ear. The former Aquilonian seized her head with his free hand and kissed her soundly before sending her away.

It was all too much for Nermesa. "I grow tired of this waiting game, Arno . . ."

"As do I suddenly, boy," returned his companion, still eyeing Marya's retreating backside. "Something's come up," he added with a chuckle.

"Arno—"

The beady eyes met his. "One thing I've got to tell you that'll make this worth your while. In a booth near the back door, sits two men. One of them is yours."

Only Arno's surprisingly swift grabbing of Nermesa's wrist prevented the knight from leaping to his feet. Bolontes' son took a deep breath to calm himself, then surreptitiously glanced toward the table in question.

And although he could not quite make out the face of

the man who sat with his back toward them, he saw enough to indeed recognize him for the rider meeting with Zoran. The garments were a perfect match, and dust from the road still coated the cloak. True, some would have still argued that Nermesa was taking much on faith, but something within told him that he *had* found his quarry.

"I'll be taking this now," murmured Arno, sliding his hand from Nermesa's to the money. Looking past the knight, he grinned. "Must be going now."

With both his ale and ill-gotten funds gathered, the informer rose from his seat. Nermesa had no doubt that he headed for Marya, who now had the captain's sympathy.

Forgetting Arno's lusts, Nermesa glanced again at the other two men. The other figure was also clad in Corinthian garb, but the knight had no interest in him. He had the look of a subordinate and, in fact, whatever Nermesa's quarry had just whispered to him filled the man with fear. The frightened Teban nodded, swallowed the last of his ale, and quickly left the table.

The man Nermesa sought rose a minute later. Even then, his face remained mostly in shadow. There was hint of a chin, some dark hair, but little more. He did not head for the front door, as his companion had done, but rather for the back.

His own drink long paid for, Nermesa abandoned his own table and started after. Now he felt grateful for the cloak that Antonus' man had insisted upon. It had protected him from identification by the mysterious rider while in the tavern and now shrouded his identity as he pursued the man out.

Hoping that the baron's horse would still be out front when he returned, Nermesa cautiously stepped through the back exit. The door there led to a wide alley where even less savory businesses sought an honest or, more likely, dishonest living. Several yards ahead, the would-be Corinthian silently hurried down an ever-darkening path.

Aware that he might be walking into a trap, Nermesa kept his hand ready at his sword. His eyes darted back and forth as he sought any figure in the shadows who might be a possible attacker.

The "Corinthian" did not seem to be heading for any horse, as Nermesa had initially feared. Instead, he climbed down a set of cracked stone steps, entering an even dingier part of the Waste than the captain had thus far seen. Nermesa waited a moment before descending, to make certain that he did not cause any suspicions on the part of his quarry.

He had not seen another soul for the past few minutes, which bothered him. Again concerned about a trap, he carefully drew his sword.

Ahead, the shadowy form of the false Corinthian hesitated at what Nermesa finally recognized as a doorway. The knight barely had time to duck out of sight as the other glanced his way. Seemingly satisfied that no one observed him, the mysterious figure lightly tapped three times on the door before planting his ear against it. Evidently hearing something inside that satisfied him, he slipped in.

Nermesa counted to twenty, then hurried to the door. He tried the handle and found to his relief that it turned.

A terrible stench greeted him as he entered. So caught up was Nermesa by the odor that he failed to notice the rail suddenly in his way. He fell forward, nearly tumbling over.

At the last moment, Nermesa righted himself, but not before his armor and his sword clattered loud and hard against the metal rail. The Aquilonian immediately froze.

He heard nothing. Silently cursing his clumsiness, Nermesa felt along the rail, discovering it led to a set of steps heading down. As his eyes adjusted as much as they could to the darkened area, he noted something below him glitter ever so slightly.

Water. Nermesa finally recognized the stench for what it was. He had entered the sewers of Tebes.

Common sense told him to turn back, that he could not possibly find his quarry down here. It was very likely that the man he hunted had heard the racket and either hurried off or lay in wait for his pursuer.

Regardless of those suspicions, Nermesa started down

the steps. This was the only opportunity he had thus far had to uncover the truth concerning the caravan attacks.

At the bottom, the knight listened to the sluggish flow of water as he decided which direction to turn. However, his choice was suddenly made for him by a brief scraping sound coming from his left. Gripping the blade tightly, Nermesa moved on.

The way was not always simple. Webs constantly befouled his face, and rats insolently darted over his boots rather than making way for him. Nermesa wondered if anyone other than he and the false Corinthian had been down here since the sewers had first been built. Several places seemed filled with rotting refuse, and once Nermesa imagined a form in the water that might have been a body long decomposing.

Deeper and deeper into the system he pursued his invisible adversary. If not for another momentary scraping sound from up ahead, Nermesa might have thought that his prey had gone in some other direction. Still, he questioned where the man's ultimate destination lay.

Next to him, the water bubbled. It had a habit of doing that, Nermesa knew, likely from air trapped by rotting vegetation and other matter deep under the surface. Nermesa had no idea just how deep the canal was, and the thought of falling in while dressed in armor was a daunting one. Fortunately, the side walkways were wide enough that he had not had to worry much so far. On occasion, there had been places where the footing had been questionable, but not enough to make him fear. Still, throughout the journey, he had clung as near to the wall as possible.

A particularly large bubble burst just next to him, making the knight pause. When he looked up again, Nermesa suddenly realized that he could finally make out the cloaked figure. The other man had paused near a set of steps leading up. Now his plan was clear; the new steps would take him to a place in a completely different part of Tebes, a clever move if he wished to avoid notice by anyone who might know his true identity.

Nermesa waited for the man to start up, but the figure did not move. After much waiting, the Aquilonian grew suspicious. He started toward the shadowed form.

When it continued to remain where it was, Nermesa picked up his pace. He all but ignored silence now, certain that he had guessed right about why the man stood where he was.

When he was about two yards away, the Black Dragon called out, "Turn around! Turn around and face me, but keep your hands from your weapons!"

When the figure continued to keep his back to the Aquilonian, Nermesa lunged forward and tore at the cloak.

The hood of the cloak ripped as it tore free from a piece of metal sticking out of the rail of the staircase. Nermesa stumbled back a step, cursing. He had been tricked, just as he had all along feared.

From the sewers came a short, harsh laugh, then something in a tongue so foreign to him that it sounded like gibberish. An unearthly red glow emanated from behind the knight.

Nermesa spun—and found himself facing the demon of the single, crimson eye.

The cloaked and hooded form stood on the other side of the canal, its twisted hands raised toward the knight. Again came the unsettling, unintelligible words . . .

Nermesa tossed aside the cloak and looked for some place by which he could quickly cross to the opposite side.

The water near him bubbled.

A wave suddenly swept over his legs. Nermesa slipped—

And, armor and all, he fell into the canal, sinking like a stone.

7

THE FLAILING KNIGHT barely managed a gasp of air before he slipped underwater. His armor—especially the breastplate—weighed him down, sending him into utter darkness. Nermesa kept praying that he would hit bottom quickly, but the canal seemed impossibly deep. Even standing with his arms outstretched above him, he knew that he would not have touched the surface.

When he did land, it was atop a soft, congealing mass whose origins he tried not to think about. Already his lungs strained for air. Nermesa grabbed at his breastplate, trying to remove it but failing.

With the knowledge of swiftly impending doom, the Aquilonian pushed toward what he hoped was the side of the canal. If he could lift himself up—

Something long, thick, and pale even in the dark waters shoved into him. The force of its collision was such that Nermesa was lifted like a small piece of rotting wood.

His head broke the surface. Grabbing blindly, Nermesa gasped for air, trying to suck in as much as his lungs could hold.

He went under again just as what seemed a tail as thick as his arm brushed past his side. Nermesa slashed at the water with his sword, but to no avail.

Aware that whatever had run into him would no doubt return very soon, the Black Dragon again sought for the side of the canal. This he finally found, but the wall proved too smooth to offer him any purchase.

His lungs again struggled for air. Nermesa shoved himself against the stone, kicking upward with his feet and fighting the deathly weight of the armor.

His head popped up over the surface . . . but he was unable to completely fill his lungs again before sinking.

And, at that moment, something monstrous snapped at his face.

Nermesa nearly exhaled his remaining air. He had a vision of a stretched skull with wild, inch-long teeth and white orbs without pupils. Had he not reacted instinctively, it might have torn off the flesh, but instead the long, broad maw missed by inches.

The Aquilonian battered at the lower jaw with his gauntleted hand. The blow was not strong, but it evidently surprised the creature, who immediately turned away.

But as it turned, what Nermesa took for a vestigial paw the size of his head shoved the knight off-balance. He tipped back.

Certain of his death now, Nermesa nonetheless reached out desperately for some salvation. His fingers caught hold of something that felt like a handle. He tugged on it, managing to maneuver himself toward the opposite side of the canal. With his last breath, he threw himself against what he hoped was the wall—

But, instead of solid stone, Nermesa felt a gaping hole. He tried to pull back from it, but a sudden rush of current sent him forward instead.

Visions of his family flashed through his weakening mind. He saw again the king honoring him, and Pallantides handing him the sword that somehow Nermesa clung to yet.

Then, as consciousness started to fade, Nermesa suddenly tumbled through into another canal. His outflung arm found air, and his body collided with what seemed a pile of rubble. However, as he sought some handhold, the current pulled at him, trying to drag the Aquilonian to what his drifting feet informed him was a much deeper section.

Somewhere, he found the strength to pull himself up until his mouth was once again above water. Unable for the moment to do more, Nermesa clung to the broken stone as best he could.

When his breathing normalized, the bedraggled knight blinked, in the hopes of making out something of his surroundings. Faint shapes formed around him, ones that did not bring to mind a place such as he had just left. This was something other than a sewer, although clearly at some point the barrier between them had given way.

The water nearby bubbled.

Gritting his teeth, Nermesa scrambled up the ruined area like a ragged spider. His free hand grabbed hold of a long piece of stone—

No. Not stone . . . *bone*.

He dropped it immediately, but in seeking some new purchase for his hand, his fingers grazed more of what had to be the remains of a large creature. A few seconds' more of desperate groping enabled him to discover just what that creature was.

A man. Not a hint of flesh remained upon the bones, and only traces of cloth still clung to the scattered remnants. However, Nermesa discovered something else in the process, several pieces of a casing that lay around the vicinity of the skeleton.

A burial box? Nermesa squinted, trying to make out what lay ahead. He stretched his fingers forward and discovered a wall with some sort of markings etched into it.

Standing, the Aquilonian felt along part of the wall, finding more markings. At an abrupt opening some height above the pile of rubble, he found what appeared a crevice in the wall.

Suspecting the truth now, Nermesa took a few tentative steps to his right. Sure enough, he found a cracked area in which his probing hand located more grisly remains.

Somehow, the break in the sewer had led him to one of Tebes' old catacombs. How old, Nermesa could not say, but perhaps if he followed along the ancient corridor, he would eventually find a way to the upper world again. Certainly, it was better than waiting here for something else to happen.

He stumbled along the edge of what had once been a walkway between the sides of the catacombs but was now a ledge over the submerged ruins of the rest of the floor. Somewhere in the past, probably long after the sewer had broken through to this place, the years of water had caused the floor to sink deep. Perhaps there was even another level to the catacombs below or maybe more than one. Whatever the case, Nermesa feared that if he fell into these black waters, he would find them far, far deeper than those he had barely escaped.

Most Corinthian city-states were built near or over rivers, and Tebes was no exception. From what little he knew of Tebes, Nermesa surmised the waters flowing through here to be from the River Olympos, branches of which fed at least two other city-states. Tebes had obviously made early use of the river and, from the looks of things, had diverted part of its course dramatically after the catacombs had been built. The sewer designers clearly had not known what lurked but a short distance from their master plan.

The way grew narrower, finally forcing Nermesa to sheathe his sword. He glanced at the dark water but saw little. Curiously, though, far ahead it seemed that there was some sort of pale luminescence, as if several hundred fireflies had gathered there.

Hoping that it was at last his way to freedom, the ragged knight increased his pace. His footing proved slippery more than once, but at last he neared the area.

To his consternation, however, the illumination turned

out not to be at all what Nermesa had expected. He had been closer to the truth when he had thought it reminded him of fireflies, for the source was indeed natural, if far different from an insect.

A vast colony—the Aquilonian knew no better word—of pale, blue lichen clustered over the vaults of the dead. Judging by their widespread reach, Nermesa believed that they represented centuries of growth. There was so much lichen that Nermesa could see some distance ahead, enough to know that the catacombs continued on much farther.

Despite his disappointment at not finding an exit, he was grateful for the light, however unsettling it was. It not only enabled Bolontes' son to better watch his footing, but revealed to him that the water's current had grown much stronger. Whether that hinted of anything, Nermesa could not say, but he swore to himself to stay clear of it.

As would be expected, debris had, over the centuries, piled up here and there. Some of it was trash from above, other parts broken segments from the catacombs. Now and then, bits of bone and such thrust out of the makeshift mounds, reminding Nermesa of his fate should he not find a way out.

Then, much to his dismay, his side of the ledge finally completely vanished. He peered across and saw that the other went on out of sight. Frustrated, but with little other choice, the Black Dragon wended his way back several yards to a particularly large deposit of debris that spread across the catacombs.

He tested out the solidity of the mass, then started to crawl across. Memories of the last time he had tried to cross running water so flashed into his mind. Then, he had been out in the Westermarck, on the one hand seeking to evade Picts and brigands and on the other trying to warn his fellow soldiers. His crossing had proven ill-fated, with Nermesa being washed down the river and nearly drowning.

But such was not the case this time. He breathed a sigh of relief as he slid over onto the other side. He paused to glance at the passage he had just made, marveling that his armored body had been supported by the haphazard mess.

On this side, he came particularly close to one of the largest growths of lichen. Even so near, the Aquilonian could not fathom how they glowed so. He had never heard of such a thing, not that the lack of knowledge meant that it was impossible. The proof lit his way in a respectable if haunting manner for which he was very grateful.

Nermesa glanced at some of the markings now visible. They were written in a script unfamiliar to him, which he assumed had to be an ancient form of Corinthian. By the appearance of some, he suspected that they were farewell wishes for the deceased, likely prayers that the afterlife would be a glorious one. Looking over his shoulder at the stench-ridden, makeshift river branch, Nermesa believed that the well-wishers would have been aghast at the fates of their loved ones.

His armor proved to be more and more cumbersome as he moved, yet Nermesa was still loath to remove any of it. Yet, the breastplate in particular became more of an annoyance than a protection, its curved design making him unable to press as close to the vaults as he would have preferred.

Finally, the Black Dragon decided to do what he had struggled in his mind to avoid. He paused and worked to remove the breastplate as quickly and quietly as he could. If he had to leave it behind, then so be it. King Conan would have been the first to tell him that it was the man, not the symbols, that were most important.

Yet, as he undid the last binding, Nermesa grimaced. Here was the armor he had dreamed of wearing, and now he had to toss it aside like so much more trash.

The water before him suddenly bubbled again, this time violently.

The huge, cadaverous head burst out of the dank water, its grotesque appearance made more so by the unnatural illumination. Seen more fully, it almost resembled a human skull with an extended, crocodilian maw large enough to easily snap Nermesa in two at the waist.

A waist now undefended by master-crafted Aquilonian armor.

The creature let out a hiss that sprayed Nermesa with both water and foul breath. Gagging, the Black Dragon raised the loose breastplate even as the monstrous thing lunged.

Teeth as long as Nermesa's fingers clamped tight against the armor. Over and over the beast bit, seeking to destroy the only obstruction to its prey.

Something slashed at Nermesa's leg, something barely deflected by the shin guard. As he maneuvered to keep the breastplate between himself and the monster, the Aquilonian saw better the upper appendages located just behind the head of the serpentlike lizard. They were stunted, as he had earlier thought, designed more for swimming through cluttered sewer canals. However, the claws at the ends were long and sharp, likely not so much for rending but for better maneuvering over the piles of refuse.

Still, they were perfect for ripping apart soft human flesh.

The jaws released the breastplate. Despite its macabre, sinewy form, the monster could balance itself well on its hind body. Nermesa supposed that the rest of the torso and the lengthy tail enabled his fearsome adversary to manage this.

Again, the subterranean horror lunged. This time it attacked the breastplate in earnest, snapping and chewing and tugging at it with abandon. The desperate knight felt his grip loosening.

Over the hissing of the lizard, there suddenly came another sound . . . muttering that sent the hair on Nermesa's neck standing.

Glancing to his left, he saw across the sunken floor the demon with the gleaming crimson eye standing atop a collapsed portion of the vaults. The bones and wreckage of the final resting places of several dead lay at the base of the hooded form's long, voluminous cloak, magnifying in their own way the evil the demon radiated.

At that moment, the beast tore the breastplate free. Raising its head high, it shook the piece of armor several times, then spat the plate out. Nermesa's armor splashed into the water, sinking out of sight.

But in that brief time, Bolontes' son kept his head enough to draw his sword immediately. Even as the pale monster hissed and lunged for the unshielded torso, Nermesa slashed with the blade across the beast's underside.

A shallow gash opened up just below the forelegs. It could not have done much harm to the creature, but the very act startled Nermesa's horrific foe. It was doubtful that much of what the beast ate ever fought back.

Encouraged, the Aquilonian thrust at the head. The serpentine creature twisted away and, with another hiss, went for his arm. Nermesa barely pulled back in time.

Twice, the jaws came at him, snapping eagerly for any bit of flesh left unprotected. Throughout his trial, Nermesa heard the cursed muttering of the demon, clearly the force instigating the foul lizard's relentless assault. Nermesa wished that he could do something to at least distract the hooded form, but he could barely hold his own against the monster.

It came at him again, but this time the knight crouched low. He cut at one of the small limbs, but only managed to scrape the claws.

Without warning, the beast sank lower, the head coming almost eye level. For the first time, Nermesa stared deep into the white, milky orbs . . . and realized that his terrible foe was blind. Accustomed to life with little if any light, it did not need to see as much as smell and feel. Only now did the Aquilonian notice the small whiskers sprouting from the tip of the muzzle and how the nostrils constantly sniffed the air.

Yet the creature moved far too well even with the last two senses surely heightened. Nermesa could only conclude that the demon of the crimson eye also guided the lizard's efforts.

Momentarily distracted by the head, Nermesa failed to

notice more movement in the water. Something shot forth and, before the startled human could react, wrapped around his leg. At first glance, Nermesa thought it a tentacle, then realized that it was the lizard's tail.

He tried to swing at it, but the tail suddenly tugged, pulling the Aquilonian from the edge. Arms flailing, Nermesa crashed into the cold, brackish water.

Fortunately, in the process, some of the tail's hold on him loosened. More by luck than effort, Nermesa kicked free. Without the heavy breastplate on, he managed to stay afloat better.

Hissing, the lizard turned to attack. Grabbing at the retreating tail, the Aquilonian allowed the fiendish creature to pull him out of reach of its jaws. Furious, the lizard pursued, in its blindness not at first understanding that in turning, it constantly kept its prey from it.

But the impasse could not last long. Before the lizard could comprehend its error, Nermesa pulled himself farther up the tail. The beast flailed its tail about, seeking to dislodge the human, but Nermesa held on tight.

The captain caught a glimpse of the cloaked demon still gesturing but had no time to concern himself with what his other foe did. Inching forward, Nermesa finally reached the end of the tail. He raised his sword with the intention of skewering the lizard through the body.

However, the subterranean creature twisted then, tossing Nermesa back into the channel. The Aquilonian collided with one side of the sunken floor and sank under the surface.

It took no guessing to understand that the lizard would be upon him. His air almost gone, Nermesa used his free hand to try to push himself up. Instead, his fingers clutched one of several brick-shaped blocks, likely parts of the former floor. What little he could see thanks to the pale illumination from above indicated that the pile continued on into the black depths, a place Nermesa would surely also go if the lizard got a good hold on him.

Even as that horrific vision came to him, he saw a shape

closing in on his position. The lizard's diabolical countenance filled his view. There was no time to flee to the surface, no matter what Nermesa's lungs demanded.

The jaws widened. The anxious officer seized the block at his fingertips and thrust it into those jaws—

He jammed it in sideways as far as it would go. The savage teeth came within an inch of snapping off his arm, metal and all.

The lizard thrashed about. It let out a hacking cough under the water, then the head suddenly darted toward the surface.

His own air gone, Nermesa had no choice but to follow suit. As he pushed up above the water, he heard a sound echoing through the ancient catacombs. The beast still struggled to free its throat from the block. It shook its head back and forth, twisted its long neck in a dozen different directions, but so far to no avail.

Nermesa contemplated escape, but knew that the creature would likely free its gullet of its burden before long, then pursue him into the dark corridors, where he would be at a complete disadvantage. There could be only one way to finish this . . . if such a feat was at all possible for the Aquilonian.

As if also aware of this, the monstrous lizard suddenly lunged for Nermesa again. That it had not yet dislodged the block meant that it could not completely clamp shut its jaws, but its fury was such that it desired nothing more than to lash out at the cause of its agony.

Even without the threat of the jaws, the creature was formidable. The teeth were sharp enough to cut—and perhaps *infect*, what with the rotting garbage the monster ate—and the force of the head striking full on would be enough to send Nermesa deep into the water. The claws on the vestigial paws were also still dangerous, as was the long, wicked tail.

Nermesa managed to bat the head away, but the lizard quickly renewed its attack. Twice, the beast almost forced its quarry underwater.

As the hacking monster once again paused to attempt to shake the block free, Nermesa judged its movements. He had a slim hope, but it had to do with the lizard's keeping its head above water, even if only by inches.

So much time in the chill waters began to have its toll on him. Nermesa knew that he had only minutes before he would grow too sluggish to defend himself properly.

Raising his sword high, the Aquilonian shouted at the lizard. The subterranean dweller paused in its efforts and turned its head in his general direction. The nostrils flared.

Still hacking, the lizard went for the human.

As the head neared, Nermesa tried his best to shift to the side of where it would strike. This he barely managed to do, the lizard somehow seeking to compensate despite its lack of eyesight.

Nermesa wrapped his free arm around the neck just below the skull. The monster instinctively lifted its head, attempting to shake the human off. However, the weakening captain immediately wrapped his legs about the long neck, making it momentarily impossible for him to be dislodged.

With an angry hiss, the lizard swung its head to and fro. As Nermesa clung for dear life, he studied the underside of the neck. It was scaled, but more softly than the rest of the body because of the need for flexibility.

Pulling his sword back, Nermesa aimed for one spot that seemed particularly soft. However, as he did, he suddenly found the neck and himself plummeting.

Striking the water was like striking rock. The force jarred Nermesa so hard that he nearly lost his hold. His legs briefly flung free before he managed to wrap them around again.

Just as suddenly, he rose in the air once more. Nermesa glanced down to see himself higher than before. He felt the lizard's body convulsing and knew that the aquatic beast was pushing itself to its limits to be rid of the thing clutching tight to it.

Nermesa attempted to cut at the throat. However, once more, he and the neck dropped like rocks. This time, though, the Aquilonian managed to brace himself. When the collision with the surface came, it still felt as if he struck stone, but now Nermesa managed to keep his hold.

He waited for the lizard to raise its head again, but, instead Nermesa felt the water rushing over him. The creature was trying a new and more lethal tactic . . . submerging.

Unable to risk waiting any longer, Nermesa aimed his blade at the nearest soft section he could see. As his head slipped below the surface, he took a deep breath and plunged his sword through the scaled hide.

Nermesa had hoped that the monster, still struggling with the obstruction in its gullet, would not dare sink too deep. With no gills and unable to shut its mouth properly, it risked drowning if it did.

His blade sank in deep. The huge lizard suddenly hissed anew and began thrashing about. Undaunted, Nermesa shoved the sword in as much as he could.

The lizard twirled on its back side as it sought to escape the sword. It pawed at the human but could not reach him. The tail whipped at Nermesa, twice striking him harshly, but not with enough to force the Aquilonian to ease up on his attack.

Quickly grabbing another lungful of air, Nermesa turned the blade in the wound, opening the bloody gap further. Dark fluids spilled from the wound.

The beast's movements grew wilder. It spun, it turned, it flipped over. Despite his best attempts, Nermesa finally lost his hold. He slipped off the bleeding monster, barely missing being swatted by one of its forepaws.

The grotesque head darted high. The lizard hacked, at last dislodging the ancient block. It turned its milky eyes toward Nermesa, its nostrils flaring—

And then the head dropped into the channel with a tremendous splash.

Nermesa clung to part of the broken edge, certain that the beast would revive. Instead, the sinewy form shuddered once, then stilled. Slowly, it began to sink . . .

At that point, the Aquilonian realized that his blade was still embedded in the neck.

Throwing himself forward, Nermesa reached out desperately for the vanishing sword. He made it to the neck just as the last of the subterranean monster sank beneath the surface.

Taking a breath, the exhausted captain dove down. He barely made out the hilt just below him.

His fingers grazed the weapon . . . then managed to seize it. Nermesa tugged—

The sword came free. Clutching the blade, Nermesa left the behemoth to its dank, watery grave.

With effort, he made it back to the edge of the channel. Sheathing his sword, the exhausted Aquilonian pulled himself up out of the water.

"Nine lives has a cat," grated a voice. "but a man only one . . ."

Shaking, Nermesa peered in the direction of the voice. There, moving toward him, was the demon with the single crimson eye.

Only now the figure was close enough that, for the first time, Nermesa saw that it was *not* a demon, not in the mythic sense, but rather a *man* ancient of flesh, and swarthy in the way a Stygian was. His features made him fit in quite well with the catacombs, for his skin was dry and contained little flesh beneath it. His foully grinning mouth was lipless, and his nose was a cadaverous beak. Greasy black hair flattened against his forehead. He stood at least as tall as Nermesa, but from the build of his skull the knight hazarded a guess that, beneath the flowing cloak, this unsightly figure was slighter in build.

Yet what was most unsettling of all was what Nermesa had mistaken for the glowing eye of a demon. Down at the base of the forehead—and nearly between where a man's eyes were—was fastened by links a large, multifaceted red jewel. It was at least as large as an egg, but tapered sharply at the top and bottom.

Although Nermesa knew that he had been mistaken to think it a true eye, he could not help, when staring deeply at it, to imagine that he *did* see an orb within it . . . but one as inhuman as that of the beast just slain.

As for the other's true eyes, they were shut tight . . . nay, they had been *sewn* together, Nermesa finally realized. He doubted that even such a figure as this would have had done such willingly.

"Nine lives has a cat," repeated the sorcerer, for what else could he be? "But a man has only one . . . and you have used your allotment twice over now."

Nermesa tried to estimate his chances of reaching the cadaverous figure and found them too slight. He would have had to race across a precarious pile of debris or swim over the sunken floor. Either way, he doubted that the fiend would simply stand there and wait for death to come.

"Twice over, I say," rasped the dark-skinned man. "A matter soon rectified . . ."

He gestured at Nermesa and the jewel suddenly flared brighter.

The catacombs rumbled, but not from any quake that Bolontes' son could detect. Instead, the shaking seemed to come from within the vaults themselves.

Gritting his teeth, Nermesa looked from the sorcerer to the catacombs.

Something burst through the vault wall behind him.

Nermesa did not hesitate. He threw himself in the water just as what felt like fingers grabbed at one leg. Nails scraped his flesh as he kicked free.

He dove deep into the makeshift channel, letting the current carry him from the vicinity of the sorcerer and his spell. The pale illumination faded behind Nermesa, but still he sensed a tremor of some kind. Despite the weight of his remaining armor, the Aquilonian pushed hard in an attempt to put as much distance behind him as possible.

When at last forced to, Nermesa thrust up to the surface for a breath. Total darkness greeted him. There was no hint of the evil he had fled, although Nermesa remained aware that it could easily lurk in the black void around him.

Taking a risk, he kept his head above the surface as he continued on. The current increased more, easing his efforts.

But then it began to grow *too* strong. Nermesa finally started toward the side . . . only to find himself unable to reach it. Weak as he already was, his latest effort made it impossible to resist the pull of the water. Nermesa was carried helplessly along.

A moment later, he heard the rush of water. The current suddenly tossed him about. Nermesa grappled for some hold, but found none—

And a moment later, was swallowed up.

8

AT SOME POINT along the way, Nermesa must have blacked out, for when he finally registered his surroundings again, he was still awash in water, but now he could see. More to the point, he could see forest, hills, and, most important of all, the *sky*.

But although the Aquilonian was free of the sewers and lost levels of Tebes, he was not free from danger. Nermesa was still caught up in a violent current. Instead of a dank, underground channel, he tumbled along a raging river. That he had survived thus far, especially unconscious for a time, was a marvel to him, but if the work of Mitra, it had been only a momentary miracle. It was very obvious that unless he made it to shore quickly, he would yet drown.

His chance came from a most unlikely source. Rapids opened up ahead, high rocks creating a violent path perfectly designed to crack open boat hulls and smash bones. The latter would surely have been Nermesa's fate if not for some underwater growth snagging his foot and slowing him. That enabled the gasping knight to seize the nearest of the rocks and use it instead for purchase. With grim determination,

Nermesa struggled from that rock to one nearer the bank, then on to one closer. His muscles shrieked, and his lungs felt as if they were filled with water, but the Black Dragon fought on.

And then, when he thought he could go no farther, Nermesa managed to plant one hand on the muddy bank. That instilled in him what he needed to shove the rest of his body forward, until all but his feet lay on somewhat dry land.

At which point, Nermesa finally allowed himself to collapse.

WHEN HE AWOKE again, the Aquilonian crawled higher, at last escaping the area of the river entirely. Shoving himself against a tree, he dared look back at the distant but malevolent flow of water. He was becoming loath to be near rivers and their like, for it seemed that Mitra or some other god was determined that he be given to such bodies to be used as their plaything.

After resting for a time, Nermesa dared test his legs. They shook, but held his weight. For the first time, he peered around, trying to get a read on his surroundings. There was nothing that Nermesa recognized about them, not that such a discovery surprised him. He could only assume that he was either southeast or southwest of Tebes. How far, though, it was impossible to say.

He had slept at least a day, of that the weary Aquilonian was certain. The sun currently hung midway between its peak and the western horizon, indicating that Nermesa had some three hours of light left to him. By the turmoil going on in his stomach, Bolontes' son knew that he would have to find some sort of food before then.

Despite his distaste for the river, Nermesa dared not leave its vicinity. Logically, the best way to return to Tebes was by following it up. That limited where he could search for food, though. True, fishing was an option, but it would take too much effort to put something together with which to fish.

At last, he determined to give himself a fixed distance

from the bank in which to search. His first foray, though, provided him with only a few bitter berries that he spat out for fear of poison. His second attempt proved no better. Nermesa cursed his failed efforts, aware that the sun was very near the horizon now.

But with his third attempt, Nermesa uncovered a surprising bounty. A rabbit squirming about in a cage trap. The Aquilonian bent to retrieve the prize, already contemplating how quickly he could build a fire and skin the animal.

But his fingers proved too clumsy and the rabbit slipped from his grip, escaping into the nearby brush. Nermesa threw himself at the animal, but to no avail.

He sat there for a time, almost ready to surrender to the elements. Then, glaring at the trap, he continued into the forest. If there was a trap, there had to be a trapper . . . or so the frustrated Aquilonian hoped.

No longer heeding his own decision to stay near the river, Nermesa hunted for any sign of the other soul. Even as darkness gradually blanketed the land, the captain journeyed farther. By now, his muddied mind had conjured up visions of a village, replete with inn, where the locals would welcome any lost traveler.

However, Nermesa found no such settlement. What he did at last confront just as the final hints of daylight faded, was a rounded hut made of branches and skins. It brought back memories of the Pict shaman, Tokanu, who had helped Nermesa against Khati for his own personal reasons. Of course, in Corinthia, it was doubtful that there were any Picts. This had to be the trapper's hut.

Far past any concern about invading another's home, Nermesa headed directly for the deerskin flap. All he cared about was finding something to eat and drink.

Ferocious barking sent him reaching for his sword. A thick-furred beast with a mouthful of teeth lunged toward him from the right of the hut—

And jerked to a halt more than a yard short as the rope acting as tether kept the animal from ripping into the hungry knight.

The brown-and-black beast resembled a wolf, but had some canine features to it. It growled and snapped at Nermesa, spattering him with saliva.

Keeping his sword sheathed, Nermesa wended his way around the snarling animal. The rope allowed the creature to stand in front of the flap, which meant that the Aquilonian could not enter unless he either slew it or created a distraction of some sort.

Not wishing to kill an innocent animal, especially one belonging to a person likely to be unwittingly sharing his food with Nermesa, the Black Dragon sought out a large, thick branch. He then approached the still-growling beast and used the branch to prod it back. The wolf-dog snapped at Nermesa's makeshift weapon, but could not get around it.

The Aquilonian pushed the creature back just enough to gain entrance . . . then, with a last swing of the branch, leapt inside.

Teeth snapped at his heels, but to no avail. Unable even to thrust its head through the flap, the wolf-dog had to content itself with barking and growling at its general surroundings.

Too famished to care about the noise, Nermesa looked around. His eyes immediately set upon a small cache of dark bread and dried meat. The Aquilonian needed no further invitation, dropping to his knees and taking a share of each.

As he stuffed some of the bread in his mouth, Nermesa saw a jug. On a hunch, he picked it up and undid the stopper. A tentative taste verified that it was water. Taking several eager gulps, Nermesa returned to his eating.

As his stomach registered the food, the knight calmed. He took a better look at his surroundings . . . his gaze freezing on an unsettling tableau to his left.

A totem had been set up, one consisting of the skulls of small, woodland creatures. The pile was an almost perfect pyramid shape, with larger skulls at the base and the tiniest—a mouse's perhaps—at the top.

Memories of the Picts resurfaced. Nermesa suddenly had an uncomfortable feeling. Finishing up his meal, he drew his sword and made for the flap. The knight prodded it with his sword, then stepped out into the darkening forest.

Too late, Nermesa realized that not only had the wolf-dog ceased barking, but it was nowhere to be seen.

A heavy object struck him on the back of the head.

THERE WERE TWO things that Nermesa—once he woke—decided that he loathed. One was rivers, a subject the Aquilonian had earlier pondered. The second was the many things that seemed to find his skull worthy of cracking.

As he shifted more into consciousness, he noted a voice quietly singing in a tongue vaguely familiar to him. A female voice. His eyes slowly registered a flickering light, which coalesced into a small fire set in the middle of the hut. Over the fire hung a well-cooked squirrel.

A shape moved near the fire, a slim form with long, brunette hair cascading down nearly to the wearer's waist. As his eyesight sharpened, Nermesa saw a dark complexion, deep, veiled eyes, and a full, firm mouth over which hung a slim, curved nose. There was something about her general appearance that reminded him of General Pallantides, as if she were related to the commander of the Black Dragons somehow.

Thought of the general reminded Nermesa of his duty. He tried to move, only to find himself bound.

His actions caught the attention of the young woman behind the fire. Eyes that glittered like black diamonds measured the prisoner. The woman rose, revealing that she wore a short skirt and tunic that barely covered her lithe form.

She said something in the language that Nermesa found familiar but could not understand. When he shook his head, she switched to another with an equal lack of success. Finally, the woman simply stared at her prisoner as if waiting.

Nermesa at last understood that she was waiting for *him* to speak. Somewhat abashed, the captain muttered, "I apologize for breaking into your home, my lady. I wouldn't have done so if it were not necessary."

The figure hesitated, then replied, "Aquilonian, you are?"

"Yes." There seemed no useful reason to hide the fact. "I am Captain Nermesa Klandes, serving his majesty, King Conan."

"Conan . . ." She glanced at the fire. "I have heard of him."

He did not doubt that, the king's exploits legendary and spanning nearly every realm. Seeing that she did not so far seem inclined toward slaying him, Nermesa sought some knowledge of his own. "You are not Corinthian."

"No," she said with a bit of pride. "I am not."

Her short response was not what the knight had hoped for. He eyed the squirrel on the stick. "I'm glad you found more food. I felt bad that I had to take what was yours. It's not my way."

"I believe you." The woman came around the fire. When she moved, her body strained her garment. She reminded Nermesa very much of a black panther on the prowl. "You did nothing to Zyr, although his barking brought me back to deal with you. That marks either a desperate man in need of food only or an absolute fool. I do not mark you as the latter, Nermesa Klandes."

"I appreciate that. Does that also mean that you might free me from these ropes?"

Her half smile taunted and teased. "In a moment, perhaps."

Turning from him, the woman took a small jug and poured a tiny bit of the contents in a wooden cup. She then added some water from the larger jug.

"You should drink this," his captor said, offering the cup to his lips.

He had watched with all too much interest as she had poured the first liquid into the mug. "What's in it?"

"Something to put you at ease . . ." When he still did not drink, she smiled and drank so that he saw that the contents did indeed go down her smooth throat.

It was still possible that the cup contained some poison to which the woman was immune, but Nermesa decided to chance it. He opened his mouth and allowed her to tip the cup toward his lips. The liquid within tasted only of water. He swallowed all she gave him.

"If you still worry," the dark figure murmured close to his ear. "It will not kill you . . . I think."

With a sultry laugh, she pulled from her waist a long knife upon whose blade were inscribed runes. As she readily sliced away at his bonds, she whispered. "And I am Malkuri . . ."

The name made him sit up straight, not because he knew of her, but because he recognized her origin now. "Ophirian! You're Ophirian? Have I flowed so far south that I'm now in Ophir?"

Again came her laugh, a sound that suddenly stirred flames within Nermesa. "No, man of Aquilonia. You are in Corinthia and not far from that place which they call *Sarta*."

"Sarta?" that confused him nearly as much as the thought of being in Ophir originally had. According to all logic, he should have been much, much farther south. "That cannot be! I was in Tebes last and the river could not have taken me up to Sarta!"

As she finished freeing him, Malkuri slid to his right onto a pile of furs. "Perhaps you were under a spell . . ."

A spell? Nermesa fought his growing desire for this beautiful woman by turning his gaze in the opposite direction. Unfortunately, that left him staring at the skulls. "A spell, you say?" he blurted. "Such as a witch could cast?"

"Be not afraid of those," the Ophirian returned, sliding across the furs until she was near enough to touch him again. "They were taken with permission, and I honor all who gave themselves for my needs. From their spirits I ask small favors, but nothing so base as to send a man into such confusion that he fears for his mind . . ."

He did not quite follow her explanation, having fixated on the fact that she *was* a witch. The last witch he had encountered had been Khati and the fact that Malkuri was as beguiling—if not more so—than the Pict did not make Nermesa any less suspicious. "What brings an Ophirian witch to the climes of northern Corinthia, if she is but a simple practitioner who troubles no man?"

Some of Malkuri's confidence eroded. Her smile faded as she looked into her own memories. "What else could, but the *House of Chelkus*?"

"Chelkus!" Nermesa breathed. Even as far away as Tarantia, rumors of the House of Chelkus made themselves known. Chelkus, reputed to spawn many gifted in sorcery or alchemy. Pallantides had once let something slip that indicated he knew more about Chelkus than the rumors, but Nermesa had never dared pursue that subject with his commander. Now he wished that he had. "You are of that House?"

"Of the weakest part," the Ophirian answered bitterly. "But carrying the blood and gift that made me a prize mare offered by the patriarch to a cousin of mine."

"A man with more of the gift?"

"Not only the gift, Nermesa Klandes, but a visage whose ugliness was only surpassed by his dark tastes! But none of that mattered, so long as the potential for a powerful child was there . . ."

The Aquilonian shuddered, aware that his own arranged betrothal had offered far less trouble than Malkuri's had and yet *he* had been repulsed by that suggested union. "But you fled Ophir before it could take place . . ."

She glared at him. "Think you *that*? Would that I could have! My protest was known and so I was kept secured until the marriage! For two years, barely out of childhood, I was his mate, his plaything . . . and the mother of his *firstborn*."

Firstborn . . . "A child?" Without realizing it, Nermesa quickly glanced around the hut, seeking some sign of a child's presence.

Malkuri must have noted his reaction, for she laughed again, but this time most bitterly. "There is no young one wandering around, playing with Zyr and climbing trees, Nermesa Klandes! He died barely three days old . . . and a good thing, for his father would have used him for his own terrible gain!"

"What?" Horror spread across the captain's face as the true meaning of Malkuri's words registered. "You mean he would have—but his own son?"

The Ophirian witch made a cutting gesture that was unmistakable in its bluntness. "To some, blood is a worthy tool of the arts, the fresher and more powerful it is."

"Monstrous!"

His exclamation made her eyes suddenly soften. Once more desire suddenly burned within him. "I mourned my child and in his death found the will to flee. Since then, this has been my home. Zyr I found abandoned near the walls of Sarta. He was only a pup, but he struggled for life that he had not first asked for . . . which is why he bears my son's name also."

Well could Nermesa understand her calling the wolf-dog by her child's name. Alone, with only the memory of the brief life she had created, Malkuri had no doubt been filled with a vast emptiness.

"I'm . . . sorry," the Aquilonian muttered, his words seeming so worthless in the face of her loss.

Malkuri abruptly leaned into him, making it impossible not to see the bounty her body offered. The eyes that looked into his burned as brightly as his desire.

"No, Nermesa Klandes, *I* am sorry . . ." Her full lips neared his as, in a whisper, she added, "but perhaps not so very much as I first thought."

He had no chance to question what she meant by the last, for then the Ophirian witch was upon him.

THREE DAYS PASSED in which Nermesa barely even left the hut of Malkuri. He knew that he had to move on, had to continue his quest, but something always drew him back to her. Nermesa suspected that it had to do with the draughts that she gave him twice each day, but the Aquilonian could not bring himself to refuse them when they were offered.

"They will give you strength a month of sleep cannot,"

the dark-tressed Ophirian promised. "They will help recoup all that was lost, Nermesa Klandes."

And each time that she offered herself, he took her with an obsessiveness that part of him questioned. It was not that she was not desirable, but another face always intruded in his mind even then. A face surrounded by a cascade of auburn hair.

Yet, still Nermesa always surrendered his will to Malkuri.

Even in sleeping, his thoughts were troubled by this. He would become determined to leave at first light, then wonder how he could abandon the woman. He would reprimand himself for such outrageous behavior, then feel the fire within stirring again.

This night, the fourth of his stay, the turmoil worsened. In addition to his troubled thoughts, his head now pounded, too. It started as a slight headache, but rapidly grew to a sensation akin to a hundred giants beating at his skull. Worse, that sensation spread to his entire body. He shifted uncomfortably, trying to rid himself of the growing pain, but nothing worked.

Then a sound intruded into his slumber. A gentle murmuring that reminded him of Malkuri. The Aquilonian focused on the sound, drawing some relief from it.

But suddenly another, more violent noise shattered any hope of peace. A crash . . . followed by another crash. Nermesa fought not to wake, but failed.

A terrible rumble of thunder shook away the last vestiges of sleep. The wind howled, and what sounded like a torrent of rain battered the small hut. Malkuri had bound the flap tight, but now it seemed to be struggling to burst inward, as if some giant invisible beast sought entrance.

Nermesa sought for his sword, but the weapon was out of reach. Malkuri's voice rose above the din, the murmuring he had heard in his slumber actually the Ophirian witch chanting over the totem of skulls.

His constant desire for her suddenly drained away as he decided that she was the cause of the storm. All this time, she had been plotting something, and now it had reached fruition. The witch had drugged him to keep him pliable for just this moment.

Pushing himself up, Nermesa reached over and harshly grabbed her shoulder. A growl rose up from the corner of the hut, where Zyr suddenly stood ready to defend his mistress. Nermesa vaguely recalled that the wolf-dog had stayed in the hut untethered throughout the knight's stay, not bothering the pair. Now, however, Zyr clearly noticed the hostility in Nermesa.

Malkuri, too, reacted to his sudden change, but not as Nermesa might have expected. She stared at the Aquilonian in concern—concern for him. The witch did not for a moment cease her chanting despite his interruption, but her gaze turned to the flap and the warring elements outside.

The entire structure suddenly shook as if some hand sought to tear it free of the ground. Yet somehow the hut stayed in place.

Releasing Malkuri's shoulder, Nermesa looked for his garments and sword. He threw on only enough to cover him, then belted on the sheath.

Zyr no longer watched him, now intent on the flap. The wolf-dog growled low, as if sensing someone outside.

The Ophirian's chanting increased . . . and now Nermesa thought he heard other sounds accompanying her foreign words. They were not human sounds, though, but rather reminiscent of the calls he heard when traveling through any forest. *Animal* calls. A wolf. Several birds, including an owl and a mockingbird. The Aquilonian even thought he heard the hiss of a snake or lizard.

He glanced back at the totem . . . and could have sworn that around it emanated a very faint golden glow. Over the skulls, Malkuri further intensified her efforts. Her arms stretched skyward, and her breasts rose and fell rapidly as she threw herself into whatever incantation she was casting.

At that moment, the flap suddenly tore open. Zyr leapt toward it, barking furiously. Nermesa charged the open entrance—

"No!" shouted Malkuri.

Just as he reached the opening, a tremendous force threw him back. But Nermesa did not simply tumble over the furs. He *flew* over them, hovering as a cloud might hover over the landscape. The walls of the hut bent in and out as if the structure breathed.

Nermesa finally landed. He grunted as the air was momentarily jarred out of him by the force of the collision.

Zyr charged out of the hut, heading into the storm.

Shoving himself to his feet, Nermesa, sword in hand, fought his way to the entrance. He felt as if cold fingers grabbed at his throat, seeking to stifle his breath. Despite that, the Black Dragon finally managed to reach the opening and follow the wolf-dog outside.

The storm wracked the forest around him. Huge trees shook and shivered, some bending over almost completely. Loose foliage swarmed around him like a mass of angry bees. Rain beat down on him. Nermesa put a hand over his face to keep from being blinded.

A growl momentarily cut through the thunder. The Aquilonian veered to the right, heading toward where he thought the animal was. He trusted the wolf-dog's natural instinct to ferret out whatever was the cause of all this.

As Nermesa entered the forest, Zyr barked wildly at something he had discovered. Picking up his pace, Nermesa tried to find the creature.

Lightning suddenly struck the tree next to him. Nermesa barely leapt out of the way as much of the upper half came crashing down.

As he rose again, a shadow moved a short distance ahead, a shadow moving on what was likely *two* legs. With an angry growl, Nermesa rushed the area. He slashed at interfering branches, tore at obstructing bushes, in order to reach his quarry.

Then, something swung across his view. In the dark, it looked like a hand made of spindly branches. It hit the Aquilonian square across the jaw, sending him tumbling back. His sword finally slipped from his hand.

And as he landed, a rasping laugh reached his ears. Over him suddenly loomed a shadowy figure.

Lightning flared . . . its illumination intensifying the glitter of the crimson jewel worn between the figure's sewn-shut eyes.

The sorcerer from the catacombs gestured at Nermesa . . .

9

A CRUSHING FORCE overwhelmed the Aquilonian. His very bones felt as if they were slowly being ground to powder. Yet, even with all that, Nermesa fought to grab his blade so that he might still save himself.

Then, out of the storm came a sleek, swift shape that leapt at the hooded figure. The sorcerer swore loudly as Zyr fell upon him. Malkuri's wolf-dog growled and barked as he and the fiend rolled out of sight.

Slowly—much too slowly for Nermesa's tastes—the crushing force eased. As soon as he was able, the Black Dragon seized his sword and struggled to his feet. In the forest ahead, he heard Zyr furiously attacking and the rasping curses of his human adversary.

But as Nermesa neared, there was a flash of crimson light, and the animal suddenly let loose with a wild, pained yowl. The light momentarily blinded the Aquilonian, and in that moment he heard ragged breathing and swift movement heading away.

The second he could see again, Nermesa rushed toward where the two had been fighting. The light had faded almost immediately after, plunging this part of the stormy forest into darkest shadow.

Nermesa's foot prodded something. An uneasy feeling swept over him. He bent down to see what lay at his feet.

Lightning flashed . . . and in it, Nermesa beheld the gruesome remains of the wolf-dog. Although only visible for an instant, it was a sight the captain doubted he could ever forget. Malkuri's loyal companion and protector looked as if he had been *flayed* alive. His fur and the flesh holding it had been torn in one great piece from the poor animal. Shock alone likely had slain Zyr, though the blood Nermesa had seen pooling over the carcass probably would have killed the wolf-dog soon after, regardless.

Disgusted at what men could be capable of, Nermesa sheathed his weapon. Had the sorcerer still remained near, he would have attacked the Aquilonian by now. Zyr had accomplished two great feats before his death—driving off the villain and saving Nermesa's own life.

Steeling himself, Nermesa bent down again and picked up the animal's body in his arms. Had he seen a man slain so on the battlefield, he would have carried the corpse back; for Zyr, Nermesa could do no less.

The wolf-dog's head lolled at an awkward angle. Grimacing, Nermesa took it by the muzzle and shifted it for better carrying. As he did so, he felt something stuck in the teeth. A piece of cloth. Without knowing why he did it, the Aquilonian took the cloth and stuffed it in his belt.

As he finished adjusting the grisly burden, Bolontes' son noticed something else. The storm had all but ceased, as if simply cut off. More curious, the only moisture on Nermesa was his sweat and the wolf-dog's blood. The Aquilonian's hair was not even damp.

Frowning, Nermesa started back to Malkuri's hut. Along the trail, he noticed a few other peculiarities. Although the dark of night hid much, his eyes had adjusted enough to tell that the many broken branches and scattered leaves that he recalled appeared to have vanished. The path was also very dry.

Most unsettling, the area where Nermesa recalled the tree being struck was clear, and the one he believed had been hit seemed entirely whole.

It was with some relief that finally Nermesa spotted the hut. As he approached, the Ophirian witch slipped out of her home. A gasp escaped her when she noticed what he carried.

"A sorcerer did this," growled the Aquilonian.

Malkuri nodded, then managed to say, "Please . . . please bring Zyr inside."

Nermesa obeyed. Malkuri entered behind him, the witch murmuring.

"Where do I set him down?"

"By the totem."

For some reason, Nermesa was not surprised. He placed the wolf-dog's corpse in front of the mound of skulls, then backed away.

Malkuri leaned down, gently touching Zyr on the top of the head. She then turned to the Aquilonian, looking him over. "You are injured?"

"Most of the blood belongs to Zyr. He saved my life from the sorcerer . . ."

"He was good." The witch returned her attention to the carcass. "Good friend and brave protector." She raised her hand, and in it Nermesa now saw a dagger. "And so you still shall be, Zyr."

Malkuri brought the blade down, cutting deep into the throat.

Startled, Nermesa watched in horrified fascination as the witch severed Zyr's head from his body. She then held up the head, pointing the ruined muzzle toward her own. Again, the Ophirian muttered under her breath.

The totem began to glow slightly.

Not wishing to see more, Nermesa silently departed the hut. With him, he carried one of Malkuri's water jugs. At the edge of the small clearing, the Aquilonian opened the jug and poured some of the water over his head and torso. He took a handful of leaves and used them to wipe off as best as possible some of the grime and blood.

It took the better part of an hour, but at last Nermesa felt himself clean enough to tolerate. He glanced over his shoulder at the shadowy hut. The witch's muttering had ceased several minutes before, but Nermesa had given himself some extra time before returning.

When he entered, it was to a scene that made him arch his brow in mild surprise. There was no sign of Zyr's corpse, not even the slightest trace of blood. Malkuri knelt by her totem, her eyes shut and her lips barely twitching.

Nermesa quietly returned to where he had been sleeping. A few minutes later, the dark woman joined him.

"Zyr thanks you, Nermesa Klandes. His spirit will join with that of the lion to watch over you."

He started. As far as he could recall, no word of his House symbol had ever passed between them. Then Nermesa recalled his sword. Likely Malkuri had studied it, possibly when he had been her prisoner.

"I thank you also," she added, suddenly leaning forward and kissing him deeply.

Vestiges of desire stirred, but Nermesa fought them down. The struggle against the nameless sorcerer had burned away most of whatever potion the witch had given him. He gently pushed her away.

Her eyes held not anger, but sadness. Malkuri nodded. "I would have stopped the draughts soon, but it has been so lonely here . . ."

"You're a beautiful woman." Nermesa gestured to the side. "Why not go to Tebes or Sarta or one of the other Corinthian city-states? There is many a man of high stature who would fall over himself for you."

"And, in doing so, my cousin's family would find me. They watch the cities, I know."

"What of your husb—your cousin? Does he also search?"

Her expression momentarily became one of grim satisfaction. "It is hard to search while rotting in a grave."

Nermesa did not have to ask the details of his death. Malkuri was a very determined woman. "You could go to Aquilonia. I've friends who would aid you there."

She shook her head. "My fate lies elsewhere, this much I have divined." The Ophirian grew much more solemn. "Something I would do for you, Nermesa Klandes. There was a force tonight of such evil that we are fortunate to be alive, much less still have our souls . . ."

"The sorcerer . . ."

"And for you to speak of him so means a familiarity no one would ask for. I did not seek the full reasons for your having wandered to my home, Aquilonian, but they involve this creature of darkness, yes?"

"Yes." He held back from saying more, though.

His reticence did not go unnoticed. "I may be able to help you know more of your enemy, Nermesa Klandes. There are ways the House of Chelkus teaches for seeking such knowledge . . ."

It was tempting. Nermesa had once thought his adversary a demon, but that a man should be so steeped in the foul arts in some ways bothered him more.

Something occurred to him. "Whoever he is, he's not as mighty as he imagines. Zyr caught him good before being so cruelly slain."

Malkuri's eyes immediately burned with anticipation. "How do you know this?"

The Aquilonian searched for the small piece of black cloth. In the light of the witch's fire, he saw for the first time how blood-soaked it was.

Malkuri snatched it from his grasp, only a moment later to gasp and toss the piece to the ground as if it had bitten her.

"Sala and Parcelsus!" she spat. "Such venom . . . it cannot be!"

Nermesa eyed the bit of garment warily. "What? What happened just now?"

Instead of answering, the Ophirian reached for the bloodied cloth again, only to halt her outstretched fingers just above it. She muttered something, then finally—defiantly—seized the piece.

"Tell me what you saw of him," Malkuri rasped. Her

eyes looked up, nearly rolling back into her head. "Tell me, Nermesa Klandes!"

He no longer hesitated. "The sorcerer wears a cloak that seems to live of its own accord. As black as his soul. In it, he appears a demon or phantom . . . but in truth, he looks far more monstrous than both. His face is as dry and pinched as from an ancient grave and—"

"And the *eyes*," she demanded. "What color are his eyes?"

"I wouldn't know." Nermesa cringed at the very memory of those eyes. "for they were *sewn up* tight! What I thought was his eyes—his *one* eye—was in fact, a gemstone the sorcerer wears over the lowest part of his forehead!"

Malkuri let out an oath in her native Ophirian. With the scrap of cloth in her hand, she crawled over to the totem. Muttering under her breath, the witch grabbed a tiny pouch and from it drew a pinch of some gray powder. This she tossed onto the cloth, which now lay before the base of the totem.

A totem that, for the first time, Nermesa noticed was now supported at that base by the freshly polished skull of an animal with both lupine and canine features.

Still muttering, Malkuri seized a tiny bottle from near the hut wall. Removing the stopper, she poured three drops of a dark liquid onto the powder.

An emerald flash caused the Aquilonian involuntarily to pull back. Green smoke rose from the cloth. Malkuri leaned forward, inhaling from the smoke.

A breath later, she began to speak . . . but her voice was deeper, almost a man's and yet something else.

"Cursed by his own, cast out by evil! Seeker of the vile treasures of Acheron! Banished from Ophir, land of the father! Reviled in Stygia, womb of the mother!" The witch convulsed, then let out a wordless cry before declaring, "It *is*! Sala and Parcelsus, it is he! The fiend, *Set-Anubis*, walks this mortal plane yet!"

The last of the smoke faded. The cloth was now a wrinkled, burned thing.

Malkuri convulsed again, then slumped forward. Nermesa moved to help her, but the Ophirian shook her head.

"Touch me not for the next few moments . . ." she rasped. "But take what is left of that cloth and toss it into the cleansing flame! Hurry!"

Nermesa wasted no time in obeying. The ruined piece was unsettlingly cold to the touch, not hot or even warm, as he had expected. With much relief, he tossed it into the small fire, where it vanished with a vile hiss.

As he turned back to Malkuri, the witch straightened. She shook her head twice, flinging her ample hair back and forth as if to shake free from it the vestiges of some nightmare.

Her eyes burned into his. "Set-Anubis haunts your trail, Nermesa Klandes! How can this be so? What could you do to so draw his interest?"

"Who is this Set-Anubis?" the captain demanded back. "He sounds Stygian." Nermesa had grown up hearing tales of mysterious, sinister Stygia, with its serpent god and dark practitioners. He knew that King Conan had faced sorcerers from that land and defeated them, but at great price. Now one was after *him*?

"Not completely Stygian, nor fully Ophirian, Nermesa Klandes, but the worst of both! He who calls himself Set-Anubis—it is said his own true name may be whispered only by demons—bears the blood of Chelkus from his father, a corrupt sorcerer himself! Yet his mother was a Stygian creature, who saw in the father the means to beget a son of dark power!" Malkuri spat. "What they begat was a monster in human form, a creature so foul that both were dead by his arts before he reached full growth!"

The Aquilonian looked aghast. "He killed his own parents?"

"In far worse manner than my *husband* would have my own baby. But those were only the first of many heinous crimes, crimes for which even the Stygian masters under whom he studied became revolted! They are the ones who sewed shut his eyes as punishment, then cast him into the deserts to die . . . but a thing as foul as Set-Anubis ever seems to find a way to survive."

"But—how, in such a state?"

Malkuri shrugged. "Some say magic, others the work of fearful demons! It is then that he is rumored to have found the ruins of lost Acheron and learned from secrets there how to bind himself to the power of certain artifacts they had left behind." With her finger, she drew a symbol in the air, one that Nermesa suspected was of protection against evil. "And there he discovered the *Eye of Charon*, which you saw adhered to his face! Legend says that it was created by a wizard of Acheron who learned all the secrets of death. Whether true or not, you see that it is aptly named, for it now gives Set-Anubis sight such as no mortal man can comprehend . . ."

A horribly fascinating tale, but still it did not explain some things to Nermesa's satisfaction. "But why is such a creature after me . . . and what can possibly defeat him? Is your magic—"

"Ha! Do not even think it! We are both very fortunate, my Aquilonian warrior! Set-Anubis is able to mix illusion with reality, and both weapons are mighty indeed! Something must have bound his skills, though . . . but he may not be long in returning. Both of us must leave here, though our paths differ!"

"So, is there no manner by which to destroy him?"

Malkuri considered. "Zyr was merely fortunate, he being a woodland presence that the foul one's sorcery did not notice until too late. Still . . . I had thought Set-Anubis once dead . . ."

Bolontes' son grasped at that straw. "And why would you believe such unless it had *some* credence?"

"Because it was said that it was the Kushites who finally slew him, using magic arts such as even Stygia only imagines. I had heard that his head decorated one of their temples and had itself become an artifact of power for those who would dare use it. A pity that it is not so."

A pity for Nermesa, especially. He leaned back, frustrated. If the powerful and relentless sorcerers of Stygia and Kush could not rid the world of this Set-Anubis, what could a simple soldier do?

Nermesa suddenly snorted in self-derision. He could do more than simply wait for his own terrible death! For much of his life, he had dreamed of serving the king and his beloved Aquilonia, and now that the utmost was demanded of him, he worried only about his own skin.

And why *was* Set-Anubis after him? Nermesa finally realized that it could only do with the attacks on the caravans. Somehow, the sorcerer was involved, although at first glance, the Aquilonian saw no reason for him to be. Surely, Set-Anubis had not been reduced to thieving . . .

"Where is the nearest town or settlement other than Sarta?" he asked the witch.

"Sonos is the nearest. Three days at good pace." With hesitation, she added, "I will take you there. They are friendly to me, for I have used my arts to heal some of their sick."

"Good. I appreciate that."

The Ophirian rose. "I do not think the fiend will return before then, but I will place wards around the area that may at least warn us if he does."

As she slipped out of the hut, Nermesa leaned back, thinking. He, too, did not believe that Set-Anubis would return this night, but they dared not wait any longer than first light to leave. Besides, it was time that he turned from the hunted back into the hunter . . .

The rustling of the flap stirred Nermesa, and he realized that he had drifted off to sleep. Malkuri had returned from outside, her expression pensive.

"I think they will do . . . I hope that they will do."

Just as a precaution, though, Nermesa drew his sword and set it next to him. Then, feeling his exhaustion taking control again, he shut his eyes. He would need all his strength, if not for Set-Anubis, then for the journey.

There was movement next to him. Nermesa heard

Malkuri's close breathing and felt the warmth of her body near his own. He prepared to reject her advance, but all she did was gently wrap one arm over his, as if seeking comfort from the darkness against which they had both just fought.

Nermesa might have lent her his other arm, too, but it already worked to comfort *him* . . . by tightly gripping the hilt of his sword.

And thus he slept for the remainder of the night.

ALTHOUGH NERMESA STIRRED before daylight, Malkuri woke even before he did. She already had everything of value to her bound up in a small sack she carried on her back. In addition, the witch held a staff that, by the manner of her grip, was clearly meant as a weapon as well as a tool . . . and likely was the item she had used on his head during their first encounter.

There were dried rabbit and berries awaiting the Aquilonian, who felt some shame that Malkuri had done so much while he had apparently slept like a rock. As her defender, he found himself far below measure.

Her skills apparently included reading thoughts, for the Ophirian finally said, "Fear not that you slept, Nermesa Klandes. You are the one on whom the fiend has set his unholy sight; the sleep you badly needed . . . and I had much to do."

One thing that that knight immediately noticed different was that the totem had vanished. Malkuri could not have put all the skulls in her sack; not only would she not have had room for anything else, but even some of the skulls would have still had to remain behind.

He dared to bring it up, to which she willingly replied, "I have returned them to the forest and ground. All save Zyr's, which is in the sack. He refused to leave me, and I gratefully accept his continued watch."

Nermesa half expected to see the ghost of the wolf-dog suddenly come inside and stand guard next to his mistress. Trying to banish such a vision, the Aquilonian pursued his

own needs, quickly gathering up what little he had and offering to carry whatever else the witch thought that she
might wish to take with her.

Malkuri bowed her head in gratitude, but declined. "I
have long learned to travel with only what I can easily
carry, Nermesa Klandes. This is not the first home I have
abandoned, nor will it be the last."

"I'm sorry to be the cause."

"There would have been another. There is always another. It is my fate." She would say no more, and he did not
press.

The sky was overcast, and so when day came, it did so
as a grudging shadow of itself. Nermesa wondered if the
clouds might be part of some new spell by Set-Anubis, but
as Malkuri did not comment on them, he chose to believe
that they were what they appeared to be and no more.

His companion led him along what at first seemed the
most awkward of paths until she explained that she followed what her skills told her was the most elusive one,
the better to keep from the mystic gaze of the sorcerer.
After what he had experienced so far, Bolontes' son willingly followed no matter how sudden and odd the shift in
direction.

The first day went without threat. Nermesa volunteered
to stand guard for a time even when Malkuri insisted
that her wards would do as well as he. Exhaustion finally
forced the Black Dragon to surrender his post for slumber,
but he continued to keep his sword ready even while
asleep.

Mitra at last seemed to smile on Nermesa, for, three and
a half days later, the pair reached the edge of Sonos.

The settlement was larger and more civilized than Nermesa had expected, with several stone-and-wood structures. There were no cobblestone streets, but the inhabitants
had covered their dirt ones with a layer of fresh straw,
which Malkuri explained was replaced every few days
per Corinthian custom.

Most of the homes were round buildings with thatched

roofs, but the two most prominent—the smithy and the meeting house—had high, sturdy roofs with wooden tiles. The meeting house, where locals gathered with the town elders to hold council, was built entirely of stone and mortar and, with its slit windows, looked as if it doubled as a place of last refuge during an attack.

Visitors were evidently not so common that their arrival did not bring many stares. Yet most of them seemed directed at Nermesa, not his arresting companion. A few locals, possibly former patients, even bowed their heads in respect to the witch.

Two men in used breastplates and wielding spears approached the newcomers as they neared the center of the settlement. One placed the tip of his spear against Nermesa's chest. The Aquilonian refrained from leaping back and drawing his own weapon, aware that, while he was capable of taking on the man, the other was only doing his duty.

"What business have you in Sonos?"

Malkuri reached a gentle hand out to the burly, bearded man's wrist, saying, "He travels with me, Herodius. Is that not enough?"

"Phillipian's ordered we take no chances. There were riders past here two days ago with the look of Sarta on them. Sonos is no vassal of Sarta and never will be!"

"I am not from Sarta," Nermesa interjected.

"And not from anywhere else in Corinthia," muttered the second guard, a reed-thin man with black eyes. Nermesa judged him the more capable fighter of the pair, despite his clearly being subordinate to Herodius. "That's an Aquilonian voice, if I mark correct!"

Malkuri stood in front of Nermesa. "And does Sonos have quarrel with Aquilonia? There was none with Ophir when I first came to Sonos."

"That's . . . different," argued Herodius.

Nermesa suspected it *had* been different. He could not see how any man could consider Malkuri a menace. The *women* of Sonos, perhaps . . .

"I swear by what goodwill I have earned that he is here

in friendship and need, Herodius. Go and tell Phillipian so. We will wait for his word—"

"You need never wait for my word or my devotion, dear Malkuri," said a voice to Nermesa's left.

All four turned to see a man nearly the age of Nermesa's father, but as lean and as capable as General Pallantides. He wore a short, dark beard trimmed just below the jaw and was clad in robes of gray and forest green. His face was round but well featured, with brown, knowing eyes that more often than not alighted on the beautiful witch.

He wore no sword and walked as if confident that he needed none. To Malkuri, the man stretched out a hand in greeting. Out of the corner of his eye, Nermesa thought he detected the slightest of blushes from the Ophirian. She took the hand in her own, holding it a moment longer than custom deemed sufficient.

"Phillipian . . ." Malkuri murmured.

"Malkuri, beautiful Malkuri . . . will you be my bride?"

His audacious question startled Nermesa, but the Ophirian simply—and perhaps sadly—shook her head. "My fate lies elsewhere, Phillipian. That you know."

"Aah, but even you admit that in that one aspect, you know not what will be . . . and so, I continue to ask and hope that your fate decides to add me to it." Before she could say more, he turned to Nermesa. "Yes, you *are* an Aquilonian, aren't you?"

"I am Captain Nermesa Klandes of the Black Dragons, my lord."

"And I am no lord, simply headman of Sonos." Phillipian took his hand. His grip was powerful. "Welcome to our home, Captain Nermesa." He turned to Herodius and the other guard. "Arrest him, will you?"

10

PHILLIPIAN TREATED NERMESA with the utmost respect, but that hardly made up for the fact that the Aquilonian now sat in what passed for a jail in Sonos. At the headman's command, Herodius and his partner marched the captain to the meeting building and a lone, iron cell situated in one corner. A wooden bench with a blanket acted as bed, chair, and dinner table.

Malkuri was not allowed to go with him. Instead, Phillipian whispered something in her ear, then guided her away.

The moment that he was incarcerated, Nermesa was forced to give up the remnants of his armor. Both armor and sword were taken by Herodius to Phillipian, no doubt—at least in Nermesa's mind—to be kept as spoils of the capture by the headman.

Herodius then came back with the simple garb of a Corinthian peasant. These he tossed into the cell, growling, "You want your life, put these on! Toss the rest out!"

There seemed no use in arguing, especially since most of the Aquilonian's garments were rags by this time. He did as the guard commanded. Herodius returned a few minutes after, grunted satisfaction, then picked up what Nermesa had tossed out and left again.

Barely had he done so when the clatter of many hooves reached Nermesa. Through the one tiny window high in his cell—so high, in fact, that he was forced to stand on his toes atop the bench to peer out—the imprisoned officer watched as a full unit of cavalry burst into the settlement. By their markings, they were from Sarta.

Nermesa cursed. Phillipian intended to turn him over to the soldiers as a peace offering. He wished then that he had not surrendered so readily, but at the time his intuition had told him to do so.

A broad-chinned giant with a hook nose and long mustache, who was clearly the officer in charge, dismounted. Herodius ran into sight, immediately taking the Sartan's reins.

"We come in search of a foreign rat, a renegade soldier from Aquilonia with ties to bandits! He was said to be sighted near here!"

"Aye, so we heard, Captain!" Herodius quickly returned, his head bobbing up and down as he spoke. "Master Phillipian—"

"Yes, where is your Master Phillipian?" growled the Sartan officer. "If he thinks to hide the scum—"

"He would be a fool to do so!" finished the headman, appearing from the left side of the window.

Nermesa almost shouted a curse at the man. He wondered how Malkuri could have such obvious feelings for one with no true sense of honor. The Aquilonian had entered Sonos in peace.

"Captain Cicero," continued Phillipian. "It has been too long since Sonos had the pleasure of your visit."

"And it's been too short since duty forced me to this dirt hole, *Master* Phillipian."

The headman bowed apologetically. "If you are thirsty, I can at least offer some of our fine local ale—"

"That swill? Bah! We'll be doing our duty and getting back as soon as possible!"

"As you wish. And I may be able to help you do just that, Captain. A body was discovered that I think was your man."

"Lead on, then." But before Captain Cicero could take more than a step, Phillipian politely indicated that he should halt.

"I have already ordered men to bring the body here. They should be on their way."

Sure enough, from beyond Nermesa's view of the left, there came a call. Both Phillipian and the captain turned in that direction. Moments later, two men carrying a covered form came into view. They tossed the body to the ground with little fanfare.

Captain Cicero bent down to uncover it. Nermesa stifled a gasp when he saw hints of armor. For a brief moment, he wondered if another Black Dragon had found his way to Sonos, only to perish, then realized it was his own equipment that he saw.

The man whose corpse pretended to be his had been roughly Nermesa's height, but his hair was a shade darker and his face more swarthy. His specific features the Aquilonian could not see, but there was some hint that they had been damaged during whatever had caused his death.

As Nermesa watched in morbid fascination, the Sartan looked over the body. He especially marked the bits of armor, grunting in satisfaction as he studied one closely.

"Where'd you find this?" the officer asked, rising.

"In a ravine a half day's ride in the direction of Tebes," Phillipian immediately replied.

"Where's his sword? I was specifically told to watch for a sword. One with lions on it."

Nermesa frowned. Someone knew much more about him than they should have.

The headman spread his hands. "No sword was found. No valuables of any sort. They even took his breastplate." Phillipian bent down and turned the body over. Much of the back of the corpse's garment was stained red. "Slain from behind. The brigands we've spoken of before, Captain. I'd wager one of them is sporting the breastplate and wielding the sword you want."

Cicero rubbed his chin in thought. "Damned scum!" He looked over the body once more, then turned to his men. "You . . . and you!" The two soldiers in question dismounted. "Secure this garbage for travel!"

As the men obeyed, Nermesa exhaled. Phillipian's plan was clear; he had arrested the Aquilonian to keep him out of sight and now used this other body as a decoy for the Sartans. The headman had clearly known of the imminent arrival of the searchers, hence his quick and, at the time, curious actions.

Phillipian bowed to Captain Cicero again. "Can I not persuade you to join us for a community meal tonight? You recall it from your last visit, I hope."

The Sartan officer's expression grew disgusted again. "Your ale's sour enough, and now you offer that black goat stew?" He turned on the men loading the body atop one of the horses. "Get moving there!"

Phillipian politely stepped back as the captain returned to his own mount. "You are welcome back at any time, Captain Cicero!"

"Never again would be too soon!" snorted the Sartan as he tugged on the reins. Turning his steed about, he waved to the rest of the soldiers. "Move out!"

With relief, Nermesa watched as the Sartans began riding off. The two soldiers finished securing the body, then mounted on the remaining horse.

As the second got on, he happened to glance in the direction of the cell window. Nermesa instinctively pulled out of sight, only after doing so realizing his terrible mistake. He would have drawn less interest if he had just stayed at the window, pretending to be a simple prisoner.

He waited, certain that the soldier would shout out a warning to his commanding officer. Instead, though, the sounds of retreating hooves drew him back to the window just in time to see the final soldiers vanishing into the forest.

The Aquilonian slumped against the wall, now at last able to breathe easy.

Several minutes went by before someone finally came for him. Herodius, a grim smile on his face, opened the door of the cell as Phillipian joined the pair.

"I trust you understand now," remarked the headman.

"You could have said something."

"There was no time for discussion . . . and if the worst case happened, I *would* have turned you over to them for the sake of the people of Sonos."

Nermesa accepted the blunt statement. Phillipian's first loyalty was to those under his care. While the Aquilonian would not have been happy with such an outcome, under the same circumstances he might have done likewise.

"Fortunately," the other man said with a more friendly smile, "they took what was before them as what they searched for."

"The body—where *did* it come from?"

Shrugging, Phillipian answered, "Much of what I said was truth, except that *he* was a brigand, not the victim of one. We caught him last night. He tried to escape earlier today and was slain. Our intention was to burn his body, as we do with all refuse." With a harsh laugh, the headman added, "But your situation came up before we had the chance. Truly, Mitra must smile over you."

Perhaps in this one instance, but Nermesa did not feel so in general. Nothing went simply for him. He had hoped to get food and rest in the hut, only to be snared by a witch and nearly killed again by a fiendish sorcerer. Then, what Malkuri had promised would be a friendly settlement had immediately tossed him into jail. Of course, the latter had been done for his own good, but he had not known that at the time.

"One thing I still don't understand. Why hide me from them in the first place. As part of Sarta—"

"Watch your tongue!" snarled Herodius.

"Easy, friend," Phillipian said to the guard. "Nermesa

Klandes is not familiar with Corinthia. We may be near enough for Sartan soldiers to come searching for wayward Aquilonians, but we are most *definitely* not a part of their city-state. We are as independent as Tebes or any other. Sonos will not become a vassal of Sarta."

"Not that we've encouraged them to want us much," added Herodius, his mood bettering. "God-awful stuff we made 'em drink and eat the last couple times!"

To Nermesa's puzzled expression, the headman explained, "We have no illusions concerning our chances should Sarta decide to annex us. But I decided to try an experiment in discouragement. Each time Sartan officers brought troops in here—Sarta was not yet the power it has become—we welcomed them with a feast and drink."

"And the worst of both," interjected Herodius.

"The *very* worst of both," agreed his leader. As Phillipian guided the knight out of his cell, he continued, "Carefully crafted, naturally. We didn't want them suspecting a ruse. The most rancid batch of ale we could brew and good goat cooked too long and seasoned with spices sure to turn a sensitive Sartan's stomach wrong."

"And it worked?"

"Visits by the patrols shrank to nearly none. The last time Captain Cicero brought his men here was nearly two seasons ago. I believe it will likely be two seasons more at least before he shows his face again." Phillipian chuckled at his own cleverness. "An army may travel on its stomach, but even it has its limits. I have no doubt that past descriptions of Sonos have left the Sartan commanders with little inclination to add such a useless backwater village to their holdings."

It was a ploy that Nermesa would have never thought of, and he suspected few others would have, either. He bowed his head to Phillipian's cunning, then dared approach the headman about a more intimate subject. "And what happens to me?"

"Malkuri speaks for you, and in Sonos her word is respected by all. Her skills have healed many who otherwise would not be alive today . . . myself included."

Nermesa did not press Phillipian on the last. "So, I am free to go?"

"With a horse, yes. The one left behind by the brigand, as a matter of fact."

As they neared the door, someone else entered. Malkuri looked at Nermesa in great relief, then gave the headman a grateful blush. Clearly, the Ophirian had feelings for Phillipian, but would not act upon them.

"Thank you, Phillipian," she said. "I am in your debt."

"Considering what you did to save my life, hardly." He guided them both out of the meeting house. "Fortunately for all of us, Captain Cicero chose not to accept my invitation, or else we'd all be dining on some rather disturbing fare instead of the fine meal awaiting us."

AND IT WAS a fine meal, as the headman had promised. The ale was robust and well flavored, while the goat was spiced in a manner the Aquilonian had never experienced, with rosemary and other seasonings that he could not identify. He sat between Malkuri and Phillipian, ostensibly because he was friend of one and guest of the other, but more because Malkuri insisted on the distance between herself and Sonos' leader.

Phillipian took her choice in stride and seemed to content himself with plying Nermesa with general questions about Aquilonia. He finally answered one of the knight's own questions, the one concerning the headman's background.

"Yes, I am part Aquilonian, though I've not seen the kingdom in many years. My father was the son of a merchant whose caravan passed near here en route to some of the more distant city-states. But one journey, he met my mother, daughter of the headman then, and chose to stay behind. Unfortunately, when I was just entering my tenth year, she died of illness, and my father returned to his homeland. I was schooled there for the next several years with the expectation that I would join the family business." With a wry grin, Phillipian concluded, "I did, just long enough to ride down here with the caravan and bid my Aquilonian heritage good-bye. I have never regretted it, either—save when that bear mauled me, and I lay minutes from death."

At this point, his eyes strayed to Malkuri, who found much of interest in her food. Nermesa marveled that a man who had been in such dire condition as his host had just hinted could be walking around looking as if nothing had ever happened.

Perhaps reading this in Nermesa's expression, Phillipian indicated his torso. He adjusted his garments just enough so that the knight could see a small portion of his chest.

What Nermesa did see was a horrific pattern of long, wicked scars from what had surely been claws.

Covering up the area again, Phillipian nodded toward Malkuri, murmuring, "Three months she stayed with me, when all others had given up."

With that, he turned to his ale, hefting the mug and quaffing a good portion of the contents.

The rest of the meal was eaten with friendly, innocuous conversation. All but a few of the inhabitants of Sonos sat at the tables set in the middle of the dirt square. Those whose turn it had been to cook and serve did so with courtesy and no complaint. Others switched off with them midway through the meal, ensuring that no one had to wait long to enjoy it.

"Is this a Corinthian custom?" asked Nermesa at one point.

It was Malkuri who answered. "No, this is a Phillipian custom."

Sonos' leader chuckled. "Once a week, to keep the community bound together. Everyone shares the responsibilities equally, including the headman."

It was the first time since leaving Tarantia that Nermesa truly felt at ease. He savored the time, well aware that it was fast coming to a close.

In fact, no sooner had the meal ended than Phillipian put a hand on his shoulder, and whispered in his ear, "Come with me."

Malkuri followed after them as they headed for a broad, square house with a stone base. Nermesa rightly assumed that this was the headman's home.

"Enter freely and unafraid," Phillipian said to the knight.

The interior was modest, more so than the Aquilonian would have expected. There were two rooms—the common area and a door that Nermesa assumed led to the place where Phillipian slept.

"As leader of Sonos, I can do no less than offer a guest my own quarters." Phillipian indicated the door. "The bed is clean and will give comfort."

"I can't accept—"

The other man cut him off. "To refuse would be an affront that might make us enemies."

Not certain exactly how true the statement was and unwilling to find out, Nermesa acquiesced. "Thank you."

"Tomorrow morning at first light, you can take the brigand's horse—saddled and with full provisions—and head along the trail you'll find on the northwest edge. Keep to it and you'll come up into Aquilonia near the pass Sarta holds. Your trail is good for a single rider, but not for a caravan, so the Sartans have paid little mind to it. Ride through that region only at night, though, to ensure the utmost safety. Is that clear?"

"Very much so. Thank you."

"Sonos is no friend of Sarta, as you know. Times are growing dangerous in Corinthia and even beyond. Before your arrival, there was word that Nemedia was sending overtures to Sarta."

Nermesa nodded. "This makes sense with what I know."

"But do you know that Ophir seeks to make a pact with Sarta's greater rivals, such as Tebes? Like Nemedia, it claims to do so because of the belief that it is the Nemedians who have attacked their caravans. The city-states are aligning themselves even as we speak . . . and I fear that this war will encompass more than my beloved Corinthia, Nermesa Klandes."

The Black Dragon could not argue with him. He had

not heard of Ophir's intentions and looked to Malkuri for verification.

"There is little I hear of the world of men in the woods," she responded carefully. "But, yes, this sounds like Ophir."

"But the trade agreement—"

Phillipian all but prodded him in the chest. "I fear that King Conan's trade agreement will soon become like dust in the wind, scattered beyond regathering. If this war happens, as it seems it will, not even Aquilonia will escape it."

"I *must* return home." Although what he would do when he did get there, Nermesa did not know. All he had was his own story of how the sorcerer, Set-Anubis, aided the brigands. How could that help solve anything?

"First light," repeated the headman. "You need the rest." He turned to the unlit stone fireplace. "And you will need this."

Reaching up into the chimney, Phillipian retrieved a long bundle. Unwrapping it, he presented the contents to the Aquilonian.

"Yours, I believe."

Nermesa could not hide his pleasure as he took the sheath and sword. As he pulled free the weapon, the knight drew comfort from it. Despite its troubles, it still gleamed.

"A brilliant piece of craftsmanship," uttered Phillipian.

Malkuri touched the flat of the blade ever so cautiously, then nodded. "The spirit of the lion has been imbued in it. It will always protect you as much as it can, Nermesa, for it has found you worthy to wield it."

Bolontes' son did not know whether that was true or not, but he did feel much better now. Sheathing the sword again, he grinned at Sonos' leader. "Thank you . . . thank you very much."

"Not at all. Now, since it is dark already, may I suggest you retire?"

"What about you?"

"I will sleep in here. There are furs by the fireplace that are quite comfortable." Phillipian opened the door, then ushered Nermesa inside. The bed was not the cot that the Aquilonian had expected, but a true one, such as Nermesa might have slept in back home.

"One of the few benefits of the nearness to Sarta is the occasional caravan that must pass this way. I admit that a bed was something I missed from Aquilonia. It was worth the haggling, trust me."

"I cannot—"

"You will." And with that, Phillipian shut the door, leaving Nermesa to reluctantly accept his gift.

The sight of the bed had a mesmerizing effect on the knight. Suddenly, he felt extremely exhausted. It was all Nermesa could do to undress and set the sheathed sword beside the bed before nearly falling onto the plush cushions.

But as he settled down and started to drift off, a sound from the other room momentarily stirred him to waking. At first, he did not know what it was, but then a feminine giggle answered all.

Malkuri had indicated that it had been some time since she had been with anyone, and so she had turned to Nermesa out of loneliness as much as anything else. However, from what he could hear, it was clear that with Phillipian, loneliness was not at all a factor. At least for this one night, Malkuri would be with the man she truly cared for but could not accept.

Turning in the opposite direction and pulling the blanket over his head, Nermesa gave them the privacy they deserved.

HE WOKE IN the dark to a hand over his mouth. His first thought was to reach for his sword, but then he noted the feminine feel of the hand. A moment later, Malkuri's throaty voice whispered in his ear.

But what the witch whispered were not words of endearment.

"The Sartans have returned," she warned.

11

CAPTAIN CICERO'S MEN rode in from the same direction that they had come earlier, but this time fanned out as they entered Sonos. From Malkuri's urgent warning, Nermesa had expected the Sartans already to be well into their hunt throughout the settlement, but the witch told him that he could thank Phillipian for the early alarm.

"When he became leader, he had sentries set up some distance around Sonos, *especially* from the direction that the Sartans would use."

Already she and Nermesa had slipped out of Phillipian's home and headed for where Malkuri said that he would find a waiting horse. Of the headman, there was no sign, and Nermesa had to assume that he had rushed out to stall the Sartan officer.

From the east, the Aquilonian heard a booming voice that had to be Cicero's and the sound of something wooden being broken. He paused, caught between his own fate and wanting to aid those who sought to protect him.

But Malkuri would not permit him to turn back. "You must go! Phillipian insists! If you are not here, he may be able to convince them that they are wrong! If they find you, then it could be worse for Sonos!"

"But what brought them back?" He envisioned the moment when the one soldier had noticed him watching from the cell. Had the man been suspicious after all and informed his superior?

"I do not know! Here, your horse!"

A figure bearing the reins of the steed materialized in the dark. Nermesa belatedly recognized him as Herodius.

"There's some small provisions in the saddlebag," the bearded guard muttered. "Best could be done."

"Thank you," Nermesa replied, as the man thrust the reins into his hand.

"Best get him goin'," Herodius added to Malkuri. With that said, the guard hurried off, no doubt to lend support to his headman.

The Aquilonian watched the man depart, aware that he had likely underestimated Herodius. The guard's loyalty to Phillipian could surely not be questioned.

There was a crash from the east. Malkuri pushed Nermesa to the horse. "Go! Leave now!"

He leapt up into the saddle. "Should you stay here?"

Even in the dark, Nermesa could sense her brief smile. "They will not find *me*. They never have. Fare you well, Nermesa Klandes. May the lion continue to watch over you."

The Aquilonian gave her a grateful nod, then turned his mount in the direction that Phillipian had earlier described and quietly rode off.

It still galled him that he had to flee rather than help the people of Sonos, but Malkuri had rightly pointed out Phillipian's belief that a lack of any sign that he had been there in the first place would do better for the locals. Captain Cicero's men would probably break a few more things and shove some of the inhabitants around; but if their search came up empty, then the headman would be able to convince them that they had made a mistake. Nermesa had to trust in the able Phillipian.

But none of that meant that the knight was better off

than his protectors. It was possible, even likely, that the
Sartan officer had also sent some men to watch the surrounding forest, which meant that Nermesa had to pick his
way carefully.

His mount proved adept at moving with caution, no
doubt a trait taught it by its former master. Nermesa gave
thanks to Mitra for the ironic twist of fate; he who had been
hunting brigands now in part owed his life to one.

The trail required care to follow, for it was not one used
by caravans. Nermesa hoped that the Sartans would over-
look it, but he dared not expect them to do so. The Aquilonian kept his sword out, ready for any sudden attack.

An hour passed, then a second. He could no longer hear
sounds from Sonos. Whether that meant that the patrol had
left, Nermesa could not say. For the sake of Malkuri,
Phillipian, and the rest, he prayed that it was so.

When what was nearly another hour had passed, Nermesa finally dared pause long enough to dig into the provisions. They consisted mainly of dried fruit, nuts, and some
leathery substance he assumed was meat. He ate a few of
the first two, but chose to save the last for when his hunger
was such that he would not mind fighting with it.

To his surprise, as dawn approached, he saw the mountains separating Corinthia from Aquilonia. From the angle,
he was also not all that far from the northeastern tip of
Ophir. He urged his horse on, his hopes of reaching home
growing as the peaks ahead did.

But midday still found him far from the beckoning
mountain range and forced at last to stop for a rest. The area
was more open here, but still enough woods and hills dotted
the landscape to give him some shelter from other eyes. He
located a shady spot near a running brook and tethered the
horse where it could lunch on tall, green grasses.

From the brook, Nermesa refilled the water sack that
Herodius had also left him and which he had emptied
along the way. He also took his fill from the brook, wiping
his face clean at the same time.

A survey of the region revealed no evidence of other

people and so the Aquilonian dared to sleep a little. He kept his sword handy, just in case somehow someone *would* come across him.

But his nap went uninterrupted and when Nermesa awoke, he saw he still had an hour of daylight remaining. After seeing to both his and his horse's needs, the Black Dragon mounted, then continued on toward the beckoning mountains.

Well into the night, Nermesa understood that he would still not reach the mountains until late into the next day. Regardless, Bolontes' son pushed forward, wanting to cut the gap as much as possible.

A short time later, though, he came to a sudden halt as flickering lights warned him of others in the area. Circling around them, Nermesa counted at least three fires.

The source of the flames did not prove to be soldiers, as he had feared, but rather a small caravan. Nermesa listened for voices but heard none. While the caravan might have been one in which he could have found transport to Tarantia, he dared not risk speaking with them. Here, they could very well be Corinthian or even Ophirian. Both would find it very curious that an Aquilonian should be traveling in stealth here. They were just as likely to slay him or, barring that, keep him bound until they could turn him over to soldiers.

Although the wagons had created a circle, he was finally able to determine that they were not headed for Aquilonia but rather another part of Corinthia. Seeing no more reason why he should risk discovery, the knight turned his mount away and quietly continued toward the mountains.

Near dawn, he paused to rest again under the protection of a gnarled ridge. Nermesa did not sleep, too eager to reach the mountains before dark. As soon as he felt both himself and the horse ready, on they went again.

When the land finally gave way to the first and smallest of the peaks, he sighed in relief. Once across them, he would be back in Aquilonian territory. Surely there would be some outpost to which he could report. If they had messenger birds, perhaps a note could even be sent to Tarantia.

Phillipian's instructions still held true. Nermesa again hoped for the best for the headman of Sonos and his people, including Malkuri. He wondered where she would move next. Perhaps, with Nermesa gone, it would be safe to return to her old hut. Certainly, doing so would keep her near Phillipian.

He was forced to shrug off any further thought of the pair, for the terrain became more and more treacherous. Despite Phillipian's warning to travel only at night, Nermesa decided it best to make what progress he could during the day. The path was well-worn, yes, but that did not mean that it did not have its threats. A recent rockfall forced Nermesa to guide his horse on foot for a time. At another area where the trail sloped alarmingly, he sighted far below the skeletal remains of a pack animal. Whether the owner's remains also lay below, Nermesa could not tell, but it was a grim reminder that home was still very far away. He could not imagine how well he would have done at this very point had he traveled in the black of night as suggested.

Much to his further frustration, the path also began winding southwest . . . away from home. He knew that it would eventually return to Aquilonia, but this meant a longer, more wearying trek. Yet, there was nothing Nermesa could do but follow it; the mountains offered no other trustworthy way.

At what was perhaps the flattest, least oppressive part of the trek, he paused to sleep. In the mountains it would not do to ride while either man or beast was overly weary. A single mistake could prove a very final one.

The next day began ominously overcast, with strong winds and long rumbles of thunder. The only good thing that Nermesa could find about the situation was that the path had just begun to wind back north again. He hoped that he would be out of the worst of the mountains before the weather turned wicked.

Some distance ahead of him, small rocks clattered onto the path. Nermesa had long grown used to being pelted by such as them, the mountains seeming constantly to shed bits of their bulk. Fortunately, only once had anything possibly deadly fallen anywhere near him.

As the wind picked up, more clatter arose from both in front of and behind him. Nermesa tugged on the reins, slowing the horse.

Up farther ahead, where he could not see, there came a particularly loud clatter. Nermesa frowned, wondering if the path was breaking apart.

Then, the head of another horse came into view.

Swearing, the Aquilonian reined his mount to an abrupt halt. He was still in lands claimed by the Corinthian city-states, especially Sarta.

Around the bend came a dour-looking rider—a soldier in Sartan gear.

He caught sight of Nermesa and his expression twisted into surprise. As the Aquilonian sought to turn his horse about, the soldier drew his weapon and urged his own mount forward as fast as it dared go.

Nermesa got his own blade out just as the man neared. As their weapons came together, Bolontes' son saw another Sartan coming up behind the first.

Despite being at an awkward angle, Nermesa proved the better swordsman. He parried two more strikes by the soldier, then cut the man on the right arm. As the soldier pulled back the wounded hand, Nermesa's blade drew a deep slash across his throat.

Not waiting for his opponent to fall, the Aquilonian urged his horse back down the path. There had been one or two possible side trails—where they came out, he could not even hazard a guess—and it was Nermesa's hope that he could lose the Sartans there.

He dared peer back long enough to see the second soldier now followed by a third and fourth. A patrol. The Sartans clearly sought to increase their hold on all commercial passage through the mountains. Phillipian had been wrong to think that they would find such a route unimportant, and now Nermesa paid the price for that false assumption.

More familiar with a path he had just taken, Nermesa

made far better time than on his way the other direction. Unfortunately, another quick look over his shoulder indicated that his pursuers, too, knew the way, certainly well enough to keep up. There were at least four behind him now, and Nermesa suspected more followed.

The hooves of his horse constantly kicked up loose rock. More than once, the animal skidded several feet. However, the Aquilonian dared not let up. The soldiers drew nearer and nearer, one of them now almost close enough to take a swing with his weapon.

A gap opened up on his right. Not certain whether it was actually one of the paths for which he had been searching, Nermesa nonetheless veered his steed toward it.

The Sartans followed right behind, the lead rider narrowing the gap more. He finally took a swing at Nermesa, only to come up short. Still, it would not take much more for the next swing to make contact.

The left edge of the trail abruptly gave way to a chasm several hundred feet deep. Nermesa kept his mount near the right, even though that meant almost constantly scraping his unprotected shoulder against the jagged side of the mountain.

The first Sartan came up on his left, by his expert handling of his horse on the narrow path clearly a man who had ridden this way before. He thrust—not at Nermesa, but rather the Aquilonian's steed. The animal let out a cry as the blade drew a shallow gash on the flank.

Nermesa swung back at the man, only to have his attack parried. The soldier thrust, but came up short. Twice more, they traded vicious strikes. The Sartan grinned as he took the upper hand—

Pulling his left foot free of the stirrups, Nermesa shoved with all his might at the other fighter's mount. The beast was powerful, and so his effort was only measured in inches.

But inches was all Nermesa had needed. The Sartan horse stumbled, lost its footing—and slipped off the path.

Both it and its rider screamed as they plummeted to their doom.

Regretting his tactics but aware that they were necessary, the knight struggled to maintain control of his own horse. The effort forced him to slow. Two more of the soldiers drew near, but they did not advance enough to take him on. That they were at the moment content to follow meant that they knew of a better point ahead at which to attack.

Nermesa urged the horse on, daring the narrow ridge more than he knew that he should have. There were still at least four men nipping at his heels and likely others out of sight.

The wind howled, and small droplets of water assailed the Aquilonian, but he did not let up. Several times, the hooves of his steed came perilously close to the edge. Once, Nermesa thought that he heard a scream behind him, but with the wind and thunder, it was impossible to verify.

At last, the trail veered off into a ravine. Nermesa had no choice but to follow it down. The ravine opened wider, finally allowing for two or more men on horseback to ride abreast . . . which was exactly what Nermesa had been hoping to avoid.

A quick glance back verified his fear. The Sartans rode with renewed energy, whipping their mounts into a frenzy as they sought to come up at him from both sides. There were seven that the Black Dragon could count, likely the full contingent at this point. He doubted that if he surrendered and tried to explain his presence, they would give him the chance even to open his mouth. All appeared to be veteran fighters, and each looked eager to take his head.

Three outpaced the rest. One in particular looked to be a serious threat. He was the oldest, leanest of the pack, and from his crested helm Nermesa suspected him to be the officer in charge. The Sartan shouted something at the man nearest him, and that soldier unexpectedly sheathed his sword.

Nermesa did not have to wonder long what the hunters planned, for the second soldier then reached back and removed a bow from behind him. With expert skill, he seized an arrow from a quiver on the other side and readied the weapon for firing.

The Aquilonian twisted in the saddle just as the archer shot. Despite the tumultuous elements, Nermesa did not fail to hear the deadly hiss as the bolt soared just above his head. Had he been sitting as he had a second before, the shaft would have buried itself between his shoulder blades.

There was nothing Nermesa could do but pray that he could present too difficult a target. He had no armor anymore, and his sword was scant protection against an arrow.

Then, up ahead he saw that the ravine narrowed again. It also rose up and split into two directions. Planting himself tight against the horse's mane, Nermesa prayed to Mitra that he would reach the narrower passage before another shot could be fired. If so, the archer would either have to risk slowing everyone down or pull back to let the others by.

Suddenly, his horse shrieked and stumbled. The animal continued on, but at a faltering pace. Nermesa could sense the loss of speed and knew that the Sartans had to be fast gaining on him.

He discovered the cause quickly. A second shaft stuck out of the horse's right flank. It had gone deep enough to draw blood and pain the beast. By the continued bleeding from the wound, the horse would only slow more, too.

Despite the arrow, Nermesa still managed to reach the narrow passage, but now the hope of gaining ground on his pursuers was gone. As the fork came up, he chose at random the one on the left. Behind him, Nermesa could hear shouts. The Sartans clearly believed that they had their prey, and he could not argue with their sentiments.

Up into the left branch Nermesa rode. His horse's breathing grew labored as the arrow wound took its toll. Behind him, the archer had given way to the patrol leader.

The path went up and around to the right, then, without warning, turned completely south. Worse yet, again the area to his left became a treacherous chasm. Nermesa could not waste any time lamenting his terrible choice, for he could already hear the hoofbeats of the foremost Sartan right behind him.

The uncertain terrain at the next curve forced him to slow. Out of the corner of his eye, the knight caught the officer's approach. The Sartan had his sword raised high, likely with the intention of trying for Nermesa's neck.

As the enemy soldier neared, the Aquilonian's horse stumbled. It crashed into the mountainside, then nearly ran off the edge. Nermesa quickly thrust his blade into its sheath and fought to keep the panicked and wounded animal from sending them both to their deaths . . .

The Sartan chose that moment for his attack. He pressed his mount against Nermesa's—indirectly assisting the knight in keeping his own steed under control—then slashed.

Nermesa bit his lip as the tip of the blade cut into his shoulder. He gave thanks to Mitra that it had not been worse. The jostling by the horses had worked to the Aquilonian's benefit.

Nermesa attempted to draw his blade again, but the Sartan pressed him too much. The Black Dragon was constantly forced to twist out of the officer's reach, something that he knew he could not successfully continue for very long.

His horse gave a mournful cry and crashed against the mountainside again, briefly pinning the Aquilonian's leg between its torso and the unforgiving rock. Nermesa grunted in pain and, in his distraction, nearly lost his head to the patrol leader.

It was clear that the horse was near collapse. The wound had been worse than Nermesa had thought. If he remained on the animal, it would either end up trapping him again between it and the mountain or crush him in its fall.

He had only one mad hope. Tensing, Nermesa tugged on the reins, allowing the Sartan to draw up beside him. The officer grinned, and Nermesa knew that he expected the fleeing Aquilonian to try to kick at the other horse as he had earlier.

Instead, Nermesa leapt at the Sartan.

His action caught the soldier completely by surprise. The knight used his weight to shove his adversary off the opposing side of the saddle. The Sartan's arms flailed, and his sword flew from his grip.

Clutching to the side of the saddle, Nermesa used his own failing steed as an added brace as he sought control of the other animal. The Sartan had all but fallen from the saddle. In desperation, he seized Nermesa's leg and with his other hand grabbed at the Black Dragon's collar.

His armored weight proved much more than Nermesa could bear in his own awkward position. Instead of gaining the saddle, the Aquilonian slid *over* it.

Both men fell from the horse. Unable to stop their momentum, they tumbled over the edge and into the chasm.

The slope here was not so abrupt as where Nermesa had sent the first Sartan and his horse to their deaths, but to fall from its height still promised certain doom. Nermesa tried to untangle himself from his foe, but for whatever reason, the officer clung tight. The two of them bounced painfully down the mountainside.

Then, at last, the Aquilonian was able to push free. He heard a desperate curse from the other fighter, then the Sartan vanished from his constantly shifting view.

Nermesa grabbed for any surface that would slow his descent, but his initial attempts only earned him fingers scraped raw and bloody. As he rolled over again, he saw that, farther down, the slope changed to a more dramatic one. If Nermesa did not stop himself soon, he would go flying off over the chasm.

His leg struck a hard outcropping with such force that he screamed. Yet, that same outcropping proved to be the hold that Nermesa had so long sought. Somehow, he managed to wrap first one arm, then the other, about it. For several seconds, Nermesa swung wildly about, then he finally stopped.

Of the Sartan, there was no sign, and Nermesa had to assume that the man had kept falling. The Aquilonian focused on his own troubles; not only did he have to worry about slipping free, but the other soldiers surely still had to be up on the trail. They would at least try to see if their commander lived.

And if they spotted Nermesa, a well-aimed shot from the archer would put an end to their quarry.

Urged on by this dire knowledge, Bolontes' son pulled himself up atop the outcropping and peered around. Some yards ahead, an overhang with a shallow depression beneath it offered some protection . . . if he could get to it and quickly.

Small rocks suddenly pelted him. Nermesa looked up, but did not see the other soldiers. Aware that he could not waste time, the Black Dragon sought some footing. When he found that, he reached with one hand to a jutting rock. Testing it and finding it holding, Nermesa shifted over.

More rocks struck him. Nermesa heard a voice. He flattened himself against the mountain, hoping that his grip and footing would remain.

When no bolt flew down at him, the Aquilonian moved on. Twice he had to adjust his feet when what seemed secure positions crumbled unexpectedly. At the end, Nermesa had to make a daring leap the final yard, and it was more by luck than skill that he kept himself from falling backward into the chasm.

Secreted in the depression, Nermesa waited. The wind battled to shove him from his hiding place, but he kept both hands tight on the mountainside.

Voices reached him. Something that sounded like an argument briefly rose above the howl of the wind and the rumble of thunder.

More rocks—a small avalanche, in fact—suddenly poured over Nermesa's location. He positioned himself as best he could beneath the overhang, hoping that the surviving soldiers had not seen him.

The rockslide grew in intensity. Another voice shouted— this time much closer.

There was a huge clatter of stone and a scream. As Nermesa gaped, a Sartan slid helplessly past him. Eyes wide with horror, the soldier grasped madly at the rock face.

His eyes momentarily fixed on Nermesa . . . and then the man tumbled into the chasm, still screaming.

Other voices above chattered angrily, excitedly. Nermesa slid one hand near his sword, although how he could use it in such a precarious position was a fair question.

Minutes slowly passed, and still no other soldier came into sight. When at last he could stand it no more, Nermesa cautiously adjusted his position and peered up around the edge of the overhang.

There were no soldiers in sight on the rock face, but his angle precluded any good view of the trail itself. Risking getting shot by an arrow, Nermesa crawled up to the top of the overhang, using it now for his footing.

When he was still not attacked, the Aquilonian decided he had to take a risk. Reaching up, he located a handhold . . .

The ascent was even more unsettling than his near fall, for the fear-stricken face of the one Sartan was burned into his memory. One slip, and he would join both him and the officer in oblivion.

Inch by inch, eternity by eternity, the knight edged up. A few loose pebbles showered him, but, fortunately, nothing larger. His fingers were raw and bled again. His path up was marked by red stains . . .

And when he planted one hand on the trail, Nermesa fully expected to be grabbed or even kicked off by the Sartans. Yet, as the bedraggled fighter pulled himself up, it was to see that the trail was *empty*.

The Sartans had abandoned the hunt, deciding that it had already cost them more than they were willing to accept. There was no hint as to which direction they had gone, but Nermesa suspected that they had turned back to report their losses. As for their quarry, he very much believed that they would report Nermesa also dead or else some other officer would have their heads for retreating from their duty.

He surveyed every direction. The last might not be far from the truth. Here he was, in the middle of the mountains without a horse, food, or shelter. He had no idea where he was or where he had to go. Nermesa no longer even had any idea which direction Aquilonia lay. All he saw around him were mountains and more mountains.

The wind renewed its assault of the Aquilonian with utter vigor. Nermesa felt a chill run through him. When he had been clad in armor, he had at least had the padding underneath to act as some sort of buffer against the elements. Now Nermesa only had the thin garments—now much torn—that Phillipian had given him to replace his own. Hardly enough to keep him warm.

But they will have to do, he told himself. *And it is said that, in his youth, King Conan crossed worse without even a shirt on his back!*

Whether that story was true or not meant nothing now, though. Nermesa had no choice but to move on. He dared not walk back the way he had come, for there was still the possibility that the Sartans had left one or two men behind to guard the area. Besides, the path ahead looked as if it descended into a more hospitable region, perhaps one where he could find shelter.

Perhaps . . . but it might also lead to a dead end.

Bracing himself and summoning visions of his loved ones and the king to encourage his efforts, Nermesa glanced one last time in the direction from which he had come, then started down the other way.

12

IT WAS LONG past the point where he should have slumped down and simply fallen asleep—and maybe never wake—but Nermesa would not permit himself to quit. Each curve ahead he told himself was the one that would finally open up into a more pastoral setting . . . or at least something less harsh.

But they did not. The staggering Aquilonian went from one winding part of the trail to another and each seemed a copy of the previous. Meanwhile, the wind did not let up, and more than once it had briefly rained. The only thing for which Nermesa could give thanks was that he had run into no more pursuit.

And then, when he thought it would never end . . . the trail finally flattened out. Minutes later, it gave way to a region sparsely covered with stunted, twisted trees and brown, low-lying grass. Even these seemed a miracle to Nermesa, but not nearly so much as the stream trickling between the rocks. From this he drank what he could, for he no longer had anything with which to carry more.

Knowing that he could go little farther, Nermesa gathered

what he could to start a fire. For shelter, the Aquilonian used a tall rock that blocked the wind. Food consisted of a spindly lizard he managed to catch and cook over the small flame.

With the fire still going and a supply of dried branches and leaves for when it started to die out, Nermesa clutched himself tight and buried his head in his arms. He muttered a prayer to Mitra which, because of his exhaustion, faded half-done into sleep.

WHAT EXACTLY IT was that woke him, at first the Aquilonian did not know. He only knew that whatever it was had been enough for him immediately to reach for his sword. Only when Nermesa saw that there was nothing in sight did he relax somewhat.

Just at the point where he began to think that the noise had merely been something out of his dreams, he heard it again.

Music?

Rising, Nermesa tried to detect the direction of the melody. While he did not recognize it specifically, it sounded like something the knight had heard back in Aquilonia.

Curious and certainly feeling as if he had nothing to lose, Nermesa followed the music as best as he could. More than once, he had to change his course, but the music gradually grew louder and more distinct. He was now certain that he *had* heard it back home and on more than one occasion.

Then lights flickered up ahead. At least four campfires, perhaps more. Nermesa immediately ducked behind a rocky mound, then peeked over the top.

A caravan . . . but not the same one that he had seen previously. This one was about as large as that which he had been assigned to protect and, judging by the men on the perimeter, as heavily armed. Still, although they were mostly silhouettes outlined by the fires that they passed, he believed the majority of the guards to be hired hands and mercenaries, not trained knights like himself.

Of course, he thought ruefully, his training had not proven to be much help when trouble had started.

Nermesa debated whether or not to walk into the camp or steer clear of it altogether. The decision was taken from him, though, by a sudden presence to his left.

The man was a driver and had clearly walked out to deal with nature's needs. Apparently half-asleep already, he almost had his pants down when he realized that Nermesa stood before him.

The Aquilonian brought the tip of the sword to the man's throat, and muttered, "Not a word unless I say so, and then it'd better be a whispered one, understood?"

The driver nodded.

"What caravan is that?"

Swallowing, the man stammered, " 'Tis one heading for the border of Ophir, to a trading market there! The caravan master is Mikonius Flavius!"

Nermesa frowned at the sound of the name. "Aquilonian?"

"Aye!" answered the driver with a nervous nod. "We all be Aquilonian and the caravan and all its goods belong to House Sibelio!"

Bolontes' son could scarcely believe his ears. "*Baron Antonus Sibelio?*"

"N-none other!"

It astounded Nermesa to run into yet another of Antonus' caravans out here. Despite the many attacks by brigands, the baron obviously still conducted much business . . . as their meeting in Tebes had also shown. Nermesa had to admire the man's determination, even if he *was* a trading rival of the knight's own House.

Lowering the sword, Nermesa ordered, "Lead me to your caravan master . . . if you please. I must have a word with him."

The driver eagerly agreed. Nermesa had no doubt that it had to do with the sword, but he did not care.

As they approached, one of the sentries called out, "You back finally, Jubal? Make a new river out—halt! Who's that with you?"

"Be at ease," the knight immediately responded. "I am Captain Nermesa Klandes of Tarantia, in service to his majesty, King Conan! I would speak with Master Flavius!"

Two more guards joined the first. From what he could see of them, they were definitely mercenaries. The one who had called out eyed Nermesa with much distrust.

"You? In service to King Conan? Aquilonia must've gone to ruins since we left, judging by you!"

"I've been through much," Nermesa said as explanation. "My interest is with your caravan master. Kindly lead me to him."

One of the others pointed a spear at the Black Dragon. "Maybe you should first kindly toss us that sword, eh? We promise to keep good care of it!"

Nermesa was not about to surrender the only thing keeping him alive. He kept the blade pointed toward the ground but ready to use should the men attack. Jubal, who also saw a confrontation coming, quickly fled to the safety of the encampment.

"If you'll not lead me to Master Flavius," continued Nermesa, "then send someone to bring him here. I will wait."

"Master Flavius will speak with you when you're good and bound," muttered the first guard. "Surrender your weapon, or we'll take it from you!"

Nermesa gritted his teeth in frustration. He had made two sensible suggestions, but all these men wanted was to fight him. Despite his travails, he readied himself for battle.

The trio spread out. Two carried spears and wore sheaths for broadswords. The third, the one who had first spoken, carried a long, well-worn blade, and Nermesa suspected him to be the most skilled.

But as Nermesa grimly prepared to defend himself, a short, beefy figure came rushing up from the center of the encampment.

"What's this? What's this?" he piped up in a reedy voice. "Cease this now, cease this now!"

"Stand back, Master Flavius," suggested the first guard. "This here man's a brigand . . ."

"Tut, tut," the caravan master waved off the fighter's concern and strode out toward Nermesa. "The man who came running into camp said something about an officer serving King Conan! That would be you, I assume?"

"I am Captain Nermesa Klandes of the Black Dragons—"

At mention of the Black Dragons, two of the guards stiffened. Master Flavius, however, found another part of Nermesa's introduction of more interest. "Klandes, you say? Klandes? Kin to Bolontes Klandes, are you?"

"I've the honor of being his son."

The beefy man turned to the nearest of the fighters. "Run and get me a proper lamp! Hurry now, hurry now!"

It said something of Master Flavius' control that the guard immediately obeyed. In but a minute, the breast-plated figure returned with a circular, brass oil lamp, which he handed to his superior.

Stepping up to Nermesa, Mikonius Flavius held up the light near the knight's countenance. At the same time, Nermesa beheld that of the caravan master. Mikonius Flavius was a round-faced, bald man roughly twice Nermesa's age. He sported a tiny mustache and beard and peered at the newcomer with narrow brown orbs. Despite being on a long journey, Master Flavius wore stately robes of white and green better suited for an elegant evening's entertainment in fair Tarantia than the mountainous wilds of Corinthia.

"Bolontes . . . Bolontes . . ." the heavyset man finally nodded. "Ah, yes, ah, yes! I can see old Bolontes in your face quite well! Recall he had a son now! Nermesa was it?"

"Yes."

The caravan master thrust out a meaty hand, which Nermesa belatedly took. "Dealt with your father in the past, I have! Know his face and manner quite well, I do! You definitely look to be his son, all right!" He shook the knight's hand with surprising vigor, then, with the lamp, gestured to the guards. "Put those silly things away, I say! This man is a guest of mine and will be treated with respect! We may be out here in the middle of nowhere, but we'll still act civilized, eh?"

The fighters did as he commanded, the lead one with the most reluctance.

Utterly ignoring the sentries, Master Flavius took Nermesa by the arm. "Come, come, my young friend! Let's get you into the camp! By Mitra! You look as if every Pict in the west had been after you! Well, we'll find you some new clothes and get you food and drink while you regale us with your tale, hmm?"

"Thank you," Bolontes' son returned with much relief. "Thank you very much."

"Tut, tut! The baron would have my head for treating a noble such as yourself with anything less than the full respect your station deserves, and *I* can do no less for the son of Bolontes, for whom I hold the highest regard . . . the *highest.*"

"I assure you, Master Flavius—"

"Mikonius, boy! Mikonius to you, Nermesa!"

The man's enthusiasm was contagious. Nermesa grinned.

Several others from the caravan stood up in curiosity as the pair neared. Many were drivers, although there were guards, cooks, apprentices to the cooks, and a few wealthy passengers with their entourages. The latter group especially found Nermesa of interest. The wealthy latched on to merchant caravans for safety when traveling and the sight of a stranger often disturbed them more than the seasoned crew.

The music had been coming from some of the drivers. One held a lyre, while another a flute.

"Continue on, continue on!" commanded Mikonius, as if he did not have an armed stranger next to him.

A scarred man with the look of a veteran driver approached the caravan master. Despite his harsh features, his eyes and expression simply held curiosity and concern. "What's with this one, Mikonius?"

"Nothing to fear, Romulo! Simply a friend of mine! Nermesa, may I present Romulo, my right hand! Romulo, this is Nermesa, son of Bolontes Klandes . . ."

The driver's eyes appraised Bolontes' son, especially the grip he had on the sword. "Aye . . . Nermesa Klandes . . . the Hero of the Westermarck . . ."

Mikonius' fat lips pursed as he looked at the knight as if for the first time. "Of course, of course! How could I forget? The Westermarck! You're a hero!"

"I survived," returned Nermesa, not at all pleased to be recalled so. "Others didn't." Briefly, the faces of his servant and friend, Quentus, General Boronius—the Boar—and even his cousin Caltero flashed through his thoughts, bringing with them renewed pain.

Romulo looked sympathetic, but Master Flavius completely missed the shift in Nermesa's expression. He slapped the younger Aquilonian on the back. "A hero in our midst! Hah! Come, my lord Nermesa! I would introduce you to my other guests!"

Ignoring the fact that he had yet to clothe or feed the "hero." Mikonius dragged Nermesa toward the nobles. He went around from one party to the next, showing off the ragged-looking captain as if the latter were a prize bull. Fortunately, most of the nobles nodded politely and even sympathetically. A few of the younger women, especially the twin, flaxen-haired daughters of one Baron Torino, eyed Nermesa with more than a little interest—to which he was careful to act oblivious.

Some of the sons and young male servants stared in open awe, they at that age when the exploits of knights and soldiers consumed their every waking moment. One boy noticed the gems on Nermesa's sword and within moments the tale of how the knight had been given the weapon by King Conan spread among the nobles . . . with most of the details utterly wrong. Nermesa, though, knew better than to try to correct the story, for he had failed in previous attempts many times before.

It was Romulo who finally saved him, the senior driver coming up behind Mikonius, and whispering in his ear, "Master Flavius, I believe your hero is about to fall over from hunger and exhaustion."

To his credit, the caravan master quickly made his apologies to the gathered nobles and escorted Nermesa back to his own wagon. Romulo assisted in getting Nermesa a tunic and pants, along with some boots, the driver locating the proper sizes from his belongings and contributions from others. The boots, in fact, came from one of the noble families and was a mark of how much Nermesa's reputation had spread throughout Tarantia and the surrounding regions.

As soon as Nermesa was dressed, Mikonius had his own cook bring the young Klandes food from his personal stock. Nermesa found the manner in which the stout man ran his caravan far different from that of Darius. Yet the Baron Sibelio clearly trusted Mikonius if the size of the caravan was any indication.

In fact, for all his bluster, Mikonius appeared well liked and respected by those who served under him. Romulo, clearly a competent man in his own right, obviously worked hand in hand with his superior without any resentment.

Someday, like it or not, Nermesa, too, would have to deal with the hiring of such men. He would also probably have to leave the Black Dragons, although it was not entirely unheard of for those in his position both to command their Houses and serve their liege.

Nermesa frowned, hoping that such a decision would be long in the future. His father was fit, and the son desired nothing more than to do his duty for king and realm. Mastery of one of the eldest, wealthiest Houses in Aquilonia could wait.

Master Flavius politely waited until Nermesa was done eating before plying him with questions concerning his

reasons for being so far from home. The knight answered
them as best he could, leaving out whatever he believed too
sensitive to reveal.

"Astounding tale, astounding tale," gasped the marveling Mikonius, when Nermesa was through. "Heard
something was being planned with one of the other caravan masters . . . didn't you, Romulo?"

The chief driver, who apparently always ate with his superior, grunted. "Aye. Figures they'd choose old Darius'.
The man was a soldier for ten years before the good baron
took him on. Darius is a crafty one."

"But so, evidently, are these awful brigands," concluded
Mikonius. "You're correct in your assumption, Nermesa! I
doubt that they think you live!"

This had continued to be a point of frustration with
Bolontes' son throughout his travails. Yet, it was not himself that he was most concerned about. "I don't even know
if the others survived . . ."

"It'd take a pack of demons to do old Darius in," replied
Romulo with a snigger.

"And you said that there were several other Black Dragons with the guards," the caravan master added. He patted
Nermesa on the shoulder. "I suspect that we'll find out that
they fought off the villains, fought them off, and made it to
Nemedia."

Nermesa looked at both men. "I wish there was some
way to find out . . . and to let those in Tarantia know I still
live, too!"

"Aah, but there is, there is! The baron keeps a number
of birds at our location at the Ophirian border! We always
send one off when we reach our destination so that he can
know as soon as possible! Also receive messages from him
wherever he might be!"

Romulo perked up. "Mikonius, can't we use the two
we're bringing with us to Ophir?"

"I would like to, yes," murmured the caravan master,
tapping his fingers together in thought. "But I've a duty to
the baron, and you know his orders are strict. These birds

are to replace the one we send and the one sent by the caretaker two months ago."

"But surely—"

Mikonius shook his head. "I am adamant in this, Romulo." He gave Nermesa an apologetic look. "I have sworn faithfully to serve the baron in all ways. You understand that, I trust?"

Nermesa knew that he *had* to understand, whether he wanted to or not. "How far are we from your destination? I fear I no longer know exactly where I am."

"Four days only, if Romulo here can be trusted to keep the pace strong . . . and he can."

Four days. Nermesa considered his options. It was possible that he might convince Master Flavius to loan him a horse. Nermesa could leave in the morning in the hopes of reaching Tarantia on his own. Of course, with his record so far, that appeared unlikely. If he did not run afoul of more Corinthians, there was the danger of bandits—not to mention the insidious Set-Anubis, apparently.

"How long before your caravan returns to Tarantia?" he asked Mikonius.

"Two months at least. We have much business to do, much business. However, you need not wait that long. The caravan run by my good friend Polythemus should be just arriving on its way up from Koth. He and I were to meet while his band refitted for the rest of the journey home."

"A caravan from Koth?" Even with the terrible threat of the brigands, it seemed that Antonus had managed to keep his business flourishing. Nermesa gave thanks to Mitra for the baron's resolve; it would enable the Black Dragon not only to get some message home, but perhaps himself as well.

Of course, once there, Nermesa would have to face General Pallantides and the king with his failure.

"Will that do, then?" his host asked hopefully. When Nermesa nodded, Mikonius fairly beamed with delight. "Splendid, splendid! Now, we must speak of your accommodations! You will take my own wagon—"

Here, the weary knight drew the line. "Thank you, but I prefer a bedroll by the fire."

"For the son of Bolontes? I should say not—"

"Master Flavius, I am an officer in the service of King Conan. If my mission has failed, I am still beholden to protecting his subjects as if they were him. I failed to aid Darius' caravan, but I willingly add my arm to those men protecting yours."

Romulo chuckled. "Don't think that you're going to argue him out of this, Mikonius!"

The caravan master looked pained but finally agreed. "I shall at least provide you with one of my own blankets. If you must sleep on the ground, then you will still sleep in comfort!"

He clapped his hands and a young, female servant rushed out of the dark to see what he needed. As she scampered off to find the blanket, Mikonius rose.

"Romulo, I leave him in your capable hands, then, eh? My lord Nermesa—pardon—*Captain* Nermesa—we shall make everything right for you the moment we reach Karphur, our destination."

Karphur. Nermesa recognized the name from his father. Klandes, too, had occasional business in the border city. Karphur actually straddled both sides of the border, but was a peculiar neutral entity owing full allegiance neither to Corinthia nor Ophir. It was a crossroads of trade not only for the two but those south and north of the kingdoms.

Nermesa briefly wondered if one of his own House's wagon columns would be there but doubted he could be so fortunate.

Once the servant brought the blanket, Romulo led Nermesa back into the main area of the encampment. The senior driver indicated the largest of the fires. "There's room there. The men know to respect the privacy of those not part of the normal crew, so don't take their silence for anything bad. They'll help you if you need it, though."

"Thank you."

"The wagon to your right has a water barrel anyone can

use. We rise before dawn. I'll come and get you for food, unless Mikonius decides you should have some from him."

Nermesa nodded. He was about to settle down when he realized that Romulo had one more thing to say.

"My brother was out in the Westermarck same time as you, Captain Nermesa. Stationed out of Scanaga, too. He was in that column you saved. He was one of those *you* saved." And with that, the senior driver turned and left.

Nermesa watched the man vanish into the dark. Despite Romulo's matter-of-fact tone, the knight could sense the driver's immense gratitude for the life of his brother.

Feeling a little better about both his situation and himself, Nermesa lay down next to the fire. He had looked over the strength of the caravan and doubted that there would be any threat to it. The worst of their journey had already passed.

He could only hope that the same was true for his.

13

KARPHUR WAS A place of mixed notions. From what Nermesa gleaned from Mikonius and Romulo, it considered itself an independent city-state, such as Tebes or Sarta. Yet, half of it existed over the official border between Ophir and Corinthia. There was a contingent of Ophirian soldiers stationed just west of Karphur and a similar group beyond the east wall organized by a band of city-states nearest to the trade center. Yet according to the caravan master, neither force had ever so much as entered Karphur's gates even during the worst years of strife between the two lands. Karphur was just too valuable to both sides as it was.

As for maintaining security in the city itself, that fell to the Karphur Guard, made up of men—and even women—born and raised there. Aware of the balance they maintained, the citizens of Karphur were zealous in their protection of their independence. It was a rare guard who took a bribe, especially since his own fellows were likely to string him up on their own.

As they entered the city through the arched gateway,

Nermesa, now riding with Romulo, studied the guards with some admiration. They wore their broad-rimmed, bronze helmets and matching breastplates with a pride that matched that of the Black Dragons. In addition to being clad in brown leather kilts with metal tips, they also had shin and lower-arm guards. Their sandals were bound all the way up the calf. Each figure watched the traffic moving in and out of Karphur with an earnestness that did them credit in the eyes of the Aquilonian.

Being of mixed heritage, Karphur naturally had its share of Corinthian traits, such as its columns, but Ophir, too, had left its mark. Gold leaf decorated many public displays, and the tunics of several of the richer citizens bore this color in some arrangement. Nermesa recalled that the tyrant Amalrus had been said to have worn armor chased with gold . . . armor that had done him little good when Sir Prospero of Poitain had cut his shoulder bone in two with his massive sword, then left the traitorous monarch to be trampled by the hooves of the Poitainians' huge warhorses.

Ophirian influence was also evident in the more rounded entrances of many of the buildings, themselves also rounded at the roof. However, Romulo explained that these were of a far older style than found in most of Ophir, which he had visited over the course of working for House Sibelio.

One curious group of people that Nermesa also spotted appeared to be miners. When he pointed them out to the senior driver, Romulo nodded. "Aye, one of the largest silver mines is located here . . . but on the Corinthian side. Of course, it's too far out for any of the city-states to trouble with. The Karphurians keep the peace by mining it themselves, then turning over a share to *both* kingdoms, with the city keeping an equal part for itself."

"That sounds overly complicated."

His companion chuckled. "Karphur will do whatever it needs to in order to remind both sides why one of them doesn't just take a chance and seize the city."

With Corinthian and Ophirian blood mixing freely, it was perhaps the look of the Karphurians that most intrigued the knight. He saw hints of the same lineage as Malkuri and, to a great extent, General Pallantides. The combination created an exotic look both dark and light at the same time. Even in Tarantia, many of the women and men would have been considered arresting.

"My favorite stop," Romulo remarked, winking at a smiling female. "No more beautiful women than those of Karphur. If I had a mind to get married, it'd be one like her." With a grin, he added, "Of course, I've not yet a mind to be married . . . not while there's still some fun to be had, eh?"

Although Nermesa smiled and nodded, no thought of such entertainment occurred to him. He was too concerned with returning home.

Their destination was near Karphur's market. While the market itself was typical of those Nermesa had seen before, the mix of people and different items for sale briefly perked his interest. Here, there were merchants from Argos and Shem and, much to the Aquilonian's distaste, Stygia. The last resembled Set-Anubis in color just enough to keep the captain wary.

The caravan stopped at a large, rounded building apparently owned by House Sibelio. With Romulo leading, the wagons lined up to be unloaded.

Mikonius met up with Nermesa and the senior driver just as they climbed down. The master beamed. "Aah, Karphur! Always among the most pleasant of stops—but you know that, don't you, Romulo?"

"Aye, Mikonius! I was trying to convince Captain Nermesa here to join me in hunting for some entertainment after we were through here, but he chose not to."

"Tut, tut! You should get *some* enjoyment out of this visit! You may never return to Karphur, my friend!"

"Actually, I was hoping to see if my own House had any representation here, Master Flavius."

The stout man's brow deepened. "Doubt it, doubt it, but you're right to want to have a look! Pity there's no envoy from Aquilonia here, or he might be able to help. My best

suggestion would be to check around the market and perhaps the nearest inns. If you don't find any information
from either, then there's no one. House Klandes would be
near the market if they're anywhere at all."

"And so you don't get lost in the process," added Romulo, "keep an eye on that one tower with the two points.
Tallest building in the area. You mark that, you'll always be
able to find your way back to here."

Nermesa shook hands with each man. "Thank you. I'll
do as you both say."

But as he started away, Mikonius took him by the arm.
"Wait a moment! Can't have you running about without
any money for food or drink!" The caravan master reached
into the neck of his robe and tore free a small pouch dangling underneath the garment. As he planted it in the
knight's palm, it jingled. "Consider this payment for helping to guard the wagons these past few days—"

From the weight, Nermesa suspected that it carried far
more than that. "I can't—"

"I insist . . . and Romulo will tell you that I will not accept any argument in this particular matter, just as you did
not when it came to sleeping by the fire."

"You'd best take it. You'll certainly need it," interjected
the driver.

With a grateful nod, Bolontes' son finally gave in. He
slipped the tiny bag within his tunic, then thanked both
men again.

Despite still considering himself on his mission, Nermesa could not help but be a bit distracted by his surroundings. The area around the market was filled with attractions
designed to entertain the merchants and their crews during
their time off. There were street performers—serpent
charmers from Stygia, undulating dancing girls from Zingara, and slim, seemingly boneless acrobats who might
have come all the way from Khitai—and booths of all sorts
offering foods from around the known world. Taverns
abounded, and each seemed to have a scantily clad Karphurian woman beckoning from the entrance.

As he walked, Nermesa kept an eye out for anyone clad in Aquilonian garb. Unfortunately, the few he noticed proved unhelpful when he asked them about House Klandes. It soon became apparent that his father did no business down here at present, clearly an oversight. Nermesa determined that he would mention Karphur if and when he saw the elder Klandes.

While Karphur offered many types of exotic foods—some of which the Aquilonian swore still *squirmed*—Nermesa settled for some familiar—and safe—bread-and-meat combinations, along with an ale. The ale proved spicy, a not-altogether-distasteful surprise.

But while his taste buds and stomach were soon satisfied, he was not. As the day faded and with it the hope of finding anyone tied to House Klandes by blood or business, Nermesa returned with some dejection to the caravan.

Romulo, clearly just on his way *out*, frowned slightly at sight of him. "No luck, Nermesa?"

"None."

The driver tried to turn him about. "You should come with me! Now's the time when Karphur truly comes alive!"

"Thank you, but I'd like nothing more than sleep right now."

"As you like. Perhaps tomorrow night . . ."

That made Nermesa think of something else. "Has the other caravan arrived?"

"Two days ago, actually. Good of you to remind me. I talked to the senior driver, and he told me that they'll be ready to leave the day after tomorrow . . . so, that doesn't leave you much time to change your mind about coming with me, Nermesa."

"Perhaps . . ." Bolontes' son bid Romulo good night, then retired to the rooms where he had been told that the drivers—assuming that they were not intending *other* arrangements as his friend was—slept during their stay. As the entrance was marked, Nermesa had no difficulty finding the area and, once inside, even less finding an open cot.

He thought that he would have trouble falling asleep, but that proved not the case. Barely had he settled down before he drifted off.

His first dreams were quite innocuous and easily forgettable. As he sank deeper into slumber, Nermesa began to dream about home, about his family, his king, and Telaria. The words of her note floated through his head, easing the day's tensions from his body. Her face smiled down on him, her auburn hair as vivid as fire in his dream.

Her lips mouthed his name; her eyes glowed bright. Telaria's hair grew redder yet, and finally became crimson and fiery.

In his sleep, Nermesa frowned and tried to reach out to her. But Telaria's face pulled back and as it did, it became less distinct. It and the hair melded into one burning flame, which then grew more narrow.

Suddenly, the flame crystallized. It gleamed brightly, but in a manner that somehow unsettled the Aquilonian. He tried to turn from it, but the crystal refused to let his gaze leave it.

And then it blinked, blinked like an *eye*.

Ra shana du karos, ashtur Charon . . . came the whisper, then. *Zeta catar Charon* . . . *Zeta catar Charon karos* . . .

Around the eye formed a specter made of cloth, a sinister phantom with claws for hands who reached out at Nermesa. As the helpless knight watched, those claws tore into his chest . . . and ripped from it his beating heart as he *screamed*—

At which point Nermesa woke with a start.

He lay on the cot, gasping for air, his heart racing faster than the swiftest charger. He peered around him, but saw that none of the others had been awakened by his actions. His cry in the dream had evidently not crossed into the waking world, for which he was grateful.

Sweat covered Nermesa. He knew that he had only been dreaming, but the presence of Set-Anubis had seemed so real, so imminent. He had heard tales of wizards reaching out to their enemies in their sleep, but never had he heard

of any such horror truly happening. Of course, who would
know if it did?

Finally, his pulse eased to normal. Nermesa inhaled,
trying to turn his thoughts to better things. It could not have
been Set-Anubis. The sorcerer was far away, somewhere
near Sarta. There would be no reason why he would still be
after Nermesa.

No reason whatsoever . . .

BUT SET-ANUBIS REMAINED on his mind even the next
day, and Nermesa grew impatient to leave Karphur. Romulo, who did not come back until the morning, promised
with a grin left over from his night's affairs that all was set
for the departure.

"I still think some companionship would do you well,"
the senior driver insisted. "I know a very sultry lass with an
equally sultry cousin. You've seen the beauty of the Karphurian women? These two make most of them dull by
comparison! It's said that they've a little Stygian in them to
add further to their mystery . . ."

Having not told either Romulo or Mikonius of Set-
Anubis, the knight could not explain that such a mix of
blood would remind him too much of the sorcerer . . . exactly the opposite of what he desired. "Thank you, Romulo,
but I'll just go and walk around the market."

"Suit yourself, Captain . . . say, you know, those female
acrobats from Khitan are said to entertain men on occasion . . ."

Nermesa departed before the driver could make any further suggestions. All he wanted was somewhere where he
could watch the activity around him until it was time to go
to sleep. Then, come the morning, he and the caravan
would head back to Tarantia.

Fortunately, there was always something happening in
the market. Today it was not acrobats, but play actors per-
forming tales for anyone willing to pay a coin. Nermesa
joined the crowd, gave his money to the youth in charge of

collecting, and watched as the actors went through one story after another. All were epic adventures shown on a decidedly unepic scale, but some of the players were fairly good even by the standards of home, and the fact that they used actual women to play women pleased him further. He had seen many plays where boys or even men had donned the feminine roles and found those wanting.

When the actors finally bid their audience good-bye, he clapped along with the rest of the crowd, then went in search of a booth selling something safe to eat. As he tried to cross toward one, though, a number of soldiers of the Guard suddenly entered the market. Led by a cloaked officer, they marched through the throng unhindered, for everyone in their path immediately pulled back.

Nermesa, who had heard enough of their reputation, did likewise. He waited patiently while the column of some twenty went by, admiring their precision and feeling some slight pity for whatever miscreant they hunted.

The crowd immediately filled the gap once the armored figures had gone. Nermesa reached the booth and purchased his food, then went to find a place to eat it.

As he was finishing, he noticed none other than Mikonius Flavius—flanked by two of his personal guard—moving with some agitation through the crowd. Although the caravan master looked as if he was on his way to some matter of importance, Nermesa dared to interrupt him.

"Master Flavius!" the knight called, disposing of the remnants of his meal. "Master Flavius! A moment, please!"

The heavy, balding man momentarily gaped at Nermesa as if Bolontes' son was an assassin come to gut him. Then, blinking, he suddenly smiled. "Ah! 'Tis you, Nermesa! 'Tis you! Forgive me! My mind was on business for the baron! I can't talk right now, but—ah, but—Master Polythemus would speak with you about your transport. Yes, that's what it was. You can find him back at our facility. By the wagons, yes. You should go now."

"Thank you," Nermesa began, Mikonius having answered in part the very question the captain had intended to ask. Nermesa had wanted to assure himself again that all was in readiness for tomorrow.

"Not at all, not at all!" called the caravan master, already hurrying off. "Go now, go now!"

Nermesa did just that, his eagerness growing. He had not met Polythemus, but assumed that the other caravan master would be easy to identify.

The crowd had thickened, slowing the Aquilonian more than he would have liked. People seemed to go out of their way to get into his. Nermesa sought to keep his impatience in check; after all, the wagons would not be leaving until the morrow.

When he finally returned, the other caravan master was already impatiently waiting. Polythemus was a direct contrast to Mikonius; a dour, gaunt man of plain clothes and plainer speech. He gave Nermesa succinct instructions as to when the knight had to be ready and where his place in the caravan would be.

"You're not ready; you don't go," Polythemus said bluntly. "You'll sleep among my drivers tonight. Antimedes will show you where."

Antimedes was Polythemus' senior driver. A sandy-haired man about the knight's age, he was broad of build, much like a wrestler. With a grunt and a nod, he led Nermesa to where the others working under Polythemus stayed.

Once his situation was arranged, Nermesa went to locate Romulo. He found the senior driver busy checking the wagons out for any last-minute repairs.

"Met Polythemus, have you?" asked Mikonius' man. "Lively sort, isn't he?"

"Not at all like Mikonius, if you mean that."

Romulo laughed. "Not at all like him, definitely! Hard to believe those two are thick as thieves, but they are!"

Bolontes' son could not imagine the pair as good friends. He shook his head at the image, then said, "I wanted to thank you for your help."

"Least I can do. I owe you many times over for my brother."

"I only did what I had to."

Romulo shrugged. "That's more than many would've done." He stepped from the wagons. "Tonight, we share an ale! You can't deny me that!"

"One, perhaps," Nermesa finally replied. "I don't want to run afoul of Master Polythemus' rules come the morning."

"Mitra forbid you should do that! Ha!"

Romulo had some tasks with which to deal, so Nermesa located a secluded area behind the Sibelio holdings and practiced with his sword. It had been the first time in many days that he had been able to do so. His muscles complained at first, then eased up. Nermesa dueled with invisible foes, going through most of the moves he had learned not only from his family instructors but from the trainers serving under General Pallantides.

He suddenly realized that he was being watched. Antimedes stood by a doorway, the driver's arms folded and his eyes taking the measure of the man before him.

"Good," he grunted. He tapped his own sheathed sword. "Want some live practice?"

Nermesa signaled his readiness with a sweep of his blade. Antimedes, clad in the plain, brown tunic of Polythemus' men, drew his weapon as he approached. From his actions, Nermesa guessed the wider man was good with the sword.

"I hear you're of the Black Dragons. That so?"

"Yes."

"I almost was." And with that, Antimedes lunged.

Nermesa barely checked the attack. He immediately discovered that he had underestimated the driver's skill. Antimedes was not just good; he was excellent. At first, it was all the knight could do to keep Antimedes from getting through his guard.

But as he became familiar with the other's moves, Nermesa not only countered better, but he began to attack. Antimedes grunted in respect as Nermesa pressed him. Their swords clanged again and again as they paced back and forth. The driver's face grew red from effort, but his eyes gleamed with pleasure. Nermesa, too, enjoyed the effort, for a skilled opponent helped hone his own abilities.

At last, Antimedes leapt back. He dropped his sword to the ground. Panting, the grinning driver said, "I yield! By Mitra, I yield!"

It took Nermesa a moment to catch enough of his breath to answer, "A good thing! I might've had to do the same myself in another minute!"

"Would that I'd known that, my lord! Would that I'd known that!" Antimedes picked up his weapon. "I'd do this again on the journey if you've an interest in it . . ."

"I'm agreeable." It would help ease some of Nermesa's impatience.

"Look forward to it, then." The driver saluted him with his sword, then sheathed it. "Just make sure you're ready. Master Polythemus don't like anyone late. You'd best retire shortly after dark, just to be safe."

"I intend that."

With another nod, Antimedes left him. Nermesa sought out a water barrel and not only drank his fill but poured some over his face. With such skill, Polythemus' second was wasted as a driver. He wondered why Antimedes had not become one of the Black Dragons. Certainly his abilities were worthy of the elite unit. Nermesa decided to ask the driver when next they had a moment.

Romulo met him as he entered. "There you are." remarked Mikonius' man. "Come! That ale's been calling to us for hours!"

He led Nermesa to a favored tavern of his, one where the women proved almost as heady as the strong drink. Scantily clad dancers leapt atop tables and swung their gauzy skirts around with wanton abandon. However, Nermesa noticed that they were also nimble enough to evade the occasional eager grab by one customer or another. The women, he soon discovered, chose the *men*, not the other way around.

Romulo was popular with them and had clearly been here several times before, judging by how more than one woman called him by name. They also seemed to take a liking to Nermesa. He accepted the company of one, buying her a drink as was expected here. Naturally, though, she left most of it untouched, her purpose not only to make the customer happy but willing to spend more than he intended. However, she also had to make certain that she kept her wits.

The one ale became two at Romulo's insistence, but when he tried to insist on a third, Bolontes' son finally had to make his excuses.

"I don't want to anger Master Polythemus," he reminded his friend. "I need to reach Tarantia."

"I suppose that's necessary." Slipping free of the woman on his lap, the driver clasped Nermesa's hand. "If our paths do not cross before the caravan leaves, I want to wish you the best, Captain Nermesa. When next I meet my brother, I'll tell him of our encounter."

Turning his own companion over to Romulo, Nermesa bid him farewell. Wending his way through the crowd, he stepped out into the relatively fresh air. The tavern was some distance from the Sibelio holdings, but even at night the towers that Romulo had pointed out could be seen, for now they were lit up.

With them as his guide, the knight started back. It was later than he had planned; at least two hours later. Nermesa prayed that nothing would go wrong and that he would indeed be prepared precisely when the imperious Polythemus insisted.

Although the market was ever active, Nermesa's route from the tavern demanded that he skirt it. Instead, he had to take side streets and even the occasional alley. The path was the one that Romulo had chosen on their way out. There were times when Nermesa thought that he should have taken a different, more straightforward direction back, but better the path he knew than trying out another in the middle of the night that might, no matter how good it seemed, lead him astray. Nermesa could ill afford to become lost in Karphur.

But lost he almost was. Nermesa hesitated at one alley-way, trying to recall which direction Romulo had earlier led him. After a moment, he turned right—

"Not that way . . ." whispered a voice in his ear. At the same time, a hand caught his shoulder.

"Romulo?" blurted Nermesa.

"Quiet!" Despite the shadows, the knight could see that his friend's face was filled with concern. "Quickly! Come this way, Nermesa!"

He all but dragged the other man in the opposite direction. When Nermesa tried to protest, Romulo immediately silenced him with a curt cut of his hand.

The knight peered over his shoulder at the alley *he* had chosen, but saw nothing. Nermesa could have *sworn* that it was the right path back.

Romulo led him around a corner, then through another alley. They made two more turns before Nermesa finally decided that he had had enough. Breaking free of his companion, he demanded, "What's going on, Romulo? Why lead me into this dark place?" The knight looked around. He now had no idea where to go, for the black buildings surrounding them hid from his view the one landmark that he knew. "What are you up to?"

In answer, the driver drew his sword. "I'm sorry to have done this, Nermesa."

Throwing himself farther back, Nermesa reached for his own weapon. But as he drew it, he heard from more than one direction soft footfalls.

Shadowed forms closed in on both sides, their faces obscured by hoods. All wielded swords.

Romulo had *betrayed* him.

14

NERMESA TURNED ON the treacherous driver. "If I'm to die, I'll take you with me!"

He leapt at Romulo who, instead of meeting his attack, left himself wide open. "Stop, Nermesa! I'm not your enemy! I admit to being part of it, keeping you out and trying to make you drink enough to unsteady your hand, but when it came time for the evil deed, I couldn't! I tried to lead you away from them, but they've followed!"

The other men were fast approaching. Nermesa counted three apiece for six. "And why should I believe that?"

"For the sake of my brother, whose life you saved!" Romulo then did the only thing that could have utterly convinced the Black Dragon of his true intentions . . . he turned away from the knight, facing three of the hooded villains. His back he left completely open to Nermesa. "For my brother, who should've been enough of a reason to refuse to be part of this treachery in the first place!"

The six were almost upon them. One on Romulo's side signaled a halt and, in a muffled voice, demanded, "What do you think you're doing, you fool?"

"I do what I must. I care not if it means I lose all."

The leader of the assassins grunted. "So be it. Then you die with him."

He lunged at Romulo. His attack was the sign for which the other assassins waited. They moved in on the duo en masse, almost forcing Nermesa and Romulo into one another.

The driver met the leader's blade, cutting and slashing with abandon. Nermesa had no time to judge his companion's skill, for his own trio of opponents struck simultaneously, leaving even the well-trained knight desperately on the defensive. He managed to parry two of the swords, but the third one slipped through, the tip licking his right arm.

Ignoring the sting, Nermesa counterattacked. His audacity startled the assassins. One momentarily backed away, giving the Aquilonian an opening against the second. He thrust, catching the villain under the arm.

Undeterred by a breastplate, the blade sank in deep. Nermesa's target let out a gasp and twisted away. As the first man returned, the wounded figure fell to the ground.

As Nermesa shifted position, he saw that Romulo, too, still held his ground. The leader had pulled back, letting his two comrades work on the driver from opposing sides. However, he had not retreated out of any fear. His stance indicated that he studied Romulo's every move, seeking weaknesses and openings.

Nermesa wanted to warn the driver of this, but his own adversaries pushed their attack again. Alternating thrusts, they nearly pinned the knight to the wall of the nearest building. Only his own superior training kept Nermesa from being skewered more than once.

"Ha!" came Romulo's triumphant cry. There was a clatter, followed by a dull thud.

But that call was followed by the muffled voice of the assassin leader growling, "Aside! I'll take him!"

"Romulo—!" Nermesa's warning got no farther, for one of the villains he fought suddenly jumped him. The knight kicked out, catching his adversary on the shin just as the man reached him. The hooded figure stumbled forward and Nermesa rewarded him with a fist to the jaw.

As the stunned assassin fell back, his comrade sought to use the struggle to his own advantage. However, Nermesa saw him out of the corner of his eye and brought up his blade.

In his haste, the last of the trio left himself open. Bolontes' son caught him across the midsection. The wound was not fatal, but surely painful. His foe retreated, one hand clutching the bleeding area.

Aware of the imminent danger to Romulo, Nermesa turned to aid the driver—

And watched in horror as the leader of the assassins plunged his blade through Romulo's throat.

Mikonius' man let out a horrific gurgle. As the hooded figure pulled free his dripping blade, Romulo, dropping his own sword, grabbed at the gaping hole with his fingers. He staggered against the wall, then into Nermesa's free arm.

"My bro—" was all the knight's companion could manage. Romulo's gaze turned skyward . . . then he slipped out of Nermesa's grip and onto the ground.

"Fool!" Romulo's murderer spat.

A fury overwhelmed Nermesa. He flung himself at the assassin. The man next to his target sought to take him instead and for his effort was rewarded with a swift thrust through the ribs and the heart.

The quick, efficient death did no more to shake the leader than Nermesa's earlier efforts against the other three assassins had. With a nod and a grunt, he met the Aquilonian's angry assault.

Nermesa had expected the villain to be good, but he was far better. Worse, he seemed to anticipate many of the knight's moves, almost getting under Nermesa's guard twice in the first few moments.

Needing to focus, Nermesa tried to back up, only to find the wall right behind him. His opponent chuckled and closed the gap immediately.

But as the furious assault renewed, Nermesa noticed

some familiarities in the man's actions. Distinct moves that he had only recently come across . . .

Antimedes.

Only then did he realize that he had earlier been played for a fool. When the other driver had come across Nermesa practicing, he had used it to test out the latter's skills . . . and weaknesses. All that so that he could be better prepared when it came time for the foul deed.

But why did he want to kill Nermesa in the first place?

Unaware that his identity was known, Antimedes attacked with relish, clearly anticipating his victory over the Black Dragon. He had claimed that he, too, had nearly been one of that august group. How true that might be was a question Nermesa would likely never know, but it also revealed some of the betrayer's shortcomings. When they had fought, Nermesa had utilized most of the tricks taught him by his instructors . . . but not *all* of them.

Antimedes suddenly grunted as he found Nermesa's weapon maneuvering in a manner unaccustomed to him. His own effort to recover momentarily evened the struggle, but then the knight countered in yet another manner.

"Mitra!" snapped the betrayer. "What did you—?"

Before he could finish, Nermesa lunged. His sword pierced Antimedes through the lung. The larger man grunted, and his sword hand twitched. He lost his weapon and staggered back.

"For Romulo . . ." snarled Nermesa.

He swiftly grabbed the falling man by his tunic and swung him into the nearest of the other assassins. Already startled by the sudden change in fortunes, the surviving attackers stood motionless. Antimedes' flailing body collided with Nermesa's target, sending both crashing to the ground.

Bolontes' son slashed at one of those he had earlier wounded, then shoved his way past. He had been fortunate to face down the group with Romulo's help, but he suspected that his troubles were not over. This trap concerned more than Antimedes; Nermesa believed Polythemus involved at the very least.

But why? And why had the caravan master simply not waited until they were out of Karphur? There were many places along the journey to Tarantia where he could have easily had the knight slain.

Confused, Nermesa ran toward the Sibelio facilities. Perhaps Mikonius could shed some light on the matter. At least he could trust *him*.

As he neared, Nermesa slowed. He carefully peered around the corner before advancing on the main building itself. There were House guards nearby—as was common for such places—but they proved easy to slip past. Until he spoke with Mikonius, Nermesa could not be certain that some of the men he confronted might not also be in the pay of Antimedes and his superior.

It still baffled him that Polythemus had chosen this sort of attack. Could the caravan master not trust his own crew on the journey?

A door creaked open. A figure carrying a lantern in one hand stepped out. Nermesa flattened against the nearest wall, then breathed a sigh of relief when he saw who it was . . . Mikonius Flavius.

The rotund caravan master was alone. He hummed to himself as he strode from the building, clearly in a good mood.

Nermesa stepped out of the shadows. "Master Flavius—"

Mikonius took one look at the knight, then at the sword. In the light of the lantern, the blood gleamed ominously.

With an oath, the caravan master threw the lamp at him.

Nermesa barely deflected the object in time. It crashed on the ground, shattering and spreading burning oil everywhere.

"Timonius! Garet! Quickly!"

Only then did Nermesa realize that Mikonius had been involved in the attempted murder. The knight froze for a moment, stunned by this revelation.

"But *why*?" he blurted to the other.

Two large men wielding long swords burst through the door. The caravan master's chief bodyguards. At the same time, Nermesa heard other shouts from within.

He could not face them all. Thinking quickly, Nermesa made a feint toward Mikonius. The heavy figure reacted as he expected, stumbling back and colliding with his own men. The collision bought Nermesa the moment that he desired. He spun about and ran toward where the horses were kept.

From behind him came angry voices. Picking up his pace, Nermesa turned toward the building in question.

Two guards stood poised near the entrance, their stances making it clear that they had heard the shouts. As Nermesa neared, he gestured behind him and shouted, "Hurry! Master Flavius is being attacked!"

He stood there as if ready to run back with them, but as the pair rushed by, Nermesa hesitated. The moment that he saw that the guards continued on, he turned back to the stables.

Swinging open the doors, the knight quickly looked around. As he had hoped, there were a few animals already saddled. Many merchants kept a handful so prepared for possible need in emergencies. His own father did the same.

Mounting up, he started out of the stables. Just beyond the doors, he nearly ran over a gaunt figure. As the knight instinctively veered his horse around the man, he saw that it none other than Polythemus.

Like Mikonius, Polythemus carried an oil lamp so that he could see where he was going. Unlike the treacherous caravan master, though, the figure before Nermesa wore an expression of utter puzzlement at sight of the rider.

"Nermesa Klandes? Why are you about at such an hour?" He did not reach for the sword at his side; nor did he call out for help. He simply stood there in confusion.

Only then did Nermesa realize that *Polythemus* was the innocent one. He had known nothing of the murder plot. Only his man Antimedes appeared to be involved, and that with Mikonius.

Nermesa thought to explain, but then decided that to do so was to risk the man's life. Better that Polythemus remain ignorant or even later assume that the knight was the villain; Nermesa did not want the caravan master's death on his hands. Once he met up with Baron Sibelio again, Nermesa could get everything straightened out.

Without a word, he urged the horse past Polythemus, who simply watched in befuddlement. As Nermesa rode out of the yard, several men came running toward him, but they were too far away to be of any concern.

But he knew that he could not stop. It would take only moments before some of Mikonius' men would mount up and be on his trail. Worse, they knew Karphur and beyond far better than Nermesa did. His present advantage would soon dissipate.

The gate through which they had arrived seemed his best bet. At least beyond them the countryside would give him a better chance of survival. He dared not seek the assistance of the Karphur Guard, for they were more likely to take the word of Mikonius—a prominent and established representative of a powerful merchant—over someone *claiming* to be a member of the King of Aquilonia's Black Dragons.

Again, Nermesa pondered the caravan master's betrayal. Why Mikonius Flavius had waited until Karphur still made no sense, but the overall reason for the assassination had somehow to involve the attacks on merchant wagons plaguing the various realms. Mikonius *had* seemed to be a very fortunate man; he had never been attacked. Could that be because he was in *league* with the villains? It was the only thing that made sense.

Antonus Sibelio must have been congratulating himself on having hired such a fortunate man as Mikonius, not suspecting that his own employee was using his position to enrich himself and his cronies. House Sibelio had lost a few caravans of its own, but not nearly as many as others. Mikonius did not want his own employer falling into ruin, for that would leave him without the means to travel to one land or another, no doubt trading information on vulnerable columns from other merchants with various cronies.

Perhaps there was more to it, or perhaps Nermesa had it

completely wrong. In his harried mind, however, it was the only course that made sense so far. Assuming he escaped Karphur, he could worry about pursuing the matter further.

It had been the knight's hope that, this late at night, he would be able to slip through the city easier. Unfortunately, the market—through which he had to ride—was as busy as ever. His steed was forced to a crawl as he fought through a drunken and entertainment-minded crowd. Briefly, his thoughts returned to Romulo, somehow forced to betray Nermesa despite what the latter had done for his brother. In the end, honor had caused Romulo to sacrifice his life for the knight, and for that Nermesa thanked his spirit. He wished that he could have done something about the driver's body, but such a hesitation would have likely meant Nermesa's undoing—not at all what Romulo had desired.

In the distance, he finally made out the darkened shape of the gate. Nermesa still had to get past the guards stationed there, but as they likely had nothing to do with those hunting him, he could not see any reason why they would hold him for long.

As he had done throughout his flight, Nermesa glanced over his shoulder to see if Mikonius' men had caught up yet. There was still no sign. That raised his hopes. Once he was through the gates, their chances of catching him would drop considerably.

An officer in the golden garb of the Karphur Guard stepped in front of him as Nermesa neared. "Halt! State your name, your country, and any articles upon you that we might find of interest."

"My name is Captain Nermesa Klandes of Aquilonia, on business for his majesty, King Conan. I have nothing upon my person save my sword."

"And why do leave at such a strange hour, Captain?" The officer looked Nermesa over, seeking some clue to the truth.

Leaning down, the knight smiled and muttered, "I spent a little too much time with a lady, of course. Now, I'll need to ride back to Tarantia with all haste if I'm to avoid punishment."

The Karphurian took him at his word. With a slight grin of his own, he gestured for Nermesa to go past. "Safe journey, Captain . . ."

But as the gates opened for him, someone farther back called out, "Stop! Stop that murderer!"

Nermesa kicked his horse, urging the animal to swift speed. He tore through the gates even as the guards sought to shut them again. Behind him, the Aquilonian heard more shouts. Someone blew a horn. Nermesa cursed, aware that he now might also have the Guard aiding his enemies in their pursuit.

But he dared not try to explain. Instead, the knight rode as hard as he could for the mountains, hoping that somewhere in them he would not only lose any hunters, but at last find his way into Aquilonia.

The dark shapes of the Karpash Mountains opened up well ahead. Nermesa focused only on them. He had to assume that he was being chased and that they would do their best to catch him. His mount raced along the road at the best speed it could surely muster.

Something suddenly whizzed past his head. It was almost immediately followed by another. There was at least one archer among the riders behind him. Despite the night, the shafts were flying too near the Black Dragon's head. Recalling what had happened in the mountains, Nermesa forced his horse to a twisting path. It slowed his progress slightly, but he hoped that it would prevent either him or the animal from ending up with an arrow through them.

A horn blared behind him. Moments later, another responded from *ahead*. Bolontes' son could only assume that there lay an outpost or lone sentry somewhere farther on. His pursuers hoped to catch him between them.

He had to abandon the path completely. Steering to the right, Nermesa headed for a lightly wooded, hilly area. In there, perhaps the night would enable him to blend in with his surroundings.

But just as he neared it, from his left there came two riders. By the glint they caused in the pale moonlight, he took them for Karphurian soldiers. Nermesa gripped his sword tight, but he was loath to use it against men whose only offense was that they mistakenly believed him to be a brigand or murderer.

Unfortunately, he quickly realized that the foremost would reach him before Nermesa managed the woods. Grim-faced, the Aquilonian met his new attacker blade to blade. Nermesa likely could have easily defeated his opponent if he sought to slay him, but because he desired only to defend, the knight soon found himself in trouble.

"I've no quarrel with you!" he finally shouted to the armored figure.

"Surrender, knave!" demanded the Karphurian in turn. "Surrender or die!"

There was no use trying to reason with his adversary. Nermesa finally brought the fight to the guard. Startled by the sudden shift in fortunes, the Karphurian desperately countered what he thought was Nermesa's main attack . . . but which was in fact a feint.

The Aquilonian's blade suddenly slipped over the guard's own. Nermesa drove the tip in deep, but at the shoulder of the sword arm, not the throat. Dropping his weapon, the other fighter grabbed at his wound.

Nermesa punched him soundly, sending him sprawling off his mount.

The second rider was nearly upon him. Seizing the reins of the first man's horse, Nermesa led the animal in front of the oncoming guard. The momentary confusion enabled the knight to gain a few precious paces on his pursuer as he headed for the woods.

The horse's heavy hooves thrashed the underbrush as Nermesa rode madly through the shadowed region. He could scarcely see ahead and hoped that the same would hold true for the Karphurians and Mikonius' villains. The landscape ahead began to rise, the first hint of the looming mountain range.

Barely had he entered when he heard the first sound of someone following him into the woods. Nermesa assumed it to be the lone guard, but then more thrashing arose. The other hunters had caught up quicker than he had anticipated.

Someone shouted. There was a crash and a groan. Nermesa took some heart from the unseen disaster, but a brief stumble by his own horse mere seconds after was a reminder that matters could change at any moment. A single misstep could spell disaster for him.

On and on Nermesa rode, his surroundings growing far more treacherous than even he had hoped. Despite those behind him, the Aquilonian was forced to pick and choose his path more and more. He prayed that none among the hunters knew the region well enough to make his forced slowness fatal.

Then Nermesa's mount tripped. The knight struggled valiantly with the reins, but the animal stumbled madly along, heading down a sharp incline.

Whether through the will of Mitra or sheer luck, the horse righted itself at the bottom. For Nermesa, Mitra or luck did not serve him as well at first. As the animal jerked to a stop, the Aquilonian was thrown from the saddle. Only quick action by Nermesa kept him from crashing headfirst into a nearby tree trunk. Instead, he rolled past it, striking his left shoulder hard against a rock but breaking no bones.

His shoulder numb and his arm momentarily useless because of it, Bolontes' son retrieved his sword—which he had lost in his fall—with his right hand. Sheathing it, Nermesa grabbed the horse by the reins and, after quickly checking the animal for possible injury, fought to mount up again.

But before he could, movement caught his attention. By the rustling of the leaves he guessed at least two, maybe three riders were in the vicinity.

Nermesa stepped down again and silently guided his horse to an area where he hoped they would blend into the darkness. Cupping the animal's mouth, the Black Dragon waited.

In the dim moonlight, murky forms that looked more like multilimbed demons than men on horseback moved through the woods. Nermesa heard the clink of metal on metal and assumed the figures to be part of the Guard. Despite his unwillingness to do battle with them, Nermesa drew his sword the moment that his arm allowed, then held it ready. However duped they might be, he would not let even them slay him—especially now that he had possible clues to his mission to pass on to General Pallantides.

"He had to come over this way," muttered one figure.

"Silence in the ranks!" hissed what had to be the voice of the commanding officer.

Several more figures slowly wended their way by, then one paused near where Nermesa waited. To the Aquilonian's displeasure, the rider urged his mount down.

But scarcely had the steed begun to descend, when it nearly fell. Only barely did the horse right itself.

With a curse that mixed Ophirian and Corinthian, the armored figure tugged on the reins, guiding his mount back up. Nermesa could only assume that since the man's own horse had nearly killed itself trying to descend so cautiously, the guard believed it impossible for their quarry to have made it down safely at any speed.

At last, the searchers moved on. Yet, Nermesa still dared not leave his shelter. It was possible that they would return the way they had come. He had no choice but to wait.

Precious minutes slipped away as he listened for any hint of either their presence or that of Mikonius' men. Finally, when he could stand it no more, Nermesa quietly started to guide his animal along in search of a better place to ride back up.

At last finding it, Nermesa led the horse on for a pace, then mounted. He heard a night bird and some small creature sniffing about the bushes, but still nothing of those giving chase.

Satisfied at last that he had escaped their clutches, Nermesa urged his mount to a steady pace. Over the trees, he could just make out the now-looming silhouette of first of the Karpash Mountains. Assuming that there were no more obstacles, he could cross them and in a few days be in outer Aquilonia.

Nermesa licked his lips. But before he could even begin to worry about the mountains, he needed water. Food he could survive without for the time being, but the chase had built up in the knight a terrible thirst. In a woods such as this, there had to be some source of open water.

It was some time, though, before he came across that needed source. Afraid to deviate from his path, he likely had missed at least one other. Still, the shallow river that Nermesa finally found looked more than ample for his needs. If not for the possibility of pursuit still behind him, it would have even made for an ideal place to camp.

Despite the tranquillity of the dark scene, the Aquilonian approached the river with caution. The Karphurian commander might have sent some of his men to follow the line of this river on the assumption that their quarry would need to pause along the way.

Within a few yards of it, Nermesa dismounted. Sword in one hand and reins in the other, he crossed the final distance. Contrary to his own hesitation, his horse immediately sought a drink. Nermesa watched the animal for a few seconds, then shifted upriver to satisfy his own thirst.

He drank slowly at first, still wary of attackers. Yet, as more time passed and nothing happened, Nermesa relaxed slightly. When he had drunk his fill, he went back to the horse and searched through the saddlebags to see what he could find. There were some dried rations, which he stored for later need, and an empty water sack. The latter he quickly filled, then hooked it onto the saddle.

Climbing back up, Nermesa eyed the mountains. He saw them only as an impediment, not a barrier. One way or another, he was determined that he *would* this time return to Aquilonia.

But whether he would make it all the way to *Tarantia* alive was another matter entirely.

15

THE KARPASH MOUNTAINS were by no means simple to cross, but cross them Nermesa did. It took him days of carefully guiding his mount over winding, precarious paths and nights of cold, unsettled slumber, where often he and the horse had only each other for warmth. The dried rations lasted him two days, the water three. Fortunately, Nermesa found water along the way, some of it melting snow. He also managed to catch a small mountain goat, which gave him the sustenance he needed to continue the trek. His horse survived on hardy mountain plants . . . and drank the water he provided.

And thus it was that, six days later by his reckoning, he finally descended into a long, grassy plain that marked the first sight of his homeland that he had had in weeks.

Nermesa came across the first *settlement*—a small village—a day later. The villagers were friendly enough and, in exchange for helping one family with their farm duties, he received a place in the barn to sleep and food to fill his grumbling belly. Out of necessity, the knight stayed for two days, but then pushed on immediately the following morning.

From his hosts, Nermesa learned that he had come out of one of the less-traveled areas of the mountains, which was why he had not run across one of the patrols constantly monitoring Aquilonia's borders. He had been told that if he stayed for three more days, one likely would have passed by, but Nermesa could not wait that long. Besides, the patrol would then have only taken him to Vanadi, an outpost several more days southwest. In the same time span, Nermesa could nearly be home.

And so, Bolontes' son continued on alone, but at least he was well fed and better clad. His saddlebags had sufficient food, and the farmer in whose barn he had stayed had told him of three points along the way where the Black Dragon could replenish his supplies before they were all used up.

Much encouraged now, Nermesa made great headway. Tarantia lay northwest of him, but before that, he would reach Corialan, a smaller—yet still-vibrant—city where there would be a military presence. They could then send word ahead for him.

Five days beyond the village, he turned onto what was the preferred route from Tarantia to Corinthia, which placed him very near the path that he and the caravan had been taking for Nemedia as well. The route should have been more active, but Nermesa saw no other travelers that day or the next. The successful attacks on the much larger caravans had made individual pilgrims fearful.

Still, he did come across a wagon driven by a priest of Mitra out seeking wayward members of the flock. The elder, balding priest was happy to give Nermesa his blessing and even happier, it seemed, to pass on news of events back in the capital, even if they might not be exactly what Nermesa wanted to hear.

"Aye, my son, I only left Tarantia a fortnight ago, so the news is not all that old. The king still seeks his trade agreement with the surrounding lands, but 'tis not likely at this point. Nemedia accuses Corinthia, Corinthia accuses Ophir—and itself, too, being of many parts—Ophir accuses Corinthia, and Kush accuses both of them. In turn, they all claim some responsibility on his majesty himself, nearly declaring that King Conan is reverting to his old ways . . ."

Nermesa had wondered when the Cimmerian's past would be brought up in this situation. "Any other news?"

"Corinthia may soon be at war with itself, and Ophir and Nemedia involved. Kush and Argos are watching this close, seeing if Ophir is ripe . . ." The old priest shook his head. "We of Mitra hear more than most . . . and more than we like, at times . . ."

The knight bid the elder farewell and rode on. Much of what Nermesa had heard from him the officer had known already. The rest had verified his earlier fears. It was bad enough that so many accusations flew concerning the brigands, but the Corinthian situation seemed ready to boil over. Had Nermesa been a paranoid man, he would have almost suspected the threats linked.

Could that be? But for such a thing to be possible would demand coordination on a scale Nermesa could not imagine. Those involved would have to have agents in every one of the affected kingdoms, agents in positions of power.

He was still pondering the subject two days later when, in the distance, he spotted the caravan.

It was long, very long, and headed toward Tarantia from the looks of it. Nermesa could not initially make out the markings or the banners, but thought that it must be Aquilonian. He debated whether or not to ride to it. Not every caravan master could be in league with Mikonius Flavius, after all. Most would be honest men.

Taking a chance, Nermesa rode closer. If he could at least identify the caravan, he would have a better idea as to whether or not to trust them.

The wagons definitely had an Aquilonian look to them. He had hoped to make out the banners, but the day was all but windless, causing the pennants to hang limply. There were symbols on the wagons, but to see them clearly he had to approach even closer.

As he did, four riders separated from the main column and headed his way. Nermesa debated turning away, but the caravan was journeying the same direction as he, meaning that it would always be in his path. To detour around it would cost him several days more.

He realized that all four riders were Gundermen. More important, as they neared, he saw that one of them was *known* to him.

"My lord Nermesa . . ." called Betavio, looking somewhat startled. "That is you, yes?"

"Aye, Betavio!" Nermesa had never been so pleased to see the Gunderman. Whatever their differences, his presence here meant only one thing—that his master Antonus also rode with the caravan. "You're a sight for sore eyes!"

"We thought you surely dead in the alleys of Tebes." The Gunderman looked him up and down as if uncertain whether or not that belief still held some merit. "The baron insisted on making the city guard search high and low for you. He felt personally responsible."

"He shouldn't. It was my own choice . . . but I fell afoul of something."

Betavio took the limited explanation accordingly. He gestured to the other riders, who still had their hands on their weapons. "Stand down. The baron will want to see this man." To Nermesa, Antonus' bodyguard said, "Please ride beside me, my lord."

As Betavio led them back, Nermesa's chest swelled with hope. Antonus would be very interested in what he had discovered concerning one of the baron's own caravan masters. More important, the other noble would surely help Nermesa get word back to Tarantia as soon as possible.

Ignoring the glances of several of the drivers and guards, Betavio guided Nermesa in among the wagons in search of Baron Sibelio. Nermesa spotted Antonus first, the baron riding astride a white charger. Antonus conversed with another man whom the knight did not recognize and assumed was the caravan master.

The baron's companion, a broad-nosed, muscular figure with long black hair and clad in the blue-and-ebony garments of House Sibelio, noticed him first. He muttered something to Antonus, who immediately turned Nermesa's way and smiled.

"Praise Mitra! Nermesa Klandes!" The baron urged his mount toward the knight, reaching out one hand as he did. He clasped Nermesa's outstretched one, then, when close enough, patted Bolontes' son on the back. "Alive and well! Truly a miracle! Truly!"

"It's good to see you, Antonus . . ."

"I'll double that! When you didn't return to my villa, I feared the worst! I should've insisted that you take Betavio with you. Things would have worked out as they should have, then."

Nermesa leaned close so that only his host could hear him. "I need to speak with you privately as soon as possible, Antonus. It is very vital."

"Oh?" Keeping his expression cheerful, the other noble replied, "It will have to wait until we make camp. I've too many things to attend to right now. Will that be all right?"

Nermesa considered. Night was only about four hours away. His news could surely wait that long. Antonus' caravan seemed under the baron's capable guidance. No bandits could be operating here. Antonus would know it quickly, and Betavio would deal with it even quicker.

"Yes, it can wait." A thought occurred to him. "Just answer me this. Do you have a messenger bird with you?"

"Of course."

Nermesa nodded. If the baron sent off a bird this evening with a note from the knight, it would surely reach Tarantia sometime tomorrow. That would be soon enough at this point.

Turning to Betavio, Antonus commanded, "Give him

food, water, and whatever else he needs. Treat him well, Betavio."

"Yes, my lord."

With an apologetic nod, the noble returned to his other companion. Betavio gestured for Nermesa to follow him.

The other Gundermen returned to various positions along the column as Betavio led his charge to what was apparently Baron Sibelio's wagon. It was large and more refined in appearance than the rest and had elegantly carved wooded shutters, with the attacking crane symbol of the House cut deep into each. Banners with the full House insignia hung from each corner of the roof. A team of white horses—each looking meticulously groomed despite the long trek already taken from Tebes—pulled it. The driver, another Gunderman, nodded to Betavio, then kept his eyes on the trail ahead.

Nermesa glanced at his guide. "I wasn't aware that so many of your people served the baron."

"The baron took them on with my recommendation."

Nermesa could certainly understand wanting to have more such fighters. After all, everyone knew that a Gunderman could be trusted to do his duty.

From the back of the wagon, Betavio secured a flask of wine, some bread, and dried, salted meat. Compared to what Nermesa had eaten over the past few days, the simple fare seemed more like a banquet. The dried meat especially did not taste at all like that to which he was accustomed. That Nermesa had to eat while riding did not bother him, either, for at last he felt as if home was just over the horizon.

The Gunderman left him with the request that the knight remain near his master's wagon. Not wanting to do anything accidentally to slow the caravan or irritate Antonus, Nermesa immediately acquiesced. He satisfied himself with organizing his thoughts in preparation for his conversation that evening with the baron. The other noble would have many questions, and it would only behoove Nermesa to be able to answer them as succinctly as possible.

It would be difficult enough for Antonus to accept that

some of his trusted men were the very brigands threatening his and others' caravans.

THEY MADE CAMP roughly two days from Corialan— the last bit of information according to the driver of the baron's wagon. After seeing to his own animal, Nermesa helped with the wagon's horses. While it was not necessary for someone of his station to do so, it kept him from growing impatient. Now that it was nearly time to meet with Antonus, the knight's patience had begun to fray. The baron had to be convinced to send off the bird as soon as possible.

Antonus came for him almost two hours after the caravan made camp. In that time, servants of the baron had set up a large tent in the center of the circle of wagons, Nermesa noticed that the fires of the other members of the caravan were set at a safe distance from Antonus' quarters and that the tent itself was surrounded by a ring of fierce-looking Gundermen.

"One can never be too careful," the baron remarked as they entered. "I've grown powerful enough to have earned my rightful share of enemies."

The floor of the tent was covered with colorful cloth sheets over which were draped rich, silken ones. In lieu of a bed, Antonus had long, flat pillows, atop which fat, round ones stood. Squat, brass oil lamps on chains hung from the ceiling, and a small wooden table with an ivory top stood in the center. Sniffing, Nermesa noted some flowery incense, well needed after a long day on the dirty road.

The Baron Sibelio indicated the table. "Please, sit there. Before we talk, we eat. I insist."

Nermesa gave in, taking up a place by the table. His host sat across from him. They did not use chairs, instead sitting cross-legged on the sheets.

"Wine first, I think." Antonus clapped his hands and a young, female servant slipped inside. In her dainty hands, she carried a golden tray with two matching chalices and a wine decanter.

As she poured lush, red wine for each of them, Nermesa could not help notice her beauty. She was slim but still curved and with black—utterly black—hair and deep emerald eyes. Clad in a gossamer gown that surely could not be the clothing in which she traveled during the day, the girl was as enticing as the women of Karphur. She gave the Black Dragon a coy smile before retreating from the tent.

"She seems to like you . . ." Antonus remarked wryly. "If you are interested, I believe that she would be willing . . ."

"Thank you, no."

The baron suddenly frowned, as if he himself had caused some offense. "Of course. Damned of me to suggest such. Telaria . . ."

Before he could stop himself, Nermesa straightened at mention of her name. Fortunately, Antonus chose then to take a sip of his wine. When he spoke it was only to say, "Our meal should be ready by now."

He clapped his hands again, and through the flap of the tent came three more servants. The two men were clad in the livery of the House, while the third, another young woman, was dressed in what Nermesa silently swore was even less than the previous one.

They brought a tray of prepared fruits and vegetables plus what appeared to be *fresh*, well-cooked goat. As one of the men sliced off a portion and put it on a golden plate for Nermesa, the knight could not help but look at his host in some surprise.

"We have a small herd of goats with us," Antonus explained as the servant put another plate of steaming meat in front of him. "They are for my use, although some is always passed on to the drivers and guards." He smiled and sipped some more wine. "There should be *some* privileges for success, especially on such journeys."

Nermesa surveyed the entire scene. "It all looks fit for a king."

That made his host smile broadly. "Doesn't it? Now, please . . . my cook is Ophirian, and they are known for their delicacies."

The goat was remarkably well seasoned and all but melted in Nermesa's mouth. He did not refuse when offered more, but the spices used demanded he also have additional drink, which was quickly poured. Bolontes' son never noticed the girl slipping back into the tent, but whenever his chalice was empty, there she was.

Before he knew it, the meal had come to an end. The empty plates and trays vanished as quickly as they had come, and again Nermesa found the servant girl filling his cup. Then, with another coy smile, she departed the tent, leaving her master and his guest alone.

But not for very long. Nermesa suddenly sensed a third presence in the tent and when he looked toward the flap, it was to find standing there the man with whom Antonus had been conversing when first the knight had arrived.

"Caius," remarked the baron, both greeting the man and simultaneously introducing him to Nermesa. "About time."

"You said not to come until you were through eating," Caius answered somewhat gruffly. "So I didn't."

Toying with his ring, Antonus frowned. "Mind your manners."

His simple words seemed to have great effect upon Caius, for the dark man grimaced, then bowed his head. "My apologies."

"Good enough. Be seated. Captain Nermesa Klandes of the Black Dragons has something very important to tell me, he says."

Caius' abrupt appearance did not sit well with the knight. "Antonus, this would be better spoken of alone."

"You may trust when I say that he will tell no one anything unless I give him permission. Is that not so, Caius?"

"Aye . . . it is so."

The Baron Sibelio turned once more to Nermesa and as he did, something glittered in the latter's eyes despite the dimming illumination of the oil lamps. Nermesa belatedly noticed that it was the other noble's emerald ring.

"Tell us what you know, Nermesa," urged his host.

Not wishing to offend Antonus by asking him to move

or cover up his favored ring, Nermesa looked at Caius for a moment.

"I've some clues to what is going on with the attacks on the caravans," he began. Nermesa tried to meet the other man's gaze, the better to judge him, but up close Caius' eyes had a strange unfocused look.

But if his eyes did not seem focused, the black-haired man's attention certainly was. "You have some idea who is responsible, do you?"

"To some extent." Bolontes' son looked again to his host and again the ring offended his eyes. This time, Nermesa refused to be cowed by the glitter. "Antonus . . . some of your own men are involved."

The baron took this in better stride than Nermesa expected. He stared steely-eyed at the captain, then lowered his chalice to the table. "You are certain of this."

Nermesa noticed that he did not phrase it as a question. He clearly respected that the knight would not have said such without being absolutely positive.

"Yes." Nermesa's head pounded, and he cursed himself for being too willing to drink each time the serving girl refilled his cup. "Some of them I discovered in the city of Karphur. I believe Mikonius Flavius and a senior driver named Antimedes are part. Antimedes is dead, though, at my hand."

"Antimedes is dead, you say?" rasped Caius with what to Nermesa almost sounded like pleasure.

"He sought my own death and failed." There was no reason to explain all the details.

"It never pays to underestimate you," remarked Antonus, toasting him. "I've come to know that."

Nermesa bowed his head in gratitude for the compliment, even if he did not feel he deserved it.

"There is surely more than that, though," added the third member of their party. Caius had no chalice, and the baron seemed uninclined to call for one for him.

"I believe that Mikonius is part of a network of caravan masters, drivers, and the like, all coordinating information between them on when other merchant columns are on journeys. I think that they know who is the easiest of targets and plan accordingly."

"That would require communication over a great distance," pointed out the baron.

"Messenger birds would suffice . . . and there may even be what some would term *sorcery* involved."

Antonus' eyes widened briefly. "Their master must be a man of genius, to have organized such an effort!"

"It's a very complex situation." Nermesa stared into the glittering facets of the baron's ring. Where it had once distracted him, it now helped the knight to focus his thoughts. All his suspicions came to the forefront, organized and ready to be told to his host. "I believe it entails other matters than just thievery."

"Oh?"

"There must be agents in all the surrounding realms, not merely caravan masters and drivers, but those in stations of power. I suspect that one of those, in fact, is Zoran, ambassador of Nemedia." Even as he made the revelation, Nermesa suddenly realized that he had said *too* much. He had not meant to name any names to the baron other than that of Mikonius Flavius and Antimedes. Zoran's involvement was no business of Antonus', even if he *was* familiar with the dignitary.

"The ambassador of Nemedia . . ." Caius shifted his unfocused gaze to Antonus. "Strong accusations."

"I saw him with a mysterious Corinthian, the same man I followed in the Waste and down into the sewers below Tebes. The same man who is a devil of a sorcerer in disguise, a fiend known as *Set-Anubis*."

Antonus lowered his chalice. He turned stone-faced. His eyes shifted from Nermesa to Caius, then back again. "Set-Anubis? Are you certain?"

Nermesa was already biting his lip for having mentioned the sorcerer. He had meant Set-Anubis' identity only for the ears of the king and General Pallantides. Clearly the wine had gone to his head far more than he had anticipated.

Rather than risk revealing something else he had intended to keep quiet, Nermesa set aside his cup and prepared to rise. "Forgive me, Antonus. I'm not feeling well. Perhaps we can finish this tomorrow evening."

"But you've not told us everything."

"My apologies, but I must go."

The baron reached up to take his arm. As he did, his ring flared bright in the knight's eyes. "You must stay."

Nermesa's legs started to fold, but the Black Dragon suddenly caught himself. Politely pulling free of his host's grip, he stood. "Good night, Antonus."

"You should not go," Caius now echoed. The dark man also rose, but for some reason he appeared a thinner than Nermesa recalled him. Caius pointed one narrow finger at the floor. "You will sit."

Again, Bolontes' son nearly did. Instead, though, he fought off the desire and started around the table. "Excuse me."

"Look at me!" rasped Antonus' man.

Against his own better judgment, Nermesa did. Despite the peculiarity of Caius' gaze, Nermesa found that it snared his attention.

"Yes, look at me . . ."

Caius' eyes filled his view. Nermesa felt a darkness begin to envelop him . . .

"No . . ." He shook his head, backing away at the same time. "No . . ." For reasons Nermesa could not explain, he reached for his sword.

And as he did, the man before him grew indistinct. It seemed that two figures stood simultaneously in the same place. One was the much more muscular Caius, while the other was wiry, much older, and clad not in the livery of House Sibelio, but some dark, voluminous cloak.

That figure became dominant. The face of Caius melted into it . . . and the eyes closed, the lids now sealed with strong fibers.

Centered between the two shut orbs, the crimson gem gleamed evilly.

"You!" Nermesa pulled free his sword. "You!"

But he got no farther. Set-Anubis, a snarl on his cadaverous visage, muttered something. The jewel flared—

Every muscle in Nermesa froze. He strained to cut the sorcerer in twain, but could not lower his arm in order to do so. The knight tried to reach with his free hand for the gaunt spellcaster's throat, yet, even that was forbidden him. He could breathe, he could see.

He could do nothing else.

"*That* did not go as planned," murmured the man behind Set-Anubis. Baron Antonus Sibelio stepped around the sorcerer and peered at Nermesa as if studying an unusual bug. "Not at all as planned."

"His will is strong, I told you that!" spat the monstrous figure. "Think you that he could have so easily survived my previous efforts?"

"I was beginning to wonder." Antonus leaned close, coming almost nose to nose with the frozen figure. "Strong, yes, but not quite strong enough."

"Not all my power is illusion. You know that. He can overcome some of what the Eye of Charon grants me, but not all. He is, after all, only mortal."

Antonus turned to the sorcerer. As he did, he raised his hand into Nermesa's sight. The emerald gem gleamed brightly. "And you, as always, should remember that *you* are, too."

To Nermesa's surprise, the terrifying Set-Anubis seemed to shrivel within his hooded cloak.

"I have not forgotten . . ."

"Not forgotten *what*?"

"Not forgotten . . . my lord." With this raspy pronouncement, the spellcaster bowed deep, as any servant would to his master.

Smiling, the Baron Sibelio turned back to his captive. He shook his head. "Poor Nermesa Klandes! So intelligent and yet so naive! I commend you on your survival skills, though. You should have died in Tebes, or in Karphur, for that matter. I'd had messenger birds sent from Tebes to those places in which you might appear if you survived the sewer trap. Mikonius can usually be trusted to see a task like that done. Pity that there's no way to convince you to join with me"— he looked over his shoulder at Set-Anubis—"or is there?"

Keeping his head low, the sorcerer answered, "As I said, his will is very strong. It would be best simply to kill him."

"A shame. Still . . ."

And as the knight watched in horror, Antonus reached to Nermesa's sword hand. The treacherous baron peeled away the fingers clutching the weapon, then took the blade.

Testing the weapon out with a few sweeps, Antonus marveled, "Such craftsmanship! Such beauty!"

Without warning, he turned so that the sword's tip ended right where Nermesa's heart was. Yet, as the baron was about to follow through with the killing thrust, a third voice interjected.

"No . . ."

The lord of House Sibelio glanced past his prisoner. "You think he should not die?"

"No, not yet," continued the other, someone whose voice Nermesa should have known but could not yet identify. "He knows more . . . or at least has suspicions worth hearing. More important, he has other knowledge of great use to you. Knowledge of things close to the barbarian."

Antonus turned the blade about, letting the point now rest in the ground. He used the weapon as a staff upon which to lean. His smile grew broader. "Yes, you're right! You serve me well, Betavio!"

The Gunderman came around to gaze at Nermesa. The cruel bent of his mouth indicated that nothing would please him more than when the knight *did* perish.

"As always, my lord, as always," the bodyguard responded quietly.

Set-Anubis showed his displeasure at any suggestion of keeping the knight breathing. "His will being strong, it may take time to break him. Much time."

"I will not be slowed," the baron insisted. "We must return to Tarantia."

Betavio nodded his agreement. With malice in his eyes, he poked at Nermesa, causing the knight to teeter danger-ously. "Aye, my lord. Nothing must prevent that. Therefore, I'll see to it that the fool is kept secreted for the rest of the journey . . . if this dog here can keep him in such a state."

"It will take much focus on my part. I will be unable to do little else in that time."

"All else goes as planned," Antonus remarked. "I see no reason that we would need your magic for anything other than this. But bind and gag him just in case, eh?"

Poking at Nermesa again, the Gunderman grunted. "With pleasure, my lord."

The Baron Sibelio held high the knight's sword. Ner-mesa silently cursed Antonus over and over as the other noble toyed with the exquisite weapon.

"I will keep this," Antonus proclaimed. "It is a fitting blade for me, isn't it, Betavio?"

"Fit for a king, I'd say, my lord."

The baron's eyes lit up. He smiled at Nermesa. "Yes, fit for a king . . . which I will soon enough be."

Betavio chuckled and, as Nermesa still stared aghast at what Antonus had revealed, pushed the frozen knight over.

16

TO NERMESA, NO hell created by any god could compare with the horrendous ordeal through which he suffered for the rest of the journey back to Tarantia. Betavio had eagerly bound and gagged him as commanded, then tossed the hapless knight into the Baron Sibelio's private wagon under a suffocating mass of rich, silken cloths. There, Bolontes' son had lain helplessly while the wagons plodded along. He could not move so much as a finger and when voices neared that he thought might belong to someone who could help, his mouth would not work.

Worse, he discovered that he could not sleep, either. Whatever mesmerism or spell Set-Anubis had cast upon him prevented the knight from doing so. For hour after hour, Nermesa could only think about his monstrous failure, think about what a fool he had been.

Once, on the very first night after his capture, he had briefly thought that he might yet free himself. Just after the wagons halted, Nermesa noticed that two of his fingers suddenly twinged. He worked on them, managing to make one bend at his will.

However, before Nermesa could accomplish any more, Betavio and the sorcerer had come for him.

"Raise him to a sitting position," demanded Set-Anubis, the insidious glow of the Eye of Charon preceding both him and the Gunderman into the darkened wagon.

"I know what to do, dog." Betavio had propped up the captive, turning Nermesa's unblinking gaze to where the sorcerer stood waiting.

"You have no choice but to look," murmured Set-Anubis to the knight. "You have no choice but to see only the Eye of Charon . . ."

It was true. Nermesa could look nowhere else. The foul crimson glow burned into his own eyes, into his very mind. He fought it as best he could, but in the end, Nermesa felt his fingers stiffening once more.

And by the time that they left him, he was in no better shape than when first ensorcelled.

Each evening thereafter, when apparently there was no fear of notice, the pair returned and Set-Anubis reinforced the spell. They never asked questions of Nermesa. From their cautious nature, he had to assume that there were others traveling with the column, others who did not share the evil secret between the three men. Like any caravan, there were probably several wealthy travelers included in it. Along with them might travel family and servants. Antonus had to be careful that none of them discovered the truth. It would be too great a risk trying to mesmerize all of them.

As for whatever foul spell Set-Anubis cast upon him, in addition to not needing sleep, the captive knight discovered that he also did not have to eat, drink, or deal with the necessary consequences of either. While his mind remained active, his entire body seemed to be in some sort of suspended animation. Only his very light breathing gave any hint that Nermesa was not dead.

He eventually lost track of the days despite his best efforts. It hardly seemed to matter, anyway. Nermesa was a helpless prisoner, doomed to betray all that he knew concerning his mission and, from what had been said in the tent, what he knew of the workings of the palace.

I have been blind! Nermesa thought over and over. He had not made the final link, though it had been there, that Mikonius and his ilk could not organize such a plan on their own. They needed someone of more cunning and of high station. Someone with a network spreading across the various realms already.

Baron Antonus Sibelio.

Nermesa had been fooled by the fact that even the baron had lost a couple of caravans. There was no consolation in knowing that so many others, even General Pallantides, had been fooled by Antonus. It had been Nermesa's task— given to him by the king, no less—to unravel the mysteries. In that he had failed utterly. If not for the fact that many others might suffer should the baron's plan unfold as expected, Bolontes' son would have almost welcomed his eventual murder. His blunders were a mark of shame on both his House and Aquilonia.

Yet there remained a niggling hope that Mitra would grant him some slight miracle, some last opportunity to redeem himself. The likelihood of that all but shrank to nil, though, when Nermesa realized that they had finally reached the capital.

He could not say exactly when they arrived in the vicinity—most sounds were muffled by the silks atop him—but the constant groaning of the wagon as it turned this way and that and the slowly rising murmur in his ears told him that they had to be near some major settlement. Still, as Corialan surely would have been behind them by now and no other sizable population center existed in between, Nermesa could only assume that what he noted were the first hints of Tarantia. He yearned for his voice, but even a shout would likely have gone unnoticed in the noise of traffic.

Nermesa had some vague hope that the guards at the city gates would inspect the wagons, but then he realized that Antonus was probably not even heading for the capital itself. The baron had a sizable holding out in the country-side, a vast estate with fields worked by scores of serfs. Nermesa had passed it once while returning from the Westermarck with the brigand, Khatak, and had even spoken briefly with the other noble during that time. It was yet another irony that while the knight had been escorting one terrible scoundrel to justice, another, even more base villain had been pleasantly chatting with him.

The wagons continued to thump over the well-worn road, jostling Bolontes' son about. Frustrated, Nermesa tried to summon some sort of physical reaction . . . and to his surprise felt his wrist obey.

Emboldened, he forced it to flex twice more, then concentrated on his fingers. They proved less amenable, his efforts, and Nermesa began to grow frustrated again. Finally, however, his thumb twitched slightly.

But, just then, Nermesa belatedly noticed that the wagon had come to a stop. Seconds later, a figure entered and began tossing aside the silks. An ugly face peered down at the frozen figure.

"You'll be happy to know that you're back in your beloved Tarantia, my *lord*," Betavio sneered.

Nermesa was cautious not to let even the slightest movement happen as the Gunderman dragged him out.

"Help me with this dog," he commanded another of his countrymen. The other Gunderman took hold of Nermesa's legs. "We take him to the lower cells."

Grunting, the pair hefted Nermesa, then carried him through an old, dimly lit corridor. Nermesa caught glimpses of arched columns covered with traces of moss. Fine veins revealed where time had begun its slow work of dismantling the structure crack by crack. The smell of mold wafted by Nermesa's nostrils, the only sense other than sight and hearing still left to the captive officer.

Other than the scrapes of his guards' boots and their heavy breathing as they lugged their burden, Nermesa heard nothing else. Familiar with some of the old, old estates of Tarantia, he knew that the type of cells of which

Betavio spoke could be several levels below the stately residence. The tender ears of jaded nobles could not be bothered with the sounds of their victims. The knight gave thanks that his own family's holdings did not, to his knowledge, include such a vile legacy.

The Gundermen abruptly halted.

"This one here," commanded Betavio.

"There's no door left on it," grumbled the other.

"The chains are all that matter. They're strong."

He was maneuvered into the darkened room, where the second Gunderman set his feet to the ground. Betavio shoved Nermesa into the other's arms. A moment later, light entered the dank chamber, and Betavio's voice said, "Over there."

On the far wall, a pair of manacles hung. They were red with rust, but when the Gunderman holding Nermesa tested one, it held.

He spun the Aquilonian about. Bolontes' son caught sight of Betavio setting a small torch in a niche just outside the doorway. Baron Sibelio's bodyguard then stepped inside and helped his comrade unbind the prisoner.

"Not quite as comfortable as the wagon, my lord," smirked Betavio. "But you won't be alive long enough to be very bothered by it."

They stood his motionless form straight, then brought one hand up to one of the chains.

But as they did, Nermesa struggled with the other. The movement he had sensed returning seemed to be spreading. If there was anything that the knight hoped to do to save himself, now was the time to do it.

Unseen, his fingers clenched. He managed to shift his hand to the other manacle.

Drawing upon every iota of strength, Nermesa seized the loose chain and swung it around. He smashed Betavio in the side of the head as hard as he could.

Grunting, the lead Gunderman dropped. His companion gaped, which gave Nermesa the chance he had been hoping for. He pulled his other wrist free, then grabbed that of the Gunderman.

As the first hand came up, Nermesa's captor moved to protect himself from what he thought was a punch. Instead, the Aquilonian used both hands to press his foe's wrist into the manacle, then clamp it shut.

Cursing, Betavio's companion grabbed for his dagger. This time, Nermesa did punch him, then threw the staggering villain hard against the cell wall. Another punch finally downed the Gunderman.

Betavio still lay stunned on the floor. Nermesa, his legs unsteady, bent down and drew the Gunderman's sword. Staggering back and forth, the knight headed for the corridor—

And nearly ran into Set-Anubis.

Both stood as if suddenly frozen by the sorcerer's insidious spell. The Eye of Charon glimmered evilly, drinking in the image of the escaping Black Dragon and his two stunned captors.

Set-Anubis chuckled. "A grand sight I will long remember! Would that it was his master that lay there at your feet . . ."

His words struck Nermesa. "You don't willingly serve the baron?"

"Would one such as *I* ever freely serve some base, opportunistic noble with petty ambitions? Fool of an Aquilonian! It is only cursed circumstance that forces me to bow to the will of this miscreant, someone whom I would willingly feed to the demons of Acheron bit by screaming bit if I could! Yet, so long as he holds the *Tear*, I must grovel even to these mongrels . . ."

"The Tear?"

"The *Tear of Charon*, you fool! That which was created by Charon to unlock the power of this, even older, artifact upon which he then also audaciously placed his name!" Set-Anubis gestured angrily at the crimson gem. "It is the baron who chanced upon it after it was stolen by the damned Kushites! They thought to slay me with it, but I struck first. Yet, one, already dying, fled with the stone and was found by your cursed baron in the deserts of Stygia!

The Aquilonian coveted the stone, and when he learned that it also had power, he kept the Kushite alive long enough to discover the truth . . ."

"And so he found out about you, too."

"Yes! As sightless as if I did not wear the Eye, I blundered into his very hands and have remained his slave ever since . . ." The sorcerer raised his hands toward Nermesa. "But some commands of his I do not mind so much to obey—"

The knight thrust up his own hand. "Wait! I can be of help to you!"

"Ha! You! In what manner?"

"Leave me be, and I'll take the ring from the baron!"

For just a brief moment, it seemed that Set-Anubis considered his offer. Then, reason returned. "And you would give it to me? How doubtful! Besides—" He extended one hand in particular. Only then did Nermesa notice that it missed the two lower fingers. They had clearly been severed, then the wounds hastily and brutally cauterized. "—even *I* have learned the price of attempting to betray him in so bold a manner . . ."

Nermesa lunged, aiming with his blade for where he hoped the sorcerer's black heart beat.

But Set-Anubis muttered a single word, and the Aquilonian's movements slowed to a crawl, then ceased altogether.

"Dolt!" Set-Anubis' insult did not seem to be focused on Nermesa, however, for the Eye seemed to look past the frozen figure. "Must I do everything?"

"Be silent, dog!" growled Betavio. There was shuffling behind Nermesa, and the lead Gunderman stepped around into view. He glared at the prisoner. "I should slit your gullet—"

"Aah, but the dear baron would not approve," cackled the sorcerer. "And I know how much you wish to keep him happy . . . for now."

Betavio gave Set-Anubis a murderous glance, then returned his attention to Nermesa. "This is your fault, spellcaster. Not mine," he muttered, peeling the sword free from the knight's grip. "Your magic wore off!"

"Yes . . . as I told the baron, this Nermesa Klandes is a mortal of great will! This new spell I have cast will not hold him long!"

Betavio snorted. "Then the better to rely on good, solid metal before that happens."

He shoved the hapless prisoner back. Nermesa collided with the wall. Betavio then went to the other Gunderman, slapping his comrade across the face.

As the second guard stirred, Betavio took a small key from his belt and worked on the manacle. With effort, he released the other Gunderman, then thrust Nermesa's wrist in. With a fateful click, the manacle shut.

"The other . . . if you can manage it."

The second guard finished locking Nermesa up as Betavio stepped back.

"Shall I begin to question him?" asked Set-Anubis.

"Not now, dog! You know that the baron wishes to be here for it and at the moment, he's got other matters on his mind . . ."

Now it was the hooded figure who snorted. "The woman . . ."

"Aye . . . the woman. Speak well of her in my presence, dog, for she is important to the plan."

Nermesa realized that they talked about Orena. Despite all that had come between them, he suddenly feared for his former betrothed. She had in part married Baron Sibelio in order to seek revenge for what she had seen as Nermesa's humiliation of her, but surely had never suspected that he had used her in turn.

The journey had given Nermesa much time to think about what Antonus was up to. He sought to weaken King Conan either by making the Cimmerian seem complicit with the brigands or too weak to deal with them. Worse, the instability caused by the growing distrust of the various kingdoms threatened total anarchy. A strong Aquilonia could hold the rest together—even those considered enemies—but without

Nermesa's homeland, the rest would soon collapse, even if they did not realize it.

Or would they? Were there indeed others like Ambassador Zoran who sought to profit from their own realm's mishaps? Like Antonus, did Zoran's ambitions reach to the throne? What about in Ophir or the larger of the Corinthian city-states?

The Corinthians . . . much of the chaos could be traced there, to when once-insignificant Sarta had suddenly gathered the wit and strength to seize power over its neighbors. The baron had many contacts in Corinthia; had he secretly instigated the seizing of the pass?

"Now this cur will stay until he's needed," Betavio remarked as he signaled the other Gunderman to come with him. They and Set-Anubis stepped out into the corridor, where Antonus' bodyguard took one last look at Nermesa. "Enjoy yourself there. The baron's entertaining tonight, so you'll have plenty of time to remember everything of value that you know . . . if you want your death to be *relatively* painless."

With Set-Anubis chuckling at this comment, the trio left. Betavio seized the torch at the last moment, plunging Nermesa into darkness.

The knight silently cursed his lost opportunity. If the sorcerer had not been in his path, he could have escaped and warned the throne. Now he was not only chained, but once more frozen.

Yet, when he was finally certain that the others were gone, Nermesa once more concentrated on regaining his ability to move. Set-Anubis had claimed that Nermesa had a strong will, one that could eventually overcome this spell. The captive officer hoped that the sorcerer had spoken true.

For the longest time, his fierce concentration on his left hand only garnered him a headache. Despite that, Nermesa continued to struggle to flex even one tiny finger. He had done it before, but now time was of the essence. Despite Betavio's words, it was possible that his captors could return at any time.

There! His index finger twitched. Although it was only a vague movement in the dark, it was the most joyous of sights to the Black Dragon. He immediately forced it to work again and again, then tried to move it in concert with the rest.

After what was surely more than an hour, most of his hand and even part of his arm responded readily to his demands. Curiously, his progress magnified with each success, almost as if the spell as a whole had had less of an effect upon him from the start.

His legs seemed the slowest to respond. Finally, though, he at least had enough control to know that he could stand on his own. Nermesa ceased focusing on them and turned to the true impediment to his escape. The manacles were rusty—that much he knew from his earlier glimpse—but still very solid. Seizing the chains, Nermesa tugged again and again, using his entire body. Yet, the chains remained solidly planted in the walls.

The placing of the manacles prevented Nermesa from using both hands on one chain. Frustrated, he stood there for a time, unable to think of what else to do. It seemed that Betavio had been right not to be at all concerned about Nermesa. At the moment, the knight was as helpless as if he was still frozen.

In mounting anxiety, he slammed his fists back against the wall.

The left manacle clicked.

Nermesa immediately tugged against it, but it still held. Yet he had definitely heard the sound, and it could only have come from the locking mechanism within. He twisted his wrist as much as possible, trying to put the lock toward the wall. When he could bring it no nearer, the knight again slammed the manacle against the stone as hard as possible.

Although nothing happened, Nermesa did not give in. Making certain that the lock was once again in position, the captive officer banged the manacle against the wall.

Still, nothing happened. Nermesa listened for any sign that someone was coming to find out the cause of the noise.

When, after a time, no one did, he had to assume that they had seen no reason to leave a guard in the vicinity.

With that in mind, Bolontes' son began hammering at the manacle with as much strength as he could muster. Over and over, he slammed the bracelet against the stone, trying to get it to unlock.

Then, just as he was about to give up hope, the manacle sprang open. Nermesa smothered a triumphant laugh and turned to work on the second.

But no matter what he did, that manacle remained locked. Seizing the chain with both hands, Nermesa let out his fury on the links. He would not be defeated so near escape—

The sound of footsteps in the corridor made him pause. Was someone at last coming to look in on him?

Nermesa quickly flattened against the wall, seizing the loosened chains and wrapping them so that it appeared that he was still held prisoner. He then froze in position.

Torchlight illuminated the corridor. Moments later, a figure appeared. Although he wore the livery of House Sibelio, he was not one of the Gundermen. The guard peered inside, then stepped up to the prisoner. With one finger, he reached out and poked the still knight in the chest. The guard had obviously heard of Set-Anubis' spell and was curious to see it for himself.

Nermesa rewarded the man's inquisitiveness by seizing him by the throat and pulling him against the wall. The torch flew to the floor. Using his chained hand to smother the guard's mouth, the desperate knight tightened his grip on the throat as much as possible.

There was a gurgle, and the guard went limp. Nermesa struggled to keep the man up with his chained hand while searching him with the other. There was no key to the manacles as he had first hoped, but the guard did have a dagger with a fine point.

Letting the body finally slip to the floor, Nermesa pried at the lock with the dagger. Had it been a new lock, he doubted that he would have had a chance, but the rust magnified his chances.

Several minutes passed . . . then the telltale click echoed through the chamber.

Nermesa forced open the manacle. Rubbing his wrist, he bent down to search the guard. The man's sword and sheath Nermesa immediately confiscated, but there was little else of value to him. He then hefted up the corpse and, after some effort, managed to chain both wrists. The body would obviously not fool anyone with a torch, but even a split-second delay would buy the knight precious time.

The only question was . . . where should he go? Peering out into the corridor, Nermesa listened. From the direction that the Gundermen had carried him, the Black Dragon heard faint sounds of men at work. Likely Baron Sibelio's servants unloading the goods. Nermesa wondered if any of it could be traced to caravans attacked. Assuming that he escaped, that was something that he and General Pallantides—along with a contingent of soldiers—could deal with later.

With so many potential foes down the one direction, Nermesa saw no choice but to enter deeper into the estate. Betavio had said that the baron was entertaining; perhaps that would keep most of the house staff and guards occupied while the knight sought a way out.

While it was tempting to bring the torch with him, Nermesa did not wish to alert anyone ahead of his approach. Therefore, armed only with the sword—a weapon of far inferior quality to his own—Bolontes' son slowly wended his way through the dark. He used the sword as a staff, quietly tapping the walls in search of any side corridor.

The corridor proved to be a very lengthy one, so much so that Nermesa wondered at one point if he had already bypassed the estate house. He had met no other guards, but voices echoed in the dark, some of them seeming quite close. As time went on, Nermesa realized that they had to come from far above in the main part of the house. One of them sounded very much like the Baron Sibelio and at least another was feminine. The Lady Orena? Nermesa wished that he could somehow warn her of the treacherous nature of her husband, but knew that his former betrothed would not believe him unless Antonus stood there and declared the crimes himself.

Then, footsteps resounded from the blackness ahead. Forgetting the baron and his wife, Nermesa sought out some alcove, someplace where he could hide from the approaching figures. Yet, wherever he ran his fingers or the sword, he found only more wall.

A faint light materialized a short distance away. Nermesa saw that it came from one of the very side corridors for which he had been searching. He heard two voices, men in argument over a past game of chance.

"The dice were weighted, I tell ye!"

"If that were so, then how come they never rolled the same twice?"

The first voice snarled. "Because that bastard palmed them . . ."

Nermesa went into a run. He prayed to Mitra that the sounds of his hasty steps would be drowned out by the guards' conversation. The corner lay just ahead of him . . .

"I don't know," went on the second voice. There was a pause, then, "What's that—?"

Nermesa spun around the corner, sword already thrust out.

He caught one of the men through the chest while the pair stared in astonishment at this sudden Fury leaping out of the dark. Even before the one guard fell, Nermesa was on the second, slashing vehemently.

But the second man used the torch he carried to parry the Black Dragon's attack. At the same time, he fumbled for his own weapon.

Aware that time was of the essence, Nermesa suddenly thrust downward, catching the guard on the thigh. As expected, the man went off-balance. Nermesa seized the hand wielding the torch and turned the flames toward his opponent.

The heat singed the other's face. The guard's cry was quickly cut off by a thrust of Nermesa's sword through his gullet.

However, barely had he finished with the last of his foes than Nermesa heard more voices coming from farther down the corridor he had originally been traversing. Quickly dragging the bodies to the side, the captain seized the torch and ran on down the side passage. He doubted that it would be much longer before his escape was discovered, which meant that he had to get out of the estate as soon as possible.

But how? Nermesa freely admitted to himself that he had no idea where he was going. For all he knew, the corridor he now headed down would lead him only to another set of dungeons. Worse, he might also run afoul of Set-Anubis again . . . and that would surely put an abrupt end to his flight.

The current corridor suddenly ended for no apparent reason. Nermesa backed up to the last side passage he had seen, then went down it. From there, he turned down two more, his patience rapidly deteriorating as the officer realized just *how* mazelike the underside of the baron's estate house was.

Worse, the passages were growing more untended. They were moist, and the walls were covered with moss and lichen. Dead vermin and refuse littered the corners. No one had been down this way in many years, perhaps even decades, but Nermesa no longer knew where to turn back.

He finally came across a set of cracked, stone steps leading up. They were so narrow that he almost overlooked them. At this point willing to take any risk if it meant getting to the surface, Nermesa climbed them—only to discover after a flight up that they ended at a wall.

Seeing no sense to such a design, Nermesa ran his hand over the wall. There had to be a handle or some sort of secret lever or maybe—

His fingers slipped into a barely discernible depression. As he probed it, the soldier heard a slight click.

The right side of the wall slid back slightly.

Shoving against it, Nermesa gradually opened up a passage just wide enough for him to enter. From the effort needed, he judged the hidden door not to have been used for some time. Still, behind it was another set of steps leading up. That was all that mattered.

Using the torch to burn away a mass of webs, Nermesa pushed on. Huge spiders, unused to any light, scuttled away. The Aquilonian kicked aside those that did not move fast enough.

The steps wound around as they rose. Nermesa's hopes increased. Surely he could not be *that* far from the top.

Then, as before, the steps ended at a wall. This time, however, Nermesa understood the system. It did not take him long to find the depression. However, unlike before, the wall did not slide open even a crack. He heard the click, but that was all.

Determined not to be foiled so close to success, the Black Dragon set down the torch and shoved against the recalcitrant wall with all his might. Again and again he threw himself into it.

Finally, it budged. Twice more, Nermesa acted as a battering ram. The gap that he achieved was very narrow, but with effort, he finally managed to slip through.

Whereupon, the Aquilonian discovered himself in a sumptuous bedroom.

Gold-and-silver silken draperies lined the windows. The bed was filled with like-colored down pillows and looked more plush than any Nermesa had ever seen. Glittering statuettes decorated wall niches and the tops of intricately carved mahogany chests. A vast mirror framed in gold leaf covered one wall across from the sumptuous bed. Glancing down, Nermesa saw that his dirty boots trod upon a delicate carpet that appeared to have been imported from Kitan, if the images of men, women, and beasts in fanciful dancing displays was any evidence.

The chamber was lit by man-sized oil lamps at each corner. Nermesa quickly counted three doors, one of which he dismissed as surely leading to a closet. Then, the nearest of the windows caught his attention, and he went over to see the view.

It was dark, as the Aquilonian had expected. Yet, by the flickering lights below and in the distance, he could tell that his climb had not only brought him to the surface, but to one of the house's upper floors. Unfortunately, it also revealed to Nermesa that he had no hope of slipping out the window and climbing down. There was no hold whatsoever, and the drop would kill him as swiftly as a dagger through his heart. He would have to go through the manor itself.

Returning to the passage, Nermesa shoved the wall closed again. He had no intention whatsoever of returning to the labyrinth below, and there was no sense giving any pursuers from that direction easy access to his present location.

It came down to a choice between the two doors. Nermesa listened at each, but heard nothing. He leaned down at the first, peering through the keyhole. When he saw only darkness, the knight shifted to the second door.

But as he did, he suddenly heard footsteps. Nermesa immediately pulled back behind the door. He kept his sword high and ready, prepared to take on every last minion of the baron's if necessary.

The door swung open, and a figure swept into the chamber.

Reacting instinctively, Nermesa wrapped his free arm around the other's throat and pulled them back to his chest. Simultaneously, he kicked the door shut again.

Only then did the knight register that his captive was female. Her clothing—a flowing emerald gown—was far too elegant for a house servant, and Nermesa immediately thought of the house's mistress . . . Orena.

But Orena was taller, and her hair did not fall past her shoulders in an auburn cascade. Nor, upon turning, would the Baroness Sibelio have gazed up with her soft green eyes and—after a moment of pure startlement—gasped in relief and even some pleasure, his name.

"Nermesa?"

Not Orena, no . . . but rather her sister, Telaria.

17

"NERMESA!" TELARIA GASPED again. "What—what are you doing here?" Her eyes moistened, and she hugged him tight. "Are you a ghost, then? I'd heard that you were slain by brigands from the queen herself! General Pallantides received the message from Sir Paulo that you were lost during an aborted attack!"

Despite his present predicament, both Telaria's face and her news gave Nermesa some heart. Pushing the lady-in-waiting back gently, he eagerly asked, "The caravan survived? The other Black Dragons live?"

"Some were slain, but most are well. They are supposedly on their way back soon from Nemedia, but there was some question I didn't understand concerning the ambassador from there . . . Zaro . . . Zoras . . ."

"Zoran . . ." His mood blackened once more. "A villain." Thinking of the ambassador also reminded Nermesa of his own predicament . . . and the further complications created by Telaria's being here.

"You must flee from here!" he whispered. "Get out before your life is in danger!"

"But why?"

"Never mind!" He did not dare reveal the truth about the baron to her. With her own sister married to the traitorous noble, Telaria might do something foolish.

Orena . . . In all good conscience, Nermesa could not leave his former betrothed here, either. Antonus' crimes were not hers.

"Telaria," the knight began more calmly. "I need you to trust me. I need you to find Orena and get her and you out of this estate. You *must* pretend that it is only for a simple journey back to the capital, but you *need* to do it."

It said much for her belief in him that the auburn-haired woman immediately nodded. "All right, Nermesa. If you say so. Shall I get the baron, too?"

"No!" The single word burst from his lips before he could stop himself. The vehemence in his tone surprised even Nermesa.

His companion was no fool. Telaria's eyes widened. She put a hand to her lips as she lightly gasped. "Nermesa . . . are you claiming that the baron—"

"Telaria—"

Now, though, she stood her ground. "Nermesa . . . tell me what is going on. Tell me!"

He opened his mouth to reprimand her for wasting precious seconds, but saw that she would not be denied regardless. As quickly but concisely as he could, Nermesa explained his travails and what he had discovered concerning the baron. By the time he was finished, Telaria was as pale as a ghost.

"It cannot be true—but I know you'd never lie!" To her credit, she did not tremble. "Orena . . . poor Orena . . ."

Those were words that Nermesa would have never thought to hear from the younger sister, who had been much abused by the baroness as a child. "Telaria, how do *you* come to be here?"

She blushed. Eyes lowered, Telaria replied, "Because of you, Nermesa. When the news reached me of your—of your—" The woman shook her head. Her gaze rose to his.

"I can't even say it now . . . but when the news came, and I thought you gone . . . I couldn't think or even breathe! The queen was very gracious, but nothing she said or did helped."

"Telaria, I—" Words failed the knight.

"Then I heard from Orena," the auburn-haired lady-in-waiting continued. "Who had heard from others in the palace. She sent me a letter filled with concern and care such as I recalled from when we were both much younger! She opened herself up to me and offered whatever consolation I needed. Orena also invited me to come see her . . . providing that I could forgive her for her transgressions."

And Telaria, naturally, had. Nermesa knew that the sisters had—to a limited extent—begun speaking to one another again even before this. His supposed death, though, had opened wide the gates between the siblings . . . and now presented Nermesa with a situation which he had not needed.

"I hesitated, but finally visited her in the city a week ago. She insisted that I join her out on Antonus' estate and so, with the queen's permission, we came here three days past." Telaria smiled bitterly. "And when the baron returned today, *he* was all sympathy and understanding, as much a brother to me as if of my own blood . . ." Telaria's eyes turned venomous. "And all the time, he had you a prisoner below, ready to be *tortured*!"

"Be calm, Telaria . . ."

Her expression changed back to one of utter sympathy for him. Telaria put a hand to Nermesa's cheek . . . then suddenly stood on her toes and kissed him soundly. Even despite the danger, Nermesa could not help but respond.

When she pulled back, she whispered, "I *had* to make certain that you *were* real." Then, more seriously, Orena's sister continued, "I'm not going to leave you here. I'll sneak you out with us!"

Nermesa had considered that scenario but had decided it too risky for either of the women. He did not want Baron Sibelio to think them complicit with the knight. There was no doubt in Nermesa's mind that the noble would consid both women expendable.

"No, it must be the two of you alone, Telaria! I can't allow you to be caught up in my mission!"

"Nermesa—"

He was adamant. "But when you do get back to the city . . . and only if you know that you're safe . . . I ask you to send word to General Pallantides. Tell him what I've discovered and that he must come with the Black Dragons as soon as possible if he hopes to catch the baron."

"But that could take far too long! I thought you dead once, I will not have it happen again . . . and know that this time it's *true*!"

Seizing her firmly by the shoulders, Nermesa pressed his point. "We've spent enough time on this matter already, Telaria! Please do what I say . . . and warn the general that there are other threats than the force of arms awaiting him here."

"What do you mean?" Her wit proved quick, for, with a brief furrow of her brow, the lady-in-waiting frowned, and said, "I saw a man with Antonus, but only very briefly. Betavio said that his name was Caius. There was something I found uncomfortable about him. Is he—"

Nermesa gritted his teeth. "Quickly! Do you know where Caius might be roomed?" If the knight could catch Set-Anubis off guard, then perhaps he could rid himself of the sorcerer before the villain could cast a spell or mesmerize him. "Nearby?"

"No." Telaria shuddered. "In the east wing. The fourth level, where Betavio and his Gundermen also keep their quarters when here."

It was not what Nermesa had hoped to hear, but at least he had some notion as to where Set-Anubis could be found. Betavio and his cohorts would surely still be busy late into the night. Nermesa thus had two choices. He could either attempt to hunt down the sorcerer or go for Antonus himself.

Then, something that Set-Anubis in his bitterness had

himself revealed made the captain's choice for him. The Baron Sibelio had utter power over someone who should have been able to slay him a thousand times over with barely the flick of a finger. Yet, two such attempts had cost Set-Anubis a pair of those fingers and created in him a healthy fear of the noble.

And all because the baron wielded a magic of his own . . . or rather, that of the *Tear* of Charon.

Surely the emerald jewel set in his ring.

"Telaria, do you know where the baron is now? Is he with Orena?" Nermesa prayed not, for that would make his task all the more daunting.

To his good fortune, she replied, "Nay. My sister's retired for the night, which is why I came back here. The baron apologized to her that he had to stay up and deal with matters of business."

Those matters likely had included the knight. "Did he say where he headed?"

"I think his study. Yes, Betavio had brought him a note said to be sent by bird, and that was what made Antonus give his apologies, then immediately depart." Without urging, Telaria described to him how to reach the study. It meant ascending to the next and highest level of the house, but also kept Nermesa from the vicinity of the sorcerer's lair.

"You saw this man, Caius, only that brief time earlier?"

"Yes."

Nermesa would have to take the chance, then, that the sorcerer would be far from Antonus at this time. That gave him some hope. Some.

He gave Telaria a hard look. "Will you do what I ask?"

With some reluctance, the lady-in-waiting finally nodded.

Satisfied, Nermesa listened at the door. Hearing nothing, he muttered, "Head straight to Orena, then. There's no reason for anyone to suspect something amiss. You merely want to see your sister again."

"What of her servants?" Telaria suddenly piped up.

The knight silently swore. "It would be wiser if it was

only the two of you . . ." His concern lessened as a face formed in his mind. "And *Morannus* as your bodyguard. He's Orena's man. He can be trusted."

Morannus would protect the two with his life, and from what Nermesa knew of the other Gunderman's skills with a sword, even Betavio would prove no match. That both were from the same land would mean nothing to either; Gundermen fought Gundermen when in the pay of others.

Telaria still stood there, eyes on him. Nermesa guided her to the entrance. "Ride swiftly but safely . . . please."

"Nermesa, is there no other way?"

In answer, he opened the door just enough for her to exit.

With no one in the hall, Nermesa allowed himself to monitor Telaria's progress until she was out of sight. He understood that Orena's chambers were not very far. Nermesa was also thankful that Telaria—long accustomed to having had to fend for herself as a child—had not been accompanied to her own rooms by two or three servants. The contrast between the sisters was ever stark. Orena likely would have come to a room filled with subordinates awaiting her every whim.

But only Morannus could be allowed to accompany them. Too many bodies would slow the journey or even bring it to an untimely end, which could not be allowed. He trusted Telaria and her sister to see to the safety of any servants the baroness deemed loyal to her, not to her husband.

Only when Telaria was long gone did Nermesa finally slip out into the hall. Whatever happened to him, it would be worth it not only if he protected the king and Aquilonia from danger, but also—and in some ways, more—her. If he had thought that he could have gotten her and Orena out himself, Nermesa would have done so, but if even one guard spotted them with the knight, it would be as if Nermesa had himself slain the two.

Many of the oil lamps in the hall had been doused for the night, but enough remained lit to illuminate his path. The stairs needed to reach Baron Sibelio's study led Nermesa in the opposite direction from where Telaria had headed, for which he was grateful.

That there were no guards here did not surprise him in the least. In his own domain, Antonus Sibelio likely believed that he had nothing to fear. From the torchlight that Nermesa had seen outside Telaria's window, the grounds were patrolled by scores of ready men. It would take an army to breach the estate house and that only after a daunting struggle with the defenders.

General Pallantides would provide that army, supposing that Telaria managed to reach him.

And by then, Nermesa would either have Antonus a prisoner or dead . . . or he himself would surely be slain.

At the banister, the knight carefully peered down. At the bottom, he noted two guards, but both men seemed to be paying attention only to the area in front of them, not the floors above. A quick glance to the next level gave Nermesa only a limited view, but one that revealed no sentries up there. Nermesa cautiously started up, aware that there might be men at the door to the study or even some within the room itself.

Each step felt like a full flight, so long did it seem to take Nermesa just to lift his foot to the next one. By the time he could at last see above the floor ahead, his heart pounded like a thousand stampeding horses. Yet not once did his sword arm quiver; nor did he hesitate. He had sworn to serve Aquilonia and the throne in whatever manner possible, and if it meant his life to put an end to the treachery of the baron, then so be it.

As with the level below, the corridor was only dimly lit. That proved fortunate for him, for near the end and stationed at what had to be Baron Sibelio's study, were two grim-faced Gundermen.

Nermesa backed down a step so as not to be seen. He had hoped that the guards would not be Gundermen, but nothing could be done to change that. What mattered was getting past them and reaching their master.

Sheathing his sword, the Aquilonian abruptly strode up

the rest of the steps and walked confidently toward the pair. They immediately straightened—but otherwise did not react. Nermesa did not wear the livery of House Sibelio, but, then, neither had some of those men working on the caravan. More important, neither of the guards were men he recognized, and so he hoped that they would, in turn, not recognize *him*.

Still, he was only halfway to the Gundermen when one drew his weapon and growled, "What're you doing here? No one disturbs the baron now . . ."

"There's something we found in the wagons that he needs to know about," returned Bolontes' son, his hand resting casually on the hilt of his sword. "I was told to make certain that he hears of it or it'll be my head."

"It'll be your head if you don't stop where you are! What's this news? Tell me, and I'll relay it to him!"

Nermesa silently cursed. He would get no farther than he was. He used his sword hand to scratch his arm, gradually working it down toward the sheath. "There was a body in one of the wagons," he explained. As he expected, hearing of such a find made both guards focus strictly on his face. Their attention was now on his story. "One of the drivers! His eyes were staring and his expression—"

Nermesa drew his sword and lunged for the nearest man.

To their credit, the Gundermen recovered more swiftly than most would have. Yet, that was not soon enough for the first to parry Nermesa's blade. The knight's expert lunge caught the lead Gunderman along the side of his neck, drawing a red line.

As the first guard clutched his bleeding neck, the second moved to take Nermesa. The Aquilonian met his blade. The swords flashed again and again as the two did battle.

The first Gunderman, his gait unsteady, sought to come at Nermesa from the side; but Nermesa shoved the weaving fighter back. The wounded guard fell hard against the door.

At that moment, Nermesa's other opponent shouted, "Alarm! Assassin in the house! Alarm—"

His cry cut off as the knight plunged his blade through a

gap in the other's armor. The Gunderman spun around and fell to the floor with a clatter.

The remaining guard struggled to rise, but he had lost too much blood. Nermesa mercifully finished him off, then barged through the door.

As he had expected, someone attacked him from the side. It was not, however, the baron, but rather *Betavio*. Fortunately, the Gunderman overreached the ducking knight. Nermesa slammed into his foe, shoving Betavio against the nearest wall and driving the air from his body. The Gunderman let out a gasp and slumped to the floor.

Nermesa immediately whirled around—and found the tip of the sword given to him by King Conan poised at his throat.

"I really do admire you, Nermesa," Baron Antonus Sibelio remarked over the hilt of the knight's weapon. "You have a determination and resilience that would serve me well when *I* am king of Aquilonia . . ."

"Aquilonia already *has* a king," growled the Black Dragon. "And his name is *Conan*."

"A wretched barbarian from *Cimmeria* of all places!" The sword did not budge in the least. "You, from one of the eldest and grandest Houses of the realm, should be able to appreciate how low that is."

"Not as low as King Namedides . . . and certainly nowhere near as foul."

The baron frowned. "At least he was *Aquilonian*. That makes all the difference." With the sword, he gestured to the right, away from the door. "Please stand by that wall . . . after you drop that weapon, naturally."

Releasing the sword, Nermesa moved to where the other noble had indicated. He eyed Antonus with such venom that the baron finally laughed.

"Such hatred! If only it could be fueled in a more proper direction . . ." He paused as they both heard shouts from some distance away. "Ah, they seem to have *finally* noticed your escape. Someone will be punished severely for this great oversight, I promise you that, Nermesa. In my own home!"

"One's own sanctum can often be the most dangerous place for him."

"Too true, which is the *only* reason you still live. You know much about the inner workings of the palace . . . and how best to get around the guards and other defenses."

Now it was Nermesa who laughed. "So that you can more easily take the king while he sleeps? Others have tried that and died quickly, Antonus! Besides, you can do nothing to make me give you such information. No torture will release those secrets from me!"

The Baron Sibelio studied him for several seconds before nodding. "I do believe that. But I never intended torture to gain what I need. I wouldn't trust the information that you finally spat out through broken teeth and a shredded tongue. No, I'd be likely to send my assassin right into the quarters of the Black Dragons, not the king's chambers."

The baron rubbed his chin thoughtfully and as he did, Nermesa noted the emerald. Recalling how Antonus had used it in the tent, Bolontes' son sneered, "And will you use *that* in a feeble attempt to seize control of my mind again?"

"This? No, the Tear of Charon is not for the likes of you; you made that abundantly clear the last time. This is useful for weak, petty men such as Lord Dekalatos or Count Stafano, useful pawns enabling me to deteriorate further relations not only between the Corinthian city-states, but with Aquilonia's present ruler as well."

"A man died because of it . . ."

"Many men have and will, and all those lives are a necessity for this to come to fruition." Antonus shifted to the side, enabling Nermesa at last to see the baron's study. Much of it resembled his father's own study—a long, oak writing table with intricately carved legs and scrollwork at the edges, row upon row of shelves filled with parchments, books, and documents no doubt pertaining to holdings of House Sibelio, and so on. There were two towering, arched windows that the knight considered briefly for escape. Standing oil lamps in each corner of the room lit the chamber. On the left side—

Nermesa's gaze froze. On the left side—and set almost as if part of a shrine—a larger-than-life-size statue of Baron Antonus Sibelio struck a heroic—nay, *majestic*—pose akin to those of the heroes of old. In his outstretched hand, the statue wielded a scepter with a flared end and cradled in the crook of his other arm was a crown with jutting points.

The baron as ruler of Aquilonia. The audacity of having had such a figure carved before the fact did not escape Nermesa. The statue wore armor akin to that of the Black Dragons save that on the breastplate was etched the Sibelio crest. The artisan had also skillfully painted the statue so that it looked almost lifelike.

"On the day of my ascension," the baron remarked, "it will be set up in the great square of Tarantia, for all to see and marvel at. The first of many!"

"The death of King Conan will not necessarily make you monarch. There would be many to contest such a thing."

His captor shook his head. "I thought better of you than that! I've planned long and hard for this, and there are many in places of influence and authority who owe me a great deal. They would sell their daughters to my men, so great a hold do I have upon them, Nermesa! The Tear helped with many, seducing them into deals that they would later regret, while others fell victim to the sorcerer's spells."

"You would seek the throne through foul witchery?"

"Through whatever way necessary. It will be for the good of all Aquilonia. The people already wonder at the king's abilities! Unable to stop most of the caravan attacks and at odds with our neighboring realms, he threatens to bring us to war and ruination. When he is dead, and I have salvaged the situation by artful diplomacy—"

"Secret negotiations with ambitious conspirators such as Ambassador Zoran to divide up the lands among yourselves!" blurted the knight.

Antonus smiled in admiration. "There is the Nermesa Klandes I expected! Yes, Zoran and others like him in Ophir, several of the Corinthian city-states—especially Sarta—and Kush, to name a few . . . all with notions of grandeur that I fueled! They will become kings for a time . . . and then vassals to the emperor of the *known* world! I will bring about a realm such as not seen since Acheron and Atlantis!"

"Apt choices to compare yourself with, especially Acheron."

A groan from near the door alerted them to Betavio's awakening. The Gunderman rubbed his head, then his stomach. His eyes burned with malice when they focused on Nermesa.

"I've changed my mind about his value," snapped Betavio to his master. "Run him *through*."

The Baron Sibelio frowned. "Remember your place! I make the decisions here."

The Gunderman lowered his head. "Yes, my lord. Forgive me. It's just that this one—"

"Is every bit the capable soldier I told you that he was." Antonus lowered his blade. "But, in the end, he is only a soldier, alas. If he was something of a visionary, he would see that I am the future of Aquilonia . . . of all lands."

"All lands . . ." agreed Betavio with much less enthusiasm. He had likely heard such speeches a thousand times before.

"Go out and alert the guards that the situation is in hand and that—"

There was a noise from without and a feminine voice raised high. A moment later, the door burst open.

Nermesa's heart nearly stopped when he saw who it was who first stepped through. Another Gunderman, but the last one that he had expected.

Morannus . . . and in his trail, her imperious manner worthy of a goddess, came Orena.

The knight swallowed back the name he wanted to blurt out, the name of the only one *not* present.

What had happened to Telaria?

Orena's gaze fixed not on her husband, but rather Nermesa. Her eyes briefly flashed, whether from shock, hatred, or some other emotion, he could not say.

"It *is* true, then. You do live."

"This is neither the time nor the place, my dear Orena," interjected the baron sternly. He glared at Morannus. "You! Guide your mistress back to her personal chambers this minute!"

Morannus looked from the baron to Betavio, then to Nermesa. The knight tried to read the other Gunderman's thoughts in his expression but failed.

"Everything's in hand here," growled Betavio to his counterpart. "Do as he says!"

Taking Orena's arm, Morannus murmured, "Come, my lady! I warned that this might not be good—"

But the baroness pulled free. "Antonus, I demand to know what is going on here! First, my sister barges into my room to tell me that *he* is alive, and then—"

"Your *sister* knows?" The baron cursed. "Where is she?"

"She kept insisting that we leave for Tarantia, but when I said that we should instead come to you, she ran off. I came here immediately—"

"The stables . . ." Antonus hissed. He glanced toward Betavio, but the Gunderman was already on the move. He shoved past Morannus, who glanced briefly at Nermesa before returning his attention to his mistress.

Nermesa started after Betavio, only to have the baron prick his throat with the tip of the gleaming sword. "Careful! This weapon is exceptionally well honed . . . as you no doubt know."

"Antonus!" began Orena again. "What is the—"

"Return to your chambers, dear Orena. Morannus, see to it that she's safe, yes?"

Again, Morannus glanced at Nermesa. His hand went to the sword sheathed at his side.

At that moment, half a dozen guards led by the Gunderman Nermesa had slugged in the dungeon poured into the study. They were followed by a figure more dread to the knight than all of them combined.

Set-Anubis.

Morannus immediately seized his mistress by the arm and ushered her to the doorway. Orena looked back at those within, first and foremost her husband and Nermesa. She gave the horrific sorcerer but a cursory glance, which baffled Nermesa until he came to the conclusion that the baroness—and likely Morannus—saw only "Caius," one of her husband's many insignificant minions.

"Shut the door," commanded the Baron Sibelio once his wife had been removed. Betavio's second gestured at a guard, who obeyed.

"So . . ." rasped Set-Anubis with a little mockery. "Cannot your legions of warriors keep *one* man prisoner without my assistance?"

"Someone will pay for this, rest assured, dog," his master returned. "And you shouldn't speak so, having lost him in the woods during the raid and underneath the streets of Tebes."

The sightless spellcaster was defiant. "For the first, I must point out that I also had to shield your men from the eyes of the defenders and, as for the second, his will *is* great. I could guide a simpleminded beast to focus on him as prey, but I could not ask him to stand there and be *eaten*. My power—"

"Has its limits." The ring hand rose so that the emerald could be seen by the Eye of Charon.

Set-Anubis had apparently been going to say something other than what the noble had, but he shut his mouth and nodded.

A horn sounded warning from somewhere outside. Nermesa started for the window, and this time the baron let him pass. When two of the guards moved to grab the knight, Antonus waved them off.

"There is no escape for him there. The bars are thick enough to prevent that."

Nermesa peered out into the night. A flurry of torches headed toward the stables while others congregated near the river flowing along the back of the estate house.

They were all after *Telaria*.

"You brought on her death, Nermesa," his captor mocked. "It's all your doing, what happens to her now."

Rage filled the Black Dragon. He spun about and lunged for the other noble. Perhaps he might have slipped past Antonus' guard or maybe impaled himself on the weapon he had himself once wielded, but Set-Anubis gestured, and yet again Nermesa felt his body slow as if trapped in liquid amber. He froze with his clutching fingers almost within reach of the baron's throat.

"You let him get closer than he should've," reprimanded the Baron Sibelio. "I might've had to kill him. And then what he knows would've been lost to me."

"A thousand pardons, my lord," Set-Anubis answered, bowing low. "His will, as I mentioned."

Antonus tapped the tip of the blade on the floor as he stood there considering the motionless Nermesa. "Yes, I think it's time to test the limits of that will. The longer we leave this one alive, the more burdensome he becomes. I want to know everything you can dig out of him, and I want it done here and now."

Set-Anubis' suddenly eager voice set Nermesa on edge as the sorcerer said, "It will be done, but I need quiet."

With a gesture, the baron dismissed all but Betavio's second and a lone guard. The Gunderman stood a short distance behind the sorcerer, expression brooding.

"I want this done quickly, dog, understand that?"

"Yes, my lord, I do." There was a pause, then, "To me, fool. To me."

Nermesa's body moved, but not by his will. Slowly it turned toward the shrouded, cadaverous form.

Toward the bloodred gemstone . . .

And as Nermesa helplessly faced Set-Anubis . . . as the Eye of Charon began to burn into his own . . . from without came the sound of another horn.

"That signal! Well," he heard Antonus remark almost pleasantly. "They've either caught her . . . or she's dead. A pity, she was a beautiful woman . . ."

Nermesa's heart filled with despair . . . and in the next instant, the Eye of Charon used that despair to break through his resistance.

The will of Set-Anubis engulfed his own.

18

NERMESA STRUGGLED THROUGH a bug-infested, mist-enshrouded swamp, aware that some party pursued him but not certain as to who they were. He heard behind him the baleful howls of hounds and the splashing of horses through the high, murky waters. Sinister horns blared, and whenever he looked back, the Aquilonian made out ominous shapes moving about in the fog.

He ran. Where he headed, Nermesa did not know. He only understood that if he ceased running, it would be the end of him. The knight had nothing with which to defend himself; the sheath at his side was empty, and there was no dagger in his belt. He did not even have any armor, merely a thin tunic and kilt that did nothing to protect him against the elements.

A pain suddenly shot through his right leg. He felt something soft squirming over the area. Reaching down, the knight tore the creature from his body. He paused to stare at a leech, but one larger and more vicious than any he had ever seen. It squirmed in his grip, seeking some area of his hand upon which to fasten its toothy sucker. Blood from his leg dripped down its thick, black body.

Revulsion filling him, Nermesa crushed the leech. It died with a piercing squeal that echoed throughout the swamp and set the unseen hounds to new, eager cries.

No sooner had he killed it, though, than another sharp pain warned Nermesa of a second leech on his knee. He tugged that free and threw it far, only to feel searing bites on several other parts of his legs.

As Nermesa quickly sought to wipe the vermin from his body, he heard harsh splashing. A glance over his shoulder revealed the shadowed figure of a monstrous steed. Atop it, clad in dark armor and an oddly shaped, visored helm, a fearsome warrior swung over his head a ball-and-chain mace. He made no sound as he rode down upon his un-armed quarry, although the horse itself snorted lustily as if as eager for the kill as its master.

The spiked ball came flying at Nermesa. He leapt aside, the foul sphere grazing his arm. The harsh pain as the spikes tore his flesh made the bites of the leeches seem like soft kisses.

Nermesa slipped under the scum-covered surface. Even there, though, he was not safe. Something hard kicked at him, just missing his head. The horse's gargantuan hooves. Again and again, they assailed the swamp, seeking the des-perate knight.

Twisting around them, Nermesa thrust out of the water near the animal's flank. He seized the rider's leg and shoved it free. Caught off guard, the armored figure slid over the other side, striking the water hard.

Bolontes' son leapt atop the horse . . . only to have the black beast rear up as if seeking to toss the interloper off. The horse spun about in the water. It twisted its head around and snapped at Nermesa as best it could, red eyes blazing with utter evil.

Red eyes, the Aquilonian belatedly realized, that were made of crystal.

Something suddenly gripped his leg. As Nermesa struggled to keep in the saddle, he saw that the rider had finally managed to rise from the waters. The fearsome warrior pulled himself up using the Aquilonian's limb.

For the first time, Nermesa saw the visored helm up close. He gasped, for it was an almost perfect representation of a spitting cobra, such as found in distant Stygia. The hood spread wide and the visor was actually the roof of the fanged mouth. Row upon row of intricate scales had been etched into the metal.

But even more unsettling were the eyes, for they were red and glowed . . . and were identical to the monstrous orbs of the horse. The crimson eyes burned into his own, and when Nermesa sought to escape their gaze by looking to the face of his opponent, he discovered that, within the helm, he could see only utter blackness.

Caught between the struggles of the horse and the attack of the rider, Nermesa was hard-pressed. At last, it proved impossible to maintain a hold. As the steed twisted again, Nermesa threw himself atop the shadowy warrior, sending both flailing into the swamp.

Somewhere, another hound howled, but Nermesa had no time to worry about other threats. He flung his full force against the armored figure, shoving his foe deep under the surface. Gauntleted hands grabbed for his throat, the grated edges of the armored fingers ripping at his skin.

As Nermesa fought, contrary thoughts assailed him from within. Even if he defeated this foe, there were others, so many others. He could never win against all of them. Would it not be simpler to surrender? To let them take him? At least there would be an end to the constant pursuit—

No! I won't! With a savage growl, the beleaguered knight pressed his assault. The serpent warrior's own attack became reckless, uncontrolled. He shook violently beneath Nermesa.

And then . . . lay still beneath the water.

Gasping, Nermesa searched around the body for the

mace but could not locate it. He felt along the unseen corpse, but there was no sword sheath, either.

A chorus of growls filled his ears. In the shrouding mist, three horrific hounds approached. Like the horse and rider, they had bloodred, crystalline eyes that blazed. The head of each stood higher than his waist, and their combined weight surely topped his own.

The hounds, their shapes indistinct save for their eyes, charged him.

Nermesa ran his fingers along the bottom of the swamp, ignoring the leeches that immediately fastened on to him. The weapon had to be somewhere near! It *had* to be!

His right hand touched a chain. The Aquilonian slid his fingers down and found the handle. He seized the mace just as the foremost of the hounds reached him.

The spiked ball cracked the animal's skull. The beast howled mournfully. It dropped limply into the swamp.

Nermesa wasted no time to see if it was dead. He had the mace up and ready as the other pair neared.

But as he glanced into the eyes of one, his strength seemed to fail him. Nermesa almost lost his grip on the mace. Only sheer will enabled him to regain control quick enough to keep from being overwhelmed by the two. With a cry, Nermesa unleashed a sweeping swing.

One hound twisted out of range, its own attack faltering in the process. The ball struck the second in the shoulder with an audible crack. The injured beast yowled as it stumbled through the dank water.

Without hesitation, Nermesa lunged at the one undamaged creature. Although there was a chill to the air, the knight's body was covered in sweat. He swung once more, forcing the hound into retreat.

But even as one foe fled him, others began coalescing in the fog. More hounds and, behind them, serpent warriors atop giant steeds as terrible as the first. Maces and swords drawn, they converged on the staggering Aquilonian.

The urge to surrender to his fate again grew strong, but

Nermesa defied it. Moreover, as he surveyed the horde gathering around him, something about it registered with his memory. Something about the many crimson eyes . . . the crystalline eyes . . .

Then, he finally recalled what they meant. A grim smile played along his dirt-covered, scarred face.

"Set them all upon me, sorcerer!" he growled toward the throng. "Send a thousand warriors and beasts at me, and I'll still stand against them! You will slay me, but you'll never get what you *truly* seek!" Nermesa glanced up into the mist-covered night, adding, "Nor will *you,* Baron!"

The hounds howled. The horses splashed loudly through the swamp. The clank of metal as the riders approached echoed in Nermesa's ears—

And, suddenly, the entire sinister tableau became a fiery swirl. The swirl petrified, turning into a huge ruby . . .

Nermesa stared at the Eye of Charon . . . and the scowling face of the sorcerer.

"You've been at this for three hours," muttered Antonus Sibelio from somewhere on Nermesa's right. "I am growing very tired with your failures—"

"Be still, cretin!" hissed Set-Anubis, leaning toward Nermesa. "Something has just happened! I would almost swear that he is—"

Nermesa fought not to show any emotion. They did not yet realize that the knight had broken free of the sorcerer's trance!

Perhaps Set-Anubis had begun to take note, but his insolent reply had turned the baron's attention to him. "Know your place, dog!" snapped Antonus. "Know how to speak to your betters!"

Although nothing visible touched the spellcaster, Set-Anubis abruptly cried out and clutched his skull. The Eye of Charon pulsated oddly, alternating between a glow as bright as the sun and a bleak dullness somehow reminiscent of death. "By the demons of Stygia and Kush!" he snarled. "Enough!"

"Perhaps not," interrupted the Baron Sibelio. "Perhaps the removal of another finger is in order. Guard . . ."

But as the nameless Gunderman left behind by Betavio moved toward the hooded figure, Nermesa acted.

Closing on Set-Anubis, the Black Dragon seized the tormented sorcerer and threw him into the oncoming Gunderman. The lone guard on the knight's left belatedly registered the prisoner's renewed animation, but not in time to keep Nermesa from barreling into him. As the two collided with a table, Bolontes' son grabbed for the man's sword. He pulled it free, at the same time striking the guard under the chin.

Even as the man fell back, Nermesa turned to face the baron.

"Yes," remarked Antonus, Nermesa's sword already pointed toward the knight. "Very impressive . . . a shame to have to slay you, but you leave me no choice."

He thrust at the officer, moving with a fluidity and skill worthy of one of Nermesa's fabled unit. The knight barely managed to meet his attack, then the one that came as quick as lightning after.

Out of the corner of his eye, Nermesa noted the Gunderman rising. Shoving aside the still-moaning Set-Anubis, the bodyguard came for the Black Dragon. Nermesa quickly maneuvered toward the baron's writing table, buying himself a moment's respite from this second attacker.

But Antonus himself was relentless, not letting up on his adversary for even an instant. He truly was as skilled as a Black Dragon, a fact that did not bode well for the weary Nermesa.

Unlike the knight, Antonus seemed to revel in the battle. No doubt he saw his superior skill against one of the king's most staunch defenders as a sign of the certainty of his ascension to the throne. As Nermesa veered to the right, he had the further dismaying image of the Baron Sibelio magnified, for the treacherous noble now stood with his back directly before his statue. It was almost as if Antonus' twin urged him on.

Noting Nermesa's distraction, the Gunderman lunged at him. Nermesa's senses were more highly attuned than the bodyguard thought, though, and as the swordsman took a cut at his head, the knight ducked under his defenses and caught his second foe through the heart.

The Gunderman fell into the table. He slid back to the floor, leaving in his wake a red trail across the piece of furniture.

Unfortunately, in dealing with the one foe, Nermesa left himself open against Antonus. The Baron Sibelio jabbed at his sword arm, cutting a red line across Nermesa's shoulder and nearly causing Bolontes' son to drop his weapon.

"Sorcery . . ." the baron all but spat. "Useful to a point, but hardly as valuable as a clever mind and a good sword arm, wouldn't you agree, Nermesa? The *great* Set-Anubis! The mongrel was good for keeping the eyes of caravan guards blind to my men and alerting me to patrols before they could become hindrances, but not much else. The Eye of Charon! Ha! Nearly all of its vast power is but illusion! Small wonder with the likes of it that the wizards of Acheron eventually fell, so dependent were they upon such empty power . . ."

Nermesa's mind flashed back to his encounters with Set-Anubis. Perhaps the savage plant warriors and the storm that had assailed Malkuri's home had been nothing but illusion, but, if so, then they had been very strong ones. Even more real had seemed the attack in the old catacombs, when the very dead had seemed ready to burst free of their vaults.

All illusion? Nermesa could not help feel that there was more to Set-Anubis' might than even Antonus understood.

But whatever threat the renegade spellcaster had posed, he now lay on the floor like a bundle of rotting cloth, his hands still clutching his head in agony. The Eye of Charon— the dread Eye of Charon—could do nothing for him now. It startled Nermesa that Set-Anubis could be laid low so easily.

But then, Antonus had the Tear, the only thing against which the Eye could not stand.

The Baron Sibelio renewed his assault, forcing Nermesa back toward the windows. The noble's face was full of confidence. Nermesa fought for breath, angrily aware that if he had not suffered through the ordeal that he had, the battle would have gone somewhat differently. Antonus was very good, but not so expert that the knight could not have beaten him.

But the truth was that Nermesa was not at his best, and it was all he could do to keep from being skewered. Worse, the baron began to play at his emotions, seeking to erode further the Black Dragon's defenses.

"We must end this soon. After all, I will have to console my dear bride, Nermesa . . . you see, she's just lost her sister, her only family . . ."

"Telaria . . ." Nermesa muttered, his anger flaring anew. "Damn you . . ."

"Don't you worry. Soon enough, you can be with her." The baron grinned. "I understand that she drowned in the river. If you like, I can toss your body in it. Perhaps you'll float to wherever her corpse lies . . ."

"Damn you!" Bolontes' son roared. He lunged, almost catching Antonus off guard. Unfortunately, the noble managed to parry his strike.

"Well played! Did your father teach you some of your swordplay? When I see him to give my condolences, I'll be sure to compliment him. It's the least I can do—"

They were interrupted by pounding on the door outside. The baron stepped back, giving Nermesa a moment of respite. Both men expected guards to come bursting through the door, but the pounding just continued on and on.

"Well?" shouted Antonus, growing angry. "Why don't you enter, you—"

A horn sounded in the distance, a signal with three short notes followed by one long one. It was not at all like the mournful dirge Nermesa had heard in the nightmarish swamp Set-Anubis had conjured in his mind. This signal he recognized, and that recognition set his heart skipping with hope.

It was the battle notes of none other than the king's Black Dragons.

"My lord!" called Betavio from without. "There is a contingent of soldiers from Tarantia approaching! If the knight is found in these walls, they'll have cause to arrest us!"

The baron lowered the sword. "Then come and take him quickly, you dolt!" To Nermesa, he mocked, "I've had my sport . . . and I'll still keep this fine weapon, even if I must hide it for a time."

Nermesa kept waiting for the guards to come barging in, but they still remained behind the door. He tried to edge around the table. If he could reach the baron before they could seize him, then at least Antonus would not live to see the knight's death.

"You know what that means, that General Pallantides and the Black Dragons are on their way," he said to his adversary. "That means that Telaria *survived*. That means that they know the truth! Even if I die, you will still end up in Traitor's Common . . ."

Bringing up the point of the sword again, the Baron Sibelio shook his head. "No . . . they will only have the word of a distraught woman who, despite the love and care of her sister and her sister's mate, finally lost her mind trying to deal with the death of the man she cared for. They will likely even give her into Orena's permanent custody . . . and mine."

Nermesa tried to think. He wanted to deny the baron's words, but they made some terrible sense. The weary knight could not be certain that things would play out just as Antonus suggested . . .

The banging on the door reached a crescendo. Betavio called out to his master.

The baron's gaze flickered toward the entrance. "What is the matter? Enter, damn you! Break down the door if—"

Now! urged a voice in Nermesa's head. *Strike now! The time is opportune!*

His thoughts filled with horrible visions of Telaria at the mercy of the man before him, Nermesa swung with all his skill and might. Yet, he did not strike for his foe's heart—as he had originally intended—but rather for one of the baron's hands.

The hand upon which Antonus wore the Tear of Charon.

The other noble let out a scream as Nermesa severed not one but *three* fingers from the hand—including that which had worn the ring. The lost fingers scattered on the floor, the one most significant tumbling toward Nermesa.

Despite the gruesome nature of his prize, Nermesa instinctively seized the ring. The baron made no move to prevent him, made no move whatsoever. He stood there, the Black Dragon's sword dropped at his feet, clutching the maimed limb with his good hand.

"I—will—have you flayed—alive, then burned, for—this outrage!"

"A very good suggestion . . ." rasped a chilling voice that made both men look to the side. "I shall take special pleasure in making use of it myself."

Set-Anubis, looking completely recovered, faced the two men. The sorcerer smiled malevolently . . . but at the Baron Sibelio, not Nermesa.

"Deal with him, dog!" snapped Antonus, evidently oblivious as to who was the focus of the hooded figure's hatred. The baron stumbled to his table, where he grabbed a decorative cloth and quickly bound it around his ruined hand. "I want nothing left to trace."

"They will only find the Baron Antonus Sibelio when they enter this chamber," Set-Anubis assured him. Yet, to Nermesa, the Eye of Charon glittered evilly at the noble. "Only the baron."

The sorcerer muttered under his breath. The flame in each lamp in the chamber froze—and then from the lamps shot forth streams of fire that arced through the air before striking their target mercilessly.

That target being *Baron Antonus Sibelio.*

The unsuspecting baron barely uttered a gasp, much less a howl of agony. The flames wrapped around him like hungry tendrils, engulfing him in a matter of seconds. He struggled to escape them, but his feet did not seem to move. The would-be king at last screamed as he sought futilely to beat off the flames.

Finally, Antonus fell to his knees. Through the fire, Nermesa could see that his flesh had all nearly been burned away. Charred remnants of his fine garments hung over the collapsing body.

The baron fell in an awful heap, yet, still the fires consumed him. He burned and burned until there was *nothing* left to burn. Only then did the flames retreat to their wicks again.

Where the Baron Sibelio had stood, there was now no sign, not even a single hint of ash.

Set-Anubis cackled. "Tell me, Nermesa Klandes . . . do you consider *that* mere illusion?"

The dumbstruck knight realized that Antonus' horrific demise had actually taken place in only the blink of an eye. Now, that same power was focused on him.

But he had the one defense that the baron had lost. Holding up the ring, Nermesa declared, "Stop! I command you to stop!"

To his dismay, Set-Anubis merely cackled more. "That fool, he knew how to use the Tear! You do not! You cannot command me, cur!" The hooded villain stretched forth the hand missing fingers. "Now give it back to me!"

That the sorcerer demanded its return—and did not simply *take* it—immediately caught Nermesa's attention. Perhaps he could not command Set-Anubis, but neither did he think that his foe could trust that a spell would work upon the soldier. For that matter, any such spell that did might damage or even destroy the very thing that the foul creature sought.

Clutching the ring tight, the Aquilonian replied, "No, I think not."

A hiss escaped Set-Anubis. "Clever, clever! Against one of your will, you know I dare not risk the Tear! But if you think to escape me thus, think again! It took me long to realize that if I could not strike directly at the baron, then I needed to do so indirectly. By his command, all his men were protected from my work and no worthy vessel for my vengeance could I find! But, in the end, you became that vessel! You brought me the opportunity, however sudden! For that, once I *have* regained the Tear, I will grant you a swift death . . ."

"You'll follow me soon after, then," returned the knight. "They will not take kindly to your having slain their master."

"Pfah! They heard nothing out there! Besides, they are fools, weak-minded fools! All they need is a baron to give them commands . . . and *that* I have . . ."

The Eye of Charon burned bright, making all other illumination dull by comparison. Nermesa tried to judge the distance between Set-Anubis and himself. If he rushed the sorcerer—

Then, behind the cackling spellcaster, there was movement. It was accompanied by a peculiar, grating sound, as when two rocks rubbed hard against one another.

A tall figure strode up next to Set-Anubis, unblinking eyes staring at the knight.

"Mitra!" gasped Nermesa, backing up a step in amazement and dismay.

Slowly, the familiar smirk spread across the chiseled features. One hand rose high, brandishing the object in it.

Brandishing the marble scepter.

"You see?" mocked Set-Anubis, the Eye blazing triumphantly. "They shall have the baron that they expect to see . . . and through him *I* will reap the benefits of my former tormentor's ambitions . . . while you . . . you shall be dead . . ."

The statue of Baron Antonus Sibelio moved toward Nermesa . . .

19

"GUARDS! BETAVIO! ENTER!"

"GUARDS! BETAVIO! ENTER!"

Nermesa stared in disbelief as the statue—still facing him—uttered a perfect imitation of the baron's voice despite having no windpipes. Within the mouth was only solid marble.

And though prior to this the men had been beating futilely at the door, they now sprang through with ease. At their head came Betavio, who glared murderously at the knight.

"This one still lives, my lord? But why?"

"Never mind!" declared the statue. "Seize him!"

This time, Nermesa saw the sorcerer's lips move ever so slightly. *Set-Anubis* was providing the voice for his false baron.

The knight considered warning the Gunderman, but saw that Betavio and the others could not tell that what stood before them was only a facsimile of a man, not the true thing. Set-Anubis had not lied.

Betavio signaled four of the men to spread out. With the Gunderman leading, they closed on Nermesa.

The Black Dragon suddenly flipped the sword up,

catching it like a spear. With equal swiftness, he threw it at Betavio.

As he expected, the Gunderman twisted to the side, at the same time using his own weapon to deflect the makeshift missile. However, the audacious act caused the oncoming guards to hesitate, giving time for Nermesa to reach his own weapon, which Antonus had earlier dropped.

The king's blade felt right in his grip, a far better sword than that which he had stolen. If he was to die, he would show them what a loyal soldier of King Conan could do . . .

In his other hand, he still held the Tear of Charon. Nermesa almost cast it way, for all the good the artifact did him now. It kept Set-Anubis at bay, but what good was that when Betavio's men would simply overwhelm Nermesa?

Yet, as he readied to drop it, Nermesa noticed an intake of breath from the seemingly confident spellcaster. He then recalled what Set-Anubis himself had said about the Tear, how it had been created to unlock the secrets of the Eye. The two were bound to one another; what would happen if the green gem was *destroyed*?

Could it even *be* destroyed? Surely the Kushites had tried, tried and failed. Yet . . .

Outside, the horns of the Black Dragons blared again. General Pallantides and his men surely had to be near the gates. All Nermesa needed to do was buy time.

But Betavio seemed to understand that also. He lunged ahead of his men, striking at the cornered knight. Nermesa deflected his blade twice, then shifted away as a second guard sought to catch him in the side. The maneuvering brought Nermesa to exactly where he wanted . . . a window.

He thrust the hand holding the ring out between the bars.

"Wait!" cried Set-Anubis, mouth twisted in outright fear.

The guards ignored him, for he was merely one of their master's jackals and a hated one at that. Nermesa kicked the table toward Betavio, sending the Gunderman back. The guard who had tried to stab Nermesa earlier attempted another thrust. Bolontes' son met his sword, coming over the man's weapon and slitting open his throat.

"Wait!"

This time, the voice sounded like that of the baron. Betavio and the others hesitated.

"How far down is it?" Nermesa demanded, gazing at Set-Anubis. "Far enough to crack a delicate stone?"

The sorcerer trembled with fury, but dared not answer directly. Clearly, he, too, was not certain as to the resilience of the smaller artifact. Through the mouth of his puppet, he managed, "Betavio! Away from him!"

"We have him, my lord Baron," insisted the Gunderman. "We can hide his body so that the soldiers will never find it! There will be no proof he was ever here!"

"Back, I say!"

Betavio turned to that which he thought his master. He peered at the false Antonus, then at Set-Anubis standing beside the regal figure.

"You heard what he said," insisted the robed villain. "Step back!"

"Something isn't right here," the Gunderman muttered. "You act as too–pleasant company for the baron, sorcerer . . . he never cared for you to be so close."

"Look hard!" Nermesa called. "Look hard at the baron, Betavio! See what treachery Set-Anubis has set in motion!"

Betavio's gaze shifted momentarily to the trapped knight.

Scowling, Set-Anubis gestured.

The marble statue swung its scepter at the Gunderman.

Only Betavio's expert reflexes saved his skull. The lead guard threw himself back out of reach of the animated figure.

"Traitor!" he snarled as he glared up at the spellcaster. Pointing at Set-Anubis, Betavio shouted to the others, "That is not the baron! It is some sort of golem! Seize the sorcerer! Quickly!"

Some of the guards hesitated, while others awkwardly moved to obey.

Muttering under his breath, Set-Anubis sent his puppet against Betavio's cohorts. One man, clearly still uncertain as to what was going on and slow to react because of it, suffered the fate the Gunderman had escaped. The top of the marble scepter crushed in his head, spilling his life fluids everywhere.

Two other guards, more trusting in Betavio's word, thrust at the statue, only to have the blades bounce off with loud clangs.

But if the golem presented a fearsome foe to his enemies, it was still not enough to suit the spellcaster. Again he muttered. The Eye of Charon flared—

The two soldiers confronting the statue suddenly eyed their own swords in horror. They dropped the swords, then fled screaming from them. What illusion they had fallen prey to, Nermesa could not say, but both men were white with fear.

Another guard helped Betavio to his feet just as the statue crushed in the head of a second man. The pair that Set-Anubis had caught in his spell continued to quiver in fear in the far corner of the study.

Nermesa had hoped that Betavio and his cohorts would give a better account of themselves, but clearly they were already in dire straits. There was only one thing to do.

Holding his closed fist to his chest, he cried, "Set-Anubis! Would you like the Tear back again?"

As he assumed, the sorcerer lost interest in all else. "Give it to me!" demanded the cadaverous villain. "Give it to me!"

Nermesa raised his fist high over his head. "Here it is, demon! All yours!"

And with that, he thrust his hand out the window as hard as he could, then released the contents.

Set-Anubis howled like a mad wolf. A savage gust of wind tore not at Nermesa, but the window. As the knight ducked, the force of that wind not only ripped open the bars, but a good portion of the surrounding wall as well.

Set-Anubis leapt toward the huge gap and as he did, his shape seemed to blur. While Nermesa could not swear to what he saw, it was almost as if the sorcerer became a winged thing resembling one of the furred howlers of the jungle forests. Without any hesitation, the sorcerer threw himself through the hole he had made—

And vanished into the darkness beyond.

But the wind did not cease blowing, and Nermesa found himself dragged toward the hole. At the same time, he saw the statue of Baron Sibelio swinging wildly in all directions. Without Set-Anubis' control, it seemed to have no focus. Like a drunken fighter, it crashed into the man next to Betavio.

That was the last that Nermesa saw, for in the next instant, he was pulled through. Unfortunately, outside, the wind died almost immediately, leaving the knight poised momentarily in midair. Then, the laws of nature took control again, and he started falling.

For once, Nermesa released his sword willingly. With both hands, he grasped for any hold. His fingers wrapped around a thick wooden bar that he realized was a pole holding the banner of House Sibelio.

But barely had he stopped his descent than the pole swayed dangerously. Nermesa heard a groan, then a cracking sound.

The pole split, swinging him down. He slammed against the wall of the estate house. The collision jarred him enough to make him lose what remained of his grip.

To his surprise, however, he fell only a few more feet before landing hard enough to briefly knock him senseless. Nermesa lay there for several seconds, trying to collect himself. He was on a lower balcony, that much he realized. Above, he could still see light emanating from the ruined wall.

Then, something blotted out that light, something that moved.

Something that *stepped out* of the study and into the air above the knight.

With a monumental effort, the Aquilonian threw himself as far as he could from the spot. Just as he did, a huge form dropped atop where he had been, crashing with enough force to shatter much of the balcony.

Even in the dim illumination of night, Nermesa could see the hand—still wielding the scepter—thrusting up over the pile of rubble that had once been the statue of Baron Antonus Sibelio.

As the clatter of the crash subsided, another sound rose to prominence. The sound of the clash of arms.

The Black Dragons had finally arrived at the Sibelio estate . . . and they were being met with resistance.

Without either the baron or Betavio to tell them what to do, the men at the gates and walls had evidently reacted as most brigands and murderers would have upon seeing an armed host approaching. They assumed that the truth had been discovered and that they now had to flee or fight for their lives. Whatever hope Betavio had kept of maintaining the pretense that all was innocence here—assuming, that was, that he had not been slain by the golem—was lost now.

But if Antonus' men were lost, there still remained a more vile, insidious threat. By no stretch of the imagination did Nermesa believe that he had seen the last of Set-Anubis. At the very least, he would come after Nermesa and, thus, after those for whom the knight cared the most. After the king and queen, General Pallantides, Nermesa's parents—

After *Telaria* . . .

"Mitra preserve me," muttered the knight. Pushing himself up, he looked around. Below him, fires marked shadowy figures caught in the throes of combat. Nowhere, though, did Nermesa see any sign of the sorcerer. Not for a moment did he believe that Set-Anubis had committed suicide when he had leapt out to retrieve the ring. The dark magicks wielded by the renegade would have somehow shielded him.

Then, something else on another balcony directly below caught Nermesa's attention. A brief gleam reflecting some of the distant fires. Almost it seemed—

Slipping over the edge of the shattered balcony, Nermesa found a handhold that enabled him to climb down farther. The second balcony coalesced as he neared it and for the first time Bolontes' son could positively identify what lay on it.

His sword.

Dropping the rest of the way, he landed in a crouching position just inches from the weapon. He seized it gratefully in one hand, then stood to survey the scene again.

This low, he could make out the battling figures better—and only then saw that there was something wrong about them. Nermesa leaned on the rail, trying to get a better look at those framed by torchlight.

He saw the armor of the Black Dragons and the liveried forms of House Sibelio's private army and although both sides fought with vigor . . . they did not always fight with each *other*. Several of them were swinging at nonexistent foes with some even seeming to take wounds from the latter. Nermesa watched in befuddlement as one Black Dragon kept backing away from nothing, yet acted as if at least three foes assailed him . . .

"Set-Anubis . . ." Nermesa muttered. Whether to cover his escape or for some other foul purpose, the sorcerer had cast an illusion over the area. The dark of night strengthened that illusion, as did the fact that neither group of fighters had expected such a sinister attack.

Cursing, Bolontes' son searched for a swift way down but found none. Below this balcony, the rest of the way was a sheer drop. With no other recourse, Nermesa kicked open the doors of the room behind him, then went charging through the house.

As he entered the corridor beyond, a woman's scream broke out from his right. Despite his desire to seek out Set-Anubis, Nermesa could not in all conscience ignore the cry. He dashed down the hallway, breaking through the pair of fine oak doors at the end.

Orena stood before him, the baroness covering her mouth with one hand. She leaned with the other against a chair that had acted in part as meager protection.

Protection, he was startled to see, from Betavio.

The Gunderman stood but a yard from her, his blade bloody. His victim had been one of Nermesa's own Black Dragons, who now lay sprawled over the chamber's luxurious carpet. A wound in the back of the knight's neck spilled its contents onto the floor and stirred anew Nermesa's rage.

"Betavio!" he shouted.

Both the Gunderman and Orena looked up. Orena let out a small gasp. Betavio, an evil grin on his face, charged the Aquilonian.

"I missed you upstairs," sneered the bodyguard. "You were a fool not to run when you had the chance!"

"I've nothing to fear from a man who can only slay a foe by striking him in the back like a cowardly knave!"

Their blades met, the clash of metal deafening. Betavio had a strong arm, and his initial momentum sent Nermesa back several paces. The knight tried to steer his foe away from the doors so as to give Orena an avenue of escape, but Telaria's sister stood where she was, seemingly mesmerized by the struggle.

"Your cause is dead, Betavio!" Nermesa growled. "Dead with your master!"

"My cause is very much alive!" snapped the Gunderman. He swung hard at the officer, who ducked back. The Gunderman's sword instead hacked away part of an ornamental wall fixture.

"Your only chance is to surrender!"

Betavio laughed. "And spend the rest of my life in the Iron Tower?"

The bodyguard's blade darted past Nermesa's defense. At the very last, Nermesa used his arm to shove the other's sword up. It garnered him a long, stinging streak across his elbow, but better that than the point through the side of his throat.

Nermesa's opponent grinned, certain of his advantage. But while Betavio was an excellent swordsman, the Aquilonian had been quickly gauging the bodyguard's skills and faults. Nermesa now had a good notion of just

what Betavio's limits were. He started a counterattack, seeing what the other man would do in response. When Betavio reacted just as he had hoped, the Black Dragon knew
that he had his adversary where he wanted him.

The sudden turn was not missed by Betavio. His grin
faded, to be replaced seconds later by a hint of uncertainty.
The sweat on his face increased.

"Surrender, I said!" Nermesa pressed the Gunderman
back to a small table, nearly causing Betavio to fall over it.
A crystalline vase slipped off, shattering. The sound jarred
the already-anxious bodyguard.

"I was a fool to suggest that you be kept alive! I
should've slain you when first we met in the streets of
Tarantia," snarled Betavio, his swings getting wilder.

"You might have had a better chance, then," Nermesa
agreed. "But not anymore."

With a guttural cry, Betavio lunged. Nermesa readily
deflected his attack, then initiated a series of quickly shifting feints ending in a thrust that buried the tip of his blade
deep into Betavio's sword shoulder. He had hoped that doing so would force the bodyguard to drop his weapon, but
the Gunderman stubbornly held on even though he could
barely grip the hilt, much less raise the sword.

Then, some movement near Orena caught Betavio's notice. Out of the corner of his eye, Nermesa saw Morannus,
crimson-tipped sword in hand, approaching.

"Stay back, Morannus," the knight ordered. "I have this
one. He'll need to be interrogated by General Pallantides'
men. There's much he may be able to tell us—"

Orena's bodyguard suddenly pointed his sword in the
direction of his countryman. "Look out!"

Nermesa reacted with the training of a Black Dragon.
Focus immediately returning to Betavio, the knight thrust.

Betavio, his sword midway up, let out a gurgle as Nermesa ran him through. The Gunderman's eyes went from
Nermesa to Morannus—then rolled up.

Crashing into the small table, Betavio dropped to the
floor.

Too late did the knight realize that he could have stopped his adversary without slaying him, but Morannus' warning had caused his reflexes to take over. "I wanted him alive!"

"A thousand pardons, my lord," Morannus said, his expression grim. "But I've seen Betavio's cunning over these many months and feared he would catch you off guard."

Nermesa could not fault the other man. Morannus had only sought to protect his life. But with Betavio dead, another danger resurrected itself in the knight's thoughts. The battle still raged without, and somewhere Set-Anubis had to be plotting. Nermesa was certain that the sorcerer was still within the estate walls.

"Watch your mistress, Morannus," he commanded the Gunderman. Nermesa headed toward the door. "Keep her here and with the doors shut behind me, understand?"

"Aye, Captain Nermesa, aye."

Satisfied that Orena would be safe in the bodyguard's capable care, Nermesa ran from the room. Locating the stairway, he quickly descended to the main floor. Bodies lay strewn about, some of them comrades of his, but most the baron's men. If not for what he had witnessed from the balcony, Nermesa would have taken heart that the struggle was nearly done.

But with Set-Anubis free, disaster was still as certain as victory.

A pair of Black Dragons suddenly burst into the house, their backs to the approaching Nermesa. He expected their foes to enter immediately after, but the two knights instead kept swinging at the open space in front of them. The pair looked much beleaguered, as if harried by twice or even three times their number.

Recognizing one of the duo, Nermesa seized him by the arm. "Thunio! Stop! You're—"

But the other soldier pulled free, crying, "Nermesa! 'Tis you! Be careful, man! You nearly got us both killed—watch out! They're coming strong!"

And as Nermesa stared, Thunio and the other Black

Dragon continued to back away from their imaginary enemies.

Seeing that there was nothing he could do for his comrades, Nermesa raced outside. The courtyard of the Sibelio estate was utter pandemonium, with men of both sides battling real and imagined adversaries. A mist that Bolontes' son had not noticed from above now enshrouded the area, surely also the foul work of Set-Anubis.

Much to his frustration, however, Nermesa still had no notion as to where the sorcerer was. He surveyed the area and finally, out of desperation, chose the stables as the most likely possibility. The entire illusion seemed designed to place such confusion over those around that surely a single rider could easily slip out unnoticed. Once beyond Sibelio's gates, the spellcaster would be able to lose himself anywhere he chose—assuming that was even what the knave wanted to do.

The trek to the stables required him to take a serpentine path, for combats of all sizes and shape popped up throughout. Nermesa was nearly run down by a liveried guard on horseback seeking to escape two mounted Black Dragons pursuing him close. A band of Sibelio guards stood in formation against emptiness, their position forcing Nermesa to skirt around them cautiously. Fortunately, they seemed entirely oblivious to the one true foe near them.

Madness! he thought not for the first time. *Set-Anubis has truly conjured madness!*

The huge wooden doors to the main stables finally beckoned to him. Peering around and seeing no more threat, Nermesa sprinted toward his goal—

And *kept* sprinting. The doors stayed as far away as ever, no matter how fast he tried to run.

Then . . . then the stables utterly faded into the mists.

Everything faded into the mists.

A harsh cackle floated through the air. Set-Anubis' triumphant cackle.

"A will so strong, yet is it strong enough?" came the

spellcaster's rasping voice. "What is real and what is illusion, Nermesa Klandes? Do even you know?"

Brandishing his weapon, the knight shouted, "I know that good steel will cut out the black heart of a sorcerer as easily as it would that of a jackal!"

"If the steel can *find* a true target, yes . . ."

Nermesa spun around. The voice had suddenly appeared to come from right behind him. He slashed at the fog but found no substance, only shadow.

Again, Set-Anubis cackled. "Wonder, do you, why I am still here? I think not. You knew that I would look for you, just as you would look for me . . ."

Now the voice came from the knight's left. Nermesa jabbed there, with the same lack of results.

"Yes, I thought that you wouldn't leave without coming after me," responded the Aquilonian. He reached into his tunic and slipped out what had been kept hidden there. "That is, if you truly still wanted *this*."

He held up the ring of Baron Sibelio, the ring containing the Tear of Charon.

The foul gemstone glittered brilliantly even despite a lack of light shining upon it. Aware of its value, especially the fact that he *might* find need of it later, Nermesa had only pretended to throw it out the window. In his frantic state, Set-Anubis had flown after nothing more than a decoy . . . the baron's severed finger. The knight had known that if the sorcerer *did* retrieve the magical emerald, nothing would be able to stop the fiend should he decide to seek revenge against all Aquilonia.

Not that Nermesa's chances seemed so good even with the Tear still his. As Set-Anubis had so rightly explained earlier, Nermesa did not know how to wield the artifact as Antonus had. For him, its power lay in the simple fact that the spellcaster feared something would happen to it if he tried to attack the knight.

"I cannot permit the Tear to remain in another's hands," Set-Anubis went on. "I must make it safe, so that the Eye, in turn, can be safe."

Nermesa paid the villain's babbling little mind. Instead, he concentrated his will as hard as he could, seeking to overcome Set-Anubis' illusion . . . if, indeed, the mists were such. Yet, whether they were real or imagined, the sorcerer *had* to be somewhere nearby. All Nermesa needed was one chance . . .

"In fact, I have decided that I will further make it safe by taking a kingdom for my *own* . . . the baron, for all his base desires, suggested the perfect thing . . . *slay* the king and take the throne . . ."

Nermesa could not help but react to *that* arrogant statement. "You said as much in the study, when you thought that a statue could play as the baron! That hardly worked, did it, knave?"

"A decision of the moment, one hastily formed." Again, the voice seemed to come from the side. "I agree, a waste of energy and power, that particular path . . . but still . . . an entire *kingdom*, aye, there I could keep the Tear safe!"

This time, the sorcerer's cackle came from in front, but Nermesa did not attack. Instead, he kept a cautious watch for any shadowed form.

Bolontes' son gritted his teeth. "Even with the Eye of Charon, you'd manage little save your death! Think you that the king is not guarded against the likes of you? If not, ask the shade of Xaltotun of Acheron, if you can . . ."

There was a flash of movement to his right. Nermesa poised. He had to strike true.

"And that is where the baron was the greatest fool!" his foe went on. "His assassins would have probably perished, yes, even with my power to disguise them! I sensed when last I passed the palace the secret enchantments surrounding it. Likely most of them the barbarian king does not even know about . . . but his most trusted *general* would, would he not? He would recall each and every one, yes?"

Pallantides! Nermesa shook with dread as he began to understand. More than a simple officer such as Nermesa, General Pallantides knew the secrets of Tarantia, especially those involving the king's sanctum. Moreover, few could gain closer access to King Conan than the commander of his elite guard.

And, because of Nermesa, Pallantides was now within the estate grounds.

Just as he thought that, Nermesa noticed movement again. The vague outline reminded him very much of the shape of the sorcerer, and, *this* time, Set-Anubis had stepped too close—to gloat at the soldier's helplessness . . .

Spinning in that direction, Nermesa thrust toward the vaguely seen form. To his relief, he felt the blade sink deep into what had to be the spellcaster's midsection. With as much strength as he could muster, the fighter shoved the weapon deeper yet. Set-Anubis had to die!

From the mists there came a sudden gasp . . . but the voice uttering it did not sound like the sorcerer's. The knight leaned closer, trying to make out more clearly his target.

"N-Nermesa?"

The blood drained from him. He shook his head in horror as, even in the dark, he managed to note the thick, long hair and the feminine form.

And the voice he had come to know as well as his own.

Nermesa had just stabbed *Telaria* . . .

20

"AHAHAHAHAHA . . ." FROM THE mists, Set-Anubis crowed with delight. "Poor Nermesa Klandes! What *have* you done, eh?"

Telaria should not have been here. She should have been safe back in Tarantia. She had done more than enough simply by escaping Baron Sibelio's men and then making it to the capital in order to seek help. *Why* had she then put herself at such risk by coming back?

Had it been because of Nermesa? That was the only reason that made sense to him at that moment. He knew how Telaria felt about him . . . and how he felt about her. They had all but said the words . . .

And now those intense feelings had brought her back to the estate . . . and brought about her monstrous death at his very own hands!

"N-Nermesa . . . I feel . . . feel cold . . ." she whispered. "So very cold . . ."

With fear and disgust at his deed—however accidental it had been—Nermesa gingerly pulled the blade free. The weapon made an awful sucking sound as it came free.

Telaria fell limply into his arms. Agony filled her expression, and that further added to his already-insurmountable guilt. He knew that there was nothing he could do to save her, yet he struggled to come up with some solution.

"Ner . . . Nermesa . . ." Her breath was ragged. "Please . . ."

More and more blood soaked the beautiful gown that he had seen her in just hours earlier. Bolontes' son stiffened as he watched the dark fluids course down the otherwise immaculate dress.

Dropping both the ring and his sword, Nermesa went down on one knee. Sobbing, he muttered over and over, "Telaria . . . no . . . no . . . what have I done . . ."

And as he cried, Set-Anubis materialized out of the mists just a few yards away, like a demon from the underworld.

On the ground, the ring—or rather, the Tear—glowed bright, as if calling to the Eye of Charon. Set-Anubis' hand slipped into his robes as he stepped within reach. From the garment, the sorcerer pulled free a jagged dagger with runes etched along the edge. It had been forged in darkest Kush and its making had required the souls of three sacrifices to make it strong.

The exposed neck of the knight was an easy target, but the ring lay even nearer. With a silence worthy of a cat, Set-Anubis bent slightly and wrapped his fingers around the ring—

And suddenly Nermesa's hands covered the Eye of Charon, blotting out the spellcaster's sight.

The knight had known that he had to time his action perfectly. He had relied on Set-Anubis' ego and intentions. More than anything, the ring—with the Tear of Charon in it—needed to be the focus of Set-Anubis' attention. The villain had to believe that Nermesa was no threat whatsoever to him, that the Black Dragon was so caught up in the horror of what he had done that he would notice nothing else.

Only . . . Nermesa had known almost immediately that he had not actually slain Telaria.

It had been her gown that had given the matter away. From everything that he had gathered from Antonus, Telaria had risked herself much to escape on her own after her sister had refused to believe the truth about the baron. If even part of what the treacherous noble had said had actually happened—and Antonus' relaxed attitude until the Black Dragons' horns had sounded had indicated that *he* at least had believed so—than surely Telaria's gown would have been reduced to rags. Just as important, even if they had somehow miraculously survived unmarred, they would have made for an ungainly ride either away from or back toward the estate. Nermesa knew Telaria well enough to understand that she would have seen the wisdom of at least changing to more appropriate and less risky attire after she had finally reached the palace and relayed his warning.

No . . . something had been amiss here . . . and Nermesa had quickly understood just what. Set-Anubis had once more sought to break his will, this time nearly succeeding through the most heinous of illusions.

And as Nermesa had thought this, "Telaria" had faded away without warning. Despite already being aware of the fact that she had not been real, the knight had breathed a sigh of relief upon seeing the irrefutable evidence of that.

But the knight had not let on that he was no longer enmeshed in the illusion. Rather, he had thrown himself into the act, letting out with abandon emotions he was certain would convince Set-Anubis of his triumph.

And it had worked. Trained to be wary of an enemy's approach, Nermesa had sensed the stealthy steps of the sorcerer. He had purposely dropped the ring far enough away so that it would shine like a beacon for the fiend, and Set-Anubis had taken to it like a moth at a flame.

Unfortunately, Nermesa had also had to drop his sword, and he had been aware that the time needed to seize it again and bring it up would not be available to him. Set-Anubis would surely strike him down first, either through the arts or through some blade of his own. Nermesa had to rely on his hands, but even those had a good chance of proving insufficient to the task. If he jumped the spell-caster or tried to throttle him, Set-Anubis would again surely have the wherewithal to cast a spell.

It was magic that Nermesa most feared against him, and so it had occurred to the Aquilonian that his one chance to save himself and disable his opponent had been to *take* the Eye of Charon just as Set-Anubis finally regained the Tear.

Thus it was that when the sorcerer picked up the ring, Bolontes' son threw himself toward the villain, both hands outstretched to seize the crimson jewel and tear it free.

As his fingers wrapped around the edges, however, an incredible heat seared them. Nermesa's first instinct was to release the Eye, but his mind overruled that, the image of a dead Telaria emphasizing what would happen if the knight failed.

Nermesa tore at the Eye of Charon, tore at the bindings that he now discovered Set-Anubis had sewn into his *skin* just as his enemies had sewn shut his eyelids. He ignored the burning, ignored the agony. Although on some level Nermesa knew that all he felt happened within only a second or two, it felt as if it were an eternity.

Then, with a horrid ripping of flesh . . . Nermesa pulled the Eye free.

He expected Set-Anubis to curse, to claw or stab at him, even to unleash any of a number of darksome spells.

Nermesa did *not* expect the spellcaster to scream so horribly that it sent shivers to the knight's very soul.

A tremendous force flung Nermesa away from his foe. With a bone-jarring thud, he landed on his back, the arti-fact still held tight in one hand. Oddly, it now felt much cooler, but, at the moment, that was a minor consideration in comparison to the scene before him.

Flinging aside his dagger, Set-Anubis clutched at his face where the Eye had once been. Blood trickled through his fingers from the ruined bindings. More monstrous, though, was the horrible mark that the dark red stone had left in its wake. There, Nermesa saw a small, crumbling layer of rotting skin perfectly shaped like the silhouette of the jewel. Beneath it could be seen hints of something white, which the knight could only believe had to be part of the sorcerer's very *skull*.

Although Set-Anubis continued to scream, he suddenly took a step toward Nermesa.

"Give . . . me . . . that . . . back!" he rasped in a voice no longer human. *"Give it . . . to me!"*

Scrambling for his sword, Nermesa edged away from the almost-demonic figure. The closer he approached, the less like any creature born of the mortal world Set-Anubis became.

Nermesa had heard that sorcerers often paid a price for tremendous power, and Set-Anubis had done just that. Either because of his long tie to the Eye or by some other spell, he had come to the point where he utterly depended upon it. How long had it been since first he had bound it to him? A decade? Two? A century or more, even? There had been tales of spellcasters who had used the arts to live for several times the life span of most men.

If so, then now, bereft of the Eye, Set-Anubis' long-held-back mortality was swiftly catching up with him.

A wind picked up, a wind that seemed to focus only upon the sorcerer. In the light of the Eye of Charon, Nermesa watched as it swirled around Set-Anubis, spinning faster and faster. His robes wrapped around him like a maddened kraken, so much so that he could no longer move. Yet still the wind's fury increased.

Dust began to fly about the sorcerer, and only after a moment did Nermesa realize that it was coming *from* the villain. More and more it gathered, until some of it began piling around the hapless figure.

As it gathered, Set-Anubis seemed to *shrivel* within himself. He grew smaller, more of a jumble of cloth and bones.

And, finally, both the sorcerer and his garments crumbled before Nermesa's astounded eyes. Set-Anubis let out a gargled sound that might have been a curse—and his body collapsed. A mound of much-decayed cloth briefly stood before the knight until it was quickly eaten away by the incessant wind.

Seconds later, there remained nothing but a thinning pile of dust. Only then did the wind cease.

Only then did Nermesa truly believe that Set-Anubis was indeed dead.

A faint glitter from the dust caught his attention. With much trepidation, Nermesa rose and went over to it. With the tip of his blade, he dug out the source.

Antonus Sibelio's ring. The Tear glowed with an intensity equal to that of the Eye. Nermesa picked up the ring.

A sense of great power coursed through him, almost leaving the knight giddy. He had a great urge to press the Eye of Charon to his heart and put the ring bearing the Tear on his hand . . .

"Mitra!" Nermesa dropped both the ring and the Eye. With utter revulsion, he brought one boot up and stomped on the former. The ring itself cracked, but when he lifted his foot, it was to discover that the gem within was still intact.

He peered around. His gaze alighted on the Eye and desperate hope arose. The knight forced himself to seize the sinister orb again. Ignoring as best he could the rush of power he felt when touching it, Nermesa raised the artifact high . . . then brought it crashing down on the smaller emerald.

This time, the Tear shattered with a very satisfactory crack. A brief flare of green energy escaped the small jewel as it broke into several pieces . . . then the light faded and the Tear became just so much more rubble.

But as Nermesa raised the Eye of Charon, with the intention of seeing if he could smash *it* somehow, he suddenly noticed another murky form stepping out of the mists. With his ready sword in one hand and the Eye forgotten in the other, Nermesa watched as it gradually coalesced into a tall figure with a slight limp. A figure very familiar to him.

"General Pallantides?" The knight exhaled in relief.

"Nermesa?" The shadowed form of the Black Dragons'

commander looked the captain up and down. Pallantides' voice had a slow measure to it, as if he were half-asleep. "Nermesa? No . . . it cannot be. 'Tis . . . another trick . . . another trick of this foul fog . . ."

And with that, the general swung at Nermesa.

Their swords rang hard as they struck one another, even a slight spark arising between them. Yet, despite this proof of substance, Pallantides did not appear to believe Nermesa real. Either that, or he suspected that some minion of the late baron stood hidden behind the illusion of his trusted officer.

Even Nermesa still had his doubts as to the reality of what was going on. Perhaps General Pallantides did *not* stand before him. Perhaps the general was on the other side of the estate. This could very well be some liveried guard or even just empty air.

Whatever the case, Nermesa had no recourse but to fight and fight against a man who—if it was indeed Pallantides— was surely far his superior in skill. Along with a handful of renowned fighters such as Sir Prospero of Poitain, Pallantides was considered one of the best swordsmen in all of Aquilonia. The veterans who had instructed Nermesa had all been trained at one point or another by the legendary general, and they had willingly admitted that they could never achieve his abilities.

Which left Nermesa in dire straits. Either he had to hope to become lucky and defeat his commander without slaying him, or Pallantides would run him through.

Unfortunately, the odds were far more likely that it would be the *latter* possibility.

The general's long blade weighed heavily on Nermesa's sword each time the weapons connected. Despite the general's limp, he seemed to move with a litheness unmatchable by his opponent. He pressed Nermesa again and again, his shadowy expression ever determined.

Nermesa had to do *something*. He had to draw Pallantides' focus, and only one way sprang to mind.

Nermesa held up the Eye of Charon. The bloodred glow from the artifact could not be ignored.

"Eh?" General Pallantides hesitated in midswing as his gaze shifted to the crimson gem. His face outlined by the unsettling red aura, the commander blinked. His eyes slowly grew more focused.

He finally seemed to see the man before him. "Captain Nermesa? It is you, is it not?"

"Yes, General! Praise Mitra that you are free of the sorcerer's illusion!"

"Illusion . . ." Pallantides shook his head as if still clearing it. "When the mists settled so quickly upon us, I sensed evil magic afoot . . . but still it was impossible to entirely ignore what I saw. Worse, everyone around me acted as if utterly insane! Men fought men, but shadows as well, and one could almost feel sympathy for the enemy, for they were just as ensorcelled."

"It was the work of a sorcerer called Set-Anubis . . ."

"Set-Anubis! When Telaria came and told me what happened, the name sent chills down my spine, for tales of him have reached my agents before!" The veteran commander looked about. "Where is the miscreant hiding? We must not let him escape—"

"Set-Anubis is dead, sir." Nermesa went into an abbreviated version of what had happened. Despite trimming the details as much as possible, he still left Pallantides marveling at him.

"Strong of sword and mind! Aye, that's you, young Klandes! So the arrogance of the cur brings him to a horrific-yet-appropriate end, I say! And what of the Baron Sibelio?"

"Dead also, but by the spellcaster's hand, not mine. The baron treated him as a slave and when finally given the opportunity, Set-Anubis paid him in full for the insult."

"And the baroness?"

"She should be well. She was not a part of this. I left her in her chambers, guarded by good Morannus." Mention of Orena allowed the knight to turn the matters to a subject more pressing to him. "General, you spoke of Telaria—how—how is she?"

"For a woman who leapt into a river to escape the

miscreants—in doing so making them believe that she was dead—then stole a horse from a neighboring estate and still managed to reach the capital as if carried by the wind itself, she is doing excellently. Admittedly, she was not suitably attired anymore for a lady-in-waiting to the queen, but Zenobia quickly forgave her."

Relief rushed through Nermesa as he listened. He marveled at what Telaria had gone through because of him . . . marveled and again felt much guilt for. Still, one question needed to be answered for him. "She did not . . . she did not ride with you, did she?"

Pallantides laughed. "It took the queen to keep her from coming, but, no, she did not ride with us. She awaits the news of what happened here back at the palace."

"Praise be!"

"And as for that news, if it is to be what we desire, Captain, then it would be good for us to see that the rest of these traitors are rounded up!"

"Yes, sir—but what of this?" Nermesa held up the Eye of Charon. It still glowed, but now just barely. It seemed to the knight that its power had begun to gradually fade—or withdraw—since the destruction of the Tear.

His superior took the sinister artifact, studying it for a moment. "What would *you* do with it, Nermesa?"

"Destroy it," Bolontes' son responded without hesitation. "Failing that, bury it where it could never be found. Even without that which can open its secrets, it is still a devilish thing."

"The fire within has almost gone. The Eye appears to be going dormant," Pallantides analytically remarked. "I wonder . . ."

As hard as he could, the general threw the Eye of Charon to the stone path.

The monstrous gem *cracked* into a thousand pieces as easily as the most fragile glass. Both men involuntarily stepped back, expecting far more.

But that was all. There was no explosion, no release of energy.

Once his nerve had returned, Nermesa shook his head in wonder. "When I used it to destroy the other, there was not even the slightest marring. How—?"

"One learns a few things about sorcery and arcane items when fighting alongside the king, trust me. The tales *he* could tell! Whatever force it contained, it either withdrew deeply into the stone or returned to the netherworld once the key—the Tear—was destroyed." Pallantides chuckled. "I was *fairly* certain that nothing dire would happen . . ."

Nermesa suddenly noticed that the mists had begun to dissipate. Without the Eye of Charon, the spell creating them could not hold. One by one, the stars reemerged overhead, joined belatedly by a half-moon.

Shouts of confusion swept across the estate.

"The illusions are no more," Nermesa realized.

"Then we must make haste! Come!"

Once again, Pallantides proved that, limp or no limp, he could move as well as any fighter. It was all Nermesa could do just to keep up with him. They rushed toward the thickest of the battle, swords at the ready.

But although many of the baron's men yet fought, they did not do so with much heart. It quickly became clear to them that their master was dead and that those who would have commanded in his name had either abandoned them or were likewise slain. A few of Betavio's cohorts attempted to make a stand, but they were no match for the numbers of the Black Dragons.

Only half an hour later, the estate was under the iron control of the king's elite, one of whom greeted Nermesa as a long-lost brother.

"Lo and behold!" Paulo cried upon seeing him. The blond knight came over to Nermesa and gave him a bear hug. "Thought you dead so long, I did! Returned but two nights previous and hoped to speak with your parents tomorrow, to console them! Then, when the news came to Tarantia, I almost couldn't believe it, not at all!"

"I've had some trouble believing it myself at times,"

returned Nermesa. Grinning, he shook his comrade's hand. "It's good to see you!"

"There'll be time for celebrations later," barked General Pallantides. "Sir Paulo! Get these ruffians lined up and ready to move! They've got a long walk to the Iron Tower—what's that?"

"That" to which the commander referred, was a sudden, intense blaze bursting out of the uppermost story of the estate house. Nermesa took a step forward, gauging where the fire burned.

"The baron's study!" he shouted. "General! I'm certain that he had information there concerning his misdeeds and with whom he was allied! Someone seeks to destroy it all!"

"You know the way? Then take some men and get in there! See what you can do! Go!"

With ten crack Black Dragons behind him, Nermesa ran back to the house. However, as he reached the entrance, he feared that it was already too late. The fire now came from other windows on that floor as well.

Two figures rushed out the doors as he tried to enter. He raised his sword, only to see that it was Orena and Morannus.

"The ceiling grew black and started to buckle!" shouted the Gunderman. "We ran into the hall! I saw two knaves in the baron's livery slipping out the side!"

Nermesa sent four of his men in the direction indicated. As he and the rest started in, Orena suddenly took his arm.

"Telaria . . . is she safe?"

"Yes. She's back in the palace."

The baroness nodded, only then permitting Morannus to lead her away. Nermesa eyed the blond woman's retreating form for a second, having expected more concern than that . . . but Orena was ever Orena.

Then a flash of flames from above stirred him to his duty again. He led the rest of his band into the house and up the staircase.

But at the third landing, they were met by a fearsome wall of fire. Ahead, Nermesa could see that part of the ceiling had already caved in. Blackened furniture from rooms above lay strewn over part of the corridor.

"Too late!" he called. "Back down!"

Even as he spoke, there was a terrible groan from above. The other Black Dragons managed to retreat down to the next floor, but as Nermesa followed, what was left of the ceiling came crashing down.

He threw himself over the railing. His sword tumbled to the bottom floor, but Nermesa caught part of the staircase just below him.

One of the other knights rushed up and lent Nermesa a hand in climbing onto the steps. Rushing down to the main level, Bolontes' son quickly seized his weapon and hurried out of the building.

Behind him, he heard the crash of timber as the remaining floors collapsed upon one another.

He and the men who had followed him in paused to breathe in fresh air. As Nermesa sought to empty his lungs of smoke and soot, a figure on horseback suddenly loomed over him.

It was General Pallantides. He stared from Nermesa to the fire, then back to the knight again.

Nermesa shook his head. "I—I'm sorry, General! The fire spread—spread too quickly! We couldn't get—to the study!" He stared morosely at his commander. "I've—I've failed the king and you!"

The commander stood in the saddle, surveying not only the burning building but the images its fiery light now revealed. Black Dragons continued to round up and march off what remained of Baron Sibelio's followers. Other knights had begun to reclaim the bodies of their own dead, which were, fortunately, far fewer than that of the enemy.

"Failed us, Nermesa?" Pallantides shook his head vehemently as he once more quickly scanned the vicinity, then turned his gaze back to man below. "Hardly that . . . hardly that . . ."

21

OVER THE WEEKS that followed, there were still raids upon the caravans, but most were easily repelled or crushed. Perhaps spurred on by earlier, easy prey, the brigands grew overconfident. Now, without the baron's guidance or Set-Anubis' sorcery, they quickly became a moot concern. Most of their members were soon dead or headed to the Iron Tower.

The threat of a war between the Corinthian city-states faded just as abruptly. Without warning, Nemedia withdrew its support for arrogant Sarta, which suddenly became quite willing to negotiate with its numerous neighbors. Nermesa could only assume that, without Nemedia or the Baron Sibelio's financial aid, Sarta could not long hold the valued pass with its limited resources. Nor could it face so many enemies.

King Conan invited the Corinthians to negotiate in neutral Aquilonia. At the same time, he invited "interested parties"—Nemedia, Ophir, and Koth—to join in the discussions. Not willing to be left out, Brythunia, Argos, and

Zingara quickly arranged for their own representatives to be added.

And, thus, the trade agreement, once thought dead, rose to new prominence. What started as merely a Corinthian concern was readily manipulated by Conan into what the Cimmerian-born monarch truly wanted. Nermesa, a party to some of the developments, watched with wonder as a man who was called by so many a "barbarian" outspoke and outmaneuvered highly trained politicians and negotiators.

Of those with whom King Conan dealt, there were many faces new to the court. Nermesa had been there when his lord and General Pallantides had sent the missives to the various other kingdoms commenting on the alliances created by the baron. What started out as an abject apology concerning the Aquilonian noble's treachery became a subtle note pinpointing those with the most ties to House Sibelio in each of those lands.

Ambassador Zoran was the first and most notable to suffer for his ambitions. The document that arrived with the *new* representative from Nemedia did not thank Conan for the information he had given to his old enemy, but did state that Zoran had been removed as the result of the misuse of his authority.

From the new ambassador had come the hint that this "removal" had involved Zoran's beheading.

Lord Dekalatos of Sarta simply disappeared, at least according to public reports. Private ones mentioned a man found floating in the city's sewers, his body unmarked save for a single dot at the neck like a bee sting. Whether natural, suicide, or something else, no one involved on the Sartan end either said or seemed to care.

As for Mikonius Flavius, once secured by Aquilonian soldiers, he willingly listed all those in league with him. For that he was spared his life and cast into the Iron Tower.

It could not be said with certainty that everyone involved in Antonus' plot—especially the nameless Aquilonian nobles he had vaguely mentioned—was captured or slain, but Pallantides and, most of all, the king appeared satisfied with the conclusion to the matter.

As for Nermesa, there was but one thing that concerned him.

Telaria Lenaro.

He had seen her but one time since returning to the capital, that the very night of his return. Along with other well-wishers in the palace, she had stood there waiting for him. Upon Nermesa dismounting, the auburn-haired lady-in-waiting had run over to him and held him so tight that he thought that he would not be able to breathe.

"I feared the worst," she had finally murmured.

"As I did about you. I should have never endangered you so."

"You never *did*," Telaria insisted. "Antonus was responsible for that . . . and do you think that I would've just stood *by*?" Her eyes had then welled up even more. "Nermesa . . . I love you."

The words had not taken him aback in the least. They were only, after all, an affirmation of what had been building up over the past year. Trying to keep his voice from cracking, he had replied, "And I you . . ."

There had been more that he had intended to say to her, and, from her expression, more from her as well, but Pallantides and the Black Dragons had at that point torn him away from her. In addition to a hastily arranged meeting with the king to tell his entire story, Nermesa had been dragged around by his commander to numerous interviews with Conan's other trusted advisors. A day had become a week, then the week two.

But finally . . . *finally* . . . Nermesa was able to arrange a rendezvous with Telaria through none other than the queen.

"Certainly, I understand," Zenobia replied after he had finally come to her. Through luxurious lashes, the queen studied the knight. "And I know that she is eager to see you, too." The queen leaned back in her chair, her gown clinging to her lush curves. Had not his own desires been turned elsewhere, Nermesa would have very much envied the king. "You are captain of the guards for this evening's ceremony honoring General Pallantides for his years of service to my husband, are you not?"

"I am." Nermesa had considered it a special honor—and a chance to redeem himself after his previous turn as guard commander—to be placed in charge of those watching over the special ceremony. Pallantides had chosen him personally, saying he could think of no better man. Nermesa only hoped that he could live up to the other's expectations.

"I will see to it that she is there, also. There should be a moment when you can step away from your duties to be with her."

Nermesa bowed deep. "I am very grateful, your majesty. Very grateful."

Zenobia nodded. "As am I to you, Captain. As we all are to you."

ALTHOUGH THE CEREMONY was to be small and private—by royal standards, anyway—those in attendance would be the most influential and trusted of King Conan's subjects. Some of the names on the list given to him by Publius were ones that made Nermesa shake his head with awe. Yet certainly the general was worthy of their greatest respect, for had he not saved Aquilonia more than once during his career?

An honor guard was to escort Pallantides in, and although Nermesa was to be in charge of security, his commander insisted that he also lead that contingent. It was another honor that the knight felt he did not deserve but could not refuse. At the general's suggestion, Sir Paulo was made officer of those already on duty in the throne room, where the ceremony was to take place.

And so, as the bells marked the coming of evening, Nermesa and a dozen crack Black Dragons stood at attention near Pallantides' quarters. Each man had polished his armor to the point of gleaming, and all wore cloaks with the king's colors. When the general stepped out to join them, he looked every inch the epic hero in his own shining outfit and plumed helmet.

"Stand beside me, Captain Nermesa," Pallantides commanded. "I insist."

Swallowing, Nermesa obeyed. He gave the signal to march, and the escort headed toward the ceremony. Along the way, guards on duty and members of the palace saluted or bowed as the men passed. Several of the onlookers seemed confused, for they not only honored Pallantides, but Nermesa as well.

Finally, the escort and its charge stood before the tall doors of the throne room. Heralds raised long horns and signaled their arrival. The doors swung open from within, and the party marched inside.

The soldiers marched between the waiting well-wishers. Among them, Nermesa saw his parents. Klandes was a House with much prestige, so he had expected them to be here. They nodded toward Nermesa and looked every bit the proud parents, forgetting that it was General Pallantides who was to be honored here, not their son.

But as the escort neared the thrones, as the swarthy Cimmerian and his queen leaned forward in expectation . . . General Pallantides suddenly fell a step behind Nermesa.

"Sir—" the knight muttered.

Pallantides only smiled, then indicated that Nermesa should look ahead.

Only then did Bolontes' son discover that it was *he* who was to be honored.

Grinning wide at Nermesa, King Conan gave his queen an arm. Rising, the two stood at the edge of the dais, looking down.

"Well fought, Captain Nermesa," Conan declared. "Well fought . . ."

And with that, trumpets blared again, and the crowd broke into applause.

When the clapping began to diminish, the king called out, "Here is a true and loyal warrior, by Crom, a man whose blade I would welcome any day beside my own! As he fought against the Picts in the west, he now fought against traitors in our midst, curs who would have placed another on the throne . . ."

"Go to the dais and kneel," murmured Pallantides.

Following the general's advice, Nermesa knelt directly before his monarch. As the knight did, King Conan drew his own sword.

"Nermesa of Klandes," continued the king, "when once before you were honored, I asked what you wanted and then granted that wish! This time, it's been suggested by others"—he glanced at both Zenobia and Pallantides—"exactly what you deserve." The Cimmerian-born monarch touched each shoulder of Nermesa with the tip of his blade. "From this day forward, half the holdings of House Sibelio—including the clan holdings in Tarantia itself—now fall to you!"

"Your maj—" Nermesa began, speechless. There had to be some *mistake*.

"And *with* it, by Crom!" Conan all but roared, drowning out the knight's protest. "Added to your other titles, that of *baron*!" The muscular giant raised his sword high as he looked to the crowd. "Hail, Baron Nermesa Klandes!"

Throughout the assembly, the call was repeated: *Baron Nermesa Klandes! Baron Nermesa Klandes!*

The king waited patiently, then, when the cries had died down, added, "And I personally add another title . . . *Caru Morgar uth Njarl*! In the tongue of my youth . . . *The Sword of the Lion!*" Conan's expression grew stern. "And let any man who thinks to do him harm know that to do so will bring down *my* wrath upon them . . ." The former mercenary grinned darkly. ". . . and no *sane* person wants that . . ."

The trumpets sounded. The audience applauded and cheered again. Conan bid Nermesa to rise. He took the Aquilonian's hand and shook it with astonishing strength.

"I mean that," the king muttered. "We are sword brothers, just as I am with Pallantides . . ."

"I . . . am . . . honored . . ."

"No . . . I am."

King Conan released him then. The Black Dragons swarmed their comrade, congratulating him. General Pallantides shook his hand. "All well deserved, young Klandes."

"Thank you . . ." Nermesa shook his head, still unable to believe what had happened. "It's all too much . . ."

"No . . . not enough. You've earned the rewards over, and you'll continue earning them. Don't think you can rest easy now. Your world will only continue to get more complicated . . . and, regrettably, more dangerous."

One thing concerned Nermesa. "General, my duties . . . I can't forgo them—"

"I've spoken with your father. He will guide your holdings, if you like. I also have others who can be of service. While he fully believes you deserve this and more for undoing this plot, the king doesn't wish to lose your good arm . . . nor the keen head that you've managed to keep."

"I followed your advice."

Pallantides chuckled. "Would that more had. Would that more had." The general suddenly stiffened. His gaze went over Nermesa's shoulder. "Your majesty . . ."

It was not Conan, but rather Queen Zenobia who stood there. She smiled at both men, then, to the general, said, "If you can relieve this fine man from duty, I have one more task for him."

"Of course, your majesty."

Zenobia guided Bolontes' son through the throng. For the queen, the way parted as if by magic.

"I trust you are pleased," she murmured.

"Why did no one tell me? Why pretend it was for General Pallantides?"

With a throaty laugh, Zenobia explained, "Because I thought it would be more fun, and the king thought it a fine jest for a worthy man. Now, no more about that. The king's granted you what he feels right and it is *my* turn to gift you with something. I did make a promise, after all!"

"A promise, your majesty?"

"And here she is now." With a sweeping gesture, the queen indicated a figure ahead.

Telaria.

As Nermesa fought for what to say, Queen Zenobia reached forward and brought her lady-in-waiting toward them. When Telaria and the knight stood face-to-face, Zenobia discreetly withdrew.

"Nermesa . . ." Telaria's face was flushed. She was clad in a gown almost as sumptuous as that of the queen. To Bolontes' son, she had never looked more beautiful. "Nermesa . . . thank you for Orena."

Under Aquilonian law, all of a traitor's holdings were seized by the throne. However, Nermesa had spoken up for Telaria's sister, insisting that she had been Antonus' innocent dupe. He had pleaded for her to be allowed to keep the baron's holdings. King Conan had finally agreed to leave all those that had once been part of House Lenaro to Orena, plus a small portion of Sibelio's, including the ruined estate. It had been a generous compromise, although, at the time, Nermesa had not known that *he* would be the recipient of the rest.

"I did what I thought correct," he finally responded.

"She'll come to understand that." Despite what he had tried to do for her, Orena had refused to speak with him personally. A sympathetic Morannus had indicated that she felt shamed and blamed not only her late husband but Nermesa as well. He had, after all, exposed Antonus' traitorous activities. That Nermesa would now inherit some of the baron's wealth and property would not sit well with her, either.

Nermesa could only hope that Telaria would eventually convince her sister to make peace with him, but he did not hold out much hope.

"I tried to come to you, Telaria. But when matters didn't keep me away, you were unavailable."

This brought a slight smile from her. Glancing in the direction of the queen, the lady-in-waiting replied, "My mistress's doing. I discovered the honor that they planned for you, and she swore me to secrecy. The only way that I could make certain I wouldn't say anything was to stay away."

The smile faded, and her eyes grew moist. "You have no idea how terrible that was!"

"I have some." And with that, he kissed her.

She met his lips with equal vigor. For a time, the noise and the crowd faded away. There were only the two of them.

When they finally separated, it was to find both of them at a loss for what to say next. It was Telaria who finally, weakly, said, "So . . . you're a baron now . . ."

Nermesa smiled. With those simple words, she had helped him figure out just how to reply.

"Yes . . . and I'll need a baroness . . . if you'll have me."

Her reply was another kiss whose meaning could not be mistaken.

Nermesa savored the bliss of the moment, aware even then that the future would be, as Pallantides had put it, very, very complicated. Antonus would surely not be the last to plot against the throne, and as one of those entrusted with the king's life, Nermesa would represent an obstacle that they would seek to remove. Still, he understood more about the workings of court intrigue now and had learned that the smiling face and outstretched hand could hide the most dire of villains. When next danger reared its ugly head, Nermesa was determined to be ready for it, whether it came from without or within.

He held Telaria tighter, and she responded in turn. For this one night, though, he could dare let down his guard. He could dare let others keep watch while he savored life.

He could simply be a man . . . and not what King Conan had called him in his Cimmerian tongue.

Caru Morgar uth Njarl . . . the Sword of the Lion.

"I don't even know how long I'll be in town."

The sadness in Abigail's voice urged Hudson to ask her who abandoned her as a kid. He hated that his heart twisted at the thought of her leaving. He needed to change the subject. "There's been something bothering me since this morning. You had another one of your extreme reactions around another De La Rosa."

He moved closer to her. Close enough to see every detail of her reaction when he asked his question. "Do you have some sort of connection with the family I should know about?"

He tended to follow his instincts, and they were screaming that she was hiding something important.

She blinked, like a deer frozen in the middle of the road, staring into the headlights. She was panicking. She was deciding how much of the truth to tell him, if any.

Leaning a hip on the table, he crossed his arms and stared at her, stone-faced. Letting her know without a word that he was not letting this go until he had the truth.

A seventh-generation Texan, **Jolene Navarro** fills her life with family, faith and life's beautiful messiness. She knows that as much as the world changes, people stay the same: vow-keepers and heartbreakers. Jolene married a vow-keeper who shows her holding hands never gets old. When not writing, Jolene teaches art to teens and hangs out with her own four almost-grown kids. Find Jolene on Facebook or her blog, jolenenavarrowriter.com.

Books by Jolene Navarro

Love Inspired

Cowboys of Diamondback Ranch

Lone Star Legacy

Visit the Author Profile page at LoveInspired.com for more titles.

Claiming Her
Texas Family

Jolene Navarro

LOVE INSPIRED

INSPIRATIONAL ROMANCE

LOVE INSPIRED®
INSPIRATIONAL ROMANCE

Recycling programs
for this product may
not exist in your area.

ISBN-13: 978-1-335-58593-6

Claiming Her Texas Family

Love Inspired
22 Adelaide St. West, 41st Floor
Toronto, Ontario M5H 4E3, Canada
www.LoveInspired.com

Printed in U.S.A.

Let your conversation be without covetousness;
and be content with such things as ye have:
for he hath said, I will never leave thee,
nor forsake thee. So that we may boldly say,
The Lord is my helper, and I will not fear
what man shall do unto me.
—*Hebrews* 13:5–6

Last year Texas went through an unprecedented winter storm. For the first time in recorded history, every county was covered in ice and snow. Without the resources and equipment to handle that type of natural disaster, first responders and many others stepped up and did what they could for their community. The needs varied, but they all demonstrated the resilience of the human spirit with bravery and hope. Thank you.

Chapter One

A strong January wind pushed at Abigail Dixon's Mercedes as she crossed the bridge from the mainland. Releasing a breath, she turned onto Shoreline Drive. The small coastal town of Port Del Mar, Texas, was a quaint mix of brightly painted stores, weatherworn buildings and blurry childhood memories.

She checked her rearview mirror, then narrowed her eyes. Was that the same black truck she saw this morning crossing into Texas? She had never seen a vehicle like it before. It was some sort of mix between a Jeep and a monster truck. Her fingers involuntarily tightened around the steering wheel. Had a reporter already found her?

Shaking her head, she forced herself to relax. Being paranoid was new for her, but after the last year, maybe it wasn't so ridiculous.

Back in Cincinnati, she hadn't been able to leave her house due to reporters shouting questions and all the angry people just spewing hatred. They believed she was as guilty as her ex-husband. Their outrage was justified, but she had been just as betrayed by Brady.

Tamping down those thoughts, she focused on the new life she was going to build. Brady was her past, but God used everything for good. Her ex-husband had given her the most precious gift. Her nine-month-old daughter.

It was a true blessing that Paloma was too young to remember any of the drama her father had brought into their lives. This would be a clean start—and Abigail would be smarter this time.

Paloma whimpered from the back seat.

"Shh, baby girl. It's going to be okay." Her sweet daughter was here because of her three-year marriage to Brady. She would do it all again for Paloma.

"I promise you will always have me, no matter what."

The goal now was to find a safe place where she could regroup and have time to lay out a plan for their future. Maybe she would take her real family's name again. Abigail released a sigh.

De La Rosa was a pretty name, and they

had a ranch here on the coast of Texas. The Diamondback Ranch was her last chance to reconnect with that family. But what if they still didn't want her?

She checked the rearview mirror again. The suspicious vehicle was still there. Could someone be tracking her down? The family ranch was miles past the middle of nowhere. If she kept driving, she would be alone with Paloma, completely vulnerable.

And after all these years Abigail didn't know anything about her family, other than that they owned the Diamondback Ranch and she was the youngest. Or she *had* been when they'd sent her to live with her great-aunt after her mother's death. Was her father remarried with new kids?

Forcing air into her lungs, she let it out slowly and relaxed each tense muscle, one by one.

Her aunt had taken her as soon as her mother's funeral was over. She had just turned nine.

To say that her mother's aunt had hated her father would be a huge understatement. The older woman had used every opportunity to make sure Abigail understood she was better off without the horrid family that had ruined her poor mother.

She'd waited for her family to come for her.

But her father hadn't even called, not once. No letters either. She had hung on to hope, but none of them had reached out to her. Would he turn his back on her and his granddaughter?

But if she didn't go to the ranch, where would she go? She was technically homeless.

Blinking back the tears burning her eyes, she gripped the steering wheel. She didn't have time to cry or feel sorry for herself. Now that she was here, her insides heaved at the thought of facing her family.

Slowing down, she scanned the four lanes of the main street. The beach wall was on her left. There were parallel parking spots with meters. But since that car was still on her tail, those were too visible.

On her right was a line of stores and restaurants. It being off-season, there weren't many people. Abigail parked in the middle of the strip, between two big trucks jacked up for off-roading. The tires were taller than her car. They gave her an odd sense of protection.

In front of her was Hope Family Health and Birthing Center that had the look of an inviting cottage, smack in the middle of businesses. At the far end, a bakery stood out with bold colors. A pink sign trimmed in turquoise and orange read Dulce Panadería in elegant script.

Clusters of ornate tables with empty chairs

under a pergola, begged people to slow down and sit. Bright paper banners and café lights trimmed the area. It looked like a cupcake waiting for a party.

The store had more of a fun Mexican fiesta vibe than a Texas coastal one. A tiny woman was sweeping the little patio area. She frowned at the sky, then disappeared back into the shop.

Abigail glanced around. Should she go in? This indecisiveness had to stop. Rolling her shoulders, she took a deep breath and held it before releasing it slowly. Finally, ready, she swung open the car door and was hit by a cold bitter January wind.

Dark glasses and hat in place, Abigail pushed herself out of the car.

Another gust of freezing air took her breath and seared her throat. Texas should not be this cold. It wasn't in her memories—but then again, she had been so young when they'd sent her away. Bundling her baby in her warm blanket, she lifted her out of her car seat and pulled her close. Diaper bag swung over her shoulder and head high, she moved away from her little red Mercedes. It was the only thing she still owned. Everything else was gone. She needed to trade it in for something more practical and less obvious.

A cup of coffee would help her figure out

her next move. Gathering information about her family before knocking on their door would probably be the smart thing to do. And could also save her a lot of heartache.

She glanced around as though she were a spy hiding from dangerous people. The problem was that she obviously didn't know how to spot the people who were bad for her. Brady Dixon was strong evidence on that front. What about her family? According to her aunt, they were the worst of the worst.

The wasps that had nested in her gut released their stingers. Reaching for the bottle of antacids in her purse, she nearly cried to find it was empty. She was too young to be living on this stuff.

The town was small. The woman in the shop had to know the De La Rosa family. Hopefully she would be able to give her some information. Showing up at the ranch without knowing what she was walking into wasn't much better than hiding in Cincinnati.

It's not like they would recognize her anyway. Her nickname had been Chunky Monkey, but the chunk had disappeared, along with the talkative hyper kid begging for attention.

At nine, her hair had been dark, almost black, and it had hung past her waist in a long braid. Her mother would plait it every morning. Now it was in a sharp, angled cut and platinum blond.

The right side of her hair fell over her eye. With a shaking hand, she tried to tuck it behind her ear. Brady had liked it this way. She should let it grow out and maybe go back to being a brunette.

A sweet, happy bell chimed when she opened the door to the *panadería*. Sugar, cinnamon and baked apples mixed with the rich aroma of coffee made her stomach rumble.

Fresh flowers of every color were gathered in a variety of vintage bottles and there were small shelves scattered around with all sorts of books. It had all the feel of coming home. The way she imagined it, anyway.

The woman who had been outside slipped in behind the counter. "Buenos días! Welcome to Port Del Mar. What can I get for you this morning?"

People this happy made her suspicious. Abigail took her time studying the handwritten menu on the chalkboard. In her peripheral vision, she glimpsed the black monster truck she had seen several times pulling into the spot in front of the bakery. Her lungs stopped.

A tall brick wall of a man stepped out of the vehicle and scanned both directions of the sidewalk before moving forward—into the bakery.

He *was* following her. Was there an emergency exit?

"Are you okay, *mija*?" the woman leaned across the counter and rested her hand on Abigail's arm.

"I think that man is following me. I know it sounds—"

"Josefina!" The woman called over her shoulder. "We might have trouble."

"Oh no. I'm probably overreacting." Abigail waved her hand to waylay the shopkeeper. She was being ridiculous and now was making a scene. "I'm sorry. Please don't—"

"It's okay. If you feel threatened, we'll work it out." She looked at the slightly taller woman who had emerged from the back. They were so much alike they could be twins. "Call Bridges."

The woman glanced back at Abigail. "I'm Margarita. This is my sister Josefina Espinoza, and she's calling our brother. He's a cop," she whispered as she leaned forward.

The two women came out from behind the counter to stand in front of her. Josefina was casually holding the largest cast-iron skillet Abigail had ever seen.

The sisters were shorter than her, but each stood at one of her shoulders, defending her. They didn't know anything about her. It would be so much easier if she just slipped out the back. And go where? Her life was at a dead end.

The bell chimed. It didn't sound happy this time. A gust of cold air pushed its way into the warm, cozy shop.

The man stopped. He was an intimidating male well over six feet tall. Abigail wasn't sure they could do much damage if he decided to try something. Even three against one the odds were not good.

Both women relaxed. Margarita gave her arm a squeeze, then stepped forward with a big grin on her face. "Sheriff Menchaca, what are you doing running around scaring innocent women?"

Sheriff? He was the sheriff? That should have reassured her, but a new dread slithered through her veins. She was not at all confident that she would fare any better with the law. Her experience with them hadn't been all that great.

He quirked one eyebrow and removed his cowboy hat. "Innocent women have nothing to fear from me. I just stopped in for my coffee and empanada." He ran his hands through dark, thick hair that had been pressed down by the hat. His gaze shifted to Abigail. "Is there a problem?"

Lifting her chin to make eye contact, she stifled a gasp. His eyes. One was a liquid gold and the other an indigo blue. Aware she was staring; she shifted her gaze down. Twisting her head to look at her daughter, she watched him from the corner of her vision.

His gaze darted between the three women, stopping on Abigail.

If he learned about the crimes in Cincinnati, would he think she was guilty like everyone else? Maybe they had called ahead and warned him. Did they do that? Was that the reason he was following her?

Those gold-blue eyes were staring at her. After a moment of silence, he lowered his chin, but his gaze stayed steady. Unsettled, she shifted her daughter to her other shoulder.

"I…um." She cleared her throat. "Were you following me?"

"Should I be?" Was that amusement pulling at the corner of his lips? The dark skin and lines at his eyes made it clear that this man didn't sit behind a desk often.

Abigail looked behind her. There was a back exit not far from where they stood.

"Sheriff, let me get your favorite coffee." Margarita nudged him to the counter, but he didn't budge.

The two sisters had jumped in because she

was scared. No one had ever stood up for her just because she had asked. Maybe this could be a place she could stay, for a few days at least. She was so tired of running.

"Ma'am?" His gaze narrowed as he studied her as if she was a problem to be solved. "Are you all right?"

His voice invited a person to sit and listen to his every word. But she couldn't afford to be lured in by another charming man.

With one step he was just a few feet from her. "Is there someone I can call for you?"

The sheriff reached out and gently touched her arm. Out of instinct, she jerked away from his touch. The diaper bag slipped off her shoulder and fell to the floor.

Abigail had been in the car for over twenty hours. She probably looked questionable, and he had every right to be concerned. But not a single word could be formed in her brain. She was exhausted.

"I'm sorry. I didn't mean to startle you." Without being asked, he dropped to his haunches in front of her and gathered her spilled items.

Well, that was a novelty. She didn't know any man who would take the blame and apologize so quickly. She wasn't even sure it was his fault.

Straightening, he took a step back and held out her bag.

Not sure what to do, she just stared at the bag.

"Ma'am. Let me call someone for you," he offered again.

Tears burned her eyes. There was no one to call. She was so alone. Without meeting his gaze, she took the bag.

Brady had been all charming at first, too. He said he would take care of her. The first year, he'd made her feel like she was the most important person in his world, but then they got married and it all changed. She had become just one more of his prized treasures to show off.

That part of her life was over. This was her chance to reinvent herself one more time. She gently bounced Paloma. Now the stakes were higher. It wasn't just her life that was impacted.

Take a deep breath. Smile. Be normal. She couldn't afford to lose control. *Pull it together.*

"What's wrong?" The sheriff had kept his distance during her little mental freak-out, but he didn't look happy about it.

With everything in place, she looked back up. "Thank you, but I'm good."

His eyes squinted as he tilted his head and scrutinized her face, doubt all over his handsome features.

Her daughter whimpered, then cried out. Abigail's heart rate spiked. Something was wrong. Had her run to Texas just put her daughter in more danger?

Chapter Two

Warning flags of every color were flying in Hudson's head. The young mother looked like she was about to bolt. Instead of following Margarita's subtle suggestion, he held his hand up to calm her. That was a rookie move.

He quickly adjusted and turned his palms up, indicating that he had nothing to hide. Then he relaxed his mouth into a smile so that he would be less intimidating. He was very aware that his size could be scary to someone that didn't know him. It was an asset in his role as sheriff, but it didn't help in situations like this.

Margarita's lips curved in a friendly expression, but her eyes were telling him to move on. Josefina stood shoulder to shoulder with the woman. He had to grin at their protectiveness.

He towered over them, but they didn't seem to notice. Somehow, they managed to look down on him. That was a true talent, since he was six foot three. The Espinoza sisters might be small, but they were fierce. No wonder their brother was one of his best deputies.

Narrowing his eyes, Hudson studied the newcomer again. She was small in a frail type of way. Like she hadn't eaten well in a long time. Her nearly black eyes were too big for her face, and her golden brown skin had an unnatural pallor. And there was nothing natural about the slick blond hair that followed the line of her jaw.

Something was off. She was either scared or guilty. He couldn't figure out which one. Yet.

His first instinct was to jump in and protect her, but that had gotten him in trouble before. The thing that threatened to tear at his heart was the way she was holding her baby girl close, protecting her child. Yeah, that got him every time. A mother protecting her child was his weakness.

He couldn't afford any weaknesses. Port Del Mar was a new beginning for him and his daughter.

This woman was a walking contradiction, and he didn't like unknowns. Only six months ago, the people of Port Del Mar had voted him in as their new sheriff without really knowing him. They had taken the word of his military buddy, Xavier De La Rosa, that he'd be a good fit for the community. But they were watching his every move and still deciding if their trust had been placed in the right hands.

So, there was a good chance he was over-reacting. Yet firsthand experience had taught him that an innocent-looking woman could cause the most damage when he let his guard down.

"Do you have a name?" he asked, making sure to keep his voice soft and as nonthreatening as possible.

Her eyes went wide for a second, then she blinked. If he hadn't been staring, he might have missed the flash of panic.

Her daughter cried out, and her head jerked down. With a soothing sound, she bounced the baby. He assumed the baby was a girl, as she was bundled in pink.

"Come on, Sheriff." Margarita coaxed him to the counter again. "I'll make you the perfect coffee for this cold morning."

This time he allowed the oldest Espinoza to lead him away. "Did she give you a name before you went to battle for her?" he asked.

Margarita ignored him as she fixed his coffee. Leaning against the counter on one elbow, he turned to keep his gaze on the stranger.

They made eye contact, and this time she

didn't look away. Instead, she lifted her chin. The corner of his mouth pulled up.

Her eyes narrowed. That only made his grin spread wider. It was all he could do not to chuckle outright at her fierceness. But those large, obsidian irises couldn't totally hide the fear.

He took a step forward, then stopped.

She *was* just a job. He had taken an oath to protect this sleepy beachside town, and his gut told him there was a problem here. Either she was trouble, or the trouble was following her here.

He popped his jaw and rolled his shoulders he tried to relax the muscles. The more obstacles she put up, the harder it was for him to let this go. But logically he knew she was probably just as she appeared. A single mother traveling with a baby. Maybe there had been a bad breakup and she needed a new start.

But why a Texas beach town so small most folks didn't know it was here? If the unfamiliar car in front of the clinic was hers, she was from Ohio. Driving a thousand miles alone with a baby couldn't be easy. Was she running from someone?

He narrowed his eyes at her again. His gut told him she was hiding something. And he wasn't leaving until he had a few simple questions answered.

It didn't take a PhD to know why he was driven to save women. Even the ones that didn't need or want saving.

The bell chimed, warning of someone new entering the bakery. A tall male walked into the store as if he belonged there. It was Margarita and Josefina's brother, his deputy, Bridges Espinoza.

Hudson nodded. "Espinoza."

"Bridges!" the sisters said in cheerful unison.

"What took you so long?" Margarita chided.

Josefina jumped in on top of her. "We could have been in real trouble by now."

Bridges scanned the area. "You called the sheriff too?" His gaze came back to Hudson. "What's going on?"

He shrugged, not sure why they had called their brother. "I just came in for coffee and an empanada."

Margarita interrupted. "We thought we might need backup, but we handled it." She pushed Hudson's coffee across the counter and went back to make one for her brother.

"This poor woman and her baby were all alone and scared." Josefina pulled out a chair and motioned the still unnamed woman to sit. "She thought someone was stalking her, but it turned out to be the sheriff. It took you a long time to get here." She gave her brother a disapproving frown.

"I'm not always in town. Which is why in a real emergency you need to call 911." He turned to Hudson. "I was out on the De La Rosa ranch."

"Any problem I should be aware of?" he asked.

"Naw. Belle called me just to have a look. There were some downed fences, evidence of trespassing. Probably bored teens. Not much to do this time of year. More important question—" Bridges tipped his coffee to him "—why were you stalking this woman?" True confusion coated his words.

A tinge of irritation tweaked at him that the De La Rosas had not called him. Even though they had elected him as sheriff, the town still acted as if they didn't completely trust him with local issues. "I wasn't. I was just following my normal routine." Why was he explaining himself?

Coffee in hand, Hudson turned from his deputy and approached the woman again. "Can I sit?" He indicated a chair opposite her.

She nodded and shifted the now fussy baby to her other shoulder.

Hudson glanced at the chalkboard wall. He turned to the woman. "Can I get you something?"

At first, she shook her head, lips pulled tight. Then she sighed and bounced the baby. "Josefina is bringing me a hot chocolate, but thank you." With her free hand, she dug into the bag on her shoulder and pulled out a half-full bottle. Offering it to her daughter, she kept her head down.

"You thought I was stalking you? Is there a reason you suspect someone was following you?" Slowly, he studied her features.

"I'm sure I was overreacting."

"Can you at least give me your name? I can help if you need it."

Her gaze shot up to his as if in surprise. "I'm... Abigail Dixon." She looked as if that should mean something. "And I appreciate the offer, but I'll be fine."

He let her name roll around in his head. It didn't click with anyone he knew. "Abigail Dixon. If that's your car with the Ohio plates, you're far from home. Traveling alone with a baby can't be easy."

She released a deep sigh. "No." Her face tightened, and she turned away from him to look at her baby. Her petite shoulders rose and fell with several deep breaths.

Something was wrong. The trouble might be *her* after all. Shifting back in his chair, he looked over her shoulder. "Sure, I can't help you?"

Her mouth pursed as her gaze darted around the room. With another heavy sigh, she finally made eye contact with him. "I might as well tell you. It wouldn't take much for you to find out anyway. I left Ohio to get away from the trouble my ex-husband caused. I want a clean start, so I'd appreciate it if that information stayed between you and me."

There was another long pause. Worst-case scenarios ricocheted through his brain.

"You might have heard of him. My ex-husband," she mumbled, hiding her gaze.

Not being able to hear, he was forced to lean closer. The soft scent of cucumbers and wildflowers teased him. Her eyes met his, and they both stilled, neither willing to break the contact. "What is it? Is it something I can help with?" Yeah, he was an idiot.

She shook her head. "Brady Dixon. He's in a federal prison for grand theft and fraud."

Whoa. The back of the chair stopped him from falling. Brady Dixon had stolen millions of dollars of innocent people's money. It had been big enough to make the national news. Hudson blinked. That man had lived the high life by taking other people's dreams. He had seen images of yachts, private planes and luxury cars. She had been living that lifestyle? The red Mercedes parked out front made more sense now. The most luxurious thing in his little coastal town was the De La Rosas' fake pirate ship.

"You were married to Brady Dixon?"

Pressing her full lips into a firm line, she shifted her gaze to the side. "I was. Not anymore."

His gut twisted. Why was she here?

She cleared her throat and tried to soothe her fussy baby. "Since you're the sheriff, you might need to know in case reporters show up or something. But as I said, I would prefer to keep it between us." She leaned forward as much as the baby would allow. "I came to Port Del Mar hoping to disappear and start anew. Yes, I was married to Brady Dixon. Yes, he is now in federal prison for grand larceny and fraud. Yes, I was investigated too, but I was never charged."

He considered her for a moment, studying the details of her features. Was there something he was missing? "I've heard of the case." Starting over somewhere new he could understand. "Why all the way down here? How did you even find Port Del Mar?"

"Would you believe me if I told you I threw

a dart at a map of the US?" The baby fussed again.

"A dart brought you to Port Del Mar, Texas? Population 378 during the off-season? I'm not sure we would even be on the map."

Swaying her baby, she shrugged.

He couldn't help but ask because she was in his town. As the sheriff, he had a right to know. "You really had no clue where he was getting his money from?"

She sighed, then lifted her chin. "No one in Ohio believed it either. But as much as they tried to dig up something on me, there was nothing to find. I'll admit I was completely guilty of being naive. It was easier than asking questions." She exhaled. "I thought that to be a good wife I needed to trust and support my husband in all matters. I learned my lesson. Look, I'm not here to cause any trouble. I promise you won't even know I'm in town."

He doubted that very much. Scanning her face, he tried to figure out the real color of her hair. With her skin tone, she had to be a brunette.

Other than the sleek platinum hairstyle, she looked like a single mom barely making it, no showy jewelry or fancy clothes. Her Mercedes was high-end, but nothing over-the-top. She was a paradox, and he didn't like it.

He knew firsthand that the best con artists didn't look the part. They slipped into a man's life all vulnerable and needy. Like his ex-wife. At their best, no one saw them coming until it was too late. "You just happened on the smallest coastal town in Texas?" Something wasn't adding up, but that was probably his suspicious nature.

"Someone somewhere mentioned it. It sounded like the perfect place to disappear. A place I could rebuild my faith and my life." She laughed. "Yeah, that didn't sound as cheesy in my head."

"There's no family that you can go to?" Hudson asked.

"No family that I can trust or that wants anything to do with me." With a tight smile, she brought her gaze back to his.

She was alone with no one in her corner she could trust. A cold sweat broke out over his body. The desire to offer her help again rammed against his chest. *Good job, Hudson, step right back into that trap you just untangled yourself and your daughter from.*

He had to keep it professional. Refer her to resources that could help her. The women's shelter was just on the other side of the bridge. As he moved to pull out his card to write the information on, Josefina brought Abigail the largest mug of hot chocolate he'd ever seen. Then she sat a plate of warm pumpkin empanadas straight out of the oven onto their table.

Balancing the bottle and holding her daughter with one arm, she twisted to get her wallet out of her diaper bag. "How much?"

"My treat," he said, before she could get into her bag. The silence fell between them again.

"Nope. I've got you both covered." Josefina smiled.

Picking up one of the warm pastries, Hudson grinned at Josefina with total boyish delight. "This is why I will never leave this town."

He slid the plate over to Abigail. "These are the best things I've ever eaten." Now he was avoiding giving her a way out of his town. Wow. He really *did* have a problem.

Biting into the warm pastry, he closed his eyes as the sweet spicy flavor flooded his mouth. So many good textures at one time.

He took another slow bite before he went back to doing his job. "How long do you plan to stay in Port Del Mar? Do you have a place?" He kept his tone casual. He was asking for professional reasons. He was.

"I'm not sure. The plan was to get here, then figure it out. Maybe find a job?" She was avoiding eye contact again and not eating.

"You traveled thousands of miles without a

plan?" Was she serious? The thought of that made his skin itch.

Josefina rubbed her hands together. "You're looking for a place to stay and a job? God must have brought you to our door today!"

"How so?" Abigail asked.

"Well, last weekend, I moved out of the apartment above the *panadería*," the woman explained. "We don't want to rent it to just anyone with it being attached to our shop. And we were just talking about getting some part-time help and maybe offering the apartment as a perk of the job. No early-morning commutes. It's hard to find a place to live here in Port Del Mar—and finding help is just as difficult."

"Really?" Abigail's full lips spread wide and became even more beautiful.

Hudson shook his head. What was Josefina *thinking*? Shouldn't he suggest they perform a background check or something before offering a complete stranger a place to live and a job?

He had heard that the Espinozas' tendency to take in strays was legendary, but this was a bit much. Even for them. "Maybe you should ask each other some questions first. Or at least get some references."

Josefina put her hand on her hip. "Sheriff, you've been stalking her and now interrogating her. Is there a reason I shouldn't rent out the upstairs apartment to her, or give her a job?"

Eyes wide, Abigail stared at him. Pleading. But for what? To keep her secret, or to give the go-ahead to Josefina.

Her moving in above the bakery wouldn't be the worst thing to happen. At least here he could keep an eye on her. Make sure she was on the up-and-up. It was better for his peace of mind to know where she was.

He lifted his hands. "I have nothing negative to say."

With a wide smile, Josefina nodded her head. "Good. I'll show you the apartment, then. It's a small two-bedroom, one bath. It has basic furnishings. Nothing fancy."

"It sounds better than my car."

"Oh, sweetheart." Josefina crossed her hands over her chest. "I'm thankful God merged our paths." She patted Abigail's arm. "It's okay. I've been in your shoes with a baby in my arms, and my family had my back. You're not alone. Let me get the keys, and I think we have a basic lease contract in the filing cabinet. I'll be right back."

The baby arched her back and whimpered.

Concerned, Hudson reached to touch the little forehead. "Is she all right?" Great, now he wanted to take care of her baby.

"I'm not sure. She's usually not fussy, but with all the traveling, maybe she's off. She hasn't had any real floor time to just play. For the last twenty-four hours, she's either been in her carrier or I've been holding her."

The bell rang, and a large group of teens filled the front of the shop. Not a few minutes went by before the door chimed again.

A young woman with three children came in. She smiled at them. "Sheriff." Her gaze moved to Abigail before she hurried the children to the counter. The little shop was filling up. The small crowd were all staring at them with different levels of curiosity.

Abigail leaned closer to him. "Is it just me, or is everyone staring and talking about us? I was getting that at times in Cincinnati, but why here?"

Her daughter let out a cry. She seemed to be done with being held.

Then the poor bell received no breaks for the next five minutes. Abigail sank deeper into her chair as each person came into the bakery. The space became even smaller as people made a point to glance their way. Some were subtle and polite; others not so much.

"Welcome to being the new person in town. And you're talking to the sheriff." He grinned.

"All sorts of stories are being spun as we sit here."

"So, if I want to stay under the radar, I should avoid being seen eating with you?"

He didn't like the sound of that, but before he could reply, Josefina returned.

Now she wore a rare frown on her face. "We just got slammed with call-in orders and the counter is busy, so I need to stay and help Margarita. Sheriff, you could show her the apartment. It would give you a chance to interview her and ask any questions you deem important, since you're obviously worried." She laid a ring with two keys on the table between them. With a wink, she turned and went back to the kitchen.

He narrowed his eyes to the retreating Espinoza. The town folk had not been subtle in their attempts to pair him up. They couldn't fathom that a single dad enjoyed being single. It wasn't even lunchtime, and he had a bad feeling that the matchmakers had a new target.

"You don't have to take me up." Abigail went back to bouncing the baby.

Standing, he grabbed the keys. "Your daughter needs a place to rest. You do too."

Abigail turned her baby around, trying a new position. The little one reached for him. He put his hand up, and her chubby fingers wrapped around one of his. "What's her name?"

"Paloma LeRae."

"Hey there, little dove." The biggest eyes blinked up at him. They danced between a gray and a dark green. "She's beautiful. How old is she?"

"You speak Spanish."

"*Sí.*" He grinned at the baby. "My *abuela* was named Paloma. It's a beautiful name."

"Thank you. She's nine months old."

"My daughter just turned six last week."

"You have a daughter?"

He chuckled. "Why do you sound so surprised? I don't look like I'd have kids?"

"Kids?" Her eyes went wide.

"No." He laughed, and people looked. "Just one. Charlotte." He nodded to the back door. "Come on. I'll show you the apartment."

He would open the door for her then leave. There was no reason for him to hang out and spend more time with this woman. The nervous energy he'd picked up from her had to do with the drama she'd left behind in Ohio.

Nothing more.

Which meant there was no need to be personally involved with her to keep an eye out for trouble. If she stayed here at the bakery, she'd be in the middle of town. In plain sight. Word spread like wildfire around here, so if she crossed the line or made a move to take advantage of any one of his people, he'd be here to stop it.

Besides, she probably wouldn't be staying long, anyway. She was used to a much grander lifestyle than a small apartment over a family bakery could offer. He gave her one month, tops, before she became restless and wanted more.

She had a bit too much in common with his ex-wife. At first, they came across as helpless and lost. But it was just an act to get what they wanted. A life of ease and glamor. He was conned once. Not again.

The town would be better off without someone like her.

Who was he kidding? With that smile and baby in her arms, he was the one in danger. But she wouldn't be here long enough to cause true damage. He hoped.

Chapter Three

The diaper bag slipped again, pulling on Abigail's shoulder. She was so tired it was all she could do to keep from falling over herself. Hudson stepped up beside her.

"Let me help." He took the heavy bag and lightened her burden. It felt nice to have someone to lend a hand, but it also scared her. Why was he being so nice? He was married, right?

In her world, men made their own rules and took whatever they wanted. She glanced over at the two women who had defended her and now offered her safety. Without even knowing her.

Their generosity was beyond anything she had ever experienced. Could she trust them? It seemed too easy. Nothing in her life had ever been easy. Not since her mother died, anyway.

In her life, when something seemed too good to be real, it usually was.

"Mrs. Dixon?" Hudson stared at her with his startling eyes.

With an attempt at a smile, she nodded. The air in her lungs became too heavy, and words were impossible to form. She blinked and cleared her throat. "Please call me Abigail. I think I'm going to drop the Dixon."

"Abigail." His voice offered so much comfort. With his warm hand on her back and her daughter's bag on his shoulder, he guided her up the stairs. She stole a glance at his profile, then quickly forced herself to look ahead.

Maybe God had led her to Port Del Mar because of the Espinoza sisters. If this worked out, it would give her time to find out more about her old family before showing up on their doorstep.

Earlier, the deputy had mentioned the De La Rosa ranch. She had wanted to ask so many questions, but she didn't know how to do that without raising suspicion.

"If you don't want to stay here, I have information about a women's shelter across the bridge."

She stiffened at the top of the stairs. "I don't need a shelter. I can pay for a place to stay." Well, for a couple of months, at least.

Clearing his throat, he opened the door, then moved back to let her in. She didn't move.

He took another step back. "I didn't mean to upset you."

"I'm not upset." That might have been a little sharper than she'd intended. "I'm sure you have better things to do than escort strangers to apartment showings."

The corner of his mouth twitched as if he were fighting a grin. "In a small town like this, the job duties of a sheriff are pretty fluid." He waved to the open door. "Do you want me to stay out here?"

"Oh, no. I'm just..." *Being ridiculous.*

Head up, she walked through the door, then paused. It was so much more than Josefina had led her to believe. The spacious living room and open kitchen welcomed her. It was perfect.

The neutral walls and floor were a soothing background for the surprises of color in the artwork and pillows that were scattered around. To her right was a clean, modern kitchen, separated from the living room by a farmer's table. The ladder-back chairs were a mix of red, blue and yellow.

The living room was cozy with a light-colored sectional and pillows that matched the chairs. And she was pleased to see there was space on the floor for Paloma and her toys. In the corner was an L-shaped desk with ceiling-to-floor shelves next to it. It had a very delicate, feminine vibe. How did a place she had never even known existed feel so much like home?

"This is nice." He walked in behind her. "It's hard to find long-term rentals in town. If a house is empty, they can make more money renting it to tourists, and there are no apartment complexes. This is a find."

"Do you and your wife have a place in town?"

"Not married. A good friend of mine, the one who encouraged me to run for sheriff, has some properties. I was able to get one with an ocean view."

So, he wasn't married. There was no reason that should be a relief. But it was.

Her daughter squirmed and made a sad crying sound. "Paloma is so tired. I just…" She looked around. What did she want?

Maybe that was what she needed to figure out first. Was this the place?

Wandering around the space, avoiding the intense stare of the sheriff, she ran the tips of her fingers along the edge of the pretty desk. This was too nice. There was no way she could afford this by working part-time at a bakery. To be this close to her dreams and watch them slip away was hard. She couldn't cry, though, not in front of him.

"The bath and bedrooms are down this

hall." Hudson's voice startled her out of her thoughts. She nodded and went to investigate, even though this place would never be hers.

The bathroom had a large tub that was begging her to take a long, warm bubble bath, but more importantly would make it easy to bathe Paloma. Across the hall was a small room where a whimsical scene of rabbits playing under the moon was painted in soft colors.

"Josefina is a single mom who has a daughter a couple of years older than mine. This must have been her room. There shouldn't be a problem finding a crib for Paloma."

Tears burned, but she couldn't let them fall. She would have to go to the shelter after all, but this was the place where she wanted to live. The last door was the larger bedroom. It was so much bigger than she was expecting. The soft blue walls and white trim were a perfect setting for the large bed. It was stripped to the mattress, but Abigail could visualize a quilt and throw pillows.

The urge to dive in and cocoon herself pulled at every tired muscle in her body. There was no way she could afford this place. Needing a hand-out made her skin itch, but maybe they would let her crash here tonight. She turned to ask Hudson, but he was gone.

Had he left? Disappointment hit her much

harder than it should have. "Come on, baby girl. I have to tell Josefina that it's a no-go."

Stepping into the living room, she found Hudson leaning on the table, scrolling through his phone.

"Oh, I thought you'd gone." She resented the giddy feeling that bubbled up knowing that he had waited for her.

"Josefina said that you can stay here for now to get some rest. There are sheets in the hallway closet. She'll come up around three to go over the details with you."

He held up his phone. "She didn't have your number, but she wanted you to know that she called her mother." He gave her an apologetic look for some bizarre reason, followed by a tight-lipped smile. "Good news…that means that before the end of the day you will have everything you and Paloma need. And the bad news? If you think the two women downstairs are a force to be reckoned with, wait until you meet their mother. Wonderful woman, but she scares me."

Josefina's mother was coming. Even after all these years, Abigail still missed her mom. Her earliest memories were of her mother calling her Gabby Girl as she cuddled her and they read bedtime stories. Then, without warning, she was gone.

Abigail, or Gabby as they called her at the time, had come home from school and found her oldest brother already there, sitting on the edge of their mother's empty bed. He told her that their mom had gone to heaven. But that didn't make sense—they hadn't finished the story they'd been reading together.

Her mother would have never left without a goodbye kiss. She had always insisted on goodbye kisses every morning.

At nine years old, she couldn't wrap her head around the fact that her mother had vanished. Abigail had been so confused and lost. To this day she didn't understand what happened or what she had done to make her father and brothers so mad that they sent her away without a backward glance.

Just like her mother, they were suddenly out of her life. It had been the first of many lessons in not trusting people who claimed to love you.

She'd barely had time to say a proper goodbye to her mom at the funeral before her great-aunt had ripped her away from her home and family. The woman had hated everything about the De La Rosa family, and she made sure Gabby knew it. Gabby De La Rosa had been erased from existence, and her aunt had dubbed her Gabriella Castillo. It was her mother's maiden name, but it was still as uncomfortable as a pair of secondhand shoes.

"Abigail? Where'd you go?"

"I can't stay here." The air wouldn't circulate through her lungs. Why did it feel like she was losing her family all over again? "I can't imagine I'd be able to make enough working part-time at the bakery for something this nice. I'll have to find something else." Logic had to keep her emotions in check, even though her heart already loved this apartment, the bakery and the sisters.

Why did she get attached to anyone who showed her the simplest kindness? Was there something wrong with her?

Hopefully they would let her stay the night. She'd use the time wisely. Going to the sofa, she pulled out the bottle and tried to feed Paloma again. Her daughter wasn't eating.

"How did you think this was going to play out, when you arrived in a small town without any connections?" His voice was low and soft, not accusatory or insulting like Brady's when she did something impulsive.

She snorted. "That is a really good question. I was born in Texas, and with everything going on in Ohio, I just had to leave. I trust that God has a plan for me." Now he was going to think she had lost her mind.

"This is ranch country," she said after a long moment. "I always thought I would love working on a ranch. There's housing for the workers, right? I heard Deputy Bridges, their brother, say something about the De La Rosa ranch. Do you know anything about them? Would they be hiring?" There, that sounded logical. She was proud of herself for working her family naturally into the conversation.

"They're a smaller ranch, family-run. They do have cabins they've been known to rent out, but I haven't heard anything about them hiring," he replied. "They tend to hire seasonal day laborers. You'd be better off trying at one of the bigger spreads, like the Wimberly Cattle Company. They have ranch hands and house staff. Several of their employees live on the property." He cleared his throat. "And there are a few other ranches in the area. If you're interested, the Espinoza sisters would be your best connection. They know everyone."

She frowned. That wasn't any help. How could she learn more about her father, brothers and cousins? Maybe the sisters would be more willing to gossip.

Wind rattled the windows. The weather was getting worse. For now, she and Paloma needed a safe warm place to stay.

The idea of asking for charity didn't sit well

with her. Voices from the past bombarded her brain. *Useless, undeserving, worthless* and *charity case* were just a few of the words. They were lies, she had to remind herself. Not a single one was from God's truth, so she closed her eyes and rebuked them.

"There's still the shelter on the other side of the bridge." His voice brought her back to the room.

Would she be able to get the information she needed if she went there? It wasn't that far, but it felt like a whole different world. She could do that and still work at the bakery, maybe. With her daughter, it was going to be hard to find a normal job.

She wanted to stay here, in Port Del Mar. It was less than a day, but it already felt more like home than anywhere else she had ever been. Was it because she was close to her family? They were within her reach, but still so far away.

"I want to find a way to stay in Port Del Mar. I think God brought us here." Her heart tightened. Fighting the urge to ask for his help, she kept her gaze on her daughter. He was not her knight in a cowboy hat.

Hudson stood watching while Abigail spread out a blanket and placed her daughter in the middle. The baby cooed at her mother as she reached for a toy.

Keeping her gaze on the baby, she smiled. "This is what you needed, baby girl."

The image of mother and daughter tugged at his heart. He was intruding on a moment he had no business being witness to. Tearing his gaze away from the personal interaction, he studied the neat but vibrant apartment. He should leave. She didn't need him here, so there was absolutely no reason for him to stay.

"Something's wrong." She said it more to herself, but he moved closer. "I wish she could tell me what was going on with her."

Yeah. He wasn't going anywhere. This just became more than a job. He was such an idiot. The last time he tried to play hero to a damsel in distress, she had wrecked him.

He was smarter now. He wouldn't allow that to happen again. The little girl scrunched her face.

Using the back of her hand, Abigail touched the baby's cheeks. "Oh, you're warm. Is this why you've been so fussy?" She finally looked at him. "Could you hand me the backpack? I might have a thermometer in there."

He grabbed the bag off the table and handed it to her.

The little arm started shaking, then the infant went stiff. Her eyes were wide-open, but they didn't have any focus.

"Paloma!" She touched her daughter's face. It didn't look right. "Hudson! Something's wrong."

He rushed to them and kneeled at the side of the tiny body. He gently rolled her to her side. His hands looked so large on the small baby. "Has she had a seizure before?"

"A seizure? No." Abigail's voice was on the edge of panic. "What's happening? She was a little fussy before but fine."

He checked his watch.

"Shouldn't we call 911?" she asked.

"Not yet. We will if it gets closer to four or five minutes."

"*Four minutes?*" She might have screamed that at him. It already seemed like an eternity. Legs tucked under her, Abigail leaned over Paloma and touched her face. "It's okay, baby girl. It's going to be okay. Stay with me. Hudson? It has to be over ten minutes."

There was a pleading in her eyes he hated.

Paloma whimpered as her little body went slack. Abigail breath whooshed out. The seizure had stopped.

"One minute and two seconds." He ran his hand over the baby's forehead. "She feels a little warm, but not too bad." His eyes went to Abigail. "Do you have that thermometer?"

She dug in the backpack, then dumped it in frustration. "It's not here." Dropping the now empty bag, she picked up Paloma and held her close. "I'm so sorry."

Tears dropped on her daughter's cheek and made him feel as useless as snow skis in Texas.

She wiped her face, then her daughter's cheek. "I shouldn't have driven all the way in such a rush."

"It's not your fault. Babies are going to do what they do." He wanted to hold her the way she was holding her daughter. Shifting back, he put more space between them.

"But I drove straight from Cincinnati hardly stopping. She's been in a car for almost twenty hours." The strangled sighs were so sad coming from her. "I'm so sorry. I hate crying. It's a total waste of time."

"You have every right to cry." Hudson stood and held his hand out. "Let's get you off the floor."

Taking her soft hand in his, he lost his breath for a moment. Gritting his teeth against the shock, he shook it off. It wasn't her. Nope. He'd just gone so long without human touch, other than his daughter. He ground his back molars.

She allowed him to help her up, then they both stepped back, away from each other.

"Thank—" another silent sob stole her breath "—you."

"Let me hold her, and you can wash your face." Arms out, he waited for her to respond. "She's safe with me, I promise."

With hesitation, she handed over her daughter. After just staring at the baby in his arms for a few seconds, she finally went to the kitchen sink. He looked down and smiled at the sweet bundle in his arms.

"Your mamma didn't want to let you go." It seemed a lifetime ago when Charlotte was this little. He missed holding her like this. Paloma reached up and grabbed his lip. He leaned in closer and made a popping noise.

At the large white farm sink, Abigail splashed her face. After wiping it dry, she turned and stared at him. "She usually doesn't take to strangers."

"She's a good judge of character." He winked. Then he turned back to Paloma, his expression growing serious. "Knowing that your child is sick and that you can't fix it is the worst feeling in the world." He brought his gaze back to her. "Just a few doors down, there's a women and children's clinic. I think you parked in front of the door. You'll feel better if we get her checked out. I can call over and see if they can fit her in."

She chewed at her bottom lip and glanced to the side, then at her baby. "That would be great. Thank you."

It didn't sound as if accepting help was an easy thing for her to do.

"One warning." He tried to look stern. "Another Espinoza sister is in charge there. Teresa. She's a PA and specializes in women and children's health."

Her eyes went wide. "A cop, two bakers and a PA? How many are there?"

His grin went wide. "There are at least two, maybe three more. Not sure."

"Wow. That's a big family. I thought—" She cut herself off.

"You thought what?" He rocked the baby as her eyelids fluttered.

"Oh nothing. Family. That's a strange concept for me." She pulled down a glass from the cupboard and filled it with tap water.

He had assumed she would be the pure-water-in-a-fancy-bottle type. Would it be safe to stop expecting the worst from her? After taking a long drink, she came back to him. For a minute, she just stared at her daughter in his arms.

Oh no. Was she going to start crying again?

"Abigail. It's going to be okay. We'll take her next door and they'll examine her."

With a nod, she held out her hands for her daughter. "Her father has never held her."

There was nothing to say to that, so he gently transferred the baby back to her.

"Oh no! What's that?" she cried out in a broken whisper. "She has blood in her ear." Eyes wide and frantic, she stared at him. "Why would there be blood coming from her ear?"

"Charlotte did that once. It was an ear infection." He got his phone out. "I'll call as we walk to the clinic." Speaker on, he grabbed the bag, then opened the door for Abigail.

So much for keeping his distance.

Chapter Four

Abigail hugged Paloma closer to her chest. Hudson had a gentle hand on her shoulder, guiding her through the door of the clinic. He stayed right next to her as they approached the counter.

The clinic wasn't what she expected. It was warm and inviting. Curved wood inlays in the ceiling were repeated in the desk. Comfortable club chairs were spaced out to look more like a reading nook than a waiting room. Plants were placed in interesting locations.

A woman with silver curls piled on top of her head sat behind the counter. Looking up, she stopped her knitting and smiled at them.

"Sheriff. Resa said you'd be coming in with a sick baby." Her curious gaze darted between Abigail and Hudson.

"Hi, Barb. This is Abigail Dixon and her

daughter, Paloma. They just drove in from Ohio."

"Oh my. I drove by myself to Lubbock once to see my son. It was just horrible—and that was only nine hours. I said I'd never do that again. You must be worn-out…and the poor little one is sick." She lifted a clipboard with a pen tied to it. "You'll need to fill these forms out, but you can do it in the room."

Abigail shifted, intending to move Paloma to one arm so she could take the paperwork, but Hudson stepped forward and took it.

"Let me help. You have your arms full, and I'm sure you don't want to disrupt her."

Barb's perfectly shaped brow arched with unspoken questions. "Well, then, you can both come this way." She was all business as she escorted them down the hall. Except for the slight smirk. Abigail couldn't even imagine what that meant.

"The PA will be in to see you shortly." Barb closed the door behind her.

The exam room had an oversize watercolor painting of wildflowers on one wall. Posters illustrating the development of a baby's first year covered another.

Three miniature rosebushes grew in the bay window. In the corner was a cozy rocking chair. A neat stack of children's books and gardening magazines sat on a vintage side table. Next to the exam table was a wicker basket full of toys.

She and Paloma were alone with Hudson in a very small room. Not knowing what to do, Abigail just stood there. Her heart rate accelerated, and her skin felt too warm. She hadn't been this uncomfortable with him before.

With a nod of his chin, Hudson motioned to the rocking chair. "Sit. Relax. She'll be here soon. I'll help fill out the paperwork while you hold Paloma, then I'll leave."

She looked at the paperwork in his hands. In bold letters at the top, it asked: Name.

"Thank you." Averting her eyes, she sat in the rocker and forced her attention to Paloma. Her daughter's thick lashes lay against her soft cheeks.

Name. That should be a straightforward question. Everyone knew their own name, but she'd had three names in her life. The one she was born with, Gabby De La Rosa. The one her aunt gave her after her mother died, Gabriella Castillo, and the one her husband gave her, Abigail Dixon. None of them really felt like her, but at the same time they were all a piece of her.

She wasn't ready to deal with the family she didn't know, but she didn't want to be a Dixon anymore either. There needed to be as much distance between them and her ex-husband as possible.

"First one is easy. Name." He printed Paloma's name, then hers. "Abigail is short for anything?"

There was nothing easy about her name. She looked to the ceiling in a futile attempt to find answers.

"Abigail?"

She didn't have the time or energy to explain her whole messed-up life. "Gabriella. But I haven't used that in years."

"Next question. Phone number."

She pulled her cell out of her pocket. "It's new. I haven't memorized it yet."

He filled in her number. "Okay. Work phone. Not yet." He put a slash through it.

She sighed. Did she even count as a full person?

He pulled his mouth to the side, then looked at her. Sympathy shadowed his piercing gaze. "Home address?"

Her lungs tightened, and the ice that had been in her lungs now burned her throat. She didn't have a home address. What was she doing here in Texas? Her daughter was sick and needed stability. She had no idea how she was going to make this work.

Coming to Port Del Mar had only made things worse. She had failed her daughter. They were homeless.

"Abigail?" He had the voice of a professional talking someone off the ledge.

Blinking, she made sure her eyes were dry before she looked up at him, but then quickly dropped her gaze. "I don't have an address. Can we skip it?"

His jaw went hard. "Abigail. Look at me."

She did, and the blue one looked deeper as the gold iris burned. It took all the strength she had, but she managed to move her gaze to the roses in the window. Such a warm, homey touch. An image of her mother trimming a climbing rosebush filled her thoughts. Was it still there? Had someone taken care of it, or had they just let it die? Her mother had loved that rosebush.

"Abigail, you can put the apartment above the bakery, or there's the shelter across the bridge. I could call and see if they have room tonight."

She shook her head. "I want to stay close, so I guess for today it's the apartment. I hope I can stay the night at least." The rosebush didn't matter now. All of her attention went to the tiny person sleeping in her arms. It was her responsibility to make sure Paloma never felt lost and alone. "I don't know if I can afford it or what they're asking for the deposit."

"I'm sure they'll work something out until you're on your feet. Her birthday?"

"She was born on July 25." That one was easy. She took a deep breath.

"Next of kin?" Her eyes went wide, and when she jerked her face up to look at him, she found his gaze was on her. Concern, or maybe pity, filled those mesmerizing eyes.

And, just like that, it got worse. They wanted an emergency contact. Next of kin. All she had was a family that didn't want her. They didn't even know she was in town. She dropped her head and closed her eyes.

"I...um." Abigail's throat threatened to close. Her aunt was glad she was gone. Would her father even acknowledge her? Two brothers and cousins she grew up with had turned their backs on her. There wasn't anyone. "I don't think an ex-husband in prison counts, does it?"

Leaning on the exam table, Hudson sat the clipboard down. "Abigail."

"No. Leave it blank. I don't have anyone I would call or who would want to hear from me." A year ago, she hadn't thought life could get worse. And now here she sat with a sick child, relying on complete strangers. Yeah, she had been so wrong.

Lifting her chin, she dared him to feel sorry for her. She was a survivor. God had gotten her through darker days, and he would get her through this as well. If only she could make better choices.

There was no shift in his expression. As a lawman, he'd probably heard all sorts of sad tales. Silence stretched between them as they studied each other.

He spoke first. With a curt nod he picked up the paperwork. "I'll put myself down for now. You might also ask the Espinoza sisters. They're good people. You can trust them."

They might be wonderful people, but she didn't see herself trusting anyone. She just wanted to be strong enough to stand on her own and be independent. The only problem was that she had no idea how to make that happen.

"Insurance?" His voice hesitated for the first time. "Do you have medical insurance?" He cleared his throat. "The clinic will work with you if you don't."

"I do." She sighed. For the next few months, anyway. She hated being a charity case, but what else could she do for now? Anger burned in her gut at everything they had lost because of Brady's greed.

Why? So he could have an even bigger house,

fancier cars and wear only shoes with red soles. It was all to impress people that didn't matter.

She had never wanted any of that.

Her dreams had been of a cozy house with a little backyard and a park within walking distance. She wanted mornings and evenings at a family table filled with love. Building a family, not an empire, had been her dream.

"Abigail?"

"Sorry. It's in the bag."

"Let me take her, and you can get your card." Hudson lowered the diaper bag off his shoulder, then one big arm slipped under hers to lift Paloma up against his chest. Her daughter snuggled into his shirt and made sweet cooing noises. She was so tiny.

Before they went any farther down the list, a soft knock brought Abigail's head up. The door opened, and a woman obviously related to the Espinoza sisters peeked in with a huge smile.

Her shoulder-length hair was pulled back, and dark curls fell around her neck. "Hello. I'm PA Espinoza. Please call me Resa." She stepped into the room and gently closed the door behind her. "Oh, hello, Sheriff. I wasn't expecting you to be in here."

"Just assisting with the paperwork."

"He was helping with the questions. Or trying to, anyway. I haven't finished. There are some… I'm not sure—" She wasn't going to cry in front of this woman.

Taking the clipboard and placing it on top of the magazines, the PA gently patted Abigail's arm. The compassion on the woman's face had Abigail on the edge of tears again.

"It's okay. Being in a new place with a sick baby is very stressful. We'll fill out the forms together after I take a look at her."

Resa was taller than her sisters but had the same dark hair and eyes. Eyes filled with compassion, the same as those of the other two women. All her focus was on Paloma as she took her temperature. "It's 99.7. A little elevated but not bad. You two have quite the fan club. I hear you had an adventure on your first day in town."

"She's never been sick before. I shouldn't have taken her on a long road trip. I only stopped a couple of times."

"Place her on the table, and we'll have a look at this precious little girl." She patted the table, and Hudson gently eased her down on top of the strip of paper. Paloma opened her eyes and looked up at him with a smile. She reached for his lip before he could get far enough away. With a chuckle, he pried her fingers away.

Abigail stood next to him and stroked her baby's hair. "She's never sick."

"She's got a healthy grip." The PA smiled

at them, then moved to examine her. "On the phone, Hudson said she'd never had a seizure before? But you've been traveling?"

"That's correct." She glanced at him. His attention was fully on her daughter. He must be a good father. She wasn't sure she even believed there was such a thing. "Is it too cold and windy for her to be out? I drove in from Ohio. I didn't even know she had a fever. She never seemed hot or uncomfortable until I was in the bakery. Was it the long trip?"

"No, I don't think so."

"What caused the seizure?"

"Since this is her first, it will be hard to say what brought it on. She might not ever have another. But if she does, we can look at common factors. It looks as if she has an ear infection."

"Is that bad?"

Hudson's eyes lifted to hers. "Charlotte had them when she was little. She outgrew them." His voice was reassuring.

Resa nodded. "The ear infection will be easy to treat. We just have to stay on top of it. Since she didn't run a fever, you'll have to look for other clues that she isn't feeling well. If they become chronic then we'll discuss other treatments."

"Treatments? If she doesn't have a fever, how will I know she's sick?" Abigail listened to every suggestion and stamped it on her brain. She'd make a list as soon as she could. "I felt so helpless."

Resa laid a hand over hers. "First rule. Kids get sick. You can't blame yourself. Two. Take a deep breath and relax. Babies are very resilient. Plus, you have Margarita and Josefina. My sisters will be mothering you until you want to go into hiding."

"What do I do now?"

"I'm going to give you some medication to start today. The pediatrician is at the clinic on Wednesdays."

"What if something happens before then? That's two days away." Hudson was frowning at the woman as if she had insulted them.

She smiled. "If they need anything, I'm only a call away. They can always find me." She scooped up Paloma and handed her to Abigail. "Go ahead and relax in the rocking chair and we'll finish the paperwork. It's mostly medical history and release forms."

Once Abigail was settled in the rocking chair, Resa pulled up a round stool with wheels and sat in front of them, clipboard in hand.

Hudson moved to the door, then stood awkwardly for a minute. "You've got this. I'm going to head out now. But you have my number, so don't hesitate to call."

"Thank you so much for your help. I don't know what I would have done if I'd been alone."

"You would have been fine, but I'm glad I was there to lend a hand. See you at the bakery." He left, gently closing the door behind him.

There was no rational reason for her to feel so alone at the click of the doorknob.

Resa touched her arm, then winked. "Now, having the sheriff as your personal escort is a pretty nice small-town service. He's a good man, but a smidge closed off as far as personal relationships go."

Abigail wasn't sure how she was supposed to respond to that. Was she being warned off? The thought was funny. Should she tell the woman she was completely closed off to any sort of relationship too?

Flipping to the second page of the paperwork, Resa asked her a few health questions. Then she put it aside and gave her another gentle smile. "You know, the mammas of this town have been trying to set him up since the day he arrived." She twisted her mouth to the side. "They might have met their match in that one. He's proven stronger than their collective power."

It took a minute for Abigail to catch up. "I'm sure Sheriff Menchaca will do whatever he thinks is right. From the moment I came into town, everyone's been over-the-top nice. It's kind of scary. Am I in one of those psychological thriller movies where nothing is what it seems to be? I'm waiting for the monster to appear and wondering how I'm going to save my daughter. Should I run now, or is it already too late?"

Resa laughed. "Oh, it's too late. Welcome to Port Del Mar. Where the danger of being smothered by love and kindness is very real."

"Everyone has been so helpful. I just want to make sure I don't do anything to make Paloma worse. I've already dragged her across the country. How am I going to make sure she stays healthy?"

"Well, first of all, you are going to get some rest. And if you need help, you will ask for it." She winked as she handed her a white paper sack. "We have some samples of antibiotics and Tylenol that you can use."

"It's safe for a baby? She has never been sick before."

"It's made for infants. I'll give you directions to follow. If you have any questions or concerns, call me. Better yet, tell my sisters. They always manage to get a hold of me." She smiled. "I know it's scary. But you're not alone."

"Thank you so much." Abigail pressed her

lips together and stood, gently shifting Paloma to her shoulder.

"My sisters can be a bit overzealous when it comes to taking care of people, but they are an incredible resource. Once you become their mission, nothing is going to stop them from taking care of you."

"But I don't want to be someone's mission. I just want to stand on my own."

"I totally get that. But sometimes we need support to get there. It's okay to get some help to build up to those first steps after we've been knocked down."

Abigail's head was swimming. How had these people just entered her life? If they were all on the up-and-up, it had to be a God thing. Could she trust them? More to the point, could she afford *not* to trust them?

The PA stood. "Okay, we're done here for now. Go get some rest. You need it as much as your girl does."

Resa went down on her haunches in front of her so that she could make eye contact. "Should I call someone to walk you back? I could check to see if Sheriff Menchaca is still out front."

She stood. "No. No. I'm good. It's just been an incredibly long couple of days that don't seem to have an end, and my brain is fried.

Getting to the apartment and taking a nap sounds like the perfect remedy. Thank you for everything."

Resa opened the door. "*De nada*. It's my pleasure. Let Barb know you'll be coming on Wednesday."

Abigail stopped by the front counter to schedule a follow-up appointment, then stepped outside. For a second, her sight blurred and there was an odd floating sensation in her head.

Sheriff Hudson Menchaca was standing not far from the door. But he wasn't alone. A pretty brunette was nodding at whatever he was telling her.

He glanced over the woman's shoulder, and they made eye contact. He instantly smiled, then frowned. His forehead creased.

The woman turned to see what had grabbed his attention. She smiled too. Both of them walked toward her.

Out of habit, Abigail pulled back slightly, then stopped herself and stood straighter. Her head did the weird, swimming, upside-down thing.

"Abigail, this is our mayor, Selena De La Rosa. She—"

Abigail didn't hear another word. Her oldest brother, Xavier, had had a girlfriend named Selena. Was this the same one? He had given the girl their pet dog.

No one had even asked her. One morning he just took Luna for a walk and came back without her. The reason? Selena had needed the dog more than they did.

But that wasn't true. She had loved that dog, and she had decided she didn't like his girl-friend. Tears welled up at the memory.

She blinked and tried to focus. It was so long ago, not now. Shadowed worms darted across her vision. She couldn't clear her thoughts. This was someone who might be a part of her family.

"Abigail?" Hudson's strong voice cut through the fog.

She wanted to ask so many questions, but she wasn't ready for this.

He was next to her. His arms protecting Paloma. She wasn't able to utter one word. The world turned upside down and then went dark.

Chapter Five

Abigail's lids didn't want to open. It was as if someone had glued them shut. Squeezing, she tried again. *Paloma!* Where was her daughter? Ripping her lids apart, she shot up. Attempted to, anyway, but there was something in her way.

Her eyes finally cooperated. Not that it helped. It was too dark to see anything. Where was she? Her fingers dug into the soft, pillowy covering of the bed where she was cocooned.

As her sight adjusted, she took in the feminine room. There was an IV in her arm. Was she in the clinic?

Her heart rate jacked up, she twisted around, searching for her daughter.

Paloma was in a crib next to the bed. Ella's pulse finally settled. Blinking, she tried to clear her head. Port Del Mar. She was in the apartment above the bakery.

She glanced at the IV bag. What had happened and why was she here instead of the clinic?

There was no sunlight shining through the curtained window. How long had she been asleep?

Falling back, she groaned and closed her eyes. It all came back. She must've fainted in front of him and the woman who might be married to her brother. Selena De La Rosa. Right in the middle of Main Street. Could this be any more embarrassing? So much for lying low and not drawing any attention.

She glanced at the needle in her arm. It couldn't be too bad if they'd brought her to the apartment, right?

Sitting up, she swung her feet to the side of the bed where Paloma lay sleeping. Had Hudson brought her to the apartment? Carried her up the steps? Was he still here?

Deep breath. *Okay, God. We are in Port Del Mar. What happens now?*

She had come here on faith alone. She needed to keep her focus on Him and let her faith guide her. Obviously, there was no way she could do this alone right now. She had collapsed. God had brought her here. She needed to trust Him. There was no person that would take care of her like her God would.

Standing on weak legs, she made it to her

daughter. Paloma had flipped onto her back with her arms above her head and her face turned to the side. Her baby girl looked so tranquil as she slept, not a care in the world. She had no clue how precarious their situation was. As her mother, it was Abigail's job to keep it that way as long as possible.

Paloma was going to be raised by a strong woman who relied on God and no one else. If her father and the rest of the family turned out to be as bad as her aunt said, then she would move on.

"Hola." A voice from behind Abigail startled her. Turning she found an older woman with a thick silver braid and the warmest smile. She stood and crossed the room. "I'm Maria Espinoza. Go get back in bed. If you need to hold your daughter, I'll bring her to you. No more falling."

"You're Mrs. Espinoza. Their mother?" This tiny woman was the one everyone had warned her was bossier than Margarita and Josefina?

The older woman laughed with a beauty that took Abigail's breath. The woman was mesmerizing, radiating pure joy. "*Sí.* That would be me. Did they tell you to run? My children have no respect for me." The wide smile said she didn't believe what she'd just said. "Do you want your baby? To be safe, you should sit while holding her. I can bring her to you."

Reluctant to go back to the bed but still feeling light-headed, Abigail did as she was told. "No. She needs her sleep. She looks so peaceful. Why am I here?"

"My daughters agreed with me this would be a better place for us to care for you than in the clinic. Your baby is feeling much better. She took a full bottle and ate some squash from my garden. Josefina steamed and pureed it. With her tummy full and the medicine Resa gave you, she is on the road to being strong and healthy. I had an extra crib no one was using, and the sheriff was kind enough to set it up. That was very nice of him, *sí*?"

"Yes. He's been very kind. So has your family." She looked up at the line attached to her arm. "Why the IV bag?"

"You were dehydrated. It was a blessing for you to fall in front of the clinic and that Sheriff Menchaca was there to help. When was the last time you ate?"

She frowned. It hadn't been that long, had it? "I don't know. Maybe an empanada." Had she eaten it?

Tsking, Maria came over to the bed and fluffed Abigail's pillows. "Everyone is very worried about you. Let me bring you some *caldo*. It's on the stove. Soup is good when you haven't eaten in a while."

"I'll go with you and sit at the table. This bed is too beautiful to eat on." She removed the needle from her arm. The bag was almost empty, anyway.

"Let me help you." The mother of all the Espinoza siblings —and seemingly the heart of the community—put her arm around Abigail's waist. The woman barely reached her shoulder, but Abigail had no doubt she was strong enough to get them both to where they were going.

When they entered the living area, Josefina and Margarita turned to them with smiles. "You look rested. Now you're ready to eat."

Settled at the table, Abigail felt her stomach rumble. The aroma coming from the stove was mouthwatering.

Maria set a glass of water in front of her. "Drink."

She drank. A large bowl of the savory soup sat on the table, next to a stack of tortillas. Before Abigail could dig in, the door opened.

The sheriff, who had seen her at her worst, stepped into the room. He carried several bags the color of a bright sunny day. Each was overflowing with groceries. He froze when he saw her.

"Uh… Sorry, I should have knocked."

"Ya, ya." Maria waved her hand in the air.

"Come in. Put this here. Oh, you've brought your special helper with you."

A little girl of about six came up behind him with two small bags. "Hi, Ms. E. Look how strong I am." She lifted the canvas tote. With a show of being very impressed, Maria took the bags from her.

"Hi. I'm Charlotte. My dad is the sheriff, and he let me help bring these bags of food in for you. Are you the lady that fainted?"

With a big yellow bow in her dark hair the little girl's smile radiated from her eyes. Standing, Abigail went to help, but Maria waved her off.

"Hello, Charlotte. And yes, unfortunately, I am the lady that fainted."

"Her name is Mrs. Dixon," Hudson gently told his daughter.

"Oh no. Please call me Abigail. I'm just Abigail."

"Where's your baby?" The little girl was now whispering. "I love babies, but Daddy told me I had to be quiet because she doesn't feel good."

"Charlotte, they're tired and don't need visitors."

Josefina and Margarita were emptying the bags Hudson had put on the counter. "We are about to leave ourselves."

Eggs, milk, bread and a wide variety of fresh

vegetables kept coming out of the totes. "Oh, I can't take all this food."

"Nonsense." Maria waved her off. "You are helping me too. My garden is too big and my chickens are too happy. I have more than I could possibly use. So, *thank you.*" She turned to the man that towered over her. "Sheriff, have you eaten?"

"Yes," Hudson mumbled, but his daughter contradicted him.

"No. We had a snack, but he said we'd pick up something on the way home." She stood on her toes to look up at the stove and sniffed. "That smells so good."

Abigail bit back a laugh as Hudson closed his eyes and sighed.

"We really should go." He glanced at her, then back to Maria.

The older woman shook her head. "Stay. We are scheduled to help organize and distribute supplies for the food bank tonight. It would be great if you were here to eat with her." She leaned closer to him. "I would worry a lot less if I knew you were here for a bit. Just long enough for everyone to eat."

Maria straightened and smiled at Abigail as if no one else had heard what she'd told the sheriff. "So, sit. I'll make you and Charlotte a bowl before we leave."

Hudson's eyes shifted to Abigail. "I um... I still have the playpen to bring up."

Maria shooed him away toward the table. "You can get that after you eat." She gestured to his daughter while making her way to the stove. "Charlotte, will you take the bowls to the table, please?"

"Yes, ma'am." The child bounced as she held her hands out. "Thank you. You make the best dinners." Guilt clouded her eyes as she turned to her dad with the first bowl. "You make good dinners too, Daddy. But Ms. Maria's have something extra."

Abigail spoke without filtering her thoughts. "It's a mother's love. It's the best ingredient." After the words were out, she lowered her head in embarrassment. She had just insulted him. Great.

"I don't think my mother ever made me dinner." Charlotte's gaze went to the ceiling as if she were trying to remember, but she didn't seem sad. "Did she, Daddy?"

"No. She didn't." With three bowls on the table, Charlotte scooted a chair in close to him. "Well, you make the best macaroni and cheese and grilled cheese. That's my favorite. And broccoli with cheese." She looked at Abigail, her bright eyes full of pure joy and innocence. "I love cheese, and Daddy does all those the best." Her eyes went wide and she wiggled in her chair.

"Daddy, I need to—" her eyes darted around the room "—I need to visit the little girls' room."

He pointed the way to the hall. "Don't forget to wash your hands. If you need help, let me know."

"I'm a big girl. I know how to wash my hands. Germs are bad."

Maria added a freshly heated tortilla to the basket on the table. "Sheriff, you are not sitting yet." She was not taking no for an answer. Apparently, there were no limits to who was bossed around.

Abigail smiled at him and pointed to the empty chair. "Might as well join me. She's not letting you leave without eating."

"Smart woman." Turning off the stovetop, Maria took off the apron she was wearing. "Come on, girls, it's time for us to leave."

"My mother doesn't offer to leave people alone very often. Better take advantage and run." Josefina put up the last of the dishes she had been washing and picked up her purse. "I'm kidding about my mother. Sort of."

"No, she's not." Margarita's mouth was in a flat line. "My mother believes it's her responsibility to take care of everyone that enters her realm."

"Then I guess y'all come by it honestly," Abigail blurted out. Hudson laughed.

"What? *Us?*" the sisters said at the same time, then groaned.

"I hate it when we do that." Josefina glared at her older sister, who just laughed. "Really, you might need to be very stern with her. She drove our older brother to Oklahoma to get away from her mothering."

Maria glared at her daughters. "He came back."

"Because he was shot!" Margarita sighed and tossed a bag over her shoulder.

"Oh no. Is he okay?" Abigail asked.

"He's fine now." Josefina was by the door now. "You met him. He's one of the sheriff's deputies. But really, our mother doesn't know when to stop."

Margarita continued the story without missing a beat. "He ended up moving out of the house and into the middle of the De La Rosa ranch with three gates to keep her out." A spark of mischief in her eyes, she hugged her mother. "We'll be downstairs loading the boxes. Mother, if you're not down in ten minutes, we will leave without you." They went out the door.

"My daughters always threaten, but they never follow through. I'm sorry if I get a little overbearing. I just need to make sure everyone is safe."

"It's okay. It's been a long time since anyone has mothered me. I appreciate it." Abigail tucked her head and stared at the food in front of her. Why had she said that? Her mouth was running all over the road without any attention to warning signs.

Which meant that she was already too comfortable with these wonderful people and was not guarding her emotions. Not good.

The chair next to her scraped the floor, and the older woman's warm hand reached for hers. "Oh, *mija,* I'm so sorry. How old were you when you lost your mother?"

Should she lie? Change the subject? But she couldn't. Her mother had loved her so much, and no one ever really wanted to hear about her. "Nine."

Maria's fingers briefly tightened around her hand. "My children lost their father at such a young age, too. That kind of tragedy shapes a person. Do you have brothers or sisters? Was your father there for you?"

Not knowing what to say, she looked out the window. "There wasn't anyone. I went to live with an older aunt."

"Oh, *mija.* I'm sorry. I don't know what I would have done without my family. This must be why God brought you to us." Her other hand came up, and she lowered her voice. "That also must be why you and the sheriff have connected so quickly. He understands loss and tragedy too. He grew up without his mother. A senseless shooting." She gripped Abigail's arm and then Hudson's, tears in her eyes. "But you both have us now. And you have God." Standing, she wiped her face. Her voice was so strong and filled with confidence. Abigail really wanted to believe her.

Hudson stiffened and looked away. He didn't say anything, but he didn't look happy about his own life being talked about. How old had he been when he'd lost his mom?

"Thank you," Abigail managed to whisper. "Your kindness means so much to me."

Maria stood. "Okay, time for me to go. Thank you for staying, Sheriff. It eases my nervous heart."

"I don't believe there is anything nervous about you, Mrs. Espinoza. But thank you for this excellent dinner. I'll make sure everything is secure before we leave for the night."

Abigail said goodbye to Maria as well but couldn't take her gaze off the man sitting across from her. He had become stiff, looking at everything but her. He was not happy at being forced to have dinner with her or was it the mention of his mother?

Charlotte bounced into the room and scooted into her chair. "I heard the baby moving around."

"Charlotte Menchaca, did you really?" Hudson lowered his chin, then he looked at Abigail for the first time since they had talked about their mothers. "She will do just about anything to be around babies. She is a little obsessed."

"No, Daddy. I promise. I came right back here." She turned her big eyes to Abigail. "Will you go get her? I do love babies. I want a little sister—or even a brother—but Daddy says I can't have everything I want."

"Give us all a chance to finish our dinner." He handed his daughter a tortilla, then offered Abigail one before taking a second one for himself. "We'll check on the baby when we're done. She isn't fussing."

"Maybe I should go check on her." Abigail looked to the hallway. He was right that Paloma wasn't crying out for her, but what if something was wrong?

Hudson grunted—or maybe it was a chuckle. Was he laughing at her? She stopped the backward motion of the chair. "What?"

"Maria was right. You need a keeper."

That caused her spine to stiffen. "I do not."

She kept her voice low and steady. Sheriff Menchaca would *not* get a rise out of her.

With a glint in his eyes, he leaned over his bowl. The left corner of his mouth quirked up. "You haven't taken two bites of your dinner and you're all ready to run. That baby is sound asleep." He eased back and tore off a piece of his tortilla. "This is the best *caldo* you are ever going to eat. Sit back and enjoy. You can't take care of Paloma if you're too weak to pick her up. We'll get your baby girl as soon as the bowl is empty."

Her skin heated. She was probably turning red. What she hated the most was that he was right. Closing her eyes, she said a little prayer for her pride to take a back seat. When she opened them, she kept her focus on the warm soup in front of her and gave thanks.

Charlotte was chatting about her day in school and asking Abigail a ton of questions about Paloma and why she came to Port Del Mar. Abigail wasn't able to keep track of the rapid-fire questions, but she enjoyed the little girl's chatter.

"How much longer will Paloma sleep? I love babies, but since I don't have a mom, Daddy says I can't have a little brother or sister." Her words were a little muffled since she also had food in her mouth. "Either would be nice, but

I think a sister would be nicer. Does Paloma have a dad?"

"Charlotte." Hudson's voice was the epitome of patience. "You can't eat and talk at the same time. And Mrs. Dixon can't eat if she is answering your questions."

"Oh! And Mrs. E. said you need to eat." With a big sigh, his daughter smiled at her, then tore off a chunk of tortilla and scooped up a piece of meat, just like her dad was doing.

Did her father eat dinner with the family? She remembered helping her mom and cousin Belle in the kitchen, but it was fuzzy. Closing her eyes, she thought of the family table, but she imagined them all grown-up. Her father would hug her, thrilled she had finally returned. He would explain how they had tried to get her back, but her aunt blocked them.

She relaxed back in her chair. They would be so happy to have her home, and she would help them make dinner. They would ask her about her life and tell her everything she had missed.

But her aunt had made sure she knew that was all just wishful thinking. Her family didn't want her. Only her mother had loved her, and she was gone.

"Abigail?" The concerned voice was low and soothing.

Blinking, she opened her lids and found Hudson and Charlotte staring at her. Smiling, she shook her head. "Sorry. Got lost in my thoughts." Thoughts that would not help her build a new life. She lifted her spoon and made a show of eating.

"I have a joke," Charlotte announced. "Knock, knock."

Hudson gave her a side-eye, but his mouth was quirked at the corner. "Who's there?"

"Booooo," she whispered.

He leaned closer. "Boo, who?"

Her small hand reached up and touched his cheek. "Don't cry. I'm here to help."

Chuckling, he leaned back, pretending he had never heard the joke before. "That's funny. Now eat or I'll cry for real."

Abigail sighed. This was what it was like to have a family. To sit at the table after a long day and enjoy each other's company. To tell silly jokes and smile. To hear about the events and people that passed through their lives. But this wasn't real either. The sheriff had been coerced into having dinner with her.

Wishes and dreams of family dinners had no place in reality—and the real world was where she had to raise her daughter.

Chapter Six

Hudson narrowed his eyes to force his attention on Mayor De La Rosa's words. His mind kept wanting to stare at the clinic door. Abigail had been in Port Del Mar for three days, and now she and Paloma were seeing the doctor.

He had made a conscious effort to stay away after they'd had dinner together at Maria's. To be fair, it had been an intense day—but still, he should not be this preoccupied with her. It was like his brain had reverted to junior high and all he could think about was the girl who had caught his fancy.

He was too old and experienced not to have better control of his thoughts.

"Sheriff Menchaca?" Selena De La Rosa, the mayor of this sleepy little town, tilted her head to gain eye contact. "Is there something going on at the clinic I should know about? You're very distracted."

With a forced smile, he shook his head. But before he could ask her to repeat her question, the door opened.

Abigail was in a long red coat, the sharp line of her blond hair peeking out from under a black beanie. She covered Paloma in the blanket before stepping out onto the sidewalk. His lame heart twisted in a strange joy.

No, he wasn't happy to see her. It was his job to make sure she didn't bring trouble into his territory. The people of Port Del Mar had elected him to protect them after all.

Her history and reasons for being here were shady at best. He didn't like unsolved puzzles. That was it. She was a riddle that needed an answer. An answer he believed.

She scanned the street, and then her gaze found his. He was on the sidewalk between her and the bakery. Her chin darted down, and she adjusted the blanket around Paloma.

Why was she just standing here? His inspection of her didn't go unnoticed. For a moment, she lifted her head and stared back at him. Her shoulders rose as she took a deep breath, then, with a straightened spine, she walked forward. The word *magnificent* echoed through his head. He bit down hard on his back molars.

"Oh, I see. There were rumors that you were taken with our new visitor and her baby. It's good to see her out and about. She looks better than she did the other day." The mayor turned to him and studied his face with a smirk. "I didn't believe it. But I've seen it with my own eyes. You're smitten."

"No. Her daughter had a seizure the first day." He shrugged and made sure to look at the mayor. "Abigail had pushed herself too far. But there are also some issues with her past, and I don't like what that could mean for our citizens. For the most part, they are hardworking, honest people, and I don't want anyone taking advantage of them."

Selena's mouth pressed into a hard line, obviously suppressing another laugh. Her gaze cut to the woman and child he was working hard to ignore. "Yes," she said with sarcastic sternness, "I can see the threat she poses."

"The most damage is done when people let down their guard, trusting that they're safe."

She leaned closer, her eyes wide. "Tell me more about the horrible mayhem this single mom and baby can wreak on our town."

Shoving his hands in his pockets, he resisted the urge to defend himself again. "I thought you were worried about the bored teens causing havoc in the area. We should go back to the station and talk with a few of the local deputies, get some ideas."

Selena pulled her lips between her teeth, obviously trying to suppress laughter at his expense. She nodded. "I agree this is important. But we should schedule a meeting and get all the right parties involved. Maybe your time would be better spent investigating the atrocities Mrs. Dixon and her little baby could bring down on the innocent people of Port Del Mar? To protect us all, you could escort her to the apartment above the bakery. As a bonus, bring back some of those pumpkin empanadas. Then we'll talk." The sly smile was emboldened with a wink. From the mayor.

She had never given him that particular expression before. He rolled his eyes to the sky. Not her too.

Turning to the woman who had been lurking in his mind without permission, he noticed that Abigail looked stronger but still stressed. Was something still wrong with Paloma?

Selena was talking. It was probably something he should be listening to, but he couldn't keep his gaze from Abigail and Paloma. Did the baby have another seizure? There was a good chance Abigail wasn't getting enough sleep or food. Was she eating?

To derail his chaotic thoughts, he turned

to stare at the ocean waves. They were high today. The wind was chilly as it came off the water. The cold stung his skin.

Selena stepped forward as Abigail approached, her hand out. "Hello. I would love to give you another welcome to Port Del Mar. I hope you are both feeling better."

His good manners forced him to stop staring at the ocean and greet Abigail. "Hi. It's good to see you. Abigail, you met the mayor of our sleepy beach town the first day you were here. Mayor Selena De La Rosa, this is Abigail and Paloma Dixson. Fresh from Cincinnati."

Abigail's smile became forced. "Mayor De la Rosa?"

"No, just Selena. Our town is way too small for the title of mayor to really mean anything. I basically just get to do all the stuff no one else wants to do. Our sheriff here is the real deal. He keeps the town moving along without any troubles."

Abigail's gaze darted between them. "I wasn't expecting to see you outside the clinic today." She bit the corner of her mouth and looked away, as if regretting her words.

"I saw Mayor De La Rosa here and needed to update her on some issues. I forgot today was Paloma's follow-up appointment at the clinic." *Okay, that was bad.* He had never been a liar. He hated liars. His head was all messed up, and over a woman. He knew better.

Abigail blinked and stared at Selena. "De La Rosa? Like the ranch?"

"Ye-es." Hesitation stretched the word into two syllables. "It's officially called the Diamondback Ranch. You've heard of it? It's a small operation."

Pulling her baby closer, Abigail fussed with the blanket, not making any eye contact. "On the first day, someone mentioned it."

Now she was looking extremely uncomfortable. Out of an instinct to protect, Hudson stepped closer. "Yeah. Bridges came into the bakery and was talking about some kids causing problems. Probably the same ones that vandalized the dock. Abigail had asked about working on a ranch."

Nodding, she kept her gaze focused on her baby. "I thought that would be fun, and I'd heard that people lived on the ranch where they worked. I needed a place to live." She pulled her bottom lip between her teeth, then looked up at Selena. "Is it your ranch? Do you live there?"

"No. My husband's family owns the ranch. He's the oldest, but we live in town. His cousin and he run several of the local businesses. Are you still looking for work? He would be able to hook you up. But rumor has it that you're working for the Espinozas' bakery. Or will be soon."

"Yes. They've been great." Her bright eyes now stared at the mayor with a new intensity. "So, his father runs the ranch? Are there many siblings and cousins? Working with family must be nice."

Hudson narrowed his eyes. What was she up to? Earlier she had asked about working on the Diamondback Ranch, now she wanted to know the family tree? "You still looking for work on a ranch? I thought you were going to take the job at the bakery and live in the apartment above the shop. Is that not working out?" He crossed his arms and leaned back on his monster Jeep.

"I, uh—"

Selena gave him a side-eye, then smiled at Abigail. "If you're still looking for work on a ranch, you can talk to Belle. She is my husband's cousin and pretty much runs the daily operations out there. But Xavier—that's my husband—does have a restaurant and a gift shop on the pier. He and his cousin have a fleet of commercial boats for sightseeing and fishing. Right now, things are slow, but by spring break it will be a whole different story."

"Belle? She runs the ranch?" Her expression

shifted, and Hudson couldn't read it. Something was up.

"Yeah. She's been in charge of the Diamondback since Xavier's father passed away a couple of years ago. Xavier was out of the country at the time."

Abigail's eyes went wide. "He's…" Her head dropped. "He died? I'm so sorry." The words were mumbled.

Selena took a step forward and put her hand on Abigail's arm. "Are you okay?"

Lifting her eyes, she nodded. The biggest, fakest smile he had ever seen was spread wide across her face. "I'm sorry to hear about your father-in-law. Um. It's cold and I need to get Paloma inside."

"Oh yeah. Sorry, I've kept you out here so long. It was nice meeting you. If there is anything I can do to help…" Selena was already talking to Abigail's back.

"Welcome to Port Del Mar," she said to herself before turning to Hudson. "What happened? That turned weird really fast, right? Or am I being too sensitive?"

"She's had an extremely hard time of it lately, and she feels guilty that her daughter got sick. She probably just realized she should get her inside. But I'll follow up and make sure everything is okay."

"I don't know." She looked after the red coat swinging around Abigail's knees. "I see what you mean by something being off." Turning back to him, she grinned. "I'll trust you to find out anything that needs to be found out. And about the mischief and vandalism in town, let's call in our community teen task force for an emergency meeting tomorrow, and we can give this new problem a solid study before it gets out of hand."

They shared a smile. "I'll be there." The committee of town busy bodies loved the important sounding title to their group.

"You might want to go check on your girl. I'll see you later."

"She's not my girl or anything else. Just part of my job."

"Uh-huh. You keep telling yourself that."

"As I mentioned before, she has some issues she's running from, which means they might be following. My number one priority is to protect this community."

She laughed. "I never doubted that, but I don't think it's the community you're worried about with the way you were watching that door. Relax, Sheriff. It's okay…you have every right to a personal life. But be careful. No one knows anything about her."

"It's not personal." He sighed. He didn't have

the time or attention to give to a life outside of his daughter or his job right now. But he did need to find out why Abigail was acting so strangely.

He thought back to their conversation about the De La Rosas. Why was she asking so many questions about them? They were a hardworking family, and they didn't need any more trouble delivered to their door. No matter how pretty the package was.

Her father was dead.

The world blurred around her, and she headed in the direction of the *panadería*. What was wrong with her knees? They were going numb. She put her free hand on the door and tried to open it, but she wasn't strong enough.

Desperation clawed at her heart. She needed to process what was happening. Of all the possible scenarios, it had never occurred to her that the giant of a man she remembered as her father would be dead.

Stumbling into the homey bakery, she reached out to brace herself on the wall. She scanned the area for a safe place to sit. It was hard to focus, but if she stayed on her feet any longer, she'd be sick. A few people lingered, but thankfully the morning rush was over.

Margarita came over and pulled her into a chair.

"Thank you," she managed to say. As much as she wanted to protest, she wasn't sure she would be able to get Paloma and herself up the stairs without collapsing.

My father is gone forever. He will never be able to explain why he abandoned me.

How could he be dead? Her brothers or cousins hadn't bothered to reach out and tell her? Memories of Belle doing her hair and helping her pick out clothes to pack flooded her mind. Belle ran the ranch now. Had they planned to send her away? She just needed a moment to get her legs back under her, then she'd go upstairs. Her brothers Xavier and Damian were in town. What about Elijah? He'd been with Belle when they gave her to their great-aunt. Had they all wanted to get rid of her?

The last few days had been great. The Espinozas had reassured her that she could take the time she needed to make sure Paloma was healthy and strong, then they would talk about the apartment and job...

"Abigail!" Margarita exclaimed from across the little table. The oldest sister grabbed her upper arm. "What's wrong, *mija*? Is it Paloma?"

"No." Her baby girl had just gotten a good report from the doctor, but Abigail didn't want to talk to anyone right now. She had come to Port Del Mar hoping to find family and friends; she hadn't wanted to be alone any longer. Now all she wanted was to be invisible.

"Why do you look as if you've lost your best friend? Did the doctor tell you something bad?"

"I'm fine. Paloma is great. We won't know what caused the seizure and she might not ever have one again. For now, we're healthy and safe. Now that I know she's fine, I think everything has finally caught up with me. I just need a bit of time to myself. You and your family have been so generous, and I don't know why." She squeezed her eyes shut, but it didn't stop the tears. "I'll never be able to repay you."

"Oh, *mija*. We all need help every now and then. We're God's hands and heart. We're happy to help you. Mom has brought over a highchair she had at the house. I have a bag of baby clothes and a few other things donated by the church. Do you want us to bring them later?"

She wiped her face with the back of her hand. How had she missed the big colorful bag on the floor between them? "Sorry. I'm a total mess. That's fine."

"No apologies. I'll find someone to help get the stuff out of my car, then I'll leave you alone. We can talk later. Do you need help getting up the stairs?"

"No. I'm—"

"I'll take the bag and Paloma." The deep voice from behind was like a jolt to her heart. What she didn't know was whether it was a lifesaving shock or a warning of danger.

"Come on. Let's get you upstairs." He gathered the bag from the floor and looped it over his shoulder, then took Paloma from her and tucked the baby into the crook of his arm. She looked so natural there.

Without saying another word, he held out his free hand to help her up, then headed to the back door.

The bag was so big but he made carrying it and Paloma look so easy. That's what fathers did, right? They carried the burdens when life got too heavy.

Part of the blanket had slipped down, and Paloma's tiny hand grabbed at his lips. He grinned and made faces at her.

In her head, Abigail had created an imaginary father holding his granddaughter for the first time and falling in love with her, unable to resist her charms.

But her father was gone. Dead. She'd never get to see him, be held in a big bear hug or hear his voice. See him with Paloma. Not ever.

Hudson paused at the back door and waited for her. The few customers that were in the bakery stared with open curiosity. She couldn't think about them right now. The upstairs apartment offered her sanctuary. If she could get behind the door, then she could safely fall apart again. Would life ever get easier?

Head high and gut pulled in tight, she followed Hudson and her daughter. She hadn't had a father in a long time; this news shouldn't change anything for her. She blinked as her eyes started to burn.

Paloma was healthy and happy. That's what mattered most, not the death of a man she barely remembered. It was just the end of a dream, one of many she'd had over the years. Dreams came and went. It was time to get a new and better one.

God had her. He was her true Father, the One that had her in His arms and would never let her go, even when she turned from Him. With a nod to herself, she climbed the steps.

Hudson struggled with the door a bit, but finally opened it and went inside. Stepping into the apartment, Abigail felt a new calmness wash over her. She didn't need the family that threw her away. The Espinozas could become her family if they'd have her. Maybe God had brought her to Port Del Mar, not for the father that abandoned her, but for these wonderful people who had truly reached out and helped a stranger for no other reason than being genuinely nice.

Kneeling, Hudson eased Paloma into the little playpen and waved a floppy pony at her. Giggling, she reached for her favorite toy and hugged it close. A little drool slipped down her chin as she chewed on the front leg.

He twisted so he could see Abigail over his shoulder. "Looks like someone's teething." He stood, then turned fully to her. "What's going on? Was it the appointment? Did the doctor give you bad news?" His expression was grim as he straightened. Was being with her the worst thing he had to do today? Or maybe, like her, he was tired. As a single dad and sheriff, the responsibilities had to be never-ending.

"It looks as if she had a strong reaction to an ear infection. And as I told the PA during the first visit, since she didn't run a fever, I didn't even know she was sick. So her body kind of did a shut-down thing. Everyone must think I'm a horrible mother. Maybe I am."

He studied her for a moment, a piercing stare. The urge to squirm tightened her muscles, but she held still. He finally moved his gaze and looked down at her daughter. "I would face a hundred hungry bobcats over my daughter being sick ever again. It's hard."

She nodded. Was he going to interrogate her now? "Thank you for helping us up the stairs. I'm still a little tired."

With a serious nod, he moved past her. He was leaving. She swatted the disappointment away. This was good. Him leaving was good.

But he didn't go to the door. Instead, he went to her refrigerator and pulled out one of the dishes Mrs. Espinoza had left. Taking off the cover and putting a paper towel over it, he popped it into the microwave. Then he put a couple of tortillas on the cast-iron skillet.

"You need to eat."

"I'm good." Why were they always trying to feed her? Crossing her arms over her chest, she tried to think of a reason to turn him down. Her stomach rumbled. *Great timing.*

A corner of his mouth quirked up, but he was polite enough not to make a comment about the noise her tummy made.

"The way you ended the conversation with Mayor De La Rosa was weird. Something happened. What was said that changed your mood so drastically?"

Heat climbed her neck, and it was hard to focus. "I don't know what you're talking about."

They stared at each other in silence. Making sure her breathing stayed steady, Abigail lifted her chin as if she didn't have anything to hide. She didn't. Her father was none of the sheriff's business.

The beeping of the timer pulled his gaze from her. With his back to her, she allowed her shoulders to fall. She was a horrible liar. Could she tell him? How well did he know the De La Rosa family?

He placed the bowl on the table and went back for the tortillas. "Sit and have a bite to eat." One more trip and he had the plate loaded with shredded lettuce, onions, lime, chilis and radishes.

She blinked at the table. No one, since her mother, had made a meal just for her—or even toasted bread. Now she had the Espinozas and Hudson cooking for her every time she turned around. "Why are you feeding me?"

He sighed and sat at the table. "Like I said, you need nourishment. And Maria told me she had her pozole up here. So, I'm making sure you eat, which means I get to eat it too." Spooning a good helping of the chicken pozole into both of their bowls, he topped his with everything but the onions.

She sat across the table and watched him.

The food smelled so good, but she wasn't hungry. Hadn't been for a while now.

He lifted his spoon to her before taking a bite.

Why was he doing this? She didn't understand his motivation. There had to be a reason he was being so nice to her. If nothing else, this was easier than thinking about her father being gone forever.

He pushed the garnishes toward her. "I promise you are about to have the best pozole this side of the border."

Finally acquiescing, she swished her spoon in the soup.

"How about you tell me what happened outside with Mayor De La Rosa."

She shook her head and took a bite. He was right—it was delicious. "I don't know. It's been too much, and it all hit me. I guess knowing Paloma was okay just let everything else hit me at once. Please tell the mayor I'm so sorry if I acted weird."

"Don't worry about her. She and Xavier, her husband, have triplets. I'm sure she understands being overwhelmed as a parent."

"*Triplets?* Wow. How old are they? Do you know them well? The De La Rosas?"

"I consider Xavier one of my best friends. The boys are somewhere between three and four. The De La Rosas are good people. Why so many questions about them?"

She shrugged and took another bite to avoid answering right away. Xavier had triplets. What were their names? Did Damian, Belle or Elijah have kids?

Belle and Elijah were her cousins, but her mother had taken them in and raised them. Did their mother ever come back? Did the others have children? That would make her an aunt.

Did they know about her, or had she been wiped from the family history? So many questions burned through her mind. Why didn't they find her to tell her that her father had died?

This wonderful lunch would be wasted on her. It would sit in her stomach like boulders. She looked up, and her gaze collided with Hudson's.

Quickly she turned away. What was blazing in those brilliant eyes of his? She shouldn't care. She didn't.

If she repeated that enough, it would become true. Maybe. There were definitely more important items on her list of things to worry about.

"Their names have come up several times, and then I find out the mayor is related to them. I don't know. I'd rather talk about other people and their families than my lack of one. Big families interest me. I always wanted one." That was the truth. She sighed, and he kept staring at her.

If she was smart, she'd keep quiet. Shifting to the side, she looked over her shoulder at Paloma playing with her toys. He was waiting for her to say more.

With a deep breath, she decided to tell him the truth. Some of it, anyway. "When people find out who I am—who my husband is—will they be as friendly? I can't even keep my daughter safe." Even just a part of the truth was hard. She would *not* cry...

"None of that is your fault." His deep voice right next to her caused her to jump. When had he moved to her side? He was close enough to her for his clean, masculine scent to tickle her nose. It was so warm and comforting, like fresh rain and cut grass. She lowered her head and bit her bottom lip.

At the slight touch of his hand on her shoulder, her nerves scrambled, then settled quickly. Determined, she warned herself not to lean on him. She had to learn to take care of herself and not wait for others to save her. It only made things worse.

He didn't stay by her side for long. Shifting back, he slid into the chair next to hers.

"As parents, all we can do is our best and

leave the rest up to God. Children get sick whether you stay in one place or travel. Would she have been better growing up where everyone knew who her father was?" He looked over at Paloma playing on the floor. "You get to tell her your story in your own time and way. Your instincts were right about leaving Cincinnati. You both need a new start. You can write the next chapter of your story."

There was a long moment of silence, then he turned to her. "Not many people know, but one of the reasons I took the opportunity to be sheriff in Port Del Mar was to give my daughter a clean slate. She wouldn't hear rumors about her mom. I get to control our narrative. Each year, I tell her a little more." He shrugged. "Some stuff I'll never tell her."

He nodded as if he were having another conversation she couldn't hear. "We love our children, and every day as parents we have to make choices that can bury us in self-doubt. At those times, I rely heavily on my faith that God has her, even when I mess up. Most of us try our best, but we're flawed. God is always perfect."

He looked so serious, but he hadn't met her gaze once while telling her about his daughter. What was his story? "Is her mother in prison?"

"No." His half smile softened his face. "Nothing like that. She wanted a life she thought I would give her. When she discovered I wanted to stay in law enforcement, she left. She walked out and didn't look back. Hasn't even reached out to Charlotte in six years."

"I can't imagine a mother doing that. I'm sorry."

"For her, a baby had been a means to an end. When she didn't get the ending she wanted, she moved on. As an adult, I can handle it. Mostly." He gave her a lopsided grin. "But kids don't understand. On the plus side, it all happened before Charlotte was old enough to remember. I get to explain it to her. You'll get to do the same with Paloma."

"I don't know how to make what her father did easier to hear. Or the mistakes I made. I don't want her to ever feel lost or abandoned." Pressing her lips closed, she cut off her verbal outpouring. He was a stranger and didn't need to know her issues.

"You lost your family as a kid." It was a statement. He tilted his head and studied her. "You told Maria you were nine?"

The lump in her throat stopped her from saying anything.

With a grim expression, he nodded. "The trauma of losing family when you're older is harder to deal with. The scars are in our memories and run deeper. That can affect us as adults."

Her heart clenched. Was he hinting that he knew she was back in town to reconnect with a family that might not want her?

The colorful place mat was a good diversion. Tracing the aqua line with her finger, Abigail studied the zigzag design. At first it looked random, but she found the intricate pattern.

Was there a pattern to her life she wasn't seeing?

He stood. "Maria asked me to bring up a few more things that she found. There's more bedding." Without waiting for her to reply, he left the apartment.

Abigail was overwhelmed with emotion and needed to be close to her baby. Across from the playpen with her back to the sofa, she stared at her daughter.

Her beautiful baby girl had fallen asleep, lost in innocent dreams. "You're never going to meet your grandpa." At their rate she might not meet any of her family.

She swallowed a lump in her throat and nearly choked on the sob that wanted to escape. Pulling her knees against her chest, she tightened her whole body into a ball. Hugging herself tight, she tried to stop the tears. It didn't work. Losing complete control, she felt the sobs take over. They came one on top of another, making her whole body ache.

Thankfully, Paloma was still fast asleep. Abigail pulled the quilt off the back of the couch and cocooned herself inside. She couldn't stop the trembles that overtook her body.

Had God brought her all this way for nothing but more heartbreak? She was so tired of hurting. All she wanted to do was sleep, but she couldn't. What if her baby girl needed her and she didn't hear her?

Hudson would be back soon. She had to get herself under control. Forcing deep breaths, she finally reduced the sobs to snuffles.

The sheriff had said to trust God. But how? Every time she trusted that things would get better, life kicked her in the gut. She couldn't let this happen to her baby girl.

But how could she protect her? What if something happened to her? Who would be there for her daughter? They had no one. The Espinozas had taken them in, but they were just a charity case, not real family.

A tear fell on the back of her hand. With a deep breath, she relaxed the death grip she had on the quilt and wiped her face dry.

Most of her memories were shadows, but she remembered her father riding on his horse. He had been so tall and handsome in his cowboy hat. Her mother had said she fell in love at first sight when she saw him at a rodeo.

Why were her memories so fuzzy? She couldn't even remember his voice.

Now she would never hear it again. She had thought that if she could get to Texas, her father would be here. In her dreams, her father would step in and fix everything that was wrong.

She had met Xavier's wife. They had triplets. What about her brother Damian or her cousin Belle? Then there was her cousin Elijah, he had looked so much like her father. He was always outside, but he had a smile for her every time she saw him. Or was she making up the memories she wanted? What if she had it all wrong?

Xavier. He had picked her up from school. She had loved her big brother so much and had looked up to him. That couldn't be made up, could it?

Xavier took her riding over the ranch. He had promised to take care of her.

At first, her faith had been unyielding. He would come for her. Belle too. Under her bed, the small overnight bag they had sent her off with was packed and ready for when they knocked on the door. They had said they loved her and would always protect her.

It took her a couple of years to reach the conclusion that they had lied. Why were they keeping her away from the ranch? Was it greed? Maybe they were fighting over the ranch and didn't want her around to take a piece. But she didn't care about the land or any inheritance. She just wanted her family.

A family that might only live in her dreams.

A half sob slipped through. No. She didn't want to cry anymore, but what she wanted had never mattered before.

The door handle jiggled. She pulled the quilt over her head and stifled any lingering cries. If she was quiet, he'd think she went to sleep and go away.

Chapter Seven

Hudson shifted the highchair so he could open the door. The knob was stuck. He'd have to get his tools and fix that before he left. What else needed to be done? Out of habit, he started a mental list of items Abigail might still need.

He liked lists. They gave him a sense of order and control in a world that turned chaotic at the turn of a knob. Yes. Lists were good. Even better when items were checked off. Best feeling in the world.

He put his shoulder to the wood to create a push-and-pull action.

Why was he even bothering making plans to fix her door? He couldn't imagine Abigail being satisfied with the bare minimum for long. She had grown accustomed to a certain lifestyle. The apartment was cozy and had the basics, but how much longer would it be before she grew restless and missed the glamorous homes and restaurants?

He gritted his teeth. Why was he making it his problem?

He had enough self-awareness to know he had issues with women who needed saving. Or, at least, who were good at acting the part. As soon as he put this highchair together, he was out of here.

But first, he had to get into the apartment. Had she locked him out?

Out of pure frustration, he put his full weight behind one last shove. The door gave, and he almost lost his balance. Inside, he froze. There was a tension in the room that had his spine stiffening.

It was too quiet. Then he heard a muffled sound, as if someone had just finished a hard cry but was trying to hide. Then it was quiet again. Had he imagined the sob?

He wasn't sure. His ex-wife always made sure he knew she was crying. It was her best performance. She had been enormously proud of her ability to produce real tears on command.

Crossing the room, he glanced into the crib. Paloma was in a deep sleep, stretched out with both arms over her head in a picture of total contentment. Her round little face was turned to the side, and she made soft sucking noises.

Not the source of the stifled sobs.

Where was Abigail? Something was wrong. She wouldn't have left her daughter alone. She had barely allowed him to hold her. Setting the box against the wall, he turned to go down the hall when he spotted the bundle on the floor behind the sofa. The quilt trembled.

Had Abigail passed out again? Blood pounded in his ears as his heart rate increased. He knelt next to the small mound and laid his hand on the corner closest to him. He thought it was her head, but he wasn't sure.

Maybe she was hiding on purpose and didn't want anyone to see her. But he couldn't leave her like this.

Frustration roiled through him. Why was he working so hard to justify staying and getting involved? It was a waste of time because he knew he was just going to do it anyway, even though it would be breaking his rule about getting involved with women in trouble.

But this was for the baby. Really, who would just walk out knowing that a mom was in no condition to care for a helpless baby? He eased further down so that he wouldn't be looming over her when he pulled the cover back.

"Abigail? It's Hudson. Sheriff Menchaca." He could at least try to keep it professional. "Are you okay? Should I call Margarita or Resa?"

She made a noise that might have meant to be no, but he wasn't sure. Gently, he pulled back the pink-and-purple-patched quilt. He hadn't even known there were that many shades of pink.

Her stylish blond cut had become a mess. He still couldn't see her face. What wasn't covered by her hair was buried in her hands. It was the most heartbreaking sight he had seen in a long time. It pulled on every string attached to his stupid heart.

After years in his line of work and one disastrous marriage, there should be no strings left to yank. He had worked hard to be detached in these types of situations. What was it about Abigail Dixon that brought out the protector in him?

Everything inside him begged to pull her into his arms and promise to make it better. But he knew reaching for her was a bad idea. Instead, his free hand went to his phone. "Abigail, I'm going to call Margarita. They'll be up in a minute to help." Then he could escape, knowing that she was not alone.

That was the best plan for them all.

"No." She popped up, her hand reaching for his. The warm skin was soft. He could have easily broken the contact, but he didn't. "Abigail, you need help."

She sat up, moving away from him as she pushed her hair out of her face. "Please don't. The idea that anyone else will see me like this is too mortifying. Please. Just leave. I'll be all right. It was just a moment. Just like after a crisis, when everything calms down. You know? The adrenaline rush that pushed you through crashes."

He did get that. "Okay. Even more of a reason for someone to come stay so you can get some good sleep in the bed. Not on the floor next to your daughter's playpen."

"No. I'm good now." Standing, she moved to sit on the sofa, pulling the quilt behind her.

"Hudson, I was so close to being homeless with a sick baby. But we have this lovely apartment, and she's healthy." She turned to look at the sleeping baby. "She doesn't have a worry in the world. It just hit me. Everyone's kindness has been too much. I'm not used to people being nice just to be nice. It was a little meltdown. It's over. I'm so sorry you had to witness it." With a deep sigh, she relaxed her shoulders and smiled at him. "I'm good to go. You can leave. Thank you for everything."

Not taking his gaze off hers, he sat on the opposite corner of the couch.

"Leaving you by yourself at this point might not be the smartest move."

"Paloma is napping. I just need a little nap too."

"On the floor? You are beyond exhausted. You've been through a life-changing event and then your daughter became sick while you were basically living out of your car. You need real rest."

With a lopsided smile, she chuckled. "*Life-changing event.* That's the nicest way I've heard it put. But you're right. My ex-husband being caught stealing millions of innocent people's retirement funds is a life-changing event. For so many people."

She looked down, twisting her lips. "There is so much wrong with everything he did, and I lived off the benefits." Palms pressed together and fingers intertwined, she pressed her knuckles to her forehead. "I didn't know about any of it, but I was there with him. Do you know he never apologized? No remorse. The last time we talked, he was worried about how he would survive without his houses, cars and boats. What he didn't understand is that those weren't his. They belonged to the people he stole from. How could I be married to a man like that? Maybe I deserve all the hate and the messed-up life, but Paloma doesn't." She shook her head and wrapped her arms around her middle. She looked down at her hands as her messy hair fell around her face.

He sat, letting her vent. He was sure she hadn't had anyone to really talk to. This was probably the first time she had put her fear and anger into words.

And, honestly, he had judged her a bit too. Some of those thoughts had been his.

"I'm sorry for dropping this on you. Please forget I said any of that. You're right. I'm exhausted."

He leaned closer to her, not touching but needing to let her know he was there. "Just so you know. Everything you say stays between us." She looked so lost and alone. He wanted to see her smile. So he gave her a grin and winked. "Unless you start confessing to crimes, then I'm obligated to arrest you."

"I would have a place to stay and three meals a day." With a huff, she flopped her head back and looked at the ceiling. "How sad is that? If it wasn't for Paloma, I would make something up just to have a place to be. Maybe she would be better off without me."

"You don't mean that."

She sighed. "Only three days and you know me so well." She turned her head and looked at her daughter. "As long as she has me, she'll have all the love in the world—but is it enough if I can't keep her safe?"

"When I talk to parents that are going

through a traumatic event, I have a piece of advice I always give. As a good parent, your instinct is to take care of your child first." This time he did reach out and waited for her to meet his gaze and take his hand.

For a split second, she looked him in the eye, then looked away again. "I'm not sure bad choices count as traumatic events. So many people say I deserve even more…" She closed her eyes and pulled her lips between her teeth.

If she was putting on a show to pull him in, it was working. He flexed his hand, inviting her to take it.

Abigail hesitated. Taking ahold of his hand would mean she was accepting his help. How would she learn to stand on her own if she kept letting others step in and take care of her?

His hand stayed in place. With her stomach in knots, she allowed her fingertips to make contact.

He released a deep breath, some of the tension leaving his shoulders. "She needs you whole and healthy. Physically and mentally." His fingers rolled around hers, surrounding her hand with a light touch. When was the last time someone had touched her with gentleness, for no other reason than to reassure her and comfort her?

He lowered his chin and held her gaze. "You've traveled, right? In an airplane they tell you to get your oxygen mask on first. Then it's safe to take care of your child. If you pass out, you aren't any good to the people counting on you."

"Think of me as your oxygen mask." He stood and offered his hand again. "I'm temporary until the cabin pressure is stabilized. Take a few deep breaths, eat, take a nap. Then I'll be gone, and you can take care of your daughter."

Was she being tested? At what point was she going to truly be independent and stand on her own without needing oxygen? "But when do I start breathing on my own? I can't keep relying on someone to come along and save me. The highchair is not that complicated. I've got this. I'm good."

"I'll get the last of the bags out of Margarita's car. Come on. You didn't eat much. Get some food in your system then take a short nap while I put the highchair together. Then you'll have enough oxygen to take care of yourself and your daughter. And I'll leave you all alone, okay?"

Her sight blurred. Her father would not be coming to her rescue, but God had sent the sheriff today.

It wouldn't undermine her independence to

accept his help. It was temporary, right? Putting her hand in his, she allowed him to lift her to her feet. He pulled out a chair for her. The room was silent as she dug into the pozole. This time she savored the home-cooked meal that had been made for her. It was the best thing she had eaten since her mother had cooked for her.

Closing her eyes, she sank into the moment and allowed the warmth of their care to pour into her.

Hudson chuckled. Her eyes shot open. Had she moaned or made some other embarrassing noise?

He was at the door. "I told you it was good. There's more on the stove if you finish that before I'm back."

Forcing her spoon down, she looked up at him. "Thank you. I appreciate you not saying anything to the sisters. They already tend to hover and worry."

Halfway through the door, he turned back to her. "I know you're trying to be independent and strong, but they don't have an agenda. They're good people, and my job is to protect them from their own generosity."

Was he warning her or comforting her? Either way she was too tired to argue. She tried to give him an agreeable expression, but her lips were tight. Everyone had an agenda. Including the sheriff. With one last frown as if suspicious of her fake smile, he walked out the door.

Chapter Eight

The sun had not yet made an appearance over the Gulf and Paloma was sound asleep in the portable crib they had set up by the back door. They had fallen into a nice routine with the sisters over the last week and half.

"Josefina!" Abigail called from the front as soon as she put the phone down. "New order. The Wimberly Cattle Company needs two dozen empanadas for tomorrow morning." She wrote the order in the spiral notebook the women kept at the register. "Half pumpkin, half strawberry." With the sharp pencil, she wrote the amount in another ledger that contained the regular customer accounts.

She should talk them into letting her update their system. It could be streamlined online. Orders placed and completed, along with payments in one place on their website. Which was another whole issue.

If they would let her update everything, Margarita wouldn't have to take paperwork home or come back at night to reconcile the accounts. It was as though they didn't live in the twenty-first century.

The first time they showed her how they took orders, tracked them and collected payments, she was floored. She didn't know anyone who did business like this anymore.

Margarita bustled in from the back, adding to the stack of boxes on the front counter. Three girls came in the back door. Angie and Nica were Margarita's two oldest, and Desirae was Josefina's only child. "Good morning, Ms. Abigail." They seemed too cheerful for the crack of dawn. Behind them came Josh, Margarita's youngest at eight. He looked as if he'd just been pulled out of bed and was not happy about the upright position.

They each took a stack of white boxes of preordered pastries to load into Jose's truck.

"The labels are on the top," Margarita explained every morning, but they nodded as if they'd never been told a million times. She took the last stack and reminded Abigail as she took them to the waiting truck. "Don't forget to put the order in the ledger so I can bill them."

"I got it. You know, this could all be done online. Your customers could place the orders and make a payment at the same time. You would have time to make more product." They sold out every day.

"Oh, people like the personal touch. And having you answering the morning phones has already increased our productivity."

"They'd still get the special treatment—it would just be more organized..." The last few words trailed off. The oldest sister was already out the door. Jose, Margarita's husband, and the kids would make the early morning deliveries, and then he would drop the kids off at school before heading to his garage. They were such a hardworking family, and Abigail knew that if they let her, they could work a little less hard.

It had been two weeks, but Abigail knew without a doubt that coming to Port Del Mar had been a God thing.

She had mistakenly assumed it was to reconnect with her family and find out why they had sent her away, then forgotten her.

But finding out her father was dead had rattled the foundation of everything she thought she knew. Her brothers and cousins didn't want her back. With her father gone, there was no reason to even tell them she was in town. No reason to set herself up to be rejected by them again.

Every time thoughts of what-if crowded her mind, she quoted Hebrew 13:6. *So that we may boldly say, The Lord is my helper, and I will not fear what man shall do unto me.*

It was posted on her bathroom mirror.

The phone rang again. As she picked it up, Josefina came from the kitchen. Smiling as she hummed a song, she put a stack of folded boxes featuring the bakery's logo under the counter, then rushed back to the kitchen. Then Margarita came in and did her morning routine. She checked all the tables and arranged the books on the shelves, then flipped the Open sign and unlocked the door.

Just like every morning since Abigail had joined them, there was a small group of people outside, waiting to come in and start their day with a perfect cup of coffee and their favorite pastry.

Abigail was convinced it was the Espinoza family's love seeped into every recipe and coating every square inch of the shop that made the difference.

How the Espinozas had surrounded her in a warm *familia* blanket of love still mystified her. At times it made her so uncomfortable that her instinct was to run.

She had no experience with this type of attention. As nice as it was, it also stressed her out. What would happen next? Something this good never lasted long.

Margarita greeted everyone and served them at the counter, then they would come to Abigail to pay. This morning, as per usual, Hudson was one of the first to come into the bakery. Sometimes he had an order to pick up, but other days he sat down to have his breakfast here. A few times, like today, he brought Charlotte with him.

Abigail's nerves went all wobbly and tingly. *Settle down, he's just getting breakfast.*

It wasn't like he went out of his way to talk to her. Over a week had passed since they'd spent any time alone together. Hudson said he would leave her alone, and he had stuck to his word. He barely talked to her now. A polite "good morning" and "thank you" was the extent of their conversation.

This morning, Charlotte pressed her face to the front of the glass, searching for the blueberry cake doughnut.

"We had a big order of your favorites this morning," Margarita told her. "A new batch will be coming out of the oven soon. Do you want to wait for hot fresh doughnuts or pick something else? The cinnamon twist was just put out. Do you want one of those?"

She shook her head, then looked up at her dad. "Can I wait for the blueberry ones?"

Glancing at his watch, he nodded. "We've got time."

He moved to stand in front of her and handed over his card. "Morning." He smiled at Paloma standing in her playpen talking to people. "Looks as if she is settling in."

Before she could reply, he turned to the opening door. "Xavier," he called out, with a warm smile for the man who walked in.

Her stomach took a nosedive. *Xavier.* Not breathing, she tucked her head down. Was it her brother? She was afraid to look up. What if it was and he recognized her? Every muscle in her body tightened. What if he didn't? That would be worse.

Twisting her head just enough to see him out of the corners of her eyes, she peered at the man Hudson was now having a conversation with. Words slipped past their moving lips, but she couldn't hear a sound.

It was him. Her brother. Sweet memories of Xavier defending her at school, helping her tie her shoes and teaching her to ride bombarded her. He had been her hero.

He was bigger now, a grown man. Selena

had said he'd been out of the country. Had he joined the military? After the weird way she had acted around Selena, she'd been afraid to ask any questions.

Now there were a ton.

"Abigail?" Hudson called her name.

Blinking to clear her thoughts, she looked at him. "Yes?" she somehow managed.

"Is there a problem with my card?" He leaned over to look at the scanner.

"Oh. Um…it's the machine." She had taken so long that it had canceled the transaction. "This thing is so old."

Xavier laughed. "I'm surprised they even take credit cards. The sisters are a little old-school."

Nodding, Hudson grinned. "Hey, at least they upgraded from the old carbon-copy machine."

She handed him his card. "Here you go. Sorry about that."

Xavier held out his hand. "Since my friend here is rude, I'll have to introduce myself. I'm Xavier De La Rosa. You met my wife, Selena."

She. Could. Not. Breathe. Her gaze darted to his hand, then to his face. He didn't know who she was.

"Abigail?" Hudson leaned closer, his forehead wrinkled with heavy frown lines. "Are you okay?"

Pull it together. He was going to think she was having another breakdown. She took Xavier's outreached hand. "Sorry, too early in the morning. Paloma didn't sleep well last night."

Hudson twisted to look at Paloma, who was carrying on a conversation, showing her cloth book to a customer. "Is she okay? Any setbacks?"

"No. Just a normal, mommy-I-want-to-play-now type of night." She wiped her hand on her jeans and avoided any eye contact with her brother. She knew she had changed a lot since she was nine. There was the growth spurt, and her hair was blond with a completely different style. And then there was the weight. She wasn't the chubby little sister he had known. But still, shouldn't there be something, like a do-I-know-you-from-somewhere kind of recognition?

The bell rang and new customers came in, pushing the two men in front of her to move on.

Xavier lifted his coffee. "Nice meeting you. It's a small town, so I'm sure I'll be seeing you around." He turned to Hudson. "Will you join me? I have some questions."

"Sure." They went to a table by the front

window. Charlotte took a book out of her backpack.

"Ma'am?"

Abigail jumped. She stopped gawking at Hudson and helped the next customer. Whenever she had a second, her gaze slipped to the table by the big window. She wasn't sure if it was Xavier or Hudson who kept pulling her attention away.

When Josefina brought out a tray of the hot blueberry cake doughnuts, she set one to the side. "Is Ms. Charlotte waiting for this?"

Margarita was laughing with a mom who had a couple of kids with her, and Josefina rushed back to the kitchen. Taking a deep breath, Abigail picked up the little plate. She could do this without acting weird.

Provided she didn't blurt out any off-the-wall questions. Hudson was already worried about her state of mind. When she was halfway to the table, Xavier stood.

"Thanks for your help. I have an early appointment on the dock. See you." Then he turned and left without a glance at her.

He was gone.

For a moment, she had the ridiculous sense of being abandoned all over again. She just stood there and watched as Xavier walked across the street.

"Ms. Abigail, is that mine?" Charlotte was politely standing next to her.

Forcing a smile, she handed the girl her breakfast. "Yes, it is." Raising her eyes to meet Hudson's was a mistake.

The wrinkled forehead was unmistakable evidence that he had questions about her odd behavior. Again. Lifting her chin, she nodded to him.

He raised one brow. What did *that* mean?

She couldn't look away. For a long moment, they stared at each other, then his phone went off and he looked away.

That was a win for her, right?

He stood and glanced around, then stepped closer to her. "I need to take this outside. Would you keep an eye on Charlotte?"

"Of course." She slipped into the chair he had just left and turned to his daughter. "Was the doughnut worth the wait?"

Cheeks full of blueberry goodness, the six-year-old nodded, her ponytail bobbing with her head. Today she wore a big purple bow.

She heard Paloma. "Little Miss Thing is ready for breakfast. Want to check on her with me?"

"Can I hold her?"

"You can help me keep her entertained while I make her bottle." Paloma smiled at them while she rubbed her eye with a tiny fist. With Charlotte talking to the baby, Abigail told Josefina that she was clocking out to feed Paloma.

She took Charlotte and Paloma to the family booth in the back of the kitchen. With the little girl sitting close to her, she let her give the baby her bottle.

Hudson came in and scanned the room for his daughter. Seeing her, his shoulders relaxed, then he turned to Josefina, who was filling and folding individual empanadas. "Josefina, I need some help. There's an incident on the other side of town, and I need to go now. Would you be able to take Charlotte to school in thirty minutes?"

"I'm sorry, but I can't. Margarita and I have a couple of special orders. One's a wedding. Maybe Abigail could. Abigail, would you be able to take her?"

"Sure. That's not a problem. I just need directions to the school." She pulled her bottom lip between her teeth. "If that's okay with you, Sheriff. I don't mind. I'm a careful driver."

"Yes!" Charlotte said. "That would be fun. I can help with the baby, then she can take me to school. My teacher would love to meet Paloma. Can she pick me up too?"

Her large eyes turned to Abigail. "Mrs. Johnson watches me when Daddy has work, but her mom got real sick yesterday. Daddy wants me to go to the afterschool camp. But I don't want to. Cody goes and he's mean."

"Charlotte." Hudson's voice had a sharp edge Abigail hadn't heard before.

"I don't mind. Paloma loves her. I can pick her up from school and bring her here or take her home and wait for you."

"Please, Daddy."

Heaving a heavy sigh, he looked at his phone. "She can take you to school this morning. We will talk abou—"

"Thank you, Daddy!" Charlotte leaped on her dad, hugging him tight around his upper legs.

He snorted and rubbed the top of her head. "Don't worry about after school. I should be able to pick her up." He kissed her. "Love you, baby girl." Then he was gone.

Charlotte was eager to help stock the white bakery bags at the front counter, and then she played with Paloma while Abigail helped a few customers.

Abigail lost track of time. She checked on the girls. They were still playing, giggling at a silly game Charlotte had made up. Her heart got the same gooey warm feeling she experienced when she watched a Hallmark movie. Margarita came out to the front with another tray.

"Hey, chica. You're going to be late if you don't get them babies in the car."

Checking her phone, Abigail gasped. How had thirty minutes slipped by so fast? She'd promised Hudson she would get his daughter to school on time and told him he could trust her.

He was going to think her irresponsible. She was pretty sure he already questioned her stability. She picked up Paloma and hustled Charlotte to the car.

When they pulled up to the drop-off spot, it was clear of cars. Of course, it was—they were late.

Putting the car in Park, she got Paloma out, then went around to help Charlotte out of the booster Margarita had given her. The little girl looked around, then up at Abigail. "Are we late? I'm never late."

"It's okay. I'll take you in and explain that it's my fault."

To get into the office, she had to press a button at the front door and explain who she was. They unlocked the door and she rushed through the lobby, ready to defend Charlotte and take the blame.

A dark-haired woman stood behind the long counter, and several others turned their way as they entered. A few seemed to drift out of the offices lining the hallway behind the counter. They were all doing something, but not really concentrating on their work. She recognized some of the faces from the bakery.

She pulled the girls closer to her, her heart slamming against her chest. Did they know about her husband, or were they merely curious as to why she had the sheriff's daughter?

"Hi, Mrs. Abernathy." Charlotte's voice was bright and cheery. "I was helping at the bakery this morning. Please don't tell Daddy I was late. This is Mrs. Dixon, she—"

"It's okay, Charlotte." Abigail put a hand on her shoulder. The six-year-old was trying to protect her. "I lost track of time. I'll let Hudson know it was my fault."

With a smirk, the brunette tilted her head. "Hudson, huh. Welcome to Port Del Mar, Mrs. Dixon. We hear the Espinoza sisters have let you move in above the bakery." She took a pink slip of paper off her desk and scribbled on it. "Here, Charlotte. Go on to class. Being tardy interrupts everyone's schedule. It's important to think of others, no matter who you are. Right, Mrs. Dixon?"

Abigail's stomach dropped. The woman knew who she was. That meant they all knew she was once married to Brady Dixon. That she had been the wife of a con man who stole other people's dreams.

Charlotte frowned for the first time. "But I wanted to introduce—"

"It's okay, Charlotte. She's right, class has already started. We can meet your teacher another day. You need to go on in."

Her little shoulders dropped. "Okay. Bye, Paloma." With a kiss on the baby's cheek and a quick hug around Abigail's waist, Charlotte disappeared.

The expressions on the faces of the women in the front office ranged from sincere kindness to open hostility. Small towns were so strange. Was it because of her ex-husband, or had she read the room wrong? Had she made a mistake in using the sheriff's first name?

He had to be one of the most sought-after bachelors in Port Del Mar. Either way, they didn't know her, so she couldn't let their negativity take away the warm joy from her morning with Paloma and Charlotte.

With a tight smile, she left.

She finished out the morning at the counter, then took Paloma upstairs. It was time to take a deep dive into the sisters' website and explore all the possibilities that would make their business run more easily and their lives better.

This would be a good time to reestablish

her own business and seek out more marketing work. She had managed to build a successful small business before her husband was arrested. Her clients had dropped her the minute word got out.

She couldn't blame them. With all the drama, she hadn't even tried to change their minds. The enormity of her husband's guilt had been too much for her to handle.

Port Del Mar was a new start, and it was time to build up a new clientele. A new name would be a good first step, but right now she didn't have the money to legally change it.

Would she go back to De La Rosa? This morning, she had come face-to-face with her oldest brother, and he hadn't even given her a second glance. She had always looked different from them, taking after her mother. Maybe she wasn't a De La Rosa. Was that the reason they had sent her away?

Nope, she wasn't even going to chase that proverbial rabbit down the hole. She had things to do. Things that she had control over and that mattered. First, the sisters' website, then some fresh branding for her and Paloma's new life.

Her daughter babbled in the back seat. "This is our fresh start, baby girl," Abigail told her.

She should forget about the De La Rosa family. They didn't know her or want her. They had obviously forgotten about her. The Espinozas, on the other hand, provided warmth and love to the whole community. Espinoza was a good name. So was Menchaca.

She shook her head. No. She was not going to fall into the trap of thinking that a man changing her name would save her.

Chapter Nine

Hudson's boots crunched the red gravel of his driveway. One hand on the smoothed railing, he paused before taking the stairs up to the beach house that he and Charlotte had called home for over a year now.

With each step, he mentally dropped the stress and ugliness of the day off his shoulders. Reaching the top of the landing, he turned and sat in the rocker. The wraparound deck had a couple of weathered rockers that had come with the house. He had added a cushioned bench and a table with six chairs. It was a great outdoor living space. They weren't on the beach, but they had a view of the ocean between the colorful houses that lined the other side of the street.

It was a restful home. The sounds of the waves allowed him to count his blessings and check in with God. On the gate, he had placed a verse his sisters had given him: *But the wisdom that is from above is first pure, then peaceable, gentle, and easy to be entreated, full of mercy and good fruits, without partiality, and without hypocrisy. And the fruit of righteousness is sown in peace of them that make peace.* James 3:17-18.

He was a peacemaker. It was his job, and today he had done his job to the best of his ability. Now he needed to let it all go and embrace all the love and joy his daughter brought him.

With his head cleared, he unlocked his door and stepped inside. His gaze narrowed. What had happened to his orderly living room?

It looked as if every blanket and sheet in the house now covered his furniture. It was a giant chaotic mess, and it put him on edge.

"Charlotte? Josefina?"

A gasp came from somewhere below the mess. "Daddy!" His daughter crawled out from under a side table and ran to him. The power of the small body colliding with his almost knocked him off-balance.

She wound her arms around him and buried her face against his pants leg. "You're home safe."

He picked her up and pulled her against him. Her heart was beating a mile a minute. "I'm sorry I'm late, sweetheart. I called Josefina… she said she'd make sure you'd get home."

His baby girl was crying now, her tears crushing him more than any physical blow could. He pulled her closer and pressed his lips against the side of her head. "It's okay. I'm home."

The blanket over the sofa was pushed back. To his surprise, Abigail Dixon stood up. "Someone at school told her about the incident that pulled you away this morning." She avoided his eye contact.

Squeezing him tighter, Charlotte nodded. "Cody told me a man was going to blow you up. He said his brother told him the man had guns and bombs."

She started crying again.

"Shh. I'm here. The man was upset, but he wasn't trying to hurt me. He wanted his wife's attention, and he wanted to hurt himself. We were there to protect his family and him. I was by my truck the whole time. That's what took so long. We didn't want anyone to get hurt. I'm so sorry, baby girl. You can't believe anything that Cody kid tells you." He wanted to talk to someone about this. That kid had been picking on his daughter for a while, but this was crossing the line.

"I told her you were going to be okay, and that Cody just had a big mouth. He sounds like a kid who likes to cause drama by talking about things he knows nothing about." Abigail's lips pressed into a hard line. "We've been staying busy. She's been fine for most of the night."

She looked as upset as his daughter.

"Thank you. Cody's older brother is a troublemaker in town, and his father isn't much better." He hadn't wanted to throw his weight around as sheriff, but that kid needed to leave his daughter alone.

"Cody says they're going to video Daddy harassing them," Charlotte told Abigail. Hudson had heard that threat from the family before.

Needing to change the subject, he walked over to Abigail and scanned the multicolored stronghold that covered his well-organized living room.

He had not expected any of this in his home. He put his free hand on his hip and tried to put a positive spin on it. Charlotte had been scared. Abigail had sacrificed his perfectly placed furniture for his daughter's sake. It had been a good call on her part.

"Wow. You built a big fort. It looks super strong."

Charlotte nodded against his chest. She was chewing on her thumb, something she hadn't done in over a year. "It is."

His heart broke. His job was to make the community safe—but was it at the expense of his daughter's mental health?

"I was scared, but Abigail prayed with me. She said when you got home, you'd be hungry after working so hard. We made dinner, then we took a bath and built a fort to hide inside until you got here. I told her you didn't like messes. That your rule is one toy at a time. But she said it would be okay. We got to show Paloma two of my favorite movies."

He glanced over at Abigail. She and Paloma had been the distraction his daughter needed.

Abigail crossed her arms over her middle and looked at his daughter. "Josefina thought Charlotte would feel better waiting for you at home. Charlotte has been a great help with Paloma, and she's a good cook. She helped make your favorite dinner."

"I did, and Ms. Josefina gave us some croissants with pecans and honey. She said after the pumpkin empanadas they were your favorite. They were sold out of all the empanadas."

Abigail had kept his daughter safe and had done everything she could to reassure her he'd be home. He treasured the feel of Charlotte's small body in his arms. In just a few years, she would be too big to hold like this. Kissing her head, he took in the smell of her apple shampoo.

"I love the honey croissants. The house smells like baked bread and lasagna." He set her down. "You said you made my favorite."

She took his hand and pulled him into the kitchen area. "We did. After I helped bathe Paloma, we washed my hair. Abigail let me layer the pasta and cheese. She poured the sauce."

"You haven't eaten yet?" he asked. "It's past your bedtime."

"Abigail said you would be home, and I didn't want to eat without you. Can they stay the night? We could all camp in the fort. There are lots of pillows and blankets."

With her baby on her hip, Abigail was pulling the salad out of the refrigerator. "I've got to get Paloma home, but you and your dad both need to eat." She placed the bowl on the table, which was set with two plates, then went to the stove.

"Why are there only two plates?"

"I told her to get three plates." Charlotte made an I-told-you-so face at Abigail. "She said they would leave as soon as you got here. I think she should stay. She helped me cook it—she should eat it too."

"I agree. We had dinner with her, and now it's her turn to eat with us. Stay. Let me get the lasagna." He moved to the oven she had opened and took the hot pads from her. She nodded and grabbed the bread basket.

His daughter already had another plate on the table and was laying out silverware. "I told you Daddy would make you stay." Charlotte smiled at them, then climbed into her chair.

"I should go. Just let me gather the blankets and straighten up."

"Sit. Y'all made the meal together, so we will eat it together. The fort can stay up tonight."

"Really? Yay! Daddy, will you camp out with me?"

"Yes. Now let's pray so we can eat."

They all bowed their heads as he said a simple grace over the food that was set before them. Afterward, Charlotte hit Abigail with a new knock-knock joke, and even Paloma laughed.

He grinned. This was nice. Sighing with contentment, he enjoyed the moment of feeling like a complete family. This was the dream he'd lost when his ex-wife had made it clear her wishes were so much grander than a simple family dinner. Zoe had been able to pretend for a while, but he had been too busy and self-absorbed and had missed the clues.

It was sad to realize that it wasn't Zoe he missed, but the feeling of returning to a family home where he could heal his heart after a difficult day in the world.

Zoe had not wanted the same things. He wanted to build what his parents had had before he got his mother killed.

Nope. Not going there. He closed his eyes and forced that ugly thought from his mind.

Talking or thinking about that day would not change the outcome. No matter what his sisters believed, analyzing his mother's death was not productive.

His thoughts now clear, he went back to the delicious meal and began asking Charlotte about her day. Abigail fed Paloma pieces of pasta in between her own bites. The meal went by too fast.

When they had finished the lasagna, Abigail put her baby girl on the blankets and started clearing the table. "Now, what we've all been waiting for! The pecan-honey pastries." She placed them on one of the fancy dishes he never used, and they all tucked into the sweet treat. Afterward, Hudson turned to Charlotte. "It's way past time to brush your teeth and get into your pajamas."

She started to protest. He held up a finger and narrowed his eyes. "We will be sleeping in your tent tonight, but no arguing. Or it's all going to be put up and you can sleep in your bed."

"Okay." Charlotte turned from him to Abigail. "Will you stay and sleep over with us?"

"No." Her response was fast and saved him from being the bad guy, something he really appreciated tonight. "I have to get Paloma home to her crib. But we'll see each other again soon. I think you've become her favorite person."

"She's mine. You won't leave without saying goodbye, will you?"

"Nope. Never." Abigail laid her palm flat against her heart. "I promise never to leave without saying goodbye."

"Enough stalling." Hudson chuckled. "Go get ready for bed. You can tell Abigail and Paloma good-night when you're done."

"All right, Daddy." She jumped off her chair and darted to the bathroom.

Hudson rose from his chair. "I'd better go check on her. You sit and relax. When I come back, we can finish the dishes."

In the bathroom, he found Charlotte peering under the sink. "What are you doing?"

"Making sure nothing bad is hiding." She stood on her pink step stool and gathered her brush and toothpaste. He pulled her hair up and braided it.

"Daddy, please let Abigail and Paloma stay the night. She could live with us, and I would have a baby sister and she could make lasagna for you every night. That would be fun."

He sighed and lowered his head so they were making eye contact in the mirror. "Charlotte. They cannot move in with us. Abigail is nice, but she is not a permanent part of our lives. She works at the bakery and is focused on her daughter. They might be our friends, but soon they'll leave town. It's just you and me, sweetheart, and that's how it's going to be until you grow up and move away. If you need anything, I will take care of it."

"I'm never going to leave you, Daddy."

He laughed, then kissed her tightly braided hair. "One day you will, and that's okay. My job is to raise you so you're ready when you want to go. Now, stop stalling and brush your teeth. After you get your pj's on, meet us at the fort."

"Okay, Daddy. I'm going to find Prancer." She turned with a huge smile. "A floppy pony is safe for a baby. Paloma will love her."

Entering the kitchen, he found Abigail washing the dishes. He took the clean plates, dried them and then put them away. This felt too right. Working together in the kitchen after a family meal had become a sad, forgotten fantasy when he'd married Zoe.

Shaking his head, he squelched the unwelcome feeling. That was treacherous territory for him and his daughter. There was no point in longing for a life that he couldn't have—not at the risk of Charlotte's trusting heart.

Apparently, he needed to have the same talk with himself that he had just had with his little girl. Clear limits needed to be set, for all their sakes.

He wasn't going to put Charlotte through the heartbreak his sisters had endured after the death of their mother.

Exhaling slowly, he put the last pot away and turned to look at the woman who had taken over his home and head tonight. She was arranging the fruit he had in a bowl.

Abigail was an unsolved puzzle. All the warm home and hearth feelings were an illusion.

She turned and found him staring at her. With a tentative smile, she leaned back on the counter but didn't break eye contact. Silence lingered, and she seemed fine with it. Most people would want to start filling the air with words. Just letting them talk was the best way to find out what people really wanted.

But Abigail just blinked and waited for him. He cleared his throat. Why was he nervous? "First, I want to thank you for giving up your evening and making sure Charlotte was safe. Being the sheriff's daughter is not easy."

"It's not a problem. She's a sweet girl. Besides, everyone's been helping me, so it was good to be able to return the favor. Being needed every once in a while, is nice."

Moving to the living room, she checked on Paloma, then turned to look at him. "I know you're not sure if you can trust me, but I'm not going to do anything to hurt your daughter. I promise."

"You might not mean to. But I think we're on dangerous ground." He looked to the window. "A few people in town seem to want to put us together." Cutting his gaze back to her, he tried a smile. "You might have noticed. And this—" he waved a hand between them "—probably won't be the last time. But I need you to know where I stand. I'm not going to ever be interested in a romantic relationship while my daughter lives with me."

She stiffened, then lifted her chin. "Good. I've tried playing the damsel waiting for my Prince Charming. It never worked out. I'm over the fairy tale. I'm not looking for any sort of relationship either."

Great. He'd offended her. "It's not personal. I have a feeling we're going to find ourselves thrown together in the coming weeks. No matter how many situations they engineer to work us into the same space, I can't go there. I don't want to hurt your feelings or confuse you."

"I get it." Wounded pride shone in her eyes before she turned away to pick up her daughter.

With a sigh, he perched on the edge of a barstool at the end of the large island. This was not how he wanted the evening to end. "I told you that my mother died when I was a kid. My twin sisters were eight. In less than a year, my dad was dating."

"Oh. That had to be hard." She sat down at the opposite end of the island.

"I'd already been dealing with anger and guilt, but then I watched each new girlfriend bond with my sisters and then leave. My sisters would be devastated, and there was nothing I could do to make them feel better. All my anger was directed toward my father and those women who wanted to replace my mother. It was a rough few years."

"I'm so sorry, Hudson. That had to be horrible. How old were you?"

"It started when I was fourteen. The reason I'm telling you this is that I want you to understand my decision. I won't put my daughter through that type of roller-coaster ride. And she's already asking you to move in with us."

The rigidity of her spine softened, and she laid her cheek on Paloma's head. "I get that. Having the people, you love leave you with no explanation is crushing to a child. I really care about your daughter, and I'd never intentionally hurt her, but kids see the world differently. They put expectations on the adults in their lives that can't always be lived up to. I don't even know how long I'll be in town."

The sadness in her voice urged him to ask her who abandoned her as a kid. He hated that his heart twisted at the thought of her leaving, and for both their sakes, knew he needed to change the subject. "There's been something bothering me since this morning. You had another one of your extreme reactions around a De La Rosa."

He moved closer to her. Close enough to see every detail of her reaction when he asked his question. "Do you have some sort of connection with the family I should know about? Something to do with your husband?" That was his biggest fear, and the only possibility he could come up with. But he couldn't connect the dots.

In his line of work, he tended to follow his instincts, and they were screaming that she was hiding something important.

Abigail blinked, like a deer in headlights. She was panicking. He could see the figurative gears moving through her thoughts, trying to figure out the best plan of action. She was deciding how much of the truth to tell him, if any. He had her.

He stood and leaned a hip on the counter, crossed his arms and stared at her, stone-faced. Letting her know without a word that he was not letting this go until he had the truth.

Her mouth opened, then closed. Turning away from his gaze, she went to the sink and grabbed a glass, filling it with water.

Her daughter on her hip, she took a few sips. He allowed the heavy silence to push at her.

She finally turned to him. "My husband has nothing to do with my life now or in the future. I just... It's so complicated. My *whole life* is complicated. I'm just asking for privacy. I get the message loud and clear, Sheriff. You don't want me around your daughter." She walked around the island to the table, giving him a wide berth. "I'll get Paloma's things and leave. If Margarita or Josefina asks me to step in again to help with Charlotte, I'll make sure to say no. I understand your mistrust."

"I don't think you do." This was not what he wanted. He reached out and gently touched her arm. Then waited for her to lift her gaze to his. "Charlotte is already falling for you. But we both know you'll leave—and then I'll have to try and explain why you didn't love her enough to stay." He sighed. "On top of that, I have the whole town to protect. And the De La Rosas are special to me. They've already had too much to deal with. They are finally finding happiness, and I don't want anything or anyone to mess with that."

"Meaning?" she asked tersely.

"Meaning… I protect the people I love. Tell me what's really going on with you."

She shook her head and stepped back. He forced his hand to drop, fighting the urge to tighten his grip and hold. Not to restrain her, but to make her tell him everything.

He couldn't help her if she shut him out. With a growl, he spun away from her and ran his fingers through his hair. Why was he worried about her? He had to take care of his family, and she could be a threat on so many levels.

"If you told me what's going on, maybe I could help." *Yes. It was official.* He'd lost his mind. He should be sending her packing, not offering her help.

Her eyes were bright, but she didn't cry. "I'm so sorry. Every time I think I have a new start, I manage to mess it up. I just want to help the Espinoza family. I'll keep my distance from you and the De La Rosa family. I'm not a threat."

He wanted to believe her. So badly. But could he?

Looking down, she rubbed her eyes. "I understand about your daughter, and I respect that. Children haven't learned to guard their hearts." She sighed and picked up her sleepy baby. "As soon as she comes in, I'll say goodbye like I promised."

This was what he wanted, so why did he want to apologize? Lips pressed tight so he wouldn't say anything, he stuffed his hands into his pockets and let her gather Paloma's things.

"I found Prancer. We're ready to camp in our fort!" Charlotte entered the room waving the stuffed pony above her head.

Abigail went down on her knees. "I love your rabbit pj's and this pretty pony. You have sweet dreams tonight. Paloma and I are going."

His daughter gave a pout that rivaled her mother's.

"Charlotte. No sulking. Say goodbye," Hudson warned.

"But I have Prancer. I'll put her in the baby's bag. Oh, her bag's in my room! I'll get it for you."

"Thank you, Charlotte."

Standing, Abigail hugged Paloma close and avoided any eye contact with him.

His daughter ran from the room and was back in a few seconds. "I have it." She lifted the pink-and-green backpack trying to stuff the toy inside, then tripped on the strap. Hudson jumped to catch her, but the bag went flying into the middle of the fort, its contents scattering.

"Charlotte." Abigail rushed over to them. "Are you okay?"

"I'm sorry I spilled your stuff."

"Don't worry about that. I should have had it zipped. I just wanted to make sure you didn't get hurt."

"Nope, I'm good. Thanks for catching me, Daddy." She moved out of his arms and started hunting down all the misplaced items. Abigail joined her.

Charlotte picked up a photo. "Who are these people?"

Abigail froze mid-movement, the package of wipes in her hand forgotten.

Hudson moved to look at the picture and frowned. It showed a teenage Xavier with his brother and cousins. There was a smaller, dark-haired girl on his shoulders. He had seen the picture before. Taking the photo from Charlotte, he flipped it over. A date and each name were printed in a faded, feminine hand. "Gabby, eight years old," was the last name on the list.

He lifted his eyes to Abigail's. "Why do you have a picture of Gabby De La Rosa with her family?" A flash of anger heated him from the inside out. Had she been playing them all?

Did she have plans to blackmail Xavier and his family—or worse?

Her eyes went wide, then narrowed. "How do you know Gabby?"

"Xavier is my friend. He's been looking for his sister. What do you know about her?"

"They're looking for her? For how long?"

What did she know?

"For a while. They started again when their father died." He studied her. What was safe to say? He twisted his mouth to the side, thinking, studying her. "Her aunt basically kidnapped he—"

"*What?* Kidnapped? No. Is that what they told Xavier?" Her eyes were wide and frantic.

"They?" What was she doing with this picture? Until she gave him answers, he wasn't going to tell her anything more.

"She didn't kidnap me. Belle and Elijah gave me to her."

He froze. Not possible. "Are you saying you're Gabby De La Rosa?"

She blinked. Tears slipped down her cheeks.

"Abigail?" His daughter went to her and hugged her as tightly as she could. "Please don't cry. Daddy, stop yelling at her. I don't understand. Who was kidnapped?"

Right. His daughter was in the room and

confused. What was he saying? He was confused too.

Abigail wiped her face and smiled at Charlotte. "I'm okay. I just seem to be crying a lot lately. I need to get Paloma home."

She took the picture from him and stuffed a few other things into the bag. But didn't seem to care that she was leaving half her items. "Thank you for the wonderful dinner. You have a good night." She hugged Charlotte and went straight for the door.

Stopping on the threshold, she turned back and finally looked at him. "Please don't say anything to the De La Rosas." She looked down. "I need to…" She glanced at Charlotte, then back at him. "We'll talk tomorrow?"

"Yes. I'll see you in the morning after I drop Charlotte off at school."

With a nod, she smiled at his little girl. "Thank you for the wonderful night. I had so much fun. You have a great dad. Goodbye."

"Thank you for being with me. Next time we can have a sleepover."

With a sad smile, Abigail closed the door.

Hudson helped Charlotte straighten the fort, but the whole time his mind was dealing with the fact that Abigail was the long-lost sister of his best friend. Abigail was the missing Gabby De La Rosa. Or *was* she?

Were they being played? He wanted to call Xavier, but she had asked him to wait until they talked. The De La Rosa family had waited years to get their little sister back. They could wait one more day. Depending on what she told him, maybe they would be better off not knowing her.

He knew. Hudson knew who her family was. She hadn't even had time to process it before she pulled into her parking spot.

I protect the people I love. His words played on repeat. She would never be the one he protected. But then she remembered what he'd told her about her family. Had they really been looking for her? Why did he use the word *kidnapped*? Had Belle lied to Xavier?

Paloma was asleep in the back of the car. He was going to make her tell them. Or he might tell them himself. She texted him. Please talk to me first before saying anything to anyone.

His reply was short. Yes. Provided we talk tomorrow. What if what he'd told her was all for show and they hadn't really wanted to find her? Would they even care she was in town?

Hudson didn't know the real story. Her aunt had not taken her from them. Belle and Elijah had stuffed some clothes in her backpack and told her goodbye. Her father and brothers hadn't been there. Did they even know what had happened to her? Or had they been part of it?

Could she trust any of them? Her great-aunt's words bombarded her mind. *The De La Rosa family is nothing but trouble.*

Abigail closed her eyes and searched her memories. She recalled seeing her father at the funeral, and that she'd been scared, but she couldn't remember why.

Then Belle had taken her to the room they shared and packed some of her clothes. She had been confused about what was going on. Afterward, Belle took her outside, where they had met Elijah. They each told her that it would be a short visit and that they would get her when things were settled. All she'd understood was that her mom was gone and now her family were sending her away.

She had cried and begged to stay. She had asked for her father. But her mother's aunt had pulled her off Elijah and put her into her car, then sped away. Abigail had twisted around in the seat belt and watched her cousins get smaller through the rear windshield. Where had her father and brothers been? Belle and Elijah had just stood there and let their great-aunt take her. That was the last time she had seen them or talked to them. Nothing since then. Had her cousins lied to the rest of her family?

With a sleeping Paloma tucked against her shoulder, she made her way upstairs to their cozy apartment. But it wasn't really theirs. How much longer would she be able to live off the charity of the Espinoza sisters? They had a business to run and their own families to take care of.

Tonight, she'd put the final changes she wanted to make on their website, then show it to them. Hopefully, they would see how it would make the daily running of the bakery smoother.

Going over to the crib, she gently placed her daughter inside and gazed down at her. She ran her hands over the railing that Hudson had put together for Paloma.

He was a good father. Had her dad been too? Had he wanted to keep her, but the others had sent her away? As more memories of herself as a little girl slipped through, she only grew more confused.

And then there was the horrible twist in her gut from losing Hudson. She had never had him, so why did the thought of not having him in her life upset her? He was right to be focused on his daughter.

She ran a finger along her sweet baby's

cheek. "I promise to always love you above all others." She hadn't realized until tonight that her dream of a traditional family still burned under the debris of her other broken ambitions.

Cooking dinner, waiting for Hudson to come home, then sitting at the table talking about the day. For a brief moment, she felt herself fantasizing that a man would make her life perfect.

God, please heal my heart and open it to finding peace with just my daughter. All I need to create joy in our lives is You.

She needed to write that down somewhere to remind herself in moments of weakness. Happiness like tonight was fleeting—and it might be all over with, anyway. Once everyone found out she had been lying to them, they would turn away from her.

It was what she was used to. She opened the laptop to work on the changes to the website.

She wouldn't be sleeping tonight anyway. The Bible told her not to worry, but that was the hardest habit to break.

Chapter Ten

Hudson's usually cheerful daughter was mad at him this morning. She had asked to go to the bakery before school, but he had kept making excuses until it was too late.

She'd wanted to see Abigail, but he couldn't let that happen. His daughter had started yearning for something Abigail couldn't give her.

He glanced at himself in the rearview mirror. Yeah, it wasn't just Charlotte who was drawn to the new girl in town. At the end of his disastrous marriage, he'd vowed not to bring women into their lives. Children needed stability and people they could trust.

Over the years, that promise had been easy to keep. No matter how many wonderful ladies the good folks of Port Del Mar paraded in front of him, not a single one had caused him to question his decision.

Until Abigail. Leave it to him to break his rule with a woman who came with more than a trainload of baggage and secrets. She had the power to break all of their hearts.

Hudson ran a weary hand across his face. His stomach was in knots, and he hadn't slept. He still couldn't wrap his brain around the fact she was claiming to be the missing Gabby De La Rosa.

Was she Gabby? The cynical part of his brain wondered if this was a con.

But she had to know that a simple DNA test could prove her a liar. Unless she was hoping to get the family to trust her and then tell them. But then why all the secrecy? Wouldn't she have been better off going to them first instead of hiding in town pretending to be someone else?

The parking lot in front of the bakery was full, so he pulled into a slot along the boardwalk and crossed the street. The morning crowd had taken just about every table. Usually, their weather was mild enough for the outside tables to be used, but the bizarre temperature drop had everyone huddled inside.

The bell above the door greeted him.

"Hey there, Sheriff. Close that door. It's colder than a frosted frog, and your lettin' 'em in," Grandpa Diaz hollered at him. The old man's family had lived here before the port was established, and, at ninety-five, Grandpa was one of the oldest members of the community.

"Hear a bad front's rollin' in tonight," another old-timer yelled at him.

Grandpa Diaz's great-granddaughter, Dawn, sat between the two men by the front window. It was a morning routine for them.

"They're predicting ice and snow. Is that true, Sheriff Menchaca?" the young woman asked, excitement shining in her eyes.

The old-timer cupped his mug in gnarled hands and laughed. "There ain't ever been snow in this neck of the woods. In 1983, it got so cold the bay froze. My boat was stuck right in the ice. Wildest thing I've ever seen. But never no snow. Those fancy weather guys just like getting people all riled up."

Hudson smiled. "That's true. But even so, we're watching the reports. It would be a good night for everyone to stay home. Even if we don't get snow, patches of ice on the overpasses can cause trouble. So order a few extra pastries and hunker down for the night."

Walking up to the counter, he gave Margarita his order, then went over to Abigail at the register. She avoided eye contact while he waited.

Margarita, on the other hand, was full of good cheer. "So, how was your evening? Abigail said she had dinner with you."

"With Charlotte and Paloma," she clarified. "I told her we all had dinner."

"Oh, that's so nice. Family dinners at the end of a long day are my favorites." Margarita subtly nudged Abigail. "Charlotte likes Abigail and the baby so much. I think Abigail watching her for you is the perfect solution while Mrs. Johnson is out of town."

He was proud of his self-discipline when he didn't roll his eyes and sigh. "My sisters are coming in today."

Margarita's face fell. It was almost comical. She leaned forward to pass him his coffee and empanada. "But they have jobs. Mrs. Johnson could be gone for weeks or months."

"They work at our dad's company. Most of their work can be done from a computer, and they plan to take turns going into the office. We're not that far from Houston." He shrugged. "I think it will be nice for them to spend more time with Charlotte. They *are* her aunts."

Why was this weird guilt making him over-explain? He clamped his lips together to stop talking.

"Of course. Family's always good." Her smile was that of a woman trying to rethink her strategy. He could take advantage of that right now.

"I'd like to speak with Mrs. Dixon alone for a bit. Is that possible?"

"*Sí. Sí.* Of course." Her real smile returned, and she waved them to the back door. "I'll keep an eye on Paloma for you."

"No need. I'll take her." Abigail moved quickly to pick up her daughter, who was stacking blocks and knocking them over. "She needs to eat and have a diaper change. But thank you, Margarita."

He followed her up to the apartment. Her gaze carried a tinge of unease as it darted to him, then back to Paloma. She talked to her daughter as she pushed the stiff door open.

She turned to him. "I really do need to change her. Can you give me a moment?"

"Sure. I'm going down to get some tools out of my truck. I want to fix your door."

"My door?"

"Yes. It's hard to open."

"Okay." Her brow wrinkled in confusion.

It didn't take him long to get back up the stairs. Kneeling at the open door, he removed the old screws and replaced them with the longer ones he had purchased.

"Fixing doors. Is that a sheriff's usual job?"

"Nope. But I like things to work properly, and

if you need to get into the house quickly with Paloma, struggling to open the door could waste precious moments. It's an easy fix, anyway."

He stood and tested the door. "There. Now you'll be able to get in and out without a problem."

"Thank you."

She had put Paloma in the high chair. He slid into the chair across from them as she cut up a banana.

She sighed, then looked at him. "You have a million questions. Do you doubt I'm Xavier's little sister?"

"I do have questions." He sighed. "It doesn't make sense. Why hide?"

She stiffened and focused on Paloma.

Hudson wanted to demand answers to the questions that had been circling his brain, but he knew that anything that felt like an attack would have her building walls. He needed her to open up, so he started over. "How about you tell me what you remember. You said they sent you away. Do you know when or why?"

"Apparently my mother had cancer. No one told me. I just knew she was in bed a lot. She started getting tired, that's what she told me. I would go and lie in her bed. Every day she'd read a story to me about a mother promising to always love her son, even when he got older.

Then, at the end, the mother is old, maybe dying, and the son holds her.

"It made her cry, but she said the tears were her love for me. There was so much that it had to leak out. She gave me a tiny little bottle. She said she put her tears inside so that I would always have her love with me."

His chest tightened, threating to crush his lungs. What would he do if he knew he was dying and had to leave Charlotte? "She was preparing you for her death."

She nodded and wiped at her face. "I don't know what happened to the book or the bottle. Late in March, one day after school, I went into her room and she wasn't there. Xavier was sitting on her bed. He said she had gone to heaven."

For a few minutes, she focused on her daughter. "It had to be hard for her. I can't imagine what I would do in her place." Setting the last of the banana on the tray, Abigail caressed her baby's soft curls. "I used to be angry that no one told me. But I get it now."

He nodded. "She wanted your time to be untarnished."

"That's what I think too. The day of her funeral, while we were getting dressed in our room, Belle packed a backpack. I didn't understand." She swallowed. "I didn't tell her about the bottle or book because I didn't know I was leaving."

"They sent you away on the day they buried your mother?" Anger flared, and he had to remember that Xavier and Belle were just teens at the time.

She nodded. Standing, she filled a sippy cup with water and gave it to Paloma, then lifted her out of the high chair. "My mother's aunt was at the funeral. I had never met her before. My mother's family cut off communication during her marriage to my dad. They didn't get along. My great-aunt told me stories that didn't make sense. She hated my father and anything to do with the De La Rosa family."

So Abigail had had years of being turned against her family. Things were making sense now. "She came to the funeral and took you away?"

With Paloma in her lap, she played peek-a-boo for a moment, then sat her daughter on the floor to let her explore. She sighed. "As a family, we all got into a black limousine. It seemed so big to me. We each put a flower on the coffin. I wanted to keep mine, but Daddy took it from me. We left the cemetery and went to the church's fellowship hall. My father was so sad. None of them were talking.

"Everyone else was, though. People were

giving me cookies and telling how sorry they were, but that my mom was in a better place now. I wanted to go too if it was a better place." She gave him a lopsided smile. "I don't think I really understood she was gone forever."

He hated the helplessness that was squeezing his insides. That little girl needed people to hold her and love her. Hudson had felt so lost at his mother's funeral. He had also been angry and had probably snarled at anyone that got close. Especially his father. That whole month had been a blur, except for the feeling of being alone. "What happened at the church?"

"Belle and Elijah—he's my other cousin—"

"Yeah. I know who he is."

"Right. You know them better than I do." She took a deep breath. "Anyway, after the funeral they took me out past the church playground to the back parking lot. She was there, waiting next to this big black SUV. Elijah handed her my backpack."

"Just Belle and Elijah were with you?"

She turned away and blinked several times. "Yeah. I don't know where my father or brothers were."

She looked back over at him, confusion filling her gaze. "I don't know if they knew what was happening. Belle leaned down and hugged me and said it was just for now. She said they would come get me when it was safe."

"Safe?"

"Yeah. That's what she said." Her bottom lip twisted. "Then my aunt took my arm and said it was time to go. I was so scared. I lunged for Elijah, and he put his arm around me."

She moved back into the corner of the couch and pulled a pillow into her lap. "I begged him to save me. I think I yelled for Xavier and my dad. I didn't know this woman and she was taking me from my family."

They sat in silence for a bit. "I wanted to stay with them. Mamma was gone and they were all I had left. I pleaded with them not to let her take me away. But Elijah didn't say anything. He didn't *do* anything. He wouldn't even look at me. Belle was crying, but she didn't do anything either. I was put in the back seat and that was it. I called out to them, still begging, but they didn't move. I twisted around to see if they were going to come after me. They stood there until I couldn't see them anymore."

The room went silent. She was lost in that little girl's trauma. She had to be Gabby. Either that, or she was the best actress he'd ever seen. There was no reason not to believe her version. It was missing the pieces that would help her make sense of the reasons why they'd sent her away. They had thought they were protecting her. But it had left a little girl lost and confused.

He went to the couch and sat next to her, wishing he could hold that traumatized little girl. Taking Abigail's hand, he gently squeezed it. "What do you remember about your father?"

She shook her head. "I remember he was tall—but back then I was small, so I'm not sure that's reliable." She pulled her hand out of his and twisted her fingers. "He would take me riding on his horse. He taught me how to sit in the saddle and use the reins. There were times when we played games in the kitchen—chutes and ladders, Candyland and card games."

"Those are good memories."

Turning in her seat, she watched Paloma scoot around the coffee table, picking up toys and chewing on them. "They seem incomplete. Since I've been back in town, there seem to be memories behind a fog. I can't clear it away."

He wanted to ask her if she was ever afraid of her dad, or if he ever violent—but those were leading questions. He wanted to know what she remembered. "Do you remember him with your cousins, your brothers?"

Wrapping her arms around her middle, she pulled into herself. Her eyes searched the room as if she would find the answers somewhere in the apartment. "Why was it only Belle and Elijah that took me to my aunt? Did my dad and my brothers know?"

Hudson rubbed his temples. He wasn't sure how to handle all this. Xavier had told him that their father was a violent drunk that abused the older kids. This was his friend's tale to tell. But there were so many gaps Abigail needed filled.

"Xavier talked to me. He and Damian knew they were taking you to your aunt. It had been set up before your mother's death. From what I understand, they had asked her to take you temporarily. Abigail, your father was a violent man. When they reached out your aunt cut them off. Then she moved and they couldn't find you."

Her head shook in denial. "That doesn't make any sense. I don't remember my father being violent. And we did move a couple of times, but we should have been easy to find." Abigail looked so lost and alone. Hudson moved closer and put his arm around her. She closed her eyes and leaned into him.

"She changed your name. Changed her phone. Mail was sent back. She went into hiding with you. From what I understand, she thought your father was dangerous and she didn't trust your brothers."

Curled up against him, she was quiet for

a long time. Paloma's babbling was the only sound in the room. "She did change my name. I never knew the ranch's number or address."

She sighed. "When I was little, Daddy was gone a lot. I always thought he was working. But when he was home, I remember the nights we had dinner together. He would tell us stories about the ranch and his dad and granddad. I wanted to be his cowgirl and work the ranch by his side. None of this is making sense. There were nights when Belle would pull me into her bed and wrap us under her blanket, holding me while a loud storm passed over the house. She said it was a storm, but there was never any rain."

She pulled her knees up and worried her bottom lip. "You said that you and Xavier are good friends. You're not from here, so where did you meet him?"

"Military. Xavier joined to get away from his father. We served together. Abigail, your father had some troubling issues when he drank. From what I know, your brothers and cousins were trying to protect you."

She took a deep breath in and laid her head against his shoulder. "My mom raised my cousins. Did you know that? Their mother left them. My childhood memories are so messed up. There were nights that Belle didn't come to our room. When I asked her where she went, she said a friend's. But we weren't allowed to go to anyone's house. Did Xavier tell you where she was? Did it have to do with my father?"

"He said there was a shed, and when he was mad at them for not doing something right, they would have to stay in the shed. Your mother would keep things from getting too violent, but when she got sick, he started using the shed more. With her gone, it got worse. Xavier told me your father went into a rage after your mother died and they were all worried that they couldn't protect you. He was unpredictable. Sending you to stay with your aunt for a few months or a year was the best option. They tried to call you but she wouldn't let them talk to you. When they went to the house, you'd moved. They tried to find you. When they finally found your aunt, she told them that you'd run away, and she didn't know where you were."

"That's not true," she protested. "When I was seventeen, she kicked me out. I stayed with friends until I went to college. I stayed in contact with her the whole time."

"She lied to you and them. You need to tell your brothers who you are."

"I don't know. It's so much to take in." She released a quavering breath. "I don't know what to think. I came here with the idea of finding my dad. And I thought if I could find him, then everything would be okay. But he's gone. I don't know who to trust."

"Abigail, they've been looking for Gabby. You need to let them know that you're here in town and that you're okay."

She shook her head. "If they'd really wanted to find me, I think they could have. How do you know their version of the story is true?"

Jaw clenched, he tilted his head back and looked at the ceiling. "They're your family. You might feel like you've been abandoned by them, but I believe Xavier when he said they did the best they could at the time. They were teenagers who had just lost their mom and were scared of their dad. Was it right to sneak you off that way? No. But now you have an opportunity to connect with your family, and you should take it."

Great. Now he was a hypocrite. When was the last time he'd had a real conversation with his father? He hadn't even invited him to his home here in Port Del Mar. But that situation was different, right?

His hand stroked Abigail's upper arm and back. Yeah, they were a mess. But she didn't know what a gift her family would be. The De La Rosas were good people.

Just like his dad. His head fell back against the sofa, and he stared at the ceiling. He was so tired of being angry about something he had no control over. Did his father still hate him?

Shifting, he laid his cheek against her forehead. "You're here in your hometown for a reason. The Espinozas have been great, but they are not your family. Don't miss this opportunity and waste any more time."

She leaned into him. He wasn't sure who was getting more comfort from the contact. They lingered like that for a moment then she gently pulled away from him.

The space between them left him cold. At the opposite end of the sofa, she tucked her legs underneath her. "There are families you are born into, then there are families you make. I've decided to make my family. If they'll let me, I want to make the Espinozas my family. I don't know the De La Rosas." She lifted her chin. "I came to town to find my dad, and he's dead. I don't know if I want to meet the cousins and the brothers who sent me away. They don't have anything that I need."

He took a deep breath. She was being stubborn. Hurt and pride had a way of doing that to a person. He should know.

Chewing on the inside of his mouth, he studied her for a moment. "I want to tell you something I've never told anyone—not even my family or my ex-wife."

His chest burned at the thought of telling this story, but she opened up a painful memory for him. Maybe this would help her.

"The day my mother was shot." His throat burned. A few deep breaths and he tried again. "That day, she hadn't wanted to stop at the convenience store. But I complained and whined that I was hungry and thirsty, so she finally took me in. While I was grabbing a drink, a man came in. I hadn't even realized what was happening when my mother knocked me to the ground."

Abigail moved back over to him and pressed a warm hand against his rapidly beating heart. "Hudson, you don't have to—"

He touched his fingertips against her mouth. "Let me tell the story." He felt hollow on the inside. A giant cavern opened. "She covered me, telling me she loved me and that it would be okay. The rest was a blur."

His throat had gone dry. Taking a moment to collect himself, he looked at his hands. "Literally nothing but motion, sounds and people screaming, then a weird silence."

He had to pause. "I didn't understand what was going on. I felt warmth and blood. We just lay there, me with my arms around my mom.

Her breathing became really labored. I don't remember how long we were like that. Someone with a uniform—maybe an EMT—took her off me. She went into an ambulance. I was taken to the hospital in the back of a police car."

The emptiness and confusion were back. This was why he never thought about this day. It was too hard. "I was alone in a room for what seemed like forever—I think people talked to me and offered me food, but I don't remember anything until my dad came in. He's the one who told me she was gone."

Abigail had moved into his arms, and he pulled her close. Holding her the way he wished he could hold on to his mom, he clung to her.

"I never told my dad that it was my fault." The words came out hoarsely; his throat was raw. "It was my fault that my mom, *his wife*, was dead. It was one moment that changed our lives. Me not wanting to wait for dinner. I don't see how he could ever forgive me. We don't even really talk anymore. It's too painful."

"Hudson. You can't—"

"Shh. Time with your family is precious. I know I have a heightened sense of protecting others. I've made it my job. But the list of people I let in is very short. I have to keep it manageable."

He took a deep breath and moved back. "Xavier, Damian, Belle and Elijah need to be given a chance to love you. You might not need them, but they need to know that you're okay. Please tell me that you'll go to them by the end of the week."

He pulled her back into his arms. Yeah, he liked to keep his list of people he cared about short. But he had a feeling that, no matter what he told himself, the distance he kept or how professional he tried to be, it was too late. He cared very deeply for Abigail and her daughter. They had made his short list.

"What if you have it wrong and they don't want me on the ranch? That I'm just another complication they would rather do without."

Leaning in and pressing his cheek to the side of her head, he whispered, "What if they love you more than you imagined and you coming home is a dream come true for them? If you hide and never ask, you'll never know."

Hope was the most dangerous thing he could give her. "If I give in to that hope, I give my family the power to destroy me when they shut the door on us."

The mental image of her standing alone on the old porch with Paloma in her arms was so vivid. The sound of a door slamming shut echoed in her brain. Her mother's bedroom door. The way her aunt had kicked her out. How the police had slammed the door when her husband had been arrested. She had been left standing alone each time. No goodbyes.

"You have proven how resilient you are. Put your hope and faith in God. But give your family the opportunity to bring you in."

"I'm so tired of being resilient." That was a level of hope that would crush her if she let it steal into her heart. If they didn't want her, she would have to leave Port Del Mar. What she couldn't speak out loud was her biggest fear.

But it was pointless to hide the truth from herself. It wasn't her family's rejection that scared her the most; it was Hudson's. He had made it clear there was no room for her in his life.

This wonderful, generous man had been hurt by his family and his wife. He wasn't going to risk his heart on her, and that made him very dangerous. Falling in love with him would be so easy to do—and would fit right into her pattern of self-destructive behaviors.

After all the hurts and disappointments she had lived through, she knew better than to rely on anyone for security. On one hand, Hudson could be her lifeline in this storm. On the other, he could be the boat that sank her.

All she wanted was peace, happiness and

family. Why was that so difficult for her to attain? What had she done wrong? What plans did God have in store for her?

Paloma banged a cup on the coffee table and yelled. Laughing, Abigail moved away from Hudson's warmth and sat on the floor next to her daughter. "Someone wants my attention. What is it? You want more? You have to ask nicely. Please."

Hudson stood. "It's time for me to head out. When are you going to tell them?"

He was so tall that she had to bend her neck to a ninety-degree angle to look up at him. "I didn't say I was going to tell them. Are you trying to intimidate me?"

With a sigh, he dropped to his haunches. "No."

Paloma handed him her cup and babbled some noises. "You want more water?" His large hand swallowed up her cup. Standing, he went to the kitchen and refilled it.

Her stupid, lonely heart wanted her to notice how terrific he was as a father. It didn't matter that he didn't want them on his short list.

Handing the cup to her daughter, he looked at her. "When are you going to tell them?" he repeated.

"Give me a week." She stood and picked up Paloma. "I want to think about how I'm going to do it. What I want to say. Maybe I'll write a letter."

"You say, 'Hi, I'm Gabby. I'm in town and would love to get to know you.'"

She rolled her eyes, then shook her head. "If it's so easy, when are you calling your dad?"

He narrowed his eyes, but before he could say anything, his phone went off. Glancing at it, he smiled. "It's my sisters. They're downstairs." He put a finger out for Paloma to grab. "Want to meet the two smartest, silliest, pain-in-my-neck women?"

Abigail had overheard a few phone conversations with his sisters, and Charlotte had gone on about how wonderful and funny her aunts were. Theirs was the kind of relationship she dreamed of having with her siblings.

"Are you coming down?" His piercing gaze held her in place and brought her back to the moment.

"Yes. Let me get Paloma's bag." She sat her daughter down on the sofa and went to get the backpack out of her room.

If she was honest with herself, she was disappointed that he'd called his sisters in instead of asking her to watch Charlotte. But he was careful about the people he allowed into his daughter's life. It was the right thing to do.

She would have doubts letting someone with her baggage watch her daughter.

She was feeling raw and vulnerable because of the deep family secrets they had shared today. Yet each time Hudson was around, she felt safe and comforted to have him close.

That worried her. There was no way she could allow herself to become dependent on him.

Coming back into the living room, she found him texting on his phone. "Everything okay?"

Looking up, he nodded. "I told my sisters that you were coming down to meet them and they screamed like teenagers at a concert. Apparently, they've been wanting an introduction for a while. Someone has told them all about you. Or should I say *several* someones have."

"Me? What are people telling them about me?" She brushed past him to reach Paloma and had to stop. The coffee table was in the way. He leaned into her as she looked up.

They froze for a second. His eyes went to her lips. Was he going to kiss her? Her lungs stopped working. The woodsy smell of him surrounded her. Inviting her to risk her heart.

He stepped back and cleared his throat. "Sorry. Didn't mean to get in your way."

She nodded and smiled. "Oh no. It's okay." But it wasn't anywhere close to being okay. It would be so easy to fall for him. But no one had to warn her how it would end. She knew. He'd leave her. Like everyone else.

Paloma on her hip, she followed him to the shop. As soon as they stepped inside there were identical women standing on each side of her.

"This must be Paloma, the amazing little girl we've heard all about." They looked from the baby to her. "Hello. I'm Madison and this is Liberty."

They were softer and a little bit lighter in coloring than Hudson, but she could see the family resemblance.

"Hi. I'm Abigail."

"We know." With a smile to light up the Texas Stadium, Liberty patted her arm. She cut a glance to Margarita and Josefina at the counter. "They have kept us updated on you and our brother. Which is good because he never tells us anything important. But we do have to check out things for ourselves you know. Someone has to protect our big brother."

"So, tell us everything about you and your plans," the other twin picked up.

Abigail blinked. "Updates?"

Hudson's sigh was so deep she could feel it. He took her free hand and pulled her away from the twins.

"How about you give her some space so we can sit down? I'll tell you everything you need to know. Not that there is anything to know." He cut a glare to the sisters behind them. And it sounded like he muttered traitors under his breath.

His sisters laughed and followed to the corner table in the back.

Liberty reached for Paloma. "Can I hold her please. I'm sure you have seen what a great father Hudson is."

"Liberty." Hudson just about growled his sister's name. She laughed and took the baby.

"How about we start with stories about Hudson as a boy. Then you can share." The sisters went on to tell her amusing stories of their childhood.

Hudson rolled his eyes, but he didn't hide the smile the memories brought.

Shared memories were a blessing of family. They knew all the weakness and ugly spots. They also knew the joys and greatest moments.

This was what her heart longed for with her brothers and cousins.

In reality some people never had this. She feared she was going to one of those.

Chapter Eleven

Abigail leaned forward to check her hair. It had been a couple months now without a trim. It was still short, but the severe edge had softened. Tilting her head, she studied how the light reflected in the new color she added last night. She had tried to return it to her natural color, but it had been so long since she started bleaching it, she wasn't sure. She looked like a stranger.

Resa bumped her shoulder and smiled. "You look great. But if we don't join the family soon, Mamma will come looking for us, and that's not good. We need to be seated before the first song starts."

Now that she was going to church with the Espinoza family, she had gained a new peace. She had a church family. Of course, it being a small town, Hudson and the De La Rosas also attended the same church.

For the first time in her life, she felt as though she had real friends and family. She had shown Margarita and Josefina the website and they were so excited about things they had never even thought about before. It had gone live, and orders and payments had increased.

As she followed Resa to the Espinoza pews, people smiled at them. Margarita had explained that the pews didn't really belong to anyone, but after so many generations, families had their spaces. And some of the old-timers got downright territorial.

Abigail loved it. She glanced over to the right side a little farther up. That's where her brothers and cousins sat with their families. Her gut twisted. She hadn't come up with a plan yet, but she ran out of time. Hudson would not hesitate to tell them if he thought she was going to keep hiding.

During her devotional on Wednesday, she'd had an epiphany. Saying she had turned everything over to God was not the same as actually doing it. She was still struggling with trusting Him completely.

A shadow fell over her. Turning, she looked up into Hudson's indigo-and-gold eyes. He nodded to her, then indicated he wanted to sit next to her. Nerves slammed into her chest. She wasn't ready to talk to him, for him to be so close. He just stood there, waiting, as people started looking at them. Resa pulled her over to make room for him.

"Thank you." He sat down and looked straight ahead. At the front of the church was a beautiful painting of a sunrise over the ocean. Rays of light came down from heaven, and a dove formed the center of the scene. The Holy Spirit. She loved the serenity it gave her. It reminded her that God was in every part of every day, from sunup to deep in the night.

She took a deep breath and relaxed.

Hudson leaned in closer. "Charlotte saw Paloma in the nursery and wanted to stay with her."

Was he concerned that their daughters had bonded? Or did he feel the same wave of contentment that she felt whenever the girls were together? Sighing, she kept her gaze forward, focusing on the dove. The service hadn't started yet, and people were still chatting and greeting each other. He leaned in again. "You told me a week. Time is up. When are you going to tell them?"

She turned and glared at him. "Soon. I have a plan." She was working on one, anyway, but she was procrastinating. Hudson didn't need to know that. That was between her and God.

"It's only going to get harder the longer you

wait. And I don't like knowing something this big and keeping it from my friends. They're good people."

Guilt hit her. She hadn't thought of how it made him feel. "I'm sorry. I promise, I'm going to do it. I just need to figure out the right time."

"What are you going to do?" Resa leaned in from her other side, a twinkle in her eye. "You two going on a date?"

"No." They both answered in a harsh whisper at the same time. People were starting to look at them.

Resa nudged her but kept looking at Hudson. "They're wondering if you're sweet on her. I mean, you are sitting with us instead of your sisters." She winked. Being in the middle of seven kids, Resa didn't think twice about teasing people and getting in their business.

The music started, and they all fell quiet. Abigail let the notes fill her and lift her heart to the heavens. In this world of uncertainty, God was the keystone.

She loved this little church. Every Sunday there was a new message that inspired her. It was as if God had a lesson ready each week just for her.

This time, the pastor talked about learning to let God's plan work in everyone's lives. He was right. Abigail knew she had to open her heart to new possibilities. Reading from the Bible and telling stories, the pastor made it sound easy. She made a note of the scriptures so that when Monday rolled around and she stumbled, the Word could pull her back onto the right path.

When the last worship song had finished, people started milling around, chatting and making lunch plans. Peace and warmth filled her.

Hudson scooted out and waited for her and Resa to join him. Abigail stood, then stepped back to let the other woman out. She glanced over at the De La Rosa family. They were in a cluster, but then Belle turned and smiled at her. All Abigail's warm, hopeful feelings froze as her cousin walked straight over to her.

"Abigail!" Belle hugged her. "It's so good to see you. I was going to go by the bakery Monday, but this saves me a trip. Well, I'll still come by for my chocolate croissant." She laughed.

Abigail didn't know what to do. Belle was standing in front of her talking like they were friends. Every muscle in her body went rigid. Her eyes darted to Hudson, and he lifted one brow and smirked at her.

She'd get no help from him. Sheriff Menchaca was enjoying this too much.

"I just had to tell you how much I love, love, love the new *panadería* website. I was told you designed and built the whole thing. It's so perfect for the bakery and so easy to use." Belle stepped back, but she kept her hand on Abigail's arm. "Anyway, it gave me some wonderful ideas."

Resa came out of the pew and joined them. "Hi, Resa," Belle greeted her. "Where are Margarita and Josefina? I wanted to talk to them too."

"They went to get the kids. We're meeting them out front," the younger Espinoza replied. "I'm heading out now. I'll see you in a bit, Abigail. Hudson, will you and your family be joining us for lunch?"

"Charlotte would be mad if I said no."

Resa squeezed his arm as she passed by. "Yeah, it's all about Charlotte." She winked at Abigail.

Heat climbed her neck. Why were people forcing her on Hudson? Poor man, he was going to start hating the sight of her.

"I was hoping we could talk about a cross-promotion." Belle was talking to her.

Good. That gave her something to focus on as she tried to ignore the man next to her.

"A cross-promotion?" She had lost track of the conversation.

"Yes. We're turning two, maybe three of our cabins on the ranch into short-term rentals. I was trying to think of ways to make it personal and homey. You had some gift basket ideas on the website." Bella's eyes lit up. "Wouldn't that be a perfect little welcome basket when someone stepped into the cabin? Sweets from the bakery along with the freshly ground coffee beans? Maybe a few things from our tackle and gift shop on the pier?" She raised her eyebrows in excitement, looking at Abigail as she waited for a response.

Abigail was still having a hard time realizing that Belle was talking to her. She managed a smile and a nod, hopefully convincing her she was listening.

Her cousin glanced at Hudson. "Have you seen the site? It makes me want to visit Port Del Mar and eat up all the goodness." She turned back to Abigail. "We could pull in other local merchants."

This was exactly what Abigail had envisioned when she had put the small gift baskets on the site. Taking a deep breath, she finally found her voice. "I have more ideas about putting together Port Del Mar baskets and using them to promote local products. It's that personal touch that brings people to a small town like this. I've been putting together some gift baskets with different themes. I can show them to you. Each season could have a different basket."

"Yes!" Belle grabbed her arm.

Now Abigail was excited too. She'd thought it would take longer to approach people about her idea. "We could also customize them if they wanted to add certain items and have them all ready when they arrive."

Belle nodded. "That sounds perfect. It's exactly what I'm thinking. Now, get the boys on board."

"The boys?"

"My brother and cousins. I run the ranch, but they have input. And they own so many local businesses, but they don't get the whole personal touches for profit. Having those small details is important to rebooking, good reviews and spreading the word. My goal is to have at least 75 percent occupancy. I think things like that are what bring people back and get them telling other people about it."

Abigail nodded. "I can bring something out to show you later today. Around six or seven?"

"That would be great! Then we wouldn't just be telling them—we can *show* them. Come out at five—the whole family will be at the ranch for dinner. We can all eat together, then hit them with the presentation."

Abigail was thinking ahead of all the different specialty shops in town she had wanted to include. "I could put three or four packages together. Some manly fishing ones and a spa-day type of basket. Really, the possibilities are endless."

Bella clapped her hands together. "Yes! Oh my gosh, I knew I loved you. That is so good—and we've got the restaurants. The fishing charters and the pier gift shop. If you need anything, let me know, or Julie, our office manager. We could really have fun with this. Let's wow the boys." Then she furrowed her brow. "Are you sure you can get something ready by tonight?"

"Yes, this is something I've already been playing around with. I have several packages sketched out."

"Sounds great! And fair warning… Sunday dinner with the De La Rosas is quite the event! There's lots of us, so it won't be a quiet affair." She looked over her shoulder as her husband, Quinn, waved at her. "The kids are getting restless. I have to go, but I'm excited to see what you bring us. Thank you, Abigail." She turned and walked off, joining her husband and their five kids.

She was going to the De La Rosa ranch.

For a moment, she couldn't breathe. She was

going to go have dinner with them. Belle had invited her into their home. She wasn't going to have to show up uninvited.

Of course, they didn't know who she was.

"Stop." Hudson's voice was low but strong. "Don't overthink this invitation. It's an informal business meeting with dinner. Before you leave, ask for a few minutes alone with Belle. Start with her. Or tell the whole family at once. But you can't deny this is a perfect opportunity that has been set at your feet."

She nodded. She had just promised to have an open door to God's plan, and then Belle came over and invited her to the ranch. "It looks that way, doesn't it? My planning is done, and now it's time to do."

Hudson chuckled. "I couldn't have said it better myself. If you need anything, you have my number. To ease your nerves, I suggest you think of the best-case scenario and a worst-case one. Go in knowing you have a plan no matter what happens."

"Yes. Thank you."

"You've got this. Trust that ultimately God is in control. And bundle up. The weather is supposed to get rough tonight with temps dropping. It might get below freezing."

She had to laugh. "Really? It was sixty-five

today. Plus, I've lived in Ohio for so many years. I can handle the cold."

He gave her a little salute. "Yes, ma'am."

The weather was the least of her worries. She was finally going to the ranch. After years of dreaming about it, it was happening.

"Abigail." His warm hand gently squeezed her shoulder. "It's going to be okay. You're about to find out how much your family loves you."

"Are you sure? They haven't recognized me. Even after I dyed my hair back to its natural color. What if they don't believe it's me? And then there's the whole mess with my ex..."

"Good. You're planning the worst-case scenario already. What will you do if that happens?"

She laughed. "Nice pep talk."

"That's why I'm here. But really, Abigail, it's going to be fine. And you'll be mad at yourself for waiting so long. But don't fixate on that. Shame and regret are a waste of time. Enjoy your family and know that God brought you to this point at *this time* for a reason."

"Thank you."

With a lopsided smile, he turned and walked out of the sanctuary. A few people were still meandering. Margarita stood at the front door with a group of Espinoza kids. Her oldest daughter held a smiling Paloma.

Margarita waved her over and Abigail joined them. She was going to spend some time with her favorite new family before heading out to meet her old one.

What was going to happen when they found out that the little sister, they had sent away was back in town—and had been for a while now?

She hoped Hudson was right and that they would welcome her and Paloma.

Halfway to the side door, Hudson saw his daughter. She was giggling at something his sister was saying. His heart twisted. He'd give about anything to protect her innocence. A twinge of melancholy clouded his thoughts.

Eventually, Charlotte would grow up and someone would hurt her, no matter how hard he tried to protect her. Liberty, the older of his twin sisters, poked her head around the edge of the door. There was pure glee shining in her golden eyes. He had a bad feeling it was at his expense. He glared at his sister.

She made an attempt to glare back, but she couldn't hold it for long and ended up grinning. "What are you so grim about?" she asked.

He stepped through the doorway and found

his other sister, Madison, waiting behind them.
They were both smiling.

"What are you so happy about?" Great, his
little sisters had him resorting to his fourteen-
year-old self.

Liberty put her hand on her hip and taunted
him with all her sass. "Wouldn't you like to
know?"

Jumping up and down, Charlotte called for
his attention. "Daddy!"

"What is it, little bear?" He picked her up.

Her small hands touched his face. "Tía Liberty said that you were making a poor attempt
at flirting." Her smile was so big, it took up
her whole face. "Were you flirting with Ms.
Abigail?"

"No. But what do you know about flirting?"
Eyes narrowed, he cut a hard glare at his sister.

"It's what boys do when they want a girlfriend.
Abigail would be a great girlfriend for us."

"I think your aunt has been saying very in-
appropriate things and needs a time-out."

Neither his tone nor his expression intimidated
her. With a smirk, Liberty shrugged. "Why aren't
you flirting? You're a decent enough guy. You're
not old. You should be flirting."

"Yes!" Charlotte agreed. "I think you're the
bestest. I would marry you, but Tía Maddy
says I can't."

Hudson tilted his head back to the ceiling. *One. Two. Three.*

He loved his sisters, but they were the best at pushing his buttons. He was an adult and not here for their free entertainment. He lowered his chin and looked at Liberty. "You shouldn't be saying these kinds of things to my daughter."

She blew out a puff of air. "I know we've both told you many times and it bears repeating. You, big brother, take yourself way too seriously."

"I'm a single dad and a sheriff. They need me to be a responsible adult."

"We're just worried about you and want you to be happy. It would help if you smiled every once in a while and were nice to people," Madison said, her expression much more serious.

"I am nice to people. All the time. Unless they are breaking a law or being a pest." He gave her a pointed look. "Stop being a pest and you'll get to meet the nice me."

"Daddy is nice. And he has the best smile." His daughter looked confused by the tension between her favorite people.

He kissed her cheek and set her on the ground. "Thank you."

"I'm hungry, Daddy."

Thankful Charlotte had changed the subject, he jumped on it. "Then it's time to have some lunch. We were invited to join the Espinozas at Bridges's house. Do you want to go?"

"Yes." His daughter squealed. This was accompanied by clapping and more jumping. "And Daddy, you can practice flirting. Abigail and Paloma are going to be there."

He let out a groan before he could pull it back. His sister was laughing out loud as she went down the hall and out into the parking lot.

"What's so funny, Tía Liberty?"

"Your daddy. He thinks he's so smart."

"He is smart."

He loved that he could do no wrong in his daughter's eyes. How long would that last?

Liberty took Charlotte's hand. "Oh, he is smart. Too smart for his own good. I think God has some plans for him that are about to shake his foundation."

"My foundation is fine, thank you very much."

"Oooh! This is going to be fun. There's a rumor going around that your single days are numbered. Wonder what they're talking about?" His sister almost danced her way to his Jeep Gladiator. "The debate in front of the feedstore this morning was about how long it'll take for you to ask her out. I guess we aren't the only ones that noticed your daddy giving Ms. Abigail goo-goo eyes."

"Goo-goo eyes?" He might have shouted. Several people in the parking lot looked over at them. Of course, his sisters were laughing so hard they doubled over.

"You're executives at a financial firm. Act like it." He took a moment to steady his breathing. He was allowing them to push his buttons again. "Never mind. Let's go home. Maybe there your *tía* Liberty and *tía* Madison can learn enough manners to go out in public."

"Please, Daddy. I want to go see Desirae, Josh and Paloma. And Angie and Nica too."

She loved hanging around Margarita and Josefina's kids as much as possible. Being an only child was tough on her.

Charlotte's eyes were big as her bottom lip puckered. It was the saddest face, but it was her eyes that got him every time. They were so much like his mom's.

Putting an arm around his daughter, he pulled her close. "I'm just being grumpy. Your aunts do that to me sometimes."

"I promise to use good manners, Daddy." She turned to look at Madison then Liberty. "You will too, right?"

"Yes. We promise to use our best manners." Liberty spoke, but both of his sisters laid their hands over their chest, trying to act innocent.

Charlotte hugged his legs. "We'll be good,

Daddy. Can we please go to the Espinozas' house for lunch?"

Hudson took a deep breath and forced his taut muscles to relax. "Fine. We'll pick up a pie and head that way. Now get in the truck."

He helped her buckle up in the back seat, then stepped out and put a hand on Liberty's door to block her. His other hand gently stopped Madison as she headed to the other side of the Jeep. He bent down to Liberty's level, going nose to nose just like when they were younger and he had to get her attention.

She was always joking and pulling pranks, while Madison would follow along. "I know you're joking and you think it's funny, but I don't want Charlotte confused. The other night she asked me to let Abigail and Paloma move in with us. She wants a sister so badly. Maybe even a mother. That's why I asked you and Madison to help me out. I can't let her get too attached to Abigail and her daughter."

Liberty blinked, moisture gathering in her eyes. "Oh, Hudson…"

"No. Don't be sad. Just stop kidding around about it. This is serious, and I don't want Charlotte hurt. You should understand that." Did she remember how much she and Madison had cried every time their dad broke it off with his latest girlfriend? His throat burned.

He had been so helpless, unable to make them feel better as they wept. "I have to take care of my daughter and protect her heart while I still can. I know you're just messing around and playing, but it can have serious consequences to a six-year-old who doesn't understand. So, stop it. Okay?"

She lifted her eyes to his, her glance so much like their mother's that his gut twisted. She touched his cheek. "We're worried about you. We miss the guy you were before Zoe tricked you into marriage, then deserted you and Charlotte."

He looked away, flexing his jaw. He hated that his ex-wife could still hurt his family. "This is not about Zoe, it's about you filling my daughter's head with ideas that won't ever materialize."

He cut his gaze to Madison.

She nodded. "We know how important she is to you. You're the best dad. But you're a person too. You're more than her father and the sheriff of this town." She took a step closer to him. "You deserve happiness too, big brother."

"I am happy." He glanced over his shoulder. His daughter was sitting in the back seat chatting to her hand. It was apparently talking back. Man, he loved that little girl. "We should go." He dropped Madison's hand and moved around Liberty.

"Hudson, I'm sorry." Liberty reached for him this time. "You know I would never do anything to hurt her or you."

He nodded as she opened her door and climbed in. By the time he walked around the front of his truck, Liberty was in the front seat and Madison was having a full-blown conversation about sea turtles with his daughter.

He was responsible for this gift God had given him. All his attention and love were hers.

Before he closed his door, he heard laughter floating across the parking lot. When he turned toward the source, he saw Abigail standing with Josefina and Noah, the youngest Espinoza. He was closer to Abigail's age.

Hudson's lungs tightened at the thought of the two of them going out on a date. Noah leaned in and whispered something, causing Abigail to throw her head back and laugh.

Josefina looked put out. He could relate. But he had zero business being any kind of jealous. If Abigail wanted to go on a date with a kid who didn't take anything seriously, well then Noah was her guy.

Charlotte asked a question and he nodded, but his mind was wrapped up in Abigail.

He knew how worried she was about telling her family who she really was. And he knew Xavier. The De La Rosas would pull her into their fold. She wouldn't need him to have her back; she'd have her family and the Espinozas. Two large families that understood loyalty and caring for others.

But then again, Xavier could also be cynical. With his history it was understandable.

If there was the slightest hesitation, Abigail would be hurt and might close down.

He should have told her he'd go with her. As he started his truck, a text came in. It was Abigail. Don't worry about Charlotte seeing me at lunch. I'm going home to get ready for tonight.

She was respecting his wishes and staying away from his daughter. He hated that that made him sad.

Chapter Twelve

Abigail leaned forward over the steering wheel. Snow flurries had started falling, but they were nothing compared to those in Ohio. As she drove, the flurries turned to huge, fluffy flakes. Then they disappeared and ice pellets pelted her windshield.

Texas had some roller-coaster weather reports. At least it was still daylight and she could see where she was going. She checked her phone. Only a couple of miles to the ranch. Glancing up at her rearview mirror, she saw that Paloma had fallen asleep.

The car slid to the right, even though she hadn't turned the wheel. She wasn't in control…they were gliding. *Ice.*

Taking her foot off the gas, she let the car coast. She knew that fighting it could make it worse. There weren't any cars on the road, so that was good.

But then her heart went into overdrive as the car veered off the road into a ditch and came to an abrupt stop. The big fat snowflakes were back, and the road looked wet with a little snow. It didn't look icy. She had hit a patch of black ice.

She twisted around to check on Paloma. She was awake and rubbing her eyes but thankfully seemed to be okay. "Looks like we're in a pickle, baby girl." And they were so close to the ranch.

"Ma. Ma. Ma," her daughter replied.

Putting the car in reverse, Abigail tried to carefully back out. That didn't work. The front grille was buried in a snow-covered dune, so there was no going forward. "We are definitely stuck." Should she call the Espinoza sisters?

Hudson would be the obvious choice, but she felt so lame. "It was just this morning I was bragging about my driving skills in winter weather." She looked at her daughter. "I could just call 911."

The dunes blocked their view of the ocean, and on the other side was flat marshy land and water. The town was ten miles behind them and the ranch was two miles ahead.

There were several blankets in the back, she should get those. She reached for the phone to call Margarita and a text came through. It popped up on her dashboard screen too.

Hudson. There was no way he was going to let her forget that a girl who'd just come from Ohio couldn't drive in Texas winter weather. Opening the door, she felt the cold wind hit her face and take her breath. Careful not to slip on the ice, she made her way to the trunk for the blankets.

She opened the text. Are you still at home? The next one was just a minute later.

Reports are warning that bad weather is hitting us. We're closing all the country roads. Where are you?

Abigail?

She was going to have to call him and admit she had underestimated the Texas weather. She'd call Hudson as soon as she got Paloma settled and warm. Her hands were already stiff; she hadn't even brought her gloves.

With the trunk opened, she gathered the three blankets. Her phone was ringing. She couldn't see who it was, but she imagined it was Hudson since she hadn't replied to any of his texts. It stopped, then started again. "Hold your horses. I'll answer you soon as I can."

She wrapped the blanket around Paloma. She was babbling and chewing on the corner of her cloth butterfly book. The phone started chiming again. Her hands now free, she answered it this time.

"Hello." Did he hear the shaking in her voice? It was so cold.

"Abigail, are y'all okay? Where are you? The conditions are getting worse by the second. Texas weather is so unpredictable."

"We're both fine." She sighed as she put him on speaker and rubbed her hands tighter. "Well, as fine as we can be in a ditch on the side of the road."

"What happened?" She could hear the deep concern in his voice.

"I hit a patch of black ice about two miles from the ranch. I was going slow and there were no other cars around. We're okay, but I don't have enough traction to get out. It's a little embarrassing since I had just been bragging about my driving skills in winter weather."

"Nothing you can do about ice. There's no way anyone can drive on it. But you're safe and warm?"

"Yes. I have blankets in the trunk. The car

doesn't seem to have any damage. Paloma is talking and reading a book."

"Hang tight. It'll take me a little longer to get there with the chains on my tires. Should be about fifteen to twenty minutes out." He hung up before she could tell him to be careful.

She turned to face her daughter. "Help is on the way. We seem to have our own cowboy who's riding in and saving the day."

The snow was coming down thicker. A blanket of white was starting to cover everything. At least Hudson should be able to see her red car. One of the things she had been most excited about when moving to Texas was the warmer winter. She hated snow. It was beautiful, but living in it was not fun.

She rested her head on the back of her seat and watched Paloma play. It'd be really easy to fall asleep. That wasn't good. "Let's sing some songs while we wait."

Paloma loved singing, so she pulled out every song she knew until she saw the big black truck driving their way.

She knew that being an independent, strong woman was a good thing, but sometimes it was really nice having someone you could count on. She wasn't sure why, but tears burned in her eyes. Hudson said that he would come, and now he was here.

As an adult, she had never had one single person she could truly depend on. This was his job, that was all, she reminded herself. She wasn't anyone special to him…and the sooner she got that through her thick skull, the better it would be for both of them.

Moments later, the black truck eased past her and stopped, its flashers on.

As Hudson walked around and inspected her car, he looked like a man in control of his world. Then his gaze came up to hers and he smiled, coming to her door.

She opened it and got out. "Thank you so much for coming to get us."

He grinned and nodded. "Seems as if even a girl from Ohio needs help when it comes to Texas ice."

He walked around to get Paloma.

"It's ice no matter where you live, Sheriff Menchaca. I just didn't think we'd have ice on the road along the beach."

He lifted Paloma and her car seat out, wrapped in a blanket. "Reports are saying that every county in Texas is under a winter weather watch. First time in history. It's going to be a big mess. Since the ranch is closer, I'll drive you over there and we'll take care of your car later. Is that okay?"

"Works for me." She looked up and down

the long stretch of road. "I don't think anyone is going to be out vandalizing or stealing cars right now."

He laughed. "You got that right. Careful." He helped her into the truck and handed her Paloma. "I'll get her car seat locked in. Anything else you need from the car?"

"Yes. The baskets. One is on the driver's side. The other two are in the back seat. Is it too much trouble to take them now? That was the whole reason I was going up to the ranch, anyway."

He lowered his chin and narrowed his eyes, the blue and gold taking her breath for a moment. Would she ever get used to his penetrating stare?

"Abigail. That is not the only reason. I would even say it's not the main reason. But it's a great excuse to go to the ranch and tell them who you are." He didn't say another word. Instead, he simply closed the door and went to the red car.

She stepped down from the truck and walked over to the passenger side of her car. Hudson already had the two larger baskets, and she grabbed the smaller one.

"Let's get going," he told her. "It's brutally cold out here."

With the baskets and Paloma settled in the

back seat, they both got into the front. She hugged her coat closer to her. His truck was so warm.

"So have you thought of what you're going to say to them?"

"About the baskets?" She sat back and grinned. He was so serious that it was easy to tease him. With the predictability of the sun rising in the east, he shot her a glare and then turned back to keep his eyes on the road.

"No. I'm thinking along the lines of you telling them that you're Gabby, their baby sister."

She pulled in closer to herself. "You do know you take yourself way too seriously, right?"

"Have you been talking to my sisters?"

Laughter bubbled up, and Paloma joined in. "You've heard that before?"

"Unfortunately, yes, but stop trying to distract me."

"From what?" she asked innocently.

"You know what." He released a breath. "We were talking about you and the real reason you're going to the ranch."

Rubbing her hands over her arms, she looked out at the quickly changing landscape. "I've gone over it a million times. Should I tell them first, as soon as I get there? Then, after dinner, talk about the baskets and the opportunity of us working together? I'm really excited about that."

She took a deep breath. "But me being Gabby might overshadow the work stuff. So, I should start with that. After dinner, I can tell them who I am. Belle said the whole family was going to be there. The kids too? Who do I tell and when do I do it?"

With a heavy sigh, she leaned back against the seat.

"I wish I had an answer for you, but I don't," he admitted gruffly. "This is a decision you have to make for yourself."

They fell into silence, and he focused on the road. Hudson gripped the steering wheel, his jaw clenched. He drew in a deep breath, his chest expanding and his shoulders falling. The black gloves fitted snugly over his large hands.

It was clear he wanted to say something more. And she didn't want him to hold back for her sake. Because deep down she needed reassurance that she was doing the right thing.

"Hudson, I understand where you're coming from, but I really want to know what you recommend. Because I can see myself completely chickening out and not saying anything. Maybe you being here is a good thing. I know you won't let me leave without telling them the truth."

"Abigail, you have no idea what a big deal this will be to them. They've been worried about you for years. I know you have different memories of what happened." He blew out a breath. "And you asked for my advice so I'm going to give it to you. After dinner, take Belle or Xavier, whomever you're the most comfortable with, and ask to speak with them alone. Let them take you back to the family and introduce you. I think it would be less overwhelming."

"Xavier's my big brother. He taught me so much. He wasn't the one that put me in the car. Maybe he didn't know. I don't know what he knew. You're right... I was a nine-year-old, and the memories are blurred. What if they don't believe me?"

He nodded. "It's a possibility. That would be the only thing that would stop them from embracing you and welcoming you home. I'll let Xavier know it's okay for him to believe you. That'll be the hardest thing for them because, just like you, good things don't come easy for them. They've been taken advantage of and lied to by family. So, they might be a little skeptical that you've suddenly shown up. But that doesn't mean they don't love you. Either way, it seems as if your faith is solid. You know God has you."

"That's true. Thank you. So, you're saying that the worst-case scenario is they think I'm a con artist like Brady?" She laughed, and as she did, the weight lifted from her shoulders. "The irony of them thinking it's a con, right? But I can deal with that. If that's the only thing stopping us from moving forward, then that I understand. Hopefully they'll give me a chance to prove who I am."

"You also deserve answers. There are pieces of information you are missing. You were just a kid who got thrown out into the world alone. They wanted to protect you, but I think it went wrong. It wasn't because they didn't love you."

Did they love her? They didn't know her. Had she ever been truly loved just for herself? The dunes disappeared and she could see the gulf. More than an inch of snow covered the sand. "Can we stop?"

He slowed. "What is it? Something wrong?"

"No. But how often is it you see a beach covered in snow? It might not ever happen again. I want to take a picture. Is that okay?"

"For social media?" He made it sound like a disease.

"No. I stay far away from all that after everything that happened with my ex… It's for Paloma. She won't remember any of this."

When he came to a complete stop and put

the truck in Park, she climbed down and made her way to the beach. A huge tree trunk was pushed up on the shore. The twisted roots were tangled with a blue rope that had to be four inches wide. Snow covered most of it. It looked like a piece of modern art, man versus nature.

Each shot had her full focus. She didn't hear Hudson come up behind her. "Let me take a picture of you."

With a small squeal, she spun around. "You scared me."

"Sorry." He didn't look sorry. Holding out his hand, he waited for her to hand over her phone.

Instead, she pointed it at him and snapped some photos. "The sheriff doing his job in an ice storm. Oh look! There are snowflakes on your hat." Lowering her phone, she scanned the winterized beach. "God is amazing. In the harshest conditions, He can show us beauty if we take the time to look around. I don't need a picture of me."

"Paloma will love seeing her mom way back when." He took her phone.

"It would be so cool to build a snowman castle. I need my gloves and scarf and earmuffs." She lifted her hands up to pose, and he took a picture of her standing in the snow in front of the ocean. He gave her the phone and started back to his truck. "Let's go. I think you might be stalling."

She scooped the snow off the top of the tree and balled it up. As he turned the corner of the truck, she struck him. Faster than she could blink, he turned to her. Muscles frozen, she stood, paralyzed. Why had she done that? Was he going to leave her here?

"Are you done?" he asked in a super calm voice. "Your daughter is waiting." He opened his door and paused for a minute. "I would return fire, but as you pointed out, you don't have the proper gear for a snowball fight."

With that, he got in the truck and waited for her. She shivered. She ran round to the passenger side and slammed the door behind her. "I'm sorry."

"You don't know how sorry you'll be for starting a war with me."

Was he grinning?

He then had the audacity to wink at her. "I might have grown up in Texas, but I've lived all over the world and I know how to win a snowball fight. I recommend you watch your back. Ambush is my favorite technique."

"You'll have to catch me first." She laughed.

Hudson wanted to chuckle out loud at her expression. How had he ever thought her pretentious and shallow? He hated to admit it, but his sisters might be right. He had become too serious.

Right now, all his focus was on his daughter. That was as it should be, but he needed balance also. Maybe he had been too narrow in his view of life. He could be friends with Abigail. That wouldn't risk Charlotte any more than making friends at school.

"How long have you and Xavier been friends?"

"About eight or nine years."

She glanced over at him. "He enlisted right after graduation? You said you served together?"

"Yep. He was such a kid. At seventeen, he was the youngest. But he was also the most determined. There was this huge chip on his shoulder, and he was the only one of us who was married."

"Selena. I remember them dating. They were inseparable. He said he was going to marry her. Are they going to be mad that I lied to them?" She turned away from him and looked out the window. His gaze flicked to the car seat in the back. Paloma was asleep.

"I don't know, but I do know he had two photos that went everywhere with him. One of Selena, and then the group picture you had. His family means everything to him, and he'd do anything to protect them. That would include you. They might be hurt that you've seen them in town and even talked to them but didn't say anything. Just like you need to give them a chance, they need to listen to you too."

He wanted to wrap her in his arms and tell her it was all going to work out, that this would have a happy ending, but he'd figured out long ago that no one could make that kind of promise.

As they rolled through the ranch gates, the back of the truck fishtailed. Abigail gripped the dashboard and turned to check on her daughter. Paloma was still sound asleep.

"Sorry." The truck straightened, and he eased forward.

"Have I mentioned I hate ice?" she said between clenched teeth. Scanning the snow-covered pastures, she tried to recall any memories, but she was coming up empty. She shook her head. "This doesn't look familiar."

"With all the snow, I don't recognize it either—and I was out here a couple of weeks ago."

"That's true. It's beautiful, but it's a lie, isn't it? It looks unblemished. The pure white blanket hides so much. I don't see any buildings."

"The main house is way back. There are several cabins. Damian and his wife have a place on the ranch. It's even farther back, closer to the coastline. I think they're out of town. They travel for her work."

"So, Damian won't be there. He's the only one I haven't seen in town." Her heart raced as they went deeper into the ranch. Snow made it surreal.

"He rarely comes to town. After he came back from the service, he pretty much became a recluse. There was an explosion during his last tour of duty, and he's a double amputee. The lower half of his left arm and leg had to be removed."

"What? That's horrible." She pulled the blanket over herself and huddled into it. "I've missed so much. Is he okay? They haven't had an easy time of it."

"No, none of them have, but they haven't let any of it hold them back. They're good people who have fought to come out on top. That's why I was a little protective of them before I knew what had brought you to our town."

She nodded. Her big eyes were sad as she scanned the landscape. "All my memories with them are good ones. Other than the last one with Belle and Elijah. That's why I was so hurt when they didn't come get me. I believed in them one hundred percent. But my aunt's constant tirades about them and them not coming to prove her wrong had me doubting my memories. I'm still not sure what's true and what's just part of my imagination." She sat straighter and pointed to the right. "Is that the house?"

"Yep." The sun was setting. Turning to drink it all in, he noted that the warm colors of the evening sky made everything shimmer in the ice and snow.

"Why am I so nervous?" Her gaze stayed on the horizon, but her hand reached for his.

He didn't think she even knew she was doing it. His fingers met hers, her smaller hand curling around them.

"You've got this." He wanted to promise her that it was going to be okay, but again he stopped short. He had no right to make any promises to her.

"Thank you for being here." She kept her face turned toward the house, but her fingers tightened around his.

It was as if she had a direct line to his heart. Why was this so difficult? He wasn't interested in a romantic relationship. So why did his heart and head act as if he had given them the go-ahead?

As soon as he knew she was safe and that the De La Rosa family had taken her in, he would be out of here. There was a county that needed him.

He didn't have time to be distracted by one lost woman. She would find her way without him. She had to.

Chapter Thirteen

"I remember the porch." Her rapid pulse was visible in her neck.

"This is it. My childhood home." She practically had her face pressed against the glass.

"The drive goes around to the back of the house and to the main barn. I'd follow my dad and Xavier and beg to get a horse. Sometimes they would take me out with them. Most of the time I was sent back to the house to help my mother." She glanced over at him with a half attempt at a smile. "I'd get so mad and kick dirt clods all the way to the kitchen door. Sometimes I'd hide in the garden just to prove they couldn't tell me what to do." She went on, eyes wide. "The garden was my favorite place. It was huge with vined-in areas that made a perfect hiding spot. I hid there a lot whenever I was mad or scared."

Sadness pulled at his heart. The idea of a small Abigail hiding hurt him. "Do you remember why you were scared?"

She was quiet for a moment, her eyes shadowed as she tried to recall the memories. Shaking her head, she looked back to the house. He eased the truck as close to the front porch as he could manage. The less she had to walk on the icy ground, the better.

She gasped and covered her mouth with her hand. "Mamma. I can see her standing on the top step."

Now he was concerned. "You see her right now?"

She laughed. "No. My memory of her standing there is so clear, it's like I could reach out to her."

He sighed in relief. At least she had more of a grin back.

"Don't worry, Sheriff. I haven't slipped into a hallucination." She pointed to the post at the top of the steps. "In the mornings she would stay there until we were out of sight. Xavier drove us to the bus stop at the end of our ranch road. In the afternoons, she would be waiting in the same spot. When I first went to school, I thought Mamma stood there all day, her life on hold until we came home. I wanted to stay with her so she wouldn't be alone, but of course they didn't let me."

"Did you tell them why you wanted to stay?"

She pursed her lips and tilted her head. "That I don't remember." She snorted. "It also didn't occur to me that a mom raising five kids needed downtime."

"Your world revolved around your mom, and you kids were her world. She probably did miss you. Xavier and the others have wonderful memories of your mother. She sounded like a very loving person."

"Thank you. Sometimes when I was in the fourth grade, she wasn't there on the porch, and I was happy that she'd found other things to do. There was always a snack waiting for us in the kitchen, and dinner would be started. I would help Belle finish it. Mamma was so tired. She would be in bed when we got home. I was so clueless. I was happy that she had so much new stuff to do that she was tired. I thought that her new stuff must really be fun if it made her go to bed so early. I would curl up with her and do my homework, and she would read to me. Every night." She took a deep breath. A tear fell on her hand, and she seemed surprised by its presence.

"Oh sorry. I didn't mean to do that." Sniffing, she wiped her face. "I wasn't expecting to be hit with emotions like this." She shook her head and tapped her cheeks with her fingers. "Do I look okay?"

"You've been stuck in an ice storm with your baby." He cupped the side of her head with his hand. His thumb wiped the trail of tears off. She was beautiful, but he didn't think she needed to hear that from him. Plus, he absolutely didn't need to be saying it, let alone thinking it.

"They're the most unjudgmental people you'll ever meet. They aren't going to think anything about this. Besides, you were so young when they sent you away. I don't think you ever got the chance to properly grieve. Do you want to tell them right away and get it over with?"

"No." She looked as if she wanted to throw up. "I need to stick to the plan."

"Do you want me to carry Paloma or the gift baskets? Which do you want to take?"

"I'll take the baskets and focus on the job. Otherwise, I might completely forget the reason I'm here. If you'd watch Paloma, that would help me stay focused. I think if I have her, it will be more personal and I'll lose it."

"It's okay to lose it sometimes." He sat back and gave her space. "Like when you're reunited with a family you haven't seen since the day you buried your mother. You were a child, Abigail. There's a lot of emotions to process."

"Now you sound like a psychologist. Is that part of your sheriff training?"

"Nope. It's years of counseling my father forced on me because I was an angry teenager and he didn't have a clue what to do with me."

Her lips quirked. "That was smart of him."

"Yeah. It was also a way to handle me without actually talking to me himself. After the murder of my mom, our relationship was rocky at best."

"Have you talked now?"

"Not really. My father is a fixer. Not much into talking about it. Just fix it and move on. He's really good at moving on." An uncomfortable tightness squeezed his chest whenever he talked about his father. He loved the man so much, but he also hated him.

Despite the therapy and his sisters, he couldn't shake the belief that his mother's death was his fault. His father had to blame him, even if he never said it. If his mother was still alive, they would never have gone down this path. "When did this become about me?"

"When you started giving me advice on talking to family."

"Smart mouth."

"My mamma would say it's better than being a dumb one."

Laughter erupted from him at the unexpected reply. Paloma's eyes opened. "Ma. Ma. Ma."

"It's okay, sweetheart. We're here."

The front door opened, and Belle De La Rosa stepped onto the porch.

"We're home." Tears hovered on the edge of Abigail's words.

"Think about the baskets for now, or you'll never get through this."

She nodded and stiffened her spine before opening her door. He got out and went to get Paloma.

Belle waved as she came down the steps. She wore thick work gloves on her hands. "I'm glad to see y'all. This weather has turned into a monster. Careful of the ice. The beautiful snow is covering it up." The whirling snow was so thick it became harder to see. "Here, let me help."

She took two of the baskets from Abigail. "This is some customer service. Let's get that baby inside where it's warm. And both of you. You are staying here where it is safe and warm."

"Thank you so much." Abigail followed Belle, and Hudson stayed right behind her.

"We'd still be stuck out there if Hudson hadn't rescued us."

Paloma was cocooned in several layers of clothes and a blanket. It was hard to tell there was a baby buried beneath all that. She definitely had her daughter prepared for the cold.

He tried to tell her that, but a gust of cold air hit and made it impossible to talk. He'd need something to cover his face if this kept up. It wasn't even nightfall yet and it would only get colder.

The snow crunched under their boots as they made their way into the house. The warm air felt good. They hadn't been out long, but the temperature had to have dropped since he checked last. "We're going to be in for a long winter night."

Belle nodded. "My husband, Quinn, and cousin Xavier, are making sure the stock has water and shelter. My brother Elijah and his wife Jazmine are adding a heater in the pump house and wrapping the exposed pipes. We also have all the tubs full of water in case the pipes freeze. They're predicting that it's going to get worse by tomorrow afternoon and that we might not get above freezing for three or four days. Not sure our system can handle that."

"We've never seen anything like this. It's

going to be a mess across the state," Hudson murmured.

"Yes. We're ready to hunker down. All the kids are snuggled in the family room under a big tent." She turned toward Abigail. "Be warned. We tend to be loud and all over the place, but I like to call it controlled chaos."

Hudson placed his hand on her back and guided her through the living room. It was warm and comforting and very lived-in. The love in the house wrapped around her.

But there was nothing from her memories; she didn't recognize it as the house she grew up in. They followed Belle into a huge country kitchen. Emotions threatened to overwhelm her. Hudson's hand slid to hers, and he gave it a gentle squeeze.

Abigail took a deep breath and grounded herself. They were here to talk about ideas for the Dulce Panadería and the short-term rental cabins. This was a business meeting so they could work together to increase traffic and outside sales.

She would put on her fake happy for a few more hours. Her ability to pretend everything was great had been honed after years of survival and trying to fit in. Once she told them the truth, she was never going to fake her way through life again.

After tonight, she was going to address any problem head-on, then move past it. No more wasting time feigning that everything was fine when it wasn't.

Yes. That was her new mantra: address the problem, then move on. She could do this. Everything inside her shook, but that was okay. This was a big event in her life. It was normal to feel uncertain.

God, I know You have this and I trust You will be holding on to me no matter what happens tonight.

Belle stopped at a large rustic farm table. That hadn't been here when she lived here. There were twelve chairs spaced comfortably around it, and the smell of fresh bread and other appetizing aromas filled the room. She saw an older woman at the stove. Belle introduced her as her mother-in-law.

The kitchen was modernized and new. She didn't remember it being this big or having an island.

"This is a great kitchen. It looks a lot newer than the rest of the house."

"It's a complete redo. We knocked out some walls and redesigned it. This is the heart of our home. I spent hours learning to cook in the old ranch kitchen with my mother. She talked about remodeling all the time. I'd like to think she'd approve."

Hudson was next to her. "Belle is a great cook. Everyone says yes if they get invited to have dinner at the ranch, even if it means re-arranging everything else. Thank you for including me."

She laughed. "You're always invited, Sheriff. I'm not sure I'm up to the Espinoza standard and I know they've been feeding you. But I don't think we had much choice tonight. Mother Nature is in charge. But I'm glad you're both here. These baskets are amazing. I can't wait to show them to everyone."

"Is that fresh bread I smell?"

"Yes. This is most certainly bread-baking weather. I've made cinnamon rolls for the morning."

The back door opened, and Abigail heard stamping feet and talking. She had met everyone in town at one point other than Elijah and Damian. She had seen them at church.

As they came in from the back porch, the room was filled with energy and laughter. "I told you he was going to do that," Jazmine was saying as they walked in.

Selena, Xavier's wife, came in from the front room, then went straight to Abigail and hugged her. "We're so glad you made it. We were worried. I've been listening to the reports." She turned to Hudson and took Paloma's hand. The baby curled her fingers around Selena's. "We've closed all the roads and asked people to stay wherever they're at. It's going to be a rough night. The bad weather came in so fast. Abigail, I know you're from Ohio, but ice always makes me nervous."

Xavier came in behind his wife and wrapped his arms around her. "When it comes to everyone's safety, she's always nervous."

She sighed and leaned into her husband. "This is true, but it's getting bad out there."

"It is." Abigail smiled at Hudson. He was holding Paloma as if it was the most natural thing in the world. "I'm thankful that the sheriff was able to get to us."

"We would have gotten you, no worries." Elijah was studying her, his head tilted. "Do I know you from somewhere? You're new to Port Del Mar?"

Hudson moved closer to her and put his free hand on her arm. "She's working for the Espinoza family and has been going to church. I want to thank you for inviting us to stay. I know Abigail doesn't want to take Paloma out in this storm."

"Oh, don't even think about it." Belle waved

him off. "We have plenty of room. It might be a little crowded, but that's better for staying warm, right? Come on, let's sit. We have a little time before the kids come in asking for dinner, so tell us about the baskets and how you see us working together."

Selena sat at the table. "If Belle had her way, everyone would live at the ranch all the time. There're never enough people on the ranch for her."

Elijah snorted as he started looking through one of the baskets. "That's the truth. I wouldn't put it past her to call up a storm just so we all have to stay longer."

Everyone laughed. Belle waved a wooden spoon in the air. "Yes. My powers are great, and I have control over the weather. If my family is wise, they will do as I say."

Elijah pulled off a piece of fresh bread and popped it in his mouth. "We already do what you say."

"Not always, but my little brother is learning well."

Jazmine wrapped her arms around Abigail and pulled her to the table. "Ignore them. Do you have siblings?"

She froze. If she said no, that would be an outright lie and she couldn't do that. "I do."

"I've got twin sisters that put any sibling rivalry to shame," Hudson said as he sat and balanced Paloma on his knee. "So why the three baskets? Wouldn't one work?"

She loved him. Wait, no. She didn't *love* him. She strongly appreciated his attempt to steer the conversation back to the business.

"Selena, Belle and I have been talking about doing something unique, and when Belle said you had been thinking the same thing but even bigger, we got very excited." Jazmine turned to her husband, Elijah. "It would even benefit our other businesses."

"That's right." Selena smiled. "We could pull in all the local shops and farms. The welcome baskets would be put together based on visitors' interests. I think one of the best parts of Abigail's idea is that people can preorder items to add to them."

Elijah pulled a paper fish from the basket closest to him. "Someone could book a deepsea fishing trip ahead and the details would be waiting for them on their arrival?"

Selena gave Abigail an apologetic look. "Sorry. I just love the possibilities of your idea."

"I'm so happy you're excited. But to answer your question, Elijah…yes, it could be a deep-sea fishing expedition. Or, alternatively, it could be a birthday party on the pirate ship.

In that case, the basket would be designed for the birthday kid. Or if it's a girls' weekend, there could be spa supplies or horse riding. I thought we could have a birthday package, a romantic weekend package, and a guys' or girls' getaway, along with the standard family vacation. I'm open to other ideas too." She paused to take a breath. "The packages could have different budget levels and, since the customers are booking ahead, there could be discounts. Everything they want would all be waiting for them in their custom basket with detailed instructions, maps and numbers. All they have to do is enjoy."

Selena stood and went to a basket. "It would really benefit the whole community and bring in more revenue."

"How would this all work? Have you talked to other businesses?" Xavier asked her.

Letting her excitement for this project take over, Abigail explained the details and how they would work together to do it. She would be the point person, organizing and delivering the final basket to each cabin. Elaborating further, she told them she'd created a forecast, a profit analysis and a list of potential problems.

Time slipped past as she answered questions and they explored all the opportunities. The De La Rosa family was going through the baskets now, making suggestions and picking out the things they really liked.

For the first time since they'd started, she looked over at the corner of the table. Hudson had made a comment or two, but he had mostly been keeping Paloma amused. She couldn't help mentally comparing him to her ex-husband, who had always needed to be the center of attention. It had been her job to make sure he looked good.

It had been clear from the first day that Hudson was nothing like her ex, but it went deeper than just being a good man of honor. When he took care of people, it wasn't for his own benefit. He truly respected and valued those around him.

He caught her staring at him and immediately grinned, then gave her a thumbs-up. Her heart kicked against her chest. *No*, she told herself, *he's just being friendly. He helps people for a living. It doesn't mean anything.*

Three of the older kids came in to save her from her spiraling thoughts. They were Quinn and Belle's oldest, asking about dinner.

Elijah and Xavier gathered dishes and Belle removed a few items from the oven and put them in a box. Everything was set for the kids to have a picnic in their fort. Jazmine and Elijah took the dinner to the other room as Belle and Quinn set the table for the adults.

Everyone worked so well together, like this big family dinner was a normal routine. They'd embraced her marketing plan, but that didn't mean they wanted Gabby De La Rosa back at their table.

She sat on the other side of Paloma. "Thank you for watching her."

"Not a problem. Charlotte is at a fun age, but I do miss her being a baby. It goes by so fast." He studied the activity in the kitchen for a minute. "Who are you going to talk to first?"

"My first thought was Xavier. He's my oldest brother, and as I mentioned, he wasn't there when I was dragged into the car. But then there's Belle. She's like a sister to me. We shared a room. She's been the friendliest."

"What are you two whispering about?" Jazmine had come back into the room and was pulling out the chair next to Abigail.

"Jazmine. Leave them alone." Belle set a platter of fajita steak on the table.

As the family joined hands to pray, Abigail had to stop herself from crying. This was a dream she had held in her heart for so long, and it had become reality thanks to Hudson.

Without him pushing her, she would have kept talking herself out of doing this. She might have still backed out if it weren't for the ice storm sending him to her rescue. God knew what she needed before she did.

Talk of the weather and what needed to be done for the ranch, a few jokes, and a plethora of shared memories kept the conversation going until everyone was finished eating.

Elijah stood and started gathering empty plates. "The sooner the table is cleared, the sooner we get dessert."

"That's true, but you also hate a mess." His wife laughed and helped him clear the table.

Hudson nodded at Abigail. She took a deep breath and went to Belle. "Is there somewhere we can talk? I have something personal to tell you."

Quinn was watching them, and Abigail almost told her to forget it. But Belle reached for her as she was backing up. "Sure. Would the front room be private enough? We could go to the screened-in porch, but it's a bit cold."

"The living room is fine." She glanced at Hudson as she followed her cousin. He was standing, bouncing Paloma. He gave her a wink, then turned to Xavier.

"Is everything all right?" Belle asked once they were alone, her voice coated with concern. "How can I help?"

"I haven't been truthful about who I am."

Leaning her head to the side, Belle narrowed her eyes. "You're not Abigail Dixon?"

"I am. But I've lived in Port Del Mar before. I'm Gabby De—"

Her words were cut off by a tackling hug. Her ears rang from the scream. Everyone rushed in from the kitchen. Everyone but Hudson.

"What happened?" someone out of her line of vision asked.

"Gabby's home!" Belle still had her in a hug. Abigail couldn't move her arms.

"I knew she looked familiar. I told you I knew her from somewhere." Elijah was next to her. "Belle, you have to let her go."

"No, I don't. I'm never letting her go." But she did. Belle was crying.

Elijah was the next to hug her, then Selena and Jazmine. "Where have you been? Why have you been hiding from us? What happened after you left, where'd you go? We've been so worried about you."

The questions came from all sides as they passed her around. Belle took her hand and led her to the couch. The kids came in wanting to know what had happened and were told that their missing aunt had come home. The children all hugged Abigail too. They had been told about her and were excited. But now they wanted to take their new cousin with them to the fort. Quinn's mother took Paloma and went with them.

Hudson stood close by, but he still hadn't said anything. Xavier, who hadn't embraced her yet, turned to his friend. "You knew?"

He gave him a quick nod. "For about a week now."

With a flick of his shoulder, Xavier glared at him. "You didn't think I would want to know that my baby sister was safe and here in town?"

Abigail stood. "As soon as he found out, he told me that if I didn't tell you, he would. Don't be mad at him."

Xavier turned to her. Something between anger and hurt was etched into his face. "Why did you have to be pressured to tell us you were here?"

She looked around at her brother and cousins, their wives. They waited for her response. "Because I don't understand the reason you sent me away. Mamma was gone and they—" she waved her hand to Elijah and Belle "—made me leave with a woman I didn't know. I clung to Elijah and begged Belle. I yelled for you. Where were you? Why did y'all send me away?" Now she was crying, almost sobbing. Hudson stood behind her and put an arm around her, holding her close to him.

"I thought you loved me. Tía said you were

all evil and that it was a good thing she saved me. I told her—" a sob interrupted her words "—I told her you were coming for me. I had my backpack hidden under my bed. You never came. Why? I didn't even know Daddy had died. Xavier, you said you'd..." She couldn't say another word.

Hudson's arm tightened around her. Xavier reached for her, his hand cupping her face. "Oh, baby girl. I said I'd always love you and protect you, and I did. Our father was a mean drunk. Mamma was afraid he would lose all control when she died, and he did. We did everything we could to keep you out of his way, but we were afraid we couldn't always be there. We asked Tía to take you for a few months until we could figure something out. It took longer than we thought." Tears rolled down his handsome face.

Belle took her hand, with Elijah right next to her. "Gabby, Xavier had the hardest time staying away that day. But he was afraid if he went that you'd ask him to let you stay and he would give in. We all decided with Mamma that you had to be safe and that the only place to send you was with Tía. We called. She would tell us to stop. We didn't. But then the number was disconnected. Nine months later, we couldn't take it anymore, so Xavier, Damian and I drove to get you and bring you home. You weren't there. We lost all track of you. We were still all in school, so there wasn't anything we could do."

Belle hugged her again, pulling her away from Hudson. "I'm so sorry you felt abandoned. I prayed that you were loved and happy. Frank just got worse. On the worse days, I'd picture you happy and loved and grateful we found you another home. He drove all the boys away. It was miserable. I was glad you didn't have to go through that." Belle released her and had to wipe the tears off her face.

Xavier took her hand and, for a long moment, everyone was quiet as he stared at her. "I should have seen it. You look like Mamma. We all look like the De La Rosa side." His eyes glistened with moisture. He glanced to the door where the kids were. "Paloma has the De La Rosa eyes."

"She does."

"I've prayed for your happiness and safety. I figured if you didn't want to find us, then you were happy. You were always in my heart, baby sister. I'm so, so sorry I didn't protect you like I promised, but I never, ever stopped loving you." He pulled her into his arms, engulfing her. Cocooned by Xavier, she clung to him.

She was home. They had not stopped loving her. Hudson had been right all along. God had brought her home.

"Damian!" Belle cried. "We have to call him. Use the video so he can see her."

It was after two in the morning before sleepiness interrupted their conversation. The kids had been put to bed hours ago, and at one point Abigail realized that Hudson had slipped out of the room. She sat at the kitchen table with Xavier, Belle and Elijah. They had just hung up from chatting with Damian.

Belle leaned in and rested her head on her shoulder. "You are not alone any longer, and you have choices. Think about what you want to do, and we'll support you."

Abigail nodded. She was overwhelmed by all the choices. No matter what she did, her daughter now had family. *She* had family.

Chapter Fourteen

It had been a long, hard week since Hudson had rescued Abigail from the embankment. He hadn't seen her for the last four days. But the sun was out, and the ice and snow were finally gone.

Walking around the side of the De La Rosa house, he found her where Belle had said she would be. Her back was to him. She was wrapped in a blanket and sitting on a bench swing that hung from the branch of a giant live oak.

The weather had been worse than anyone had predicted. The snow and ice had been unprecedented across Texas. Several times he'd been thankful that he had brought her out here to the Diamondback Ranch.

The utilities in town had been down and the water lines had frozen. The ranch had been more prepared for off-grid survival than her apartment.

He watched her for a while. She had no clue what an amazing woman she was. Most people would have crumpled under her burdens. The morning sun was highlighting the red in her dark hair. It fell in loose waves around her neck, natural and beautiful.

He took a step closer and she turned. A smile glowed in her eyes. "Well, hello, cowboy. Long time no see. Everyone safe in the county?"

"Back to normal for now. Hard to believe that this was all covered in snow and ice less than twenty-four hours ago."

She scooted over, giving him room to sit. "It's surreal. I was afraid that when the snow melted, I would find myself alone again." She smiled and took a sip of her coffee. "I don't think I have to worry about that anymore. Belle's trying to get me to move out here."

He tried not to frown, but his first thought was that she would be farther from home. Farther from him. Biting back a growl, he turned his gaze to the ranch. A few horses were standing at the fence, enjoying the sun.

When had he started associating her with home? He sighed. Falling in love with her was a mistake; he wouldn't make it worse by telling her. He knew better than anyone that life wasn't easy and that you rarely got what you wanted. "So, are you moving out here?"

"Oh no." She laughed. "I love them, but I've gotten really used to quiet. There is nothing quiet about this house."

A truck came up the drive. When she turned to see who it was, it put her closer to him. He fought the urge to pull her against him.

"It's Xavier." She didn't seem to notice that she snuggled into him. He waved and they waved back. They watched in silence as he made his way to the house.

"You know, I've never actually been on my own. I thought it would be horrible. But I've enjoyed settling in at my apartment with Paloma. I love that we have our own space. It means even more now that I know my family loves me."

With a nod, he draped an arm over her shoulder. She fit against him so naturally.

"Thank you, Hudson. I have so many options now."

"I didn't do anything." Her gratitude made his skin too tight.

"Do you know that the De La Rosas had set aside an account for me? I own a part of the ranch, which I haven't actually wrapped my brain around yet. But there's money for me to go back to finish college. It's all a bit over-whelming."

Everything inside him stilled. She was going even farther away?

"Where would you go?" The question burned his throat.

"I don't know, that's the beauty of it. I could go anywhere. I could finish at Ohio State. I had two semesters there before I moved in with Brady."

He kept his focus on the horizon. Yeah, her moving to the ranch would have been a better option than Ohio. But for the first time, she was able to make choices for herself. This was important. So, he made sure to nod and keep his voice casual. "You're a Buckeye?"

"I guess. But I'm not really feeling it." She took a sip of coffee. "It's the obvious choice, but it feels like going backward. I don't have any good memories there, other than Paloma."

His next breath came a little easier, the tight-ness in his chest loosening. "Options are al-ways good. You have an amazing talent. I saw it in action earlier this week. You've basically started your own business with nothing. Is there a reason that you want to finish school?"

"I've never done anything on my own ex-cept leave for college. I had applied for a ton of scholarships and I had to work really hard, but then I let Brady save me. Of course, looking back, I know now he wasn't doing me any favors."

Hudson wrapped his arm tighter around her and pulled her in. He kissed the top of her head. What he really wanted to do was protect her from the world. But everyone had lessons to learn, choices to make, a life to figure out. This was her time for that.

Shifting in her seat, she turned from the horizon to him. For a long moment, she just studied him.

His heart hit against his ribs. The stupid thing didn't understand that he couldn't have her. "What is it?"

"You know, when Brady came into my life, I thought he was saving me. But he wasn't—it was just another trap and I owed him. In exchange for his—" she paused and made air quotes "—'love,' I had to perform. I gave up everything I really was to make sure that I made him look good. That's all I was. But you…" She blinked a couple of times, and he looked away. She obviously didn't want to cry in front of him.

He gave her arm a quick squeeze and pressed his lips to her temple.

With a deep breath, she started again. "Thank

you for rescuing me time and time again but not expecting anything in return."

She was breaking his heart. "We all need some help every once in a while. You helped me too."

She slapped him on the arm. "Liar. How have I ever helped you?"

"Several ways." He couldn't tell her that she'd brought his heart back to life when he hadn't even known it was hibernating. "You called me out and reminded me to talk to my dad. There was so much unsaid between us because it was difficult. I'm not using that as an excuse anymore. I called him and made some big steps in getting him back into my life.

"You also showed me that it's okay to make new friends. My list doesn't have to be short if I trust God. Trusting others, even God, to take care of the people I love is a hard thing to do. Thank you."

She bit her lip and nodded, then turned back to the horizon. "It's not easy to trust others, to open up and let them know you need help. It's so much easier to go about pretending everything's okay. It's hard to be honest, even with yourself, about not being okay."

Twisting to face him, she tilted her chin up. Her gaze holding his, she pulled him closer to her. He reached up and cupped his hand around her neck.

He didn't want to think about the past or future. This moment was all he wanted. He lowered his head slowly, and their lips touched, dancing with the softness of snowflakes on the breeze. He traced kisses to the corner of her mouth and back to the center. She was sweeter than even his imagination. Until this moment, he hadn't realized how much he had missed this kind of connection, but it wasn't just the kissing. It was her.

Abigail made him want to risk his heart all over again. To fall into the bottomless gulf. No, he couldn't do this to either one of them. They were going in different directions.

He forced himself to pull away, but he wasn't strong enough to completely break contact. So he rested his forehead against hers. This had to stop, but his heart was singing. She could be his if he asked, but that wasn't fair to her. Not now, when the whole world was at her door.

"Hudson?" Her soft voice was unsure. He had done that.

"I'm sorry. That was a mistake." He stood, keeping his back to her. If he stayed that close, he'd start kissing her again, so he stared at the vast horizon. "I had your car driven to your apartment. The water and electricity are back on too. Are you ready to go home?"

"Yes."

Her touch on the sleeve of his Carhartt coat brought him back to her. "Hudson? What just happened?"

"It's been a long week, and I'm running on fumes. Let's go get Paloma and you can tell everyone goodbye. Unless you want to stay longer."

"I'm ready to go home."

Abigail's world was forever changed. Her family had been looking for her and loved her. Then Hudson had kissed her. Not just any kiss either. At least not for her. Maybe to him it was just an accident, but that kiss had shaken her foundation.

The trip back to town was thick with silence. How did they get back to their friendly conversations? She had shared more with him than she had with anyone else, but he had made it clear he wasn't interested in a relationship of any kind. And then he had talked about his list getting longer and kissed her.

She was so confused. With another glance at his profile, she tried to figure out what to say or do. Did this mean there was a chance that he was open to more from her, or was she looking for hints that weren't there?

His phone chimed. He reached over and hit Accept on his dashboard. "Hey, Madison."

Sweet laughter came over the speakers. "I tricked you, Daddy. It's me, Charlotte! I have a surprise for you. When are you coming home?"

"I'm going to drop Abigail and Paloma off at their place, then I'm coming home. Everything okay?"

"Yes. Please bring them. I want them to see my surprise too."

He glanced at Abigail with his brows raised in question. She nodded. "Sure." The word stuck in her dry throat.

"Yay!" Charlotte asked them questions and chatted for a while.

"Hey, little bear. I'm going to hang up now. I love you and we'll be there soon."

Silence fell over them again. She checked on her daughter. Breathing was becoming hard. She had to say something or explode. He might be the strong and silent type, but she needed words.

"Why did you kiss me?" Heat burned her neck. *Great*. In the next few minutes, her face would be red. This was why she never confronted anyone. It was so embarrassing.

The only indication that he had heard her

was the flexing of his jaw and the white knuckles gripping the steering wheel. She waited. There was no backing out now.

"Hudson… I'm confused."

He sighed, his big shoulders falling. "Me too. I was tired, you were … I don't know. It shouldn't have happened, and I'm sorry. You have so much to decide right now. The last thing you need is me throwing more on your plate."

"Maybe I can make room. It's a big plate."

He grinned for the first time since he broke the kiss. "My issues are too big for anyone's plate. You have new fresh choices to make."

Her heart thumped. Was he saying he wanted to be one of her options? "Hudson."

"No. I have to focus on my daughter. She's only six, and she deserves my full attention. We're friends. That's all we can be."

"Did you just friend-zone me? A man who claimed he didn't want any more friends?"

He rolled his eyes as he drove slowly past the row of brightly colored beach homes. He pulled his truck under his pretty turquoise one with the white trim. She might love his house as much as she loved him.

She smiled, admitting to herself that she loved *him*. For the first time, she thought that maybe there was a chance.

He frowned, looking over her shoulder. Turning, she followed his gaze. "What is it?"

"That's my dad's Land Rover." He didn't seem happy that his father had made a surprise visit.

"I thought you said you called him."

"I did. But I didn't invite him over." He shook his head.

"But this is good, right?" she asked.

Getting out of the truck, he handed her the diaper bag and went to get Paloma. "I hope my sisters are all right."

She hadn't thought of that. "I just assumed he was the surprise Charlotte was excited about."

He nodded. "You're right. But why is he here?" Unlocking the tall gate, he held it open for her.

"Because his son called to have a real conversation after too many years?"

He grumbled under his breath as he followed her up the steps. "It's just weird. He's never been here before. The least he could have done was let me know he was coming."

Hudson opened the door for her. Inside, his family was waiting. "Surprise!"

Abigail blinked. There were balloons, a sign and a cake. "It's your birthday?"

"No." Shaking his head, he lifted his daughter with his free arm as she threw herself at him.

"Happy Birthday, Daddy!" She hugged his neck and kissed his cheek.

Abigail lifted a brow and took her daughter from him. "It's not?"

Madison and Liberty rushed over to them. They hugged her, then their brother. "His birthday is Monday. But he probably forgot. He does that when he's busy. He forgets everything."

He sighed. "It's true."

They led him to the table, where his dad stood, not looking very sure of his welcome. "Son. Happy birthday. Your mom always thought this day should be a big family celebration. You joining us and all."

"I remember."

Abigail's heart hurt. His birthday had become another reminder of what they had lost.

"PaPa brought the cake. He said German chocolate was your favorite. Margarita made it for you. She said it won't be as good as your mom's, but she did her best. Right, PaPa?"

"Yes, ma'am. I suspect it will be super close. Is it okay? Me, being here—"

Hudson cut his dad off with a real hug this time, and the two men clung to each other. The sisters, close to tears, made themselves busy getting plates and drinks.

Stepping back, Hudson wiped his face. "Thank you, Dad. This is great."

"PaPa, this is Paloma and Ms. Abigail. They're our new friends. Paloma and I want to be sisters." His family laughed. Abigail and Hudson did not.

Cake was served and funny stories of Hudson were shared. Then Charlotte wanted to show Paloma the new doll and clothes her aunts had given her.

Liberty had whispered to Abigail that Hudson and their father had ignored their birthdays since their mother died, confirming what Abigail had suspected. Remembering his birthday was painful for both father and son.

Abigail was reluctant to leave Hudson's side. Was it her imagination, or had he leaned on her several times during the little celebration? She wanted to help him like he'd helped her. But he had just told her that he had to focus on his daughter, and she understood that. He had offered her friendship, and she'd have to be happy with that.

He had his own wounds, just like she did. With Paloma in her arms, she followed the girls to Charlotte's room. She paused once to glance back at him. She thought she caught him looking at her, but then he turned to his father so fast she thought maybe she had imagined it.

Then again, even the people who seemed the most put together could have scars hidden under all their perfect layers.

Chapter Fifteen

Abigail had just caught him staring at her. No wonder she was confused. He was sending her so many mixed messages and he had to stop. Set his mind right. Abigail was amazing, but if he started a relationship with her and then she left, his daughter would pay the highest price.

"That's quite a girl you got there." His dad pulled him back to the present.

"Not my girl."

"Well, that's a shame. Your sisters speak highly of her, and your daughter won't talk about anyone else but Ms. Abigail and Paloma."

"But we know how that will end, don't we?"

His father furrowed his brow. "I'm not sure I understand. You think she's a user and leaver like Zoe?"

"No. She's nothing like her." Hudson may have thought that the first week or so, but after spending time with her, he knew she had nothing in common with Zoe.

"Then how do you think it has to end?" His dad put down his fork and turned to him. "It's been a long time since we truly talked. Thank you for calling me the other day. I know it will take more than one conversation, but I want us to move forward. Being open and honest can be…difficult. But it was long overdue." He sighed and lowered his head for a bit. Then, with a deep breath, he locked his gaze with Hudson's.

"I thought about everything you told me. It was nothing I didn't already know. The police report contained everything you said. But I had no idea you blamed yourself for your mom's death. Or believed I held you responsible." His voice cracked. "I was dealing with a lot of grief, but I never, ever blamed you, son. It was just too painful to talk about and you were so angry. Emotions are hard. It was easier to send you to therapy."

"Thank you for that. I know at the time I yelled and fought, but overall, I can't imagine the choices I would have made if I hadn't had my therapist to guide me through the worst of it."

"But I still needed to talk to you. I was a coward." His father's lips were tight as he stared off into space. "Don't believe for a minute that your mother would've been okay coming home without you. I lost my partner, my best friend, the love of my life, but to lose a child? I thank God and your mother every night for making sure you came back to me."

Hudson's chest was tight. He had never thought of it that way. His father gripped his shoulder. "You have a daughter, now. What would you do to protect Charlotte?"

He'd lay down his life for his baby girl. Blinking back tears, he thought of his mother.

"Don't let her love for you get lost in bitterness and guilt. Be happy and love every minute of this life she gave you, twice. That's what your mother wanted for you."

His father gripped the back of his head and pressed their foreheads together before pulling him into a bear hug. "Son, I love you so much."

Hudson didn't know how long they cried. But all the tears that had been pushed down and locked away were freed. They fell until his dad's shirt was saturated. Pulling back, he went to the sink and splashed his face. Going back to his dad, he offered him a clean towel.

His phone pinged. Pulling it out, he read the message and smiled. "The girls decided to go for a long walk on the beach."

His father nodded. "You know this was your

mom's favorite time of year to visit the coast. She loved the off-season."

"I remember." Hudson nodded to his living room wall, where he had several family pictures. "Those are some of my favorite memories."

"Is your mom's death the reason you avoid real relationships?"

"Dad, I've been married. You were there. I know you never liked her, but that was a relationship. While it lasted, anyway."

"I never believed you were in love with Zoe," his father said. "She was a liar and con artist. You were tricked into that marriage, but we have Charlotte. So, like the Good Book says, God works it all for His good. But I'm talking about you falling in love, really caring for a woman. Putting yourself out there."

Hudson shrugged. After this emotional black hole they had just climbed out of, he owed it to his dad to be honest—but really, how much could they take in one night?

He sighed. On the other hand, maybe tonight was the night to get it all off their chests so they could finally move forward.

"Zoe messed me up some, but it's more than that, or Mom's death. It's a promise I made to Charlotte when she was born." He paused.

Would this destroy the fragile communications they just started?

"Son. I want to help make this right. Talk to me."

Hudson leaned back. "After Mom died, you started dating right away."

Frowning, his dad shook his head. "It was close to a year. Maybe a little less. But I wasn't really dating. Clair was the first...she was a friend of ours and I could talk to her about your mother without feeling guilty."

"It looked like dating to me. You went out to dinner and movies. You even went dancing. You used to dance with Mom in the kitchen, and then you replaced her without a blink."

"Oh, Hudson." His brow wrinkled in a deep frown. "I'm sorry. I never thought about it like that. I missed your mom so much. I was drowning in darkness, but I had you kids, so I couldn't let it pull me down. I needed someone to talk to like I used to with your mom. I missed having a companion. I had you three kids and you were so angry that I had to figure out a way to stay present for y'all."

He shook his head. "Son, I've never stopped loving her. I'll never stop grieving her loss. But, um...dating, for lack of a better term, helped me. Do you remember me and your mom had date nights every week? Clair knew this. She'd come over and drag me out of the house. She wanted to be there for your sisters too. She was a good friend.

"I got better and even went out on some real dates. I think Abby lasted the longest, but the woman sitting across from me was never my wife and we'd always end up as friends. We can always use more friends, right? I also thought the twins could use some trusted female advice. They were coming to an age that feminine issues would need to be addressed. I grew up with brothers. Maybe that was a reason I was so drawn to being around women. I enjoy their company. But I couldn't do a long-term commitment."

Hudson sat back, processing. His perspective was changing, but there was still the twins. "Didn't you realize that every time one of your girlfriends left, the twins would cry? Each time, they said they thought she was going to be our new mother. I couldn't stand it. I didn't know how to help. They would come to my bedroom and want to sleep with me because they were so sad. I would tell them they didn't need a new mom, that they had me."

Putting his hand over Hudson's wrist, his father squeezed it. "I'm so sorry. I knew they were struggling, but I didn't know they went to you."

"They didn't want you to feel bad. The twins made me promise not to ever tell you."

Hudson looked down. "When Zoe left, I promised I'd never bring anyone around Charlotte who wouldn't be in her life forever."

Eyes wide, his father looked shocked. "Have you talked to the twins about this since? I didn't realize they went to you crying. After each initial conversation, Clair, Abby and even Monica called the girls. They developed friendships that they still have today." His face relaxed into a smile. "They helped your sisters with their first dance and prom. Even with the first year at college. When there were boy issues, they were a lot more helpful than I could ever be."

Hudson was confused. "What? Why didn't anyone tell me about that?"

"Because you had made it very clear you did not want those women in our house. I'm thinking the girls didn't want to upset you when they continued being friends with them. Not bringing people in and out of your child's life makes you a good parent, but you're not doing that. Being a responsible parent doesn't mean you can't have adult relationships."

A part of him was mad at his sisters, but they didn't know his secret vow not to date or why. "They still talk to these women?"

"Yeah. Till this day, they are in their lives. If

you don't believe me, ask your sisters. Truthfully, you were just so angry when they were around that it was difficult for all of us. We were all trying to protect you."

The air left his lungs. They were trying to protect him.

"That girl seems to be a keeper. You're not being stupid, are you?"

"I'm not sure."

His father got up, then went to the door and opened it. "Your mother wanted nothing more than for you and your sisters to be happy. If that girl makes you happy, go get her."

"What if I love her more than she loves me?" Was that his real fear? Had he just been hiding behind his daughter?

"You won't know if you don't ask."

Heart racing, Hudson stepped out onto his deck. Which direction did they go?

"Are you looking for us?" Madison's voice pulled him to the left. There they were. But Abigail wasn't with them.

He ran down the steps and across the street. "Where's Abigail?"

"Margarita called and wanted to know if she would be able to help out. They've been slammed with orders. She went to the *panadería*."

"But we're going to keep Paloma." Charlotte clapped.

"Don't worry, brother, we didn't kidnap her. We're just babysitting her for an hour or two." Liberty grinned at him.

He looked at his sisters. "So you still have relationships with the women Dad dated?" Their identical looks of confusion answered his question.

"Yes." They looked at each other, then back to him. "Is that a problem?"

"I… no. I need to talk to Abigail."

"Finally." Liberty rolled her eyes.

"If you're looking for Abigail, she—"

He didn't stay long enough to hear the rest of Madison's sentence. Abigail had left without telling him and he had an urgent need to reach her, to tell her everything before another minute slipped by.

Hudson's heart was pounding in his ears, and his lungs burned as he ran. Cutting up from the beach, he hit the boardwalk. People honked as he ran. They were probably thinking their sheriff had lost it.

He had. His heart was in Abigail's hands. He couldn't waste another moment with her thinking she wasn't worth the risk. He needed to let her know she was. That he was willing to risk it *all* for her.

The bakery was across the boardwalk. He stopped at the curb, resting his hands on his knees as he tried to steady his breath. His lungs protested. Sprinting down the beach had not been his best idea.

Every parking spot was taken, and people were coming and going into the Dulce Panadería. After the weeklong freeze, everyone was craving their hand-ground coffee and fresh pastries.

Well, he clearly had not thought this out. He stood looking right and left, waiting for the cars to pass, then crossed the street. It seemed a lifetime ago when he'd opened that door and saw her standing there.

He hadn't known she was going to change his life. He smiled. Change was scary, but it was good.

A few more people left the bakery, some waving to him. A couple of cars had pulled away. He paused in front of the door. With one last deep breath, he opened it and walked in. He smiled at the happy little bell that announced his arrival.

Abigail looked up from the cash register. A frown wrinkled her forehead. "Is Paloma, okay?" Emerging from behind the counter, she approached the front of the store, her gaze searching his. "Hudson, tell me what's wrong."

He was here, but now he had no clue what to say. He swallowed. "You didn't say goodbye."

She tilted her head, narrowing her eyes in confusion. "I don't understand."

"You promised never to leave without saying goodbye. You left. You didn't say goodbye."

Everyone in the bakery had gone silent. Josefina and Margarita stood at the counter. Yes, he was making a scene.

"You said that when you love someone you should always tell them goodbye. Every single time."

Her eyes went wide. "I did say that."

The pounding in his ears was so loud, she had to hear it. "There are a lot of things I should have said to you on the swing. I lied. I wasn't sorry I kissed you. That was the best kiss I've ever experienced. I want to kiss you good morning every day and every time one of us leaves. But you have your whole life in front of you. I don't want to get in the way."

She smiled. "I'm glad you're not sorry. But all the other stuff doesn't mean anything if I don't have you to share it with. You make my life richer, Hudson, fuller than I ever thought possible. Stop being so heroic. Please."

He blinked a couple of times. With both hands, he cupped her face and pulled her to him. Or maybe she fell into him. He wasn't sure who went where, but they met in the middle. Their lips touched, and he knew it was right. Then he pressed his lips to her forehead, and everyone around them cheered. Pulling back, he kept his gaze on her. "I forgot we had an audience." He took her hand and led her out the front door and over to the beach.

Under the pier, it was quiet except for the crashing waves. "Abigail, I love you so much, but I need to know what you want."

"I—I don't understand this sudden about-face. Just this morning, you said all we could be was friends."

"Because I'm an emotional coward. I was afraid you would hurt me and my daughter when you left."

"Oh, Hudson. I'm not going anywhere."

They stared at each other for a long moment. "It's okay if you do. I'll still love you."

She cupped his face with her hand. "I love you so much. There are so many things I want to do, but I want to share it all with you. But are you sure you want to take me on? I come with a lot of baggage. As sheriff, should you be hanging out with someone who was married to a convicted con artist?"

He wrapped his arms around her. "Our pasts don't matter. It's what our future holds that makes you the perfect girl for me."

She laughed. "There is nothing perfect about me. I'm as flawed as they come."

"And that's why I love you. Will you be my forever girl?"

"I'm not sure I know how to be a forever girl."

"Then I'll come to Dulce Panadería every morning until you figure it out."

She leaned into his chest, her ear against his heart. "I love you. Everything I want is right here in Port Del Mar. When God put me on the road home, I was so scared. I had no idea how wonderful it would be."

"You woke up my heart. Thank you, love."

Stepping back, she looked to the beach. "I should get back to the *panadería*."

Over her shoulder, in the deep shadow of the pier, was a clump of pure, untouched snow. He smiled. Reaching over, he scooped it up in one hand and made a ball.

"Abigail."

She turned. Her brows raised in question. He threw the snowball. "Caught you." He tossed her words from the beach back to her.

She brushed the snow off her chest. "You did. You caught me." Tilting her head, she gave him a sly smile. "Or have I caught you?"

He gathered up more snow and she ran, laughing. He followed her. He would follow her anywhere.

Epilogue

Abigail shifted in the saddle. The chestnut mare underneath her waited patiently. From atop his gray gelding, Xavier reached over and took her hand. There was a shine in his eye as he smiled at her.

"Are you ready?" he asked gruffly.

"I've been ready my whole life." Excitement had her heart pounding in double time.

"More like your life got you ready for this." Winking, he sat up and adjusted the reins.

That was true. If her path had been easy, she wouldn't have seen the true gift Hudson was and she wouldn't have been able to bring what he needed to his life. Then there was Paloma. Her daughter was the true treasure. "God works it all for good."

"That He does. It's good to take it slow.

Rushing into something never ends well. You and Hudson, you are going to end well."

Over the rise, the music changed. "That's our cue."

With a nod, she urged her horse forward and fell in step with Xavier. The breeze caught her veil and for a moment her vision was hazy. Straightening it, she froze. Her lungs stopped working. Everyone that had become an important part of her life was standing and looking at her. Her lost family, her new family, and now her very own family.

Her new life was richer than anything her ex-husband had given her.

As they approached the last row of chairs, they stopped the horses and Xavier dismounted to come help her off her horse.

A couple of the Espinoza boys took the horses.

Her brother laid her hand over his arm.

She looked up at him and smiled. "Thank you for walking me down the aisle."

"My baby sister is marrying one of my best friends. My family is all in one place, safe and happy. There is nowhere else I would be today. Thank you for coming home and trusting us. I don't say this enough, but I love you. I'm honored you asked me." He turned to the east. "I think someone wants us to hurry." He winked at her.

She searched for Hudson. He stepped closer to the pastor and smiled at her. The wonder in his eyes made her feel beautiful and cherished. He was waiting for her and behind him the sun was coming up over the ocean.

When he had asked her to marry him, she knew it had to be in the morning facing the ocean. Just like the mural at church. Now here they were, close to the spot they were going to build their house on the family ranch.

A few people questioned the time of day, but Hudson understood.

He was going to be her husband and she was going to be his wife.

She squeezed Xavier's arm and nodded.

They stepped forward. At the end of the aisle Charlotte held Paloma's hand. Paloma looked up from throwing rose petals and seeds and squealed. "My mamma."

Standing to the left were Belle and Hudson's sisters. Next to Hudson was his father, Damian and Elijah.

He wanted Xavier to be his best man, but she said that was the only person that would give her away. The whole world faded the closer she got to Hudson.

His gaze stayed on her. They stopped before the pastor. Xavier laid her hand in Hudson's. Leaning in close he whispered, "I'll always be here. You're never going to be alone again, but now you'll build your own family." He kissed her forehead and with a nod to Hudson he stepped away. The rest of the ceremony was a blur. All she remembered was staring at Hudson, into his incredible eyes, holding his hands and feeling an abundance of love.

As the sun rose into the sky the kiss of the rays warmed them. Abigail didn't know what the future held but hope and love filled her now and she knew that would guide them on this new journey together.

Once the final vows had been spoken, Hudson leaned over to kiss her, and she reached up and cupped his face as his arms went around her.

The pastor introduced them as husband and wife. Her hand in Hudson's, they walked down the aisle, passing the people who filled her life with faith, love and joy. Leaving for Port Del Mar had been one of the darkest days in her life but now God had brought her into the light.

Hudson helped her back onto the horse, then swung up behind her. She laughed. "What are you doing? You have your own horse." She pointed to the one Xavier had ridden from the stables.

Reins in one hand, he held her close with the other. "Nope. I caught you and I'm not letting go."

* * * * *

If you enjoyed this story,
look for these other books by
Jolene Navarro:

Dear Reader,

Thank you so much for joining me on this trip to Port Del Mar. If you read the other De La Rosa stories you know that Gabby is the baby sister they have been looking for. It was so satisfying to get to bring her home. It took a little bit longer because we had to find the perfect hero. Those don't always come around as easily as you would think. But Hudson was there waiting for her and waiting for me to write their story. Elijah can be found in *The Texan's Secret Daughter*, Xavier's story is in *The Texan's Unexpected Return*. Belle and Quinn are in *The Texan's Promise* and Damian's is *The Texan's Unexpected Holiday*.

Not long ago, the whole state of Texas was actually covered in snow and ice for a week. I was driving from Colorado ironically, when it hit. Highways were closed; electricity and water were not easy to get. It was an incredible week beyond anything in the history books.

Writing about something that I had just experienced was interesting. I love talking to readers, so please look me up on Facebook at Jolene Navarro, Author, or email me at jnavarro32@gvtc.com.

Hope to see you in the next book. We'll be hanging out with the Espinoza family. I'm excited to get to know them better. They're a fun family.

Jolene Navarro

Get 4 FREE REWARDS!

We'll send you 2 FREE Books plus <u>2 FREE Mystery Gifts</u>.

FREE Value Over **$20**

Both the **Love Inspired®** and **Love Inspired® Suspense** series feature compelling novels filled with inspirational romance, faith, forgiveness, and hope.

YES! Please send me 2 FREE novels from the Love Inspired or Love Inspired Suspense series and my 2 FREE gifts (gifts are worth about $10 retail). After receiving them, if I don't wish to receive any more books, I can return the shipping statement marked "cancel." If I don't cancel, I will receive 6 brand-new Love Inspired Larger-Print books or Love Inspired Suspense Larger-Print books every month and be billed just $5.99 each in the U.S. or $6.24 each in Canada. That is a savings of at least 17% off the cover price. It's quite a bargain! Shipping and handling is just 50¢ per book in the U.S. and $1.25 per book in Canada.* I understand that accepting the 2 free books and gifts places me under no obligation to buy anything. I can always return a shipment and cancel at any time. The free books and gifts are mine to keep no matter what I decide.

Choose one: ☐ **Love Inspired**
Larger-Print
(122/322 IDN GNWC)

☐ **Love Inspired Suspense**
Larger-Print
(107/307 IDN GNWN)

Name (please print)

Address   Apt. #

City   State/Province   Zip/Postal Code

Email: Please check this box ☐ if you would like to receive newsletters and promotional emails from Harlequin Enterprises ULC and its affiliates. You can unsubscribe anytime.

Mail to the Harlequin Reader Service:
IN U.S.A.: P.O. Box 1341, Buffalo, NY 14240-8531
IN CANADA: P.O. Box 603, Fort Erie, Ontario L2A 5X3

Want to try 2 free books from another series? Call 1-800-873-8635 or visit www.ReaderService.com.

*Terms and prices subject to change without notice. Prices do not include sales taxes, which will be charged (if applicable) based on your state or country of residence. Canadian residents will be charged applicable taxes. Offer not valid in Quebec. This offer is limited to one order per household. Books received may not be as shown. Not valid for current subscribers to the Love Inspired or Love Inspired Suspense series. All orders subject to approval. Credit or debit balances in a customer's account(s) may be offset by any other outstanding balance owed by or to the customer. Please allow 4 to 6 weeks for delivery. Offer available while quantities last.

Your Privacy—Your information is being collected by Harlequin Enterprises ULC, operating as Harlequin Reader Service. For a complete summary of the information we collect, how we use this information and to whom it is disclosed, please visit our privacy notice located at corporate.harlequin.com/privacy-notice. From time to time we may also exchange your personal information with reputable third parties. If you wish to opt out of this sharing of your personal information, please visit readerservice.com/consumerschoice or call 1-800-873-8635. **Notice to California Residents**—Under California law, you have specific rights to control and access your data. For more information on these rights and how to exercise them, visit corporate.harlequin.com/california-privacy.

LIRLIS22

Get 4 FREE REWARDS!

We'll send you 2 FREE Books plus 2 FREE Mystery Gifts.

FREE Value Over **$20**

Both the **Harlequin® Special Edition** and **Harlequin® Heartwarming™** series feature compelling novels filled with stories of love and strength where the bonds of friendship, family and community unite.

YES! Please send me 2 FREE novels from the Harlequin Special Edition or Harlequin Heartwarming series and my 2 FREE gifts (gifts are worth about $10 retail). After receiving them, if I don't wish to receive any more books, I can return the shipping statement marked "cancel." If I don't cancel, I will receive 6 brand-new Harlequin Special Edition books every month and be billed just $4.99 each in the U.S or $5.74 each in Canada, a savings of at least 17% off the cover price or 4 brand-new Harlequin Heartwarming Larger-Print books every month and be billed just $5.74 each in the U.S. or $6.24 each in Canada, a savings of at least 21% off the cover price. It's quite a bargain! Shipping and handling is just 50¢ per book in the U.S. and $1.25 per book in Canada.* I understand that accepting the 2 free books and gifts places me under no obligation to buy anything. I can always return a shipment and cancel at any time. The free books and gifts are mine to keep no matter what I decide.

Choose one: ☐ **Harlequin Special Edition**   ☐ **Harlequin Heartwarming**
                      (235/335 HDN GNMP)   **Larger-Print**
                                                                          (161/361 HDN GNPZ)

Name (please print)

Address   Apt. #

City   State/Province   Zip/Postal Code

Email: Please check this box ☐ if you would like to receive newsletters and promotional emails from Harlequin Enterprises ULC and its affiliates. You can unsubscribe anytime.

Mail to the Harlequin Reader Service:
IN U.S.A.: P.O. Box 1341, Buffalo, NY 14240-8531
IN CANADA: P.O. Box 603, Fort Erie, Ontario L2A 5X3

Want to try 2 free books from another series? Call 1-800-873-8635 or visit www.ReaderService.com.

COUNTRY LEGACY COLLECTION

19 FREE BOOKS IN ALL!

EMMETT
Diana Palmer

COURTED BY THE COWBOY

THE RANCHER AND THE BABY

Cowboys, adventure and romance await you in this new collection! Enjoy superb reading all year long with books by bestselling authors like Diana Palmer, Sasha Summers and Marie Ferrarella!

YES! Please send me the **Country Legacy Collection!** This collection begins with 3 FREE books and 2 FREE gifts in the first shipment. Along with my 3 free books, I'll also get 3 more books from the **Country Legacy Collection**, which I may either return and owe nothing or keep for the low price of $24.60 U.S./$28.12 CDN each plus $2.99 U.S./$7.49 CDN for shipping and handling per shipment*. If I decide to continue, about once a month for 8 months, I will get 6 or 7 more books but will only pay for 4. That means 2 or 3 books in every shipment will be FREE! If I decide to keep the entire collection, I'll have paid for only 32 books because 19 are FREE! I understand that accepting the 3 free books and gifts places me under no obligation to buy anything. I can always return a shipment and cancel at any time. My free books and gifts are mine to keep no matter what I decide.

☐ 275 HCK 1939   ☐ 475 HCK 1939

Name (please print)

Address   Apt. #

City   State/Province   Zip/Postal Code

Mail to the **Harlequin Reader Service:**
IN U.S.A.: P.O. Box 1341, Buffalo, NY 14240-8571
IN CANADA: P.O. Box 603, Fort Erie, Ontario L2A 5X3

*Terms and prices subject to change without notice. Prices do not include sales taxes, which will be charged (if applicable) based on your state or country of residence. Canadian residents will be charged applicable taxes. Offer not valid in Quebec. All orders subject to approval. Credit or debit balances in a customer's account(s) may be offset by any other outstanding balance owed by or to the customer. Please allow 3 to 4 weeks for delivery. Offer available while quantities last. © 2021 Harlequin Enterprises ULC. ® and ™ are trademarks owned by Harlequin Enterprises ULC.

Your Privacy—Your information is being collected by Harlequin Enterprises ULC, operating as Harlequin Reader Service. To see how we collect and use this information visit https://corporate.harlequin.com/privacy-notice. From time to time we may also exchange your personal information with reputable third parties. If you wish to opt out of this sharing of your personal information, please visit www.readerservice.com/consumerschoice or call 1-800-873-8635. Notice to California Residents—Under California law, you have specific rights to control and access your data. For more information visit https://corporate.harlequin.com/california-privacy.

50BOOKCL22

COMING NEXT MONTH FROM
Love Inspired

THE AMISH MATCHMAKING DILEMMA
Amish Country Matches • by Patricia Johns

Amish bachelor Mose Klassen wants a wife who is quiet and traditional—the exact opposite of his childhood friend Naomi Peachy. But when she volunteers as his speech tutor, Mose can't help but be drawn to the outgoing woman. Could an unexpected match be his perfect fit?

TRUSTING HER AMISH HEART
by Cathy Liggett

Leah Zook finds purpose caring for the older injured owner of an Amish horse farm—until his estranged son returns home looking for redemption. The mysterious Zach Graber has all the power to fix the run-down farm—and Leah's locked-down heart. But together will they be strong enough to withstand his secret?

A REASON TO STAY
K-9 Companions • by Deb Kastner

Suddenly responsible for a brother she never knew about, Emma Fitzgerald finds herself out of her depth in a small Colorado town. But when cowboy Sharpe Winslow and his rescue pup, Baloo, take the troubled boy under their wing, Emma can't resist growing close to them and maybe finding a reason to stay...

THE COWGIRL'S REDEMPTION
Hope Crossing • by Mindy Obenhaus

Gloriana Prescott has returned to her Texas ranch to make amends—even if the townsfolk she left behind aren't ready to forgive. But when ranch manager Justin Broussard must save the struggling rodeo, Gloriana sees a chance to prove she's really changed. But can she show Justin, and the town, that she's trustworthy?

FINDING HER VOICE
by Donna Gartshore

Bridget Connelly dreams of buying her boss's veterinary clinic—and so does Sawyer Blume. But it's hard to stay rivals when Sawyer's traumatized daughter bonds with Bridget's adorable pup. When another buyer places a bid, working together might give them everything they want...including each other.

ONCE UPON A FARMHOUSE
by Angie Dicken

Helping her grandmother sell the farm and escaping back to Chicago are all Molly Jansen wants—not to reunite with her ex, single father and current tenant farmer Jack Behrens. But turning Jack and his son out—and not catching feelings for them—might prove more difficult than she realized...

LOOK FOR THESE AND OTHER LOVE INSPIRED BOOKS WHEREVER BOOKS ARE SOLD, INCLUDING MOST BOOKSTORES, SUPERMARKETS, DISCOUNT STORES AND DRUGSTORES.

LICNM0722

Visit
ReaderService.com
Today!

As a valued member of the Harlequin Reader Service, you'll find these benefits and more at ReaderService.com:

- Try 2 free books from any series
- Access risk-free special offers
- View your account history & manage payments
- Browse the latest Bonus Bucks catalog